I0576984

Sydney Dobell, Emily Jolly

The Life and Letters of Sydney Dobell

Vol. II.

Sydney Dobell, Emily Jolly

The Life and Letters of Sydney Dobell
Vol. II.

ISBN/EAN: 9783337017057

Printed in Europe, USA, Canada, Australia, Japan

Cover: Foto ©Raphael Reischuk / pixelio.de

More available books at **www.hansebooks.com**

SYDNEY DOBELL'S WORKS.

———— ·:·←——

THE
POETICAL WORKS OF SYDNEY DOBELL.

With an Introductory Notice and Memoir by JOHN NICHOL,
M.A., LL.D., Professor of English Literature in
the University of Glasgow.

2 vols. crown 8vo., with Photographic Portrait.   21s.

THOUGHTS ON ART, PHILOSOPHY, AND RELIGION.

BEING SELECTIONS FROM THE UNPUBLISHED PAPERS OF
SYDNEY DOBELL.

With an Introductory Note by JOHN NICHOL, M.A., LL.D.

Crown 8vo. with Portrait.   7s. 6d.

London: SMITH, ELDER, & CO., 15 Waterloo Place.

SYDNEY DOBELL

VOL. II.

THE

LIFE AND LETTERS

OF

SYDNEY DOBELL

EDITED BY E. J.

With Steel Portrait and Photographic Illustrations

IN TWO VOLUMES

VOL. II.

LONDON

SMITH, ELDER, & CO., 15 WATERLOO PLACE

1878

[All rights reserved]

CONTENTS

OF

THE SECOND VOLUME.

BOOK VII.

1866 TO 1871. AGED 12 TO 17.

BOOK VIII.

1871 TO 1874. AGED 17 TO 50.

ILLUSTRATIONS.

BOOK IV.—*continued.*

CHAPTER VII.

THIS year began anxiously for Sydney Dobell. The improvement in his wife's case showed itself to be less radical, and more temporary, than he had dared hope. His own health was breaking more and more under the constant mental strain to which the conditions of his life exposed him.

The book he published in the course of this year—a collection of Ballads, entitled 'England in Time of War,'—the writing of which he had regarded as the mere filling in of an interval before a more settled and organised existence should permit work of greater magnitude, and of a more consecutive kind—proved to be his last considerable literary venture.

The lately arrived guest, poor young ——, was too ill to be moved; and his presence in such an invalid household could not but cause a good deal of fatigue and harass during the few ensuing

B 2

weeks. That he was cared for as a brother would have been, it is needless to say.

At the end of the time Mr. Dobell wrote, to his mother :

B—— left us on Monday, and arrived without fresh cold at his friends, in Yorkshire. . . . The additional shade that this anxiety threw into her atmosphere was very unfavourable to E——, and she has gradually sunk in strength day by day. . . . I think I could, if necessary, finish the book in a week or two, but I would prefer lingering over it. . . .

The tone in which he wrote to his departed guest shows the brotherly intimacy that had grown up in the weeks they had lived under the same roof.

In one of the earliest letters, answering enquiries about his wife, he says :

Yesterday she could hardly speak from weakness ; but this morning, upon my proceeding to demonstrate conversationally that the people called 'cannibals' are an ill-used race—gentlemen of peculiar opinions, perhaps, but otherwise irreproachable— against whom (chiefly in consequence of an odious commercial conspiracy among the butchers) we civilised nations have indulged unjustifiable prejudices, she roused up—you know her naïve earnestness—and took the other side of the question with a success—diverging into an episodical onslaught upon 'unassisted reason'—that was the happiest of omens. . . .

To D. B——, *Esq.*

One line of hearty congratulation on the resolve in your note of yesterday. Depend upon it you never did a more manly and sensible thing than you will do on the day you re-enter Devonshire, and place yourself again under those conditions on which God had set the imprimatur of such past blessings. I am eager to know you have actually started, and that this interval of mild weather is not lost. You are right in thinking that a retreat is more glorious than an unreasonable continuance of the contest—remember Torres Vedras and Xenophon. Be sure, my dear fellow, you take the wisest care in the mode and process of your return. Recollect that expenditure in such a case is the truest economy. And I shall believe you have no true friendship for me—that you like your own pride a thousand times better—if you scruple (in case there is the least difficulty in getting ample funds) to let me know what cash to send you. I put it in this plain way, because it is a plain duty which you ought not to neglect when such great matters are at stake. . . . I am afraid from some things you say that you caught cold on your journey, notwithstanding all precautions. Have you the prescription for the cough-mixture? Tell me if you have lost it, that I may send another.

E—— joins me in much anxiety regarding you.

Give our kind messages to your sister when you write, and believe me, in haste, my dear fellow,

Yours affectionately,

SYDNEY DOBELL.

A number of brief notes written about this time to the same correspondent, relate almost exclusively to the literary and physical concerns of Mr. B———. But in one, dated towards the end of March, Mr. Dobell speaks of a serious and protracted illness of his wife, and says :—

I have been so long recovering the over-strain of mind that all poetry has been impossible for weeks past. . . . I have an accumulation of MSS., and six new printed volumes, from various friends, lately arrived, so I won't promise to read your critique for a few days, but it shall *not* wait for its turn. . . . Let the new hopes and accomplishments, with regard to your health, make you resolve all manner of patience in finishing your book. A few weeks, or even months, more or less are now of no consequence, while even a few new beauties are of much. . . . We expect to remove from Granton next week for a glimpse of spring and a change of air and scene.

The hope of a visit 'home' during this spring or summer was spoken of in some of his letters, early in the year :

One knows that such plans are not only provisional, but Providential, (he wrote), and that in scheming for

what is beyond the present, one can only be like him who
drops leaves into a running stream and prejudges by the
curves, and eddies, and rapids, the course they are likely
to take; and, alas! how often there are ground-swells, and
freshets, and hidden drifts that make the upper seeming of
the stream no true evidence of its actual forces—as A——
and I found that memorable day when we nearly drowned
poor Jeannie. Poor little Jeannie, I wonder if she will
remember us, and how Maida will put up with her tiny
rival: Maida who could swallow her whole, and who loves
us with a kind of passionate delight that is almost pathetic
to see.

They were, however, compelled to abandon
any thought of so long a journey.

In answer to a request for his own and his
wife's signature to some 'Woman's Rights Petition,'
he wrote, before leaving Granton:—

The subject of that petition is one far too difficult, I
think, to be decided upon without a twelvemonth's deep
previous consideration, and without much more knowledge
of all its bearings than will be possible to four-fifths of
those who sign it. There is no doubt of the sufferings of
those to whom it alludes—no one can feel for them more
deeply than I; but there is very great doubt whether such
legislative enactments as the petition requires would not
be substituting a greater evil for a less. The subject of
marriage and marriage duties is so infinitely difficult that

the wisest and most impartial heads in the kingdom are
not likely to solve its problems—and any others are certain only to complicate them. The very argument on
which the petitioners rely seems to me against them.   It
would be difficult to over-estimate the *mental* evils produced by that very law of settlements to which they
refer; and any amount of physical misery is better than
even a comparatively small result of spiritual injury.
But the whole matter, as I said before, is one on which no
one should come to a conclusion without a year's previous
study, and you won't wonder, therefore, that your paper
returns to you unsigned.

To a Brother-in-law (in answer to an announcement of
the birth of a daughter).

April 1856.

If you had given us face to face the most happy news,
which your letter has just brought, there would probably
have been but few *words* on either side. . . . I could
hardly fancy such tidings more completely all one could
most hope for than as they have come to us in your brief
despatch just arrived.   A little girl-child! the very idea
is the most exquisite of poems. . . . A child-daughter—
wherein it seems to me that the spirit of all dews and
flowers and springs and tender sweet wonders 'strikes its
being into bounds.'

To his Father and Mother.

Bridge of Allan: April 5th.

I have no hope of answering these birthday letters,
and will not do injustice to the reception they have had

by making even an attempt at a reply. Every year I live shows me more conclusively that speech is not a natural language, and all the noise that goes on with us outwardly seems to bear less and less relation to the feelings and thoughts within. We speak and write, speak and write, with wonderful industry; but whether briefly and stammeringly, as some men—whom people pity for having 'such difficulty of utterance,'—or amply and fluently as others—in whom hearers and readers admire 'so great a gift of speech,'—there sits the soul in the midst of it all for ever desiring—and just as vainly—to be expressed. You know what love—and what other precious things—those letters represented, and you can understand from those realities of yours by what realities of ours they were received. I can tell you we cried over them—in pleasure and in great thankfulness, but I could sooner write a book than try to tell you 'the why and the wherefore.'

To a young Sister.

Bridge of Allan: April 10th, 1856.

With regard to good deeds, remember that good deeds are only valuable in as far as they indicate certain good things in the mind from which they come. This is the Scripture doctrine of 'Faith' and 'Works.' Good works are only valuable if they prove the existence of faith—*i.e.* of a certain state of mind. That 'state of mind' can hardly ever exist without being accompanied by 'works' of some kind, because it is the nature of that particular

state of mind to work, but the truth remains the same,
that the works are only important inasmuch as they
demonstrate the state of mind to exist. So with all good
works : they are precious only as they evidence the good
qualities in your own mind. Do them without those
qualities—or from any other qualities—and you lose your
reward.

A machine, or a workhouse, or a soup-kitchen can feed
the poor as well as you ; a government commission, or a
public institution can teach them better than you ; you
can see in any gallery better pictures than you are likely
to paint, and can hear at the next concert better music
than you will ever play. Yet you ought to feed the poor
and to teach them, and to pursue painting and to cultivate music, because these things are the proper exercise
and result of certain good qualities in your mind, and no
other method but that of your own personal activity will
suffice to exercise those qualities. But the moment you
do them from any quality that is not in itself a good one,
you had better leave them undone. . . . It can never be
too constantly remembered that we shall be punished or
rewarded according to what we *are.*

In order to be good, therefore, take care that your
good deeds always arise from good qualities : and in order
to be beautiful, take care that both good deeds and good
qualities be exquisite. The good qualities, intense, un-
mixed, vital, abounding, unsullied, blooming, dewy—exquisite. The good deeds, sincere, earnest, gracious, harmonious, exuberant, unwearied, angelic—exquisite. And
I mean by 'angelic,' self-repaying, delightsome, disinte-

rested, done for and by the pure love of doing. And remember that a woman's first 'mission' in this world is to be beautiful; and that if women become less than beautiful, we had better have none but men; for there is nothing on earth we cannot do better than women, except be beautiful. Therefore, my dear sister, God give you to grow in all sweetness of nature and action; in all height and depth and grace and delicateness of love and faith, and in all fair congruity of gentle, lovely and all true performance: teach you, indeed, to delight in every good and perfect work; but teach you also that the feeding of a thousand beggars will not compensate for one unkind thought or deed towards any of those you love; and that you shall do more to instruct mankind by growing, yourself, into loveliness than if, without that, you should endow a whole country with schools.

Are you tired with my long sermon?

Writing in April, from Bridge of Allan, to the Rev. J. B. Paton, he says:

Perhaps I deserved the pain with which I read your 'dear Mr. Dobell' (substituted for a less formal style of address), and yet I think not; for, after all, my chief fault has been an over confidence in your faith and patience.

After speaking, with some detail, of what had been done and suffered since he had last written, in the summer of the previous year, he goes on— à propos of there being always a tax of correspond-

ence which, under any circumstances, he felt himself obliged to pay :

The friends of those who write poetry do not sufficiently
remember that poetry is the exuberance, the self-pressed
wine, of the mind. . . . Who was it that said 'a little
thing makes perfection, and perfection is not a little
thing ?' A letter may be a trifle in itself, but a string
the tenth of a note out of tune is enough to spoil the
whole symphony. . . . The 'book' of which I have spoken
is a collection of about forty ballads, exponent of the
Home feelings of England on the subject of the War. All
are now written but one, and the book will probably
appear about midsummer. The title will be, I think,
' Time of War, or What they said in England.'

To the Same.

May 5.

How I wish you were in reach of the hearty hand I
would lay on your shoulder! Your letter was so
thoroughly all I expected from your brave, warm, true-
souled self, that I can hardly bring myself to regret the
accident which has been the means of confirming my best
faith in you. That that faith is unimpaired, indeed, I am
going to give you the most unmistakeable of proofs—I
am going to give you something to do for me. It is on
behalf of that young poet in whose nearly mortal illness
when on a visit to us this winter you felt so much interest.
A word or two of his history will not make you less concerned in him. . . . Literature seems the only path open

to him, as his *physique* forbids all business occupation. I laid a MS. volume of his Poems before ——— ———, and that fastidious judge was so much impressed with their power as to pronounce for publication, which is to take place in good time. Meanwhile, poetry is not a paying commodity; and as the powers that can produce such verse must be competent to admirable prose, he is about to write reviews. Herein it strikes me you can probably help him. . . . He has just written an article on novels generally, and on Miss Mulock's in particular: it would make an admirable introduction, probably, to a review on her new work, 'John Halifax.' . . . Suppose you were to get him an order to do it for 'The Eclectic.' . . . I go at once *in medias res* in this fashion, because I know how anxious you will be to 'bear a hand' in such a case

To his Father and Mother.

Bridge of Allan : April 25.

You will forgive no Sunday letter to-day, for ——— arrived last night. This, to anyone who knows him, must seem a reasonable sentence, but to you it must look rather ludicrous. . . I had gone in to tea with the Brewsters, next door. Meanwhile, dear ——— (who had not come by his appointed train, and whom therefore we did not expect till to-day) arrived; and, hearing where I was, came to find me. . . . Leaping upon Sir David, like an enormous Newfoundland dog, and nearly startling the ladies through the window by the rapidity of his motions, he sat down to the tea-table, talking all the while, sipped a little, ate a

little, sprang up, dashed at some ornament on a side-table—
still talking—examined it, upside, downside, sideways and
everyways—still talking—dashed back to his seat, sipped
again, ate again—still talking—rose, caught up a chair,
hurled it towards the fire, sat thereon almost into Miss Brewster's lap, after nearly upsetting the tea-table—and still talking! Surely such a feverish spirit was never appointed
to wear out a harassed body. You may fancy the kind of
social consternation he produced—the ladies of the family
not having been accustomed to him; and how the courtly
Sir David eyed his plunges with a mixture of terror and
amusement entertaining to behold. . . .

Besides being a pundit of learning, he is a bundle of
talents of various kinds; and I have had, since I have been
in Scotland, opportunities of knowing passages (not from
himself) of his private history, which show him to have
qualities more precious than either talents or learning.
Next Tuesday, if all goes well, we shall move to the ' Mine
Farm,' a cottage midway between here and Blaw Lowan,
with a full southern exposure and a view of the whole
valley.

To the Same.

The Mine Cottage, Bridge of Allan: May 3.

I was too much occupied yesterday to write before
post-time. . . . I had a long morning's work upon my
last ballad, and as the Brewsters go to-day I spent the
evening with them.

When I say my ' last ballad,' it merely means that said
ballad completes the scheme of the book, but, I daresay,

before it has passed through the press, I shall add several others. This 'last' was a ' Meditation of the Spirit ' completing the trio of prayers—the prayer of the heart (a battle-prayer for victory), the prayer of the understanding (' Thy will be done '), and the prayer of the spirit (' Thy Kingdom come '). I hope to finish this morning.

We removed to this pretty cottage last Tuesday, and already feel the increased vitality of the blessed southern light. . . . The cottage stands in a pretty garden, and the landlady seems excellent even among Scottish hostesses. —— left us some days ago, having to lecture at a distant town. He seemed to enjoy his stay, but caught a bad cold the last day by fishing not *by* the water but *in* it, and then refusing pertinaciously to change his stockings. There was no actual necessity to go into the water, but the same unconquerable restlessness that hunts him through his every waking moment seemed to chase him into the stream. Certainly if ever a poor body was possessed by seven devils—only they are all *good* devils—and worn to shreds in ' seeking rest and finding none,' it is his good, thin, feverish incarnation of perpetual motion. Even his voice is never still. He is the only man I ever heard sing to himself without knowing well enough that he was doing so. His morning Greek studies are worth going to see. While he was with us he had a new Greek book to prepare for the University classes, and every morning he sat down to it. As soon as he was in deep the house began to ring; and a succession of fragmentary tunes—ahs and aws supplying the place of words—alternating with a

profound three minutes of silence, for the rest of the
séance.

The sudden lapse into silence gave one the feeling of
falling out of window ; *e.g.*

> Scots wha hae wi' Wallace bled,
> Scots whom Bruce hae often led,
> Welcome ——

profound stillness,

> And for bonnie Annie Laurie
> I ——

dead silence for five minutes. Fancy this going on for
hours in a voice that could be heard all over the house!

I write you gossip because I want to keep my head for
work.

I enclose poor S——'s letter. I do not see that I can
act on my father's suggestion to 'write him a conciliatory
letter.' I concluded our correspondence [1] with an affectionate assurance that, whenever he felt ready to open it
again, he would find me ready to take up our friendship
again at the place where it was broken ; and if he wishes
to renew it, he knows therefore it can be done. The time
when things are again *couleur de rose* with him is not the
time in which I ought to make advances. If he were in
great misfortune, I would willingly come forward. The
best way would be for you to tell him that you know I
have every good feeling towards him, and that if he feels
what he says he had better take measures accordingly.

---

[1] A long and multifariously interesting correspondence, of which
none of Mr. Dobell's letters have been obtained.

To M——.

When I said I wished the new book to be popular, it was not from any increased respect for the populace. I am quite certain that they know nothing about poetry, and that the worst testimony any poem could receive would be that they, unled, and of their own mere emotion, voluntarily adopted and admired it. Even in the case of poetry which, when the mind of the masses has been conducted to it by the voice of their intellectual superiors, has become popular, the popular element is chiefly the non-poetry which exists in every poem, and never the differentiæ, by virtue of which the poetry is poetry.

I am sorry to see you catching up the pass-word of those half-thinkers who take refuge in rhetorical generalities because, while their intellects are too negligent for science, their fancy stops short of that imagination which alone can accurately reproduce the facts of nature. 'The mob has a great heart somewhere to be reached.'

It is quite true that a mob, an assembly of men temporarily brought together, are sometimes, under extraordinary circumstances, by the passing excitement of mental action and re-action, stimulated to a higher collective moral being than belongs to any individual among them in his cool and separate moments. But—what has this fact to do with the popular reception of a book which must of necessity be taken individually, and is usually

taken even by the individual under the most individuali-
sing circumstances? The heart of the mob in any literary
sense is, therefore, the heart of the integers that make it
up, and you should, therefore, never allow yourself to use
a metaphor which is calculated to mislead you. Instead
of saying 'the great heart of the mob,' always say, ' I will
confide the selection of my poetry to Mr. So-and-So the
cobbler in the next alley, or John the butcher's man, or
Mr. Such-and-Such the draper's shopman, or Jones the
grocer;' and instead of saying, that 'the great heart is
honest, impartial, and bound to no authority,' say ' I am
certain they will not be at all influenced by what " The
Family Herald " or " Reynolds's Journal " may write, but
will, with inscrutable instinct, detect true poetry by the
very *cover*, and go to it on the book-stall, true as needle to
the pole.' Always recognise the *personality* of the people
you speak of, and take that personality at random from
the nearest specimens, that you may have a chance of
hitting the main truth. And (if you do this *really*) you
may extend the term 'mob' to the majority of every
conventional class, without materially increasing your con
fidence in their likelihood to discriminate poetry. And if
you wish for general facts to confirm particular results,
you may then ask the publishers of Martin Tupper's
twenty-eighth edition, and Satan Montgomery's twenty-
seventh, for the statistics of actual sale.

The truth that, even in poetry, ' the great soul of the
world is just,' misleads careless thinkers into supposing
that the 'great soul' is the *bulky* soul of the world. The
'great soul' is just, because it comprehends the few high-

est as well as the multitude of lower minds, and––in the course of generations––the one or two yet higher even than the usual highest. In the process of years the verdict of the highest re-echoed by the grade below, whose echo is again reverberated through all the descending scale––is finally reflected as a matter of mental obedience from the great *Populus consentiens* of mankind. But the '*Populus*' in these cases is always not *sentiens*, but *consentiens*. And even when the consent is the most unanimous you will find, on examination, that the unanimity is in the verdict, not in the grounds of it, and that the thing dearest to the people is usually the least valuable element in what they value. . . .

. . . I wish my book to be popular by its appealing, too irresistibly to be withstood, to the underlying sense of justice in those rarer spirits who lead the mob.

To his Mother.

The Mine Cottage, Bridge of Allan: May 21.

I write a hasty line to thank you for letting us know of poor Wager's state.[1] Instead of forestalling his allowance as you propose, be so kind as to continue it weekly as usual, and to make him a present on our account of a pound towards paying his debts. I am sure they would never have been incurred, if he could have helped it. Could he not raise the amount either by gifts or loans, and so get free of S——? Please to see that he is not 'sold up,'

---

[1] An old man who had been the Coxhorne gardener.

for I would sooner pay the whole amount than the poor old fellow should have that addition to his trials.

You will be glad to know that I hope and think the book is finished, though not quite copied. I hardly like to confess to myself that it is so, for I could spend another year upon it without exhausting the field or satisfying my wishes.

I shall of course do my best to get strong in the interval between the completion of this and commencement of the next : but there is too much to be done to make it possible to wait very long. The mere intellectual labour of a book would not be too much for me, if other conditions were favourable. It was that labour added to the great anxieties of my darling's relapses, and her long winter illness, that overthrew me so often.

I don't quite understand your idea of ' God's harvest-field,' nor what better *description* of work I could do in it (I am not now speaking of the *execution*, but of the *kind* of that work) than I am doing.

Do not fear, dearest mother, that I should over-tax myself. I gave you the fairest version of the Dr.'s verdict ; he made reservations which are quite sufficient to keep me from being too confident. . . . All ' plans ' with us are impossible till we know what the summer is to do for E——. As yet we project nothing more definite than to stay here till the place is too hot.

To his father about this time, regarding his youngest brother, he wrote :

It has often struck me, and I think it must have occurred to you, that with a lad of ——'s temperament and inherent longing for travel, the most prudent course for those who have his fate in their keeping is to make gratification legitimate, by uniting it with the performance of duty. . . . Have you considered the great advantages that are implied in A——'s offer? Lightly, with the grace of his own fine instinct, as he made the offer, it is as valuable a one as a place under Government. . . . Dangerous as an exile of that sort may be under any circumstances, I think there can be little doubt that he will, be the conditions what they may, get into equal dangers in his course through youth and, probably, if affairs go ill with him, under influences and moods less likely to surmount them. I know from his own confession to me the craving that exists—well curbed and bravely met, as he hoped it to be —for foreign experience, or at least for a life less wholly ordinary than the common routine of minor business. I confess—often as I have looked round the horizon with him in my thoughts—I can see no path open which seems so promising for the particular nature with which we have to do.

Of Kossuth, who delivered an address, at Stirling, on the occasion of ' the great Wallace demonstration,' he wrote, June 28, 1856 :

We had a little chat before the lecture began : and I had a long close view of his head, of course, during the two hours' oration. His head is a wonderful puzzle. I

should like to know its measurements. The face is an
equal puzzle. . . . With his hat on (when he appears to
far more advantage than when the receding forehead is
shown, which, however, may recede from prominence of
the perceptions) he reminds me more of one of Landseer's
best pictures of a Newfoundland dog than anything else.
The peculiarity of his head is the immense physical *base*
on which it is built, which accounts for his enormous power
of mental *work*. The lecture was good, but not extraordinary, the passages of high eloquence being spoiled by
his excessively foreign pronunciation, which made him
constantly unintelligible. The *character* of the eloquence,
so far as the matter of it was concerned, was the very
highest. The manner was not particularly good. The
kingly dignity of his attitude being sometimes injured
by stiff movements of the arms. The fact of the very
high character of what he said made the fault of pronunciation additionally lamentable; because some of the
most telling points in the speech were in so few words, and
said with such an intentional quietness, that people missed
them or misunderstood them. He says his best things so
quietly, as if they dropped unawares. Somebody in the
committee-room, before going on the platform, asked him
in the name of another town if he could lecture there a
few weeks hence. He did not know: other duties might
prevent him: lecturing was well enough, but he would
sooner fight. The 'I would sooner fight' being said in
the manner in which he might ask if you had seen his
gloves, after which indeed he seemed to be looking about
when saying it.

Illness and anxiety had to be the frequent theme of the home letters, but they were dwelt on lightly, and the most was made of any humorous aspect of things. He wrote, still from the Mine Cottage, Bridge of Allan :

To my consternation a family, who had some time ago engaged the other half of this cottage, suddenly arrived with—seven boys! They came when I was out for a walk, and on my return I thought my poor little patient was on the verge of a nervous fever. Her first acquaintance with the new lodgers was the rush of a schoolboy into her bedroom, who having had his stare at so rare a joke as a lady in bed, forthwith called ' seven (or five) other devils worse than himself.' You may fancy that this first experience of our new friends made me anxious enough as to how we should manage; and though they are better arranged now, I don't think it will be bearable. The incessant swarming of fourteen feet, before, behind, on each side, and overhead, has an ubiquity like a plague of lice. . . . I had no way of providing against the visitation, for the father, who came to take the lodgings, was a most unsuspicious gentlemanly looking person. Who would have guessed that so decent a man could be guilty of so many boys? I can't think what people mean by these large families. All boys, too! But though we try to make a joke of it, it is really a very serious matter— would be bad enough to a healthy person.

The same letter speaks somewhat anxiously of

business and money affairs—says : ' I know I seem
to spend a good deal of money ; but the expenses
of this nomadic way of living are so great, that I
really can't afford to do with less.'

The nature of a considerable proportion of this
expenditure may be conjectured from facts already
incidentally mentioned.

Sums of money—not always small in proportion to the income from which they were claimed
—(on one occasion a request for an immediate
loan of twenty pounds drained the available
finances and caused slight temporary embarass-
ment), ' borrowed ' on some sudden emergency,
and not repaid, amounted to something considerable
in the course of a year ; as did many more direct
gifts. The business from which Mr. Dobell drew
his income, was, of course, in spite of the kind
supervision of his father, carried on at disadvantage during his protracted absence from its neighbourhood.

CHAPTER VIII.

'ENGLAND in Time of War,' published about Midsummer in this year, was received with much hostile criticism, but, also, with much appreciative admiration.

The volume contained many poems which have proved themselves thoroughly popular—having been read and re-read in public, quoted again and again, and included in many books of selections, and poetical treasuries.   Among these are 'An Evening Dream,' 'Home, wounded,' 'How's my Boy?' and 'Tommy's dead.'

Mr. Tennyson selected 'Grass from the Battlefield' for special approval; and the note containing this opinion from one towards whom, as the greatest poet of our time, Mr. Dobell always proclaimed his allegiance as of a clansman to a chief, gave him keen pleasure.

Of the little poem entitled 'The Wold'—which has again and again been selected by reviewers for

ridicule—a friendly but fastidious critic wrote
to him : ʻI was delighted with your lyric ʻThe
Wold.ʼ It blows weirdly in one's ears and sweeps
one before it.ʼ The same pen continues :

ʻThe Market Wife's Song,ʼ ʻLady Constance,ʼ ʻDead
Maid's Pool,ʼ ʻThe Evening Dream,ʼ ʻThe Gaberlunzie's
Walk,ʼ ʻA Psalm of the Heart,ʼ ʻA Shower in War Time,ʼ
ʻHome, wounded,ʼ and ʻGrass from the Battle-field,ʼ are at
present my favourites. . . . My simple reply to anyone
who did not share my admiration for these gems, would
be to decline any discussion with him as to examples of
poetic genius . . . When I say that I am not yet clear
of the difficulties which I felt as to the repetitions, and
that in some cases the arguments and forms of expression
seem to me more subtle than the general reader can
apprehend with facility, I have discharged all that I have
to say in the way of exception, and give myself up to unrestrained admiration.

To C. B. Ker, Esq., M.D.

The Mine Cottage.

You did well to be certain how heartily I must always
sympathise in any welfare of yours. And the blessing
which you tell me has befallen you is precisely that form
in which I could most rejoice to see your good fortune.
You remember I was always a preacher of matrimony :
and every year I live I perceive more clearly how essential
is Love—I mean Love as distinct from Charity—and
usually married love, to the full development of a Chris-

tian; and how fatally dangerous (putting all its coarser
perils out of the question) the life of bachelorhood, (except
in those cases where

> 'Tis better to have loved and lost
> Than never to have loved at all),

to everything which is best and rarest in human (another
way of saying Christian) character.

Every year makes me *feel* more thoroughly what we
all recognise in theory—that there is no happiness but in
being good and doing good, and that *self* is in all men
the great obstacle to both these things. Now love is the
great means of self-negation: and you will find that you
may accurately test the health and quality of your love
by the degree to which self grows imperceptible to you.
And your happiness will be in proportion to this 'health
and quality.' That ecstasy of the old Alexandrians, by
which they fancied to escape into the Infinite, may really
be accomplished by him who totally and truly loves; for
he learns to live in the joy of another, which, since he
cannot know the bounds of it, is, *quoad se*, boundless.
There is no perfect love or perfect happiness till this
thorough transmigration of souls has taken place: and
herein it seems to me is the wonderful divineness and
glory of marriage—when rightly realised—that it makes
total self-oblivion (the imperative condition of all high
beauty and virtue) consistent with that temporal good,
and personal welfare, without which (as we see in the
great mistakes of Monachism, &c. &c.) the body becomes
too arid a desert to nourish the best flowers of the soul.

In the case of married lovers each may safely forget that
self which is so wholly cared for by the other, and there
is possible therefore to the dual being a combination
impracticable to any unit—*blessedness and happiness*,
earth and heaven at once. But this is a subject too
inexhaustible to be entered in a letter. God make you
master of it, my dear friend, in the sweet school of experience. I know you well enough to believe you will
graduate rapidly. . . .

I have more than once noticed Bafford[1] in passing by,
and remember especially approving its delicately kept
lawn. I fear, indeed, your fair one will hardly find a daisy
to leave ' rosy.' You remember that exquisite passage in
one of Tennyson's best works—' Maud ' ?[2]

Poetry reminds me that I hope in a few days to send
you a volume which ought to read well in those Charlton
fields which were so often in my mind while writing it.
And the mention of those fields recalls your questions
concerning these on which I am now looking. I know
right well all the beauties you speak of—none of them
so lovely to me perhaps (because so English) as those
'grounds of Kippeaross.' I walked through them last
with a noble old Scotchman, of whom I have seen a good
deal lately. If you don't know him—Sir David Brewster
—let me give you an introduction when he comes to the

---

[1] The home, at Charlton, of his correspondent's *fiancée.*

[2] This opinion of the comparative merit of ' Maud ' was, it will be
remembered, at variance with the general verdict. Among Mr.
Dobell's papers were found notes for an answer to some of the more
hostile reviews of that poem.

British Association. We young men of the new time do well to know the veterans of 'the age of the giants.'

I need not tell you how thoroughly E—— is one with me in every good wish and hope for you—as in all other things. She is again recovering from another serious relapse. I will not make you unhappy by recounting the many vicissitudes of her slow and painful restoration. Enough for your sympathy and my gratitude, that I dare believe it *restoration*.

Not very long after the preceding letter was written, Mr. and Mrs. Dobell returned to Edinburgh. They went first to the house of a dear and kind friend, Mrs. Stirling, sister of Mr. Hunter of Craigcrook ; a lady of exceptional gifts, and well known as the authoress of a successful novel, entitled 'Fanny Hervey.' Afterwards they went to Trinity, from whence the next home letter was dated :

Although Edinburgh is so empty at this time of year that it looks more like a toy city, or model of some kind, than the habitation of so many thousand families, we have had an influx of strangers and others, passing through towards the north, who have, with other matters, so much taken up my time that my despatch must be short.

I have little literary news to give you. There have been some good reviews of 'England in Time of War,' which I hope to send when I get copies. You saw, of course, 'The Leader's' article of last week. Its objections may be answered by the simple fact, that the book is a

book of things to be *sung*, and that in all songs the great
desideratum is to relieve the attention as much as possible
from all unnecessary work, by conveying the requisite
thoughts and feelings in the least possible variety of
phrase.   That is, the least variety consistent with the
thorough and poetic conveyance of those thoughts and
feelings.

To Professor Nichol (author of ' The Architecture
of the Heavens ').

George Street, Edinburgh.

You and I must surely be very awful stars indeed, for
the Fates are evidently obstinate against our conjunction.
But the greatest human affairs, you know, have always
been brought about through all manner of obstruction,
and when we *do* meet, if something extraordinary doesn't
happen I'll have no more faith in the philosophy of
history.

Seriously—and it is really a serious thing to lose so
pleasant a gathering, and at your house, as that to which
you invite me—there seems to be something curiously
unfortunate in the circumstances under which your
welcome invitations always reach me. . . .

. . . I must again look forward to that week in
Glasgow which I still hope to spend, and before your son
returns to college, one of the first pleasures of which will
be, I hope, a walk to the Observatory.   I am right glad
you like my new book.   People think me callous to all
criticism ; but the truth is that, in proportion to my care-

lessness of the ordinary oracles, is my value of the few
verdicts which are likely to be verdicts.   I hope that in
reading it you have borne in mind that it is a book of
things *sung* rather than said.   Most of the printed
objections (*e.g.* anent 'repetitions') that I have seen may
be answered by this fact.   The instinct of a song-writer
teaches him to express what is necessary in the least
variety of phrase, in order that no exertion of the intellect
may subtract from the full force of the feelings.   The
exertion of the intellectual apprehension takes from the
sum of that *vis vivida* which would otherwise be available
for the passions.   *Labor vincit amorem.*

But, as a song which made no appeal to the intellect
would be too narrow to be thoroughly human, one is in-
stinctively led to accustom the perceptions to an idea and
phrase in one portion of a lyric, and then to repeat them
in other parts, with slight variations, or under fresh conditions of context, &c., &c.   And this instinct of the
song-writer has led to the same results in all times and
circumstances.

In some of his letters this summer Mr. Dobell
spoke of 'the Philosophy of Poetry' as a subject
which was occupying his mind, and on which he
entertained the idea of lecturing.

The hope of going home for a month or two,
'that our eyes and hearts may be refreshed, by a
sight of all the dear faces, for a new patience of
absence and waiting,' looked to as a 'cloud and

pillar of fire,' had been gradually extinguished, ' and now,' he wrote towards the autumn,

burns so low that it can hardly be said to be alight. There seems no prospect of so long a journey being possible to E—— before winter; and then—but 'then' will bring its own decisions.

'Meanwhile,' he wrote from Portobello,

we have changed our lodgings, and have surrendered any more ambitious designs, in favour of the very mild rusticity of this suburb of dingy villas. . . . We felt it wiser to sacrifice the longings that drew us to the fields and hills.

There is a subordinate advantage, too, in being near Edinburgh, that, now we *are* fixed, I feel to be of some importance. My young men friends are returning from their summer rambles, and the new Review is therefore in active process of formation.

Of Ruskin, in connection with the Art department of this projected Review, he said:

Ruskin may not be wholly right, but he is more nearly right than anybody else who has given the same pains to the inquiry and won the same right to an opinion. *Apropos* of 'young men friends,' Alexander Smith has just returned from Skye—having wooed and won there the Flora Macdonald who gave us the hound—I hope heartily the match will be a happy one or a blessed one to the dear fellow, and I look with some considerable anxiety to the lady's advent in Edinburgh. Report speaks well of her, but it is no ordinary 'well' that should qualify her for a poet's wife ; and Alexander's marriage will be a crisis of his career, for his nature is unwrought gold, and only a great love would stimulate his indolence to work it. . . . One great effect of his marriage will be, probably, to add a great prose author to literature. He will find prose more lucrative than poetry, and he has the power, I believe, to do great things in it.

Speaking of prose authors, we spent some hours with Carlyle two or three days ago as he passed through Edinburgh, and went as far as Granton with him on his way to Fife. You should have seen the looks of the people in the train as he rolled forth (swaying to and fro the while, with the restlessness of some wild creature), the most idiosyncratic denunciations of railways, nineteenth centuries, steam-engines, cheap literature, 'clever' people, and civilisation generally. Though of course they had no notion of who he was, he gradually got them into a sort of mesmeric possession that stilled every voice but his own and stretched every eye. . . . In the midst of all this thunderous lava he was very kind and sweet to us, and his last words to E —— were a spontaneous assurance that he should seek us out when he returned from the North. All of his face that his moustache and thick beard left bare had a ruddy health upon it which contrasted pleasantly with his morbid London looks, and which showed that the weeks in the moorlands near which he was born ('covered in with solitude and silence,' and out of reach of any human being that knew him), where he had just, he declared, been spending the 'most altogether blessed days he could remember,' had been of more than mental benefit. I must not continue this scribble, having to go to Edinburgh presently, and having some unavoidable letters to write this morning. Death is again going up poor ——'s long stair, I fear; my little namesake was nearly dying when I saw him last.

To M——.

Portobello: September, 1856.

Believe me, there is no serious 'loss of strength' implied in the disability to write letters. I feel no diminution of power in other respects; it is merely that the faculty by which the mind is *compelled* to this thing or that seems to have been overtired by long exercise without leisure. Letter-writing, you know, is the greatest of all labours to me, yet it is the one thing in which for years I have (I may almost say) never given myself a day's holiday. Because it is not called 'work' I have not treated it as work, though practically it is more fatiguing to me than the most profound speculation or the most passionate poetry. My brain is a machine that naturally works according to the essential relationship and *ordo* of ideas. To compel it to bring things together that are not essentially like, and to pass from one subject to another, without any natural and necessary relationship, is a wrenching of the machine from its purposes—a reversing of the paddle-wheels, and a winding backward of the

watch, which cannot be done but on strict compulsion and
with sore wear and tear. And this I have been doing
every day of my life for four or five years, and counting it
the mere metope and intercalation of actual work, and
now I am surprised to find the poor machine creaking out
its protest against me! And said machine has a stronger
case, *pro* itself and *contra* me, because the great overstrain
which years ago brought on rheumatic fever was precisely
an over-work of the same power—the power that compels
attention to unspontaneous subjects at definite times and
under all manner of non-harmonious conditions. Therefore, do not feel anxious, as if there were some inexplicable
decay of *me*: it is a mere case of local fatigue, easily to be
cured by rest.

Unhappily this 'rest' was never given. The
work done, both of letter-writing and other kind,
became less and less; but only because the absolute possibility of work became less and less.

To the Same.

You overrate the 'construction' of my letters: I
would willingly have constructed them well if I could, but
I came long since to the demonstrable conclusion, that a
good letter is simply impossible, and all I have ever done
in letter-writing has been but a long syllogism with this
corollary. A perfect letter would be—as you will see
whenever my Lectures are finished—a great epic. Therefore I have—for years past at least—never even attempted a

good letter; but have, nevertheless, as I explained last
week, done violence to the mechanism of my brain by
setting it to make out of two or three sticks, straws, and
stones, damnable little images of Kosmos. . . .

. . . God be praised that this storm did not arrive
while —— was on the sea! A ship is even now in distress on this shore. I wish I could discover who wrote
that verse,

> And for love and for victory
> One welcome was in store,
> In the lull
> Of the waves
> On a low lee shore.

I read it seventeen years ago, and it has washed upon the
' low lee shore ' of memory ever since.

I am going down to the beach presently, to see the
rollers and the beating ship, ' the noise of the captains and
the shouting.' Of all descriptions of waves and wrecks
none seems to me to approach—in the mixture of heaven
and sea and the nightmare sense of infinite engulphing
possibilities—the shepherd's [1] few words in the ' Winter's
Tale.' Don't suppose I could be writing if the ship were
really in great danger, but she has ridden out the night,
and to-day is gentle in comparison. . . .

.   .   .   .

Poor —— ! How long I shall remember that wintry
Wednesday in summer when I stood by the brink—the
dribbling brink—of his sapped and sodden grave, and saw
the oozy mud shovelled in upon him. The most infelicitous

---

[1] Clown's?

day was but one—any one—of all the days of his so many
years. The very September rain hardened into hail as it
fell on him, and his funeral was decreed in that hour
when it was necessary that the most irreverent wind should
hustle and hurry him into the earth ; but this was no more
than in keeping with the inexplicable and inveterate un-
prosperity of his life. It seemed as if, for years, he had
been out of step with Nature, and the wheels and beams
which expedite the welfare of all others, moved for him
but to lacerate and bruise.

Of the same friend, he said, to another correspondent :

He was as unparalleled in the wealth of his powers
(*no man ever so much impressed me with the sense of
many jewelled brilliancy*) as in the inexplicable poverty
of his accomplishment, the adverse machinery of a fate
that seemed constructed to counteract him.

Thackeray somewhere says, 'Heaven will be
full of the men who have failed here,' or words to
that effect. Belief in some such theory indeed
seems necessary to those who, believing in the
absolute goodness of God, look thoughtfully upon
lives which seem one protracted struggle of fruit-
less aspiration, of frustrated ambition, and of
thwarted endeavour.

In a letter home, about this time, he wrote :

Death has been so exacting near me these last weeks that all earthly separation looks by contrast but like another form of union.

He enquired anxiously for the latest news of a scheme which threatened the Charlton valley with being traversed by a railroad :

We have a dear dream, which may prove 'only a dream,' but meanwhile is too precious to be surrendered easily. It is this. You know that place at the top of Salt's Farm, where he intended to build a house? A mud cabin stands there now under a tall tree. We hope, whenever we may return home, to buy one acre at that spot and to build on it such a cottage as we lived in at Bridge of Allan, one about the size and character of the gamekeeper's cottage on the London Road. I obtained long since the estimate for such (or rather something more trustworthy than 'estimates,' the actual amount of what such a cottage was built for), and it may be done well for three or four hundred pounds. The acre of land and the cottage upon it would be under five hundred.

In October, Mr. and Mrs. Dobell returned to Granton, to the same house they had occupied there in the previous winter :

It is a solemn thing, (he wrote home) to return to old rooms—even old lodgings—after the vicissitudes of many absent months. At first there is the sense of distance and outsideness : you see everything, as it were, from an opposite shore, and each remembered object seems to need a *Te Deum*. But the shores are moving, the sea between them lessens, till past and present seem to meet, and as you sit down into the old chair you sit back into the former life. Here is the little table with the old cloth upon it, inked with so many of those songs which the external world are now reading and reviling, but which as I sit by it again I can hardly believe are printed. Speaking of these 'songs,' you will like to know that there are favourable notices in the 'Westminster' and 'British Quarterly.'

Of an article in some other review, he says:

It is cleverly written, but it should have commenced with the sentence with which it finishes: 'We have no patience with the whole school to which Mr. Dobell belongs.' . . .

. . An intimate and interesting friend of Tennyson's — Woolner, the sculptor—found us out at Portobello, and spent part of two days with us. . . . The announcement of Smith's new book is premature. You may look out for Massey on the twentieth of this month. (Pray buy as many copies as you can, for he publishes at his own risk).

Granton: October 10.

I am going to revenge myself for the family silence, by writing the merest bulletin. I take for granted that if any serious cause for taciturnity existed, you would have contrived directly or indirectly to let us know, and I may allow myself, therefore,—thank God—to be as retaliative as I please. . . .

From all I have heard, and a little I have seen, ——'s new book seems to abound in fine things, and to contain the most flagrant breaches of good taste. . . .

I suppose dear C—— has left you ten days since for the Academy. No one has told us any more of the picture he was painting. Did he finish it, and where did it appear? I should have often enquired about it, but I could hardly speak much without expressing an opinion, and I did not wish to influence him by mine, which is, and was, that it is unwise to paint or exhibit so early. . . .

With regard to the lecturing, be so kind as not to let Dr. —— ask me. I have set aside my intention of lecturing even to the Edinburgh Philosophical; and it would cost me as much thought to prepare a lecture to the working men as one for a cultivated audience—indeed, perhaps more. If 'England in Time of War' had met a roaring popularity, I should have arranged differently; but all it has done is to advance me a step forward in literary position. . . . It is necessary, therefore, to set about my next book with a less interval than I intended, and as the book (a portion of 'Balder: Part II.,' which I hope to publish in portions before publishing it as a whole) will require a great deal of study, in preparing the materials, before I begin the work of forming it, I have no brains or energy to spare for subordinate exertion.

'That he did not approach his task,' writes his friend Professor Nichol, in the Introductory Note to 'Thoughts on Art, Philosophy, and Religion,' without adequate preparation, the copious historical, biographical, antiquarian, and literary references in his common-place books abundantly testify. He had studied the leading characters, the prevalent superstitions—the Alchemy, Astrology, and Demonology—all the salient manners and customs of the age, and made himself master of the issues at stake with an amount of research and judgment which might have qualified him to write a great historic poem.

About this time occur a few short letters to the young poet, D. B—— (whose death was nearer than any of his friends seemed to apprehend), chiefly occupied with plans for the publication of the book, the longing to see which printed and published was like a strong passion in the dying man.

' I confess, my dear fellow,' Mr. Dobell writes,

that your resignation of all present designs upon Italy was a relief to me: for you are aware how serious a matter I always thought it for such an invalid *in posse* to exile himself from sister, friends, and country. Moreover, the omens, just now, promise some great change there; and if—as seems probable—the Popular party oust the Pope, and come to rule in Rome, you might reside there under much more favourable circumstances.

' Your letter of this morning,' says another despatch.

sat on my shoulders for a long time after reading it.
God help you, my dear fellow. It is vain for me to say
anything in reply to the accumulated and complicated
ills of which you tell me. . . . But I won't lose a day in
making you sure that your wishes shall be fulfilled with
regard to ' The Eclectic,' and that, in case of a refusal
there, another resource is probably at command. . . .

To M——, (after speaking of extreme specimens of the
'strong-minded woman' type).

Granton: October 7.

They are more to be pitied than blamed because, like
hypochondriacs, lunatics, and fanatics, the very conditions
of their disease disable them from perceiving the truth
from which they have fallen. They are like a favourite
dog gone mad, whom one deplores, appreciates, pities—but
is obliged, affectionately—to poison. Among a hundred
illustrations of what I mean I was amused the other day
with one which I give, not as more characteristic than
others, but merely as the latest I remember. . . .

. . . One of the pleasantest specimens of the type,
because having so much intellect as to be able to carry it
off with a gentle manner, called on me and we had a long
talk on the subject. I concluded it by saying that however people may differ as to the theory and logic of the
case, there was a *fact*, independent of all theories, which
seemed to me of serious importance. That I am certain,
from all I know of human—and manly—nature, that if
women became what the 'strong-minded' party would

make them, there would be one inevitable consequence—
that no first-class man would or could *fall in love* with
them. He might admire them as curious and interesting
phenomena, but could not feel towards them that inexpres-
sible emotion we call *love*. The unavoidable result would
be that they must either die spinsters or fall to the lot of
the inferior orders of men. She seemed perplexed at this
outlook ; but, after thinking a little, said she hoped it was
not true, for she hoped both to be married and to have
children, because unless she passed through both these
experiences *she should not think her whole nature developed.* Never dreaming—alas ! poor clever girl—that
the maiden who had arrived at so much self-consciousness
on such subjects as to be able to rationalise upon them
as useful ' developments of her nature,' had lost already
—without the power of knowing it—one of the most
exquisite attractions to a high-natured man, and one of
the most delicious differences of her sex.

To his Father and Mother.

Granton : October 31.

By throwing letters into disconnected memoranda, and
so doing away with the congruous succession of ideas, I
can decrease the labour of writing, and I am sure therefore you will not object to the dislocated state in which
my ' Sunday despatches' will in future appear. In poetry,
that which legitimately and necessarily *grows* is the very
desideratum, but in letter-writing the whole skeleton to
which a bone belongs is not always desirable ; and time

and thought are often wasted, therefore, in discovering
some other bit of osteology to decently succeed it. . . .

I suppose you have seen ——'s last book; but do you
know of its wonderful popularity? 'The Examiner,'
'The Athenæum,' 'The Press,' and many Scottish papers
have already given it enthusiastic reception, and the sale
the first week of its appearance exceeded the number of a
usual edition. I rejoice from my heart . . . bad as the
book is—and so bad a book was hardly ever *written by a
poet*, I think,—if it will sell, it is fortunate he did no
better. That he did as well is doubtless wonderful under
the circumstances . . . but—to paraphrase Johnson—
however curious it may be that a bear should dance that
does not make the dancing itself any better. With the
exception of a few lovely things here and there, it seems
to me that such books might be made *ad infinitum* by
putting roses, gold, kisses, dews, sunshine, marriage, and
blossoms, into a hat, and shaking them together. . . . So
much for popularity. . . .

To M——.

And you actually thought Maida was a maid? What
troubles will that name bring me into next? The owner
of it used sometimes to stray away from me in the town,
and when I shouted for her, Princes Street looked round.
This phenomenon occurring when I was walking with
Mrs. —— (a charming child-woman—no, that's an ugly
phrase, and suggests charwoman, but the fact for which it
stands is right lovely and lovable), she solved the difficulty,

by perceiving that *maida* was a dialect of *murder*, and
suggested I should avoid the public alarm by giving the
Spanish name its Spanish intonation. But, on trying the
experiment, the old effect followed—this time, however,
with a notable specific difference. For, whereas on former
occasions the street *en masse* had righted-about-face, in
this instance it was only every lady within hearing—*i.e.*
of course from the Wellington Statue to 'the Mound'—
that turned, like a marionette, upon her axis. And it was
not until 'half a mile of females,' as Mr. Weller would
have said, had been several times submitted to this
simultaneous and spasmodic volution that I discovered—
what you may discover by repeating the name *à l'Espagne*
—that whereas to my consciousness I had been holla-ing
Maida, a cognomen of nothing but my hound and a
foreign city, to the ears of those dear creatures I had been
shouting 'My dear,' with what they doubtless considered
to be 'that delicious English accent !' Think of what each
must have suffered as, slowly becoming sensible of the
terrible truth, she turned to husband, lover, brother, and
'the light of common day.' Feeling that I had no right
to be the cause of such continued human misery, I have
been obliged to discontinue taking Maida into the town.
She follows me everywhere in the country though, as you
may infer from the following complimentary anecdote.
Wishing to go down a grand old avenue, I asked a farmer
if there would be any objection, and, receiving a favourable
answer, thought it necessary to point to Maida, and ask
again—'Even though I had her with me?' 'Na, na,'

quoth Sandy, ' ye'll no be the waur o' that ; for *when the laird sees yon dog, he'll ken ye're somethin' genteel.'*

I was interrupted yesterday, and in resuming this morning will dismiss Maida with a reference to Landseer's deer-stalking pictures, for a better notion of her than I can give.

As I was dressing, the post brought me the new number of the ' National Magazine,' and my mind ever since has been full of Burd Helen—not the picture, though that is good, but the fact. Oh, wondrous miracle of woman-hood that—as the stars are seen in the deeps of a well—in its lowliest humility is most divine! Strange and inscrutable problem that it is at the moment of her most perfect self-abasement that the proudest of us feel ready to kiss the dust beneath her. That when, to herself, she is most wholly meritless, ' our comeliness is turned into corruption ' before her unconscious eyes.

We look with indifferent approbation, amused patronage, or · at most—affectionate esteem, upon the ' highly cultivated' modern young lady, whose well-kept faculties, in the prettiest canter, do really sometimes get neck-and-neck with the foot-pace of the rough horse of manhood. We bow our heads in humbled and hopeless homage—homage whose wonder can neither question, envy, nor compete—before Griselda and Burd Helen. It is from want of knowing these and other secrets of man's nature, that the ' Rights of Women ' ladies must blunder on to the perdition of womanhood, and that no assertion by female pens of the excellencies, or claims, or superiorities

of women can do anything but increase every evil they
deplore.

To ——.

November 6, 1856.

I felt that I should best thank you for your book [1] by
fulfilling literally the request that preceded it that I
should read it without delay. It had not been a day in
the house before it was begun. I enclose the few notes I
made. They are few, not from negligence or haste, but
from a reason that gives me, I think, almost as much
pleasure as it will give you. I soon found that the faults
of the book were subordinate errors, and its merits of such
sustained equality as to give but little opportunity for
special praise.

I know no novel by a young author of such quiet,
substantial, unmitigated excellence, or that, while fresh
and original (in the sense of being always 'at first hand'),
is so thoroughly free from every kind of youthful melo-
drama or extravagance, and from that incompleteness of
conception which usually marks the best efforts of youth.
Indeed, if I had not seen your powers grow so steadily
and notably, I should feel this fine balance and sobriety a
bad sign—as indicating a premature character. But with
such a signal growth as your literary experience has been, it
is an augury of the happiest interpretation. I am in hopes,
too, from the fact that your men are more manlike than
the men of most lady novelists (who are almost invariably

---

[1] The first novel of a young writer, on whose MSS. he had spent
much time and care.

mere women in costume and talking in *mezzo-basso*) that
you possess that power of self-transmutation, which is so
rare among women (*happily* rare, unless they are authoresses), and for want of which our female writers so soon
play out their *rôle* and are tedious ever after. . . . I am
sure you will not allow any 'success' to make you careless,
or to hurry you into omitting in future works those qualities of painstaking truth and delicate fidelity to the things
heard and seen in the imagination by which you have
gained what you now show to the world. . . .

Among the enclosed notes occur the following :

It is not the excess, but the *imperfection* of love that
ever makes it selfish.

There is no strength so strong as absolute goodness :
directly 'strength' shows itself recognisably and separ-
ately as strength, it is imperfect. White light is white,
not by deficiency but by completion : and in proportion as it
is coloured must it somewhere or other be defective. The
mistake is in calling a character 'good' which has merely
some elements of goodness in excess, (by comparison with
its other constituents) and in calling a character 'strong'
because its strength is so badly combined as to be noticeable.

To his Father and Mother.

Granton : November 8.

I have not seen or heard Thackeray yet—being unable
to go out at night. . . . The crush has been great at his
Lectures, and the enthusiasm among the more liberal

Edinburghians very warm; but, with a curious want of
tact, in so wise a man, he ran foul of the local prejudices
by an unnecessary attack on Queen Mary, and has roused
bitterly hostile feeling throughout the Aytoun party. . . .
He behaved with admirable ability when, upon his attack-
ing Queen Mary, the Tories present got up a storm of
hisses. Instead of seeming angry or confounded, he began
to laugh and appeared to find it such excellent fun, that
it recoiled upon the heads of his opponents. Aytoun,
however, next day at dinner, turned the tables upon him,
by a similar presence of mind. 'Can you tell me,' said
Thackeray to the company, 'who Percy Jones is?'[1] 'Oh,'
said Aytoun, instantly, 'he's a d—d rascal who lives at
Ipswich.'

The same letter explains that illness had also
obliged him to decline, what he would have liked
to accept—a courteous request to open the session
of the Eclectic Society :

It was just the kind of address I should like to give,
but I know that to get it ready with my brains in their
present state would knock me up for the winter ; and, as
I could not do less than my best, I was forced to decline.

November 16.

. . . I see you think I did ill to miss 'such fine opportunities' as the delivery of the Eclectic address and the
hearing of Thackeray's Lectures. I think you don't consider that it often requires more strength and judgment to

---

[1] The name under which Professor Aytoun published 'Firmilian.'

resist than to embrace an opportunity.   It is better to do
nothing than to do other than well.   In public matters, as
in war, the game is to him who makes the fewest blunders :
and the self-knowledge which refuses a flattering opportunity, when it comes under circumstances which do not
ensure that it shall be successfully accepted, is among
the most valuable of talents.   I went to Thackeray's last
Lecture.   It was good—from its strong, honest, unflinch-
ing demolition of that bundle of fine rags, George IV.—but
(except for a few turns of his peculiar manner) would not
have attracted attention from a man not eminent.   I had
a good study of his side face—sitting very near him—and
was interested to remark how the countenance had improved
in moral power since I saw him lecture six years ago.   All
the good he thinks and does is creditable, in no ordinary
degree, for the great head is a mass of contrariety, and his
inner life must have been an enormous chaos in which,
through long agonies, duty is slowly working towards a
Cosmos still far off.   The greatest hall in Edinburgh was
crammed, and the platform was well laden with brains.
There were some odd conjunctions, *e.g.*, Aytoun and I sat
side by side.   Curiously enough I had met Aytoun in the
morning (when walking with ——, who stopped to speak
to him) for the first time for more than a year.   After the
first salutations, I laid my hand on his shoulder and said,
very quietly and slowly, so that he should not lose a word,
but looking good-humouredly into his face, that he should
understand I was not ill-willed : ' I was much pained to
hear from our friend, Francis Russell, that you thought
me the author of a vulgar attack on you which appeared

in the American papers some time ago. I wish you to be good enough to bear in mind that if I should ever find it my duty to attack you, it will be in open field and with the weapons of a gentleman.' I was glad of an opportunity of making him distinctly aware both that I had nothing to do with the anonymous insult, and that I might, if necessary, use other modes of warfare.

To the same.

Granton: November 23.

I have had more writing than usual this past week, for, in addition to other matters, poor —— chose to declare war against me a few days ago, and, as he did it pen in hand, I thought better to put what I had to say on record, than to trust the memory of such a very impulsive person. He is an amusing belligerent, poor fellow, for he fights and borrows almost in the same breath. . . . Some time ago B—— got me to write a sketch of Dr. Simpson for his 'Men of the Time.' As I wished —— to have the money for it, and —— had commissions to do other portraits for B——, I sent my sketch to B—— through ——; who, in addition to giving it to B——, used it in a New York paper. There was no great harm in that, if B—— was 'agreeable,' but —— did more; he inserted in my sketch —inlaying them so that no one could suppose they were interpolated—slanders upon some of my best Edinburgh friends (the Blackies). This article is copied from the New York paper into the Edinburgh papers, and actually posted up in the shop windows. A part of the article was

known to be mine (from my having applied to Dr. Simpson
for sundry medical statistics contained in it) : it appears as
though I had been guilty of libelling in this cowardly
fashion some of the very people with whom I am on
the best terms, and—if possible, worse still—of *abusing*
Aytoun, upon whom a personal attack is also inserted.

Happily the Blackies know me too well not to enter in
an instant into the real explanation ; but the case is a fair
specimen of the want of gumption—and things more
valuable even than gumption—which makes poor ——
such a dangerous friend. . .

Nothing shall make me give him up, but the affair
(which is only one of several in which he has mixed me
up with his public follies) showed me the time was come
for speaking distinctly : and he has taken offence, for the
time, at least.

The first portion of the following letter to
his father, relates to the placing of his youngest
brother at the Agricultural College at Cirencester ;
a step which was, of course, a departure from the
educational traditions of the family :

Granton : November 27.

I thoroughly understand, and enter into, what you feel
about Cirencester. At the same time perhaps its very
temptations, being but modified forms of the temptations
of the open world, may be a good school: for he meets
them there under controlling influences (home and other),

and in a favourable frame of mind.   And since, of course,
the great object of all education is, not to *eradicate*, but to
modify and direct, it is likely that circumstances under
which the natural dispositions of the particular character
are able to have exercise and satisfaction, without violating
the conscience, will be more favourable to your ultimate
aim than a less congenial sort of discipline. . . .

. . . With regard to Robertson, dearest Pater, concerning whom your iterated requests forbid me to be longer
silent, I have said nothing, because I so thoroughly entered
into your admiration for the moral character of the man,
that I did not like to disappoint you by differing with your
estimate of his intellect.   I have read the Lecture on
Poetry carefully through, and find in it evidence of a most
sweet nature and a fine æsthetic taste ; but if you deduct
from it all that is really Emerson's, Carlyle's, Goethe's, &c.,
you leave nothing for the creation of his own intellect.
He seems to me a case of a poet's brain diminished below
creation point, but having taste and fine discrimination
enough to gather the best thoughts of others, and being by
temperament disposed to make selection from the newest
thinkers of his time.   But, intellectually, he is merely an
early and ready disciple of greater men, reproducing their
thinking in a captivating manner, but having no claim to
the power of creation or discovery on his own account.   I
see this to be his type unmistakeably in the Lecture on
Poetry.   At the same time, the moral nature seems of that
exquisite kind which is appropriately united to talents so
tasteful and beautiful. . . .

CHAPTER IX.

1856.

SOME time during this year, 1856, Mr. Dobell—at special request—prepared an Address to the Edinburgh medical students, the following notes for which were found among his papers :

Notes of an Address to Medical Students.

You have graduated—literally, you have *taken steps.* But what steps? Steps on that Jacob's ladder of human improvement whose base rests on earth, indeed, but whose top should be in heaven. Let the success that has attended you in these first stairs of the ascent be the stimulus to such a noble ambition as shall not rest till the highest rundle be gained. . . .

The active and individual life of each of you may be said to commence from to-day. I wish, therefore, to speak briefly of the three principal facts which make up the practical life of every individual in a civilized community : his social position ; his pecuniary resources ; and his private character. On each of these I shall say a word,

and first of *Social Position.*   At a time when the Continental world is divided into two great contending parties
—representing the opposite extremes of opinion : the one
crying frantically for *Liberté, Egalité,* and the other sworn
to uphold a system of conventional and unreal distinctions
—you are about to occupy a peculiar and very interesting
place.

You—Med. Doctores—are going out, a titled few, into
the midst of the untitled many : and you have received
your honourable titles in a University whose motto is,
Palmam qui meruit ferat.

Let your future life and conversation be in keeping
with this commencement. Let it be yours to show, on the
one hand, that rank is natural and inherent in mankind,
that human society can only healthily exist by a due and
happy ordination of degrees ; but to vindicate, on the
other hand, the great and irresistible truth, that title should
be the outward sign of inward superiority, that dignity in
name should be the mere index to dignity in fact, and
that social distinctions are then only just and venerable
when those who bear them are of Nature's aristocracy—
' Nobles '—in the words of a great Scotchman, spoken of
your Covenanting forefathers—' Nobles by right of an
earlier creation, priests by the imposition of a mightier
Hand.'

With regard to *Pecuniary Resources,* the situation of
the physician is so special and so important that it becomes
me to speak and you to think upon it with no ordinary
attention.   The whole monetary business of the physician
is, by necessity, of an exceptional kind.   In the ordinary

transactions of the market-place the commodity transferred to the buyer bears some calculable proportion to the price received by the seller. But it is the quality of purely intellectual labour that it admits of no such bargain and sale. You cannot *pay* the author ' whose thoughts '—in the phrase **of** our Laureate—' enrich the **blood of** the world : ' you cannot *pay* the advocate **who** wins you your inheritance or vindicates your fame : you cannot *pay* **the** physician who steps between you and the grave, or snatches a beloved from the open jaws of death, or restores to a faint and fading life the health that gives **vigour to** duty and rest **to** enjoyment. **In** all **these** cases the greatest monetary return that can be made by the recipient of an incalculable benefit is no more **than an** *acknowledgment* **of** its receipt, a recognition of a **debt that can** never **be** paid. Let this fact have its due effect on **the mind of** every one of you. Remember that, in its sphere, commerce is noble, honourable, and beneficent : **but that** the spirit which is to animate you is a spirit higher than the commercial.

The calculations which adjust the commodity given to **the** price received are not those on which you are now going **forth to** distribute your science, **your** talents, and your sympathies. You will show your consciousness that what you impart **is** inestimable by forbidding yourselves to entertain the very notion of an estimate. Whatever your hand finds to do will be done with your might. While in other departments of industry the quality of the workmanship is in proportion to the remuneration of the workman, **it is** the pride of the physician **to** emulate the operations

of the great optimist—Nature—and never to do less than
his best.   It is his divine privilege to imitate that 'Good
Physician' who gave 'without money and without price,'
and to bestow on the poor man for his thanks and the
rich man for his fee the same deepest learning, the **same**
highest skill, and the same most excellent patience.

If it be 'more blessed to give than to receive,' how
favoured his function who gives what can never be repaid!
how god-like his vocation whose life is one impartial bene-
ficence—who causes the **sun of** his cheering influence **to**
shine upon the **evil and** the good, and sends his healing
rain upon the just and the unjust!

I am now speaking to *you*—Med. Doctores—and point-
ing out your duties. If I were addressing the world at
large, I should perhaps have occasion to descant as emphatically **upon the duties of the** patient **to the Doctor as I**
have now done on those **of** the Doctor to the patient.   **Or,**
perhaps, I should rather say in each case, on the duties
that every man owes to himself and to Right.   Which
leads me to the third element in your public lives, your
Private Characters.   And leaving the more solemn aspects
of the subject, and dealing with it professionally, I recognise
as the first of scientific maxims **the** great moral precept,
Physician, heal thyself.   Omitting those higher considerations which are nevertheless peculiarly imperative on
those **whose** daily duties are **in** the house of affliction and
by the bed of death, and who, by the specialities of their
position, will have to enter more than other men into the
secrets, sorrows, and temptations of suffering humanity,
and taking my stand-point on the lower levels of science,

I find that the moral excellence which religion demands is the highest guarantee of philosophical success. 'To do justice, and to love mercy, and to walk humbly,' is the ethics at once of Science and Religion. The just man, whose soul is itself in constant equilibrium, will best perceive the exquisite justice of nature, and understand those fine compensations by which material stability is balanced and maintained. He who is himself merciful is best prepared to appreciate that atmosphere of mercy which surrounds the solid necessities and harder provisions of creation : to detect the defensive contrivance that sheathes an operative function, to observe the restorative powers which accompany the susceptibility to disease, and to recognise —in all that ample variety which Science reveals to the eye attempered to receive it—'the silent magnanimity of Nature.' And the humility of the Christian is not less valuable in the hospital, the class-room, or the study, than in the common paths of life. The first condition of real success in any natural science is, that it be approached devoutly, in the attitude not of the dogmatist but of the disciple. The great secret of the modern attainments, and the ancient failures, in these scientific fields is the fact, that *we* are humble and *they* were proud.

Nature—like Falstaff—will not 'give a reason on compulsion.'

Ancient philosophy came to facts, and squared them on that bed of Procrustes—an *à priori* theory. *Modern* philosophy is thankful for the facts, and waits till they make a bed for themselves.

The one 'called spirits from the vasty deep;' *the other*

was content to analyse water and enquire the causes of the tides.

The one sought, as a master, to 'bind the sweet influences of Pleiades and loose the bands of Orion;' *the other* was satisfied, as a pupil, to wait upon the courses of the stars.

The one launched the thunderbolt from the hand of an arbitrary Jove, and strove to avert its terrors by the hecatomb and the human sacrifice; *the other* sent a child's kite into the cloud, and held the lightning in a woman's silken thread. Yet *the one* left science an empty boast, a brilliant sophism, an ambitious superstition; and *the other* traverses the earth, with the strength of Titans and the pace of the once-worshipped winds, measures and weighs the planets that were held divine, adds new universes to the empire of intelligence, passes on its electric wings the magic messenger of Prospero, and unites in bodily intercourse or mental communion the most distant families of man. In a word, the dispensations that govern us are consistent with themselves; and he who would excel in the investigation of Nature will find his best apprenticeship in the school of Revelation. The subject of his study is a production of the Divine Essence, and no man will understand it less for approaching the character of the Divine. 'Blessed are the pure in heart, for they shall *see* God;' and the great Canon is of universal application whether we would behold Him in the cosmos without or the microcosm within.

.   .   .   .

We have, as it were, studied geography together; you

are now going on your travels upon the face of the real
world. The marks on the map stand for very stern realities.

Hills, high and difficult—but then what a prospect!

Rivers, dangerous and deep—but then how fertili-
sing!

Roads, long and weary—but leading to what gorgeous
cities!

—And trod with what sweet companions!

We have gone—as it were—through the grammar and
vocabulary--and you are now to speak and hear the
living language. Those of you who have been in foreign
lands can testify to the seriousness of the task, and that
the well-learned syntax of the desk or the class-room is
but too often at fault in the ten thousand quick necessities
of daily circumstance. But then how delightful the
sound of the spoken tongue! How full of new meanings
and interests! How warm with human passions! How
sacred—(it may be)—with Divine Intelligence! May
those travels, guided by the science you take hence, be
fruitful to yourselves and beneficial to mankind! May
that language learned at the knees of Alma Mater be the
mother-tongue of truth and goodness! We have spent
three years together in military discipline, and you have
practised yourselves thoroughly in the use of weapons.
You are now about to enter upon the seas and fields of
practical duty, and to reduce the Cronstadts and Sebasto-
pols of actual human ill. Remember that the battle of
life is as much above your quiet exercises within these
peaceful walls, as Trafalgar above the sham-fight at South-

ampton ; and that all the learning, talent, virtue, and courage of the greatest and the best among you, will not be too much to bear the flag of Science triumphant, and prove yourselves worthy of those gallant predecessors, who placed it in the van of the world.   I am confident that while our soldiers and sailors in the North and in the East are shedding their blood in the cause of enlightenment, and winning for their country that proudest title of a free nation, 'the stay of the weak and the friend of the oppressed,' you, in other but not less glorious contests, will as faithfully uphold the honour of the British name. Recollecting that, as ' Peace hath her victories as well as War,' in either conflict 'England expects every man to do his duty,' and all worldly prudence and all true religion are summed up in that saying of the great Christian warrior : ' Trust in God, and keep your powder dry ! '

CHAPTER X.

His own words may most fitly begin such history
as belongs to this year: the earlier part of which
saw his residence in Scotland brought to an abrupt
close by the break-down of his health.

Granton: January 1, 1857.

Dearest father and mother, God indeed bless and love
and keep you in the year to come and in all after time!
On New Year's Day I cannot begin a letter without these
words; though, so far as what they contain is concerned,
there is no day in the year which is not New Year's Day.

'New Year's Day'—how strange it is to bring the
holy English feeling which surrounds it in contact with a
people who approach it from another side. With the
Scotch it is the one safety valve to a year of high pressure,
and the flesh, let loose for twenty-four hours, takes its
revenge with a fierceness of carnal resolution that 'must
be seen to be understood.' You should have been in
Edinburgh to-day, and seen the great army of the Body
that debouched inexhaustibly through all its main streets
—a roaring parti-coloured river, where a fallen child or a

blind beggar made an instant mob—as in a stream at
flood so much as a walking-stick set straight will make an
eddy. It was curious to walk up the same streets where
on Monday I walked after Hugh Miller's hearse, and to
think what different causes could produce the same 'pomp
and circumstance' of populous life. Never since the
death of Chalmers has Edinburgh been so unanimous in
honour. Even Christopher North's funeral was sectional
and cold by comparison. The shops were shut, the common people drew up in thick masses on each side of the
streets where the cavalcade was to pass; and through this
flesh-and-blood corpus, as it were, all the mind of the
city followed, in long-drawn procession, half-a-mile in
length, the hearse of 'the stone-mason of Cromarty.' The
whole thing was national as distinct from popular. To
make the day complete Nature herself spread over it the
robe of innocency—but, as it were, of a dabbled innocency,
snow and thaw together. You saw, of course, the result of
the post-mortem examination, which showed a brain past
responsibility. A terrible example of what mental work
can do even to such a physical giant as Hugh Miller. The
last time I saw him I felt suspicious that his mind was
shaken, for such tottering nervousness in so vast a frame
(for he really looked quite colossal) seemed more than
ordinary *mauvaise honte*, and he complained much of his
broken health.

You must excuse the memoranda character of my
letters, for I find it necessary to escape every avoidable
exertion, and of all others that of letter-writing tires me
most. . . . The day before yesterday I had to talk for

many hours, with hardly any intermission, on subjects often the most difficult, and with a succession of fresh and well-furnished interlocutors, and was less fatigued than I should be in constructing an ordinary 'Sunday letter.' I forget if I have mentioned this state of things before. . . .

If our dear hope of going south in spring is fulfilled, what a new-old world of unknown-well-known little people we shall find coming up in the light of the familiar faces!

I had not seen the *Times* article when your note mentioned it. It is a very valuable one for Smith and me; more so than any other form of eulogy. I recognise in it ——'s cardinal mistake—which he and I have argued over so many a time—of taking *oratory* for *poetry*. Oratory thinks of an audience; the first essential and differentia of the Poet is that he thinks of nothing but his subject, and embodies it in the forms and language that are essentially the *best* expression of it, because essentially the most congruous with its nature. His works, therefore, are universal and immortal, because whenever a great mind arises anywhere it recognises the essential truth of what he has done.

I understand there is an attack on me in this month's 'Blackwood.' See there a beautiful poem ('Maid Barbara') by a young M. D., whom I was describing some letters back.

January 10.

Dear -——'s book is progressing well through the press. I forget whether I told you that, a few weeks ago, I wrote

to Smith, Elder, & Co., to say I was sure its success would
be risked by his dedication of it to me, and that, if they
thought so too, I would take the responsibility of cutting
it out.   This placed them in an amusing predicament, but
they had the good sense ‘reluctantly to be obliged to
agree’ with me.   ——[1] will be disappointed not a little ;
but, in the present hot state of party criticism, I should
have d——d his book by accepting it.   Speaking of
books, I don't know whether you can assist me in a
matter I am much interested in just now.   Poor B——,
of whom I have frequently spoken, is at last dying.   He
has written a small book of Ballads, of which Marston
thinks highly, and the only happiness the poor fellow can
receive in this world (and he pants for this with a kind of
desperate morbid thirst) is to see his book out before he
goes. . . . I have found a publisher, who will take it in
hand, if twelve friends will each order a pound's worth of
copies. . .

Apropos of poems, have you read ‘Aurora Leigh’?
It is not a great *poem*, and illustrates in an interesting
manner the great fact that no female author ever wrote, or
ever will write, one ; but it is a magnificent modern Saga,
and contains some of the finest poetry of this century.
The authoress is as much superior to every other woman
who ever wrote, or, probably, ever will write, as Shakespeare
was to other men ; and, critically speaking, it is most
curiously instructive to note how the head and top of
feminine intellectual eminence is necessarily inferior to

---

[1] A young friend, who had gone abroad leaving his first book—
poem—to pass through the Press under Mr. Dobell's supervision.

'he head and top of masculine. . . You will see a Sonnet
on her, which I sent a few days ago to the ' National Magazine.' *Apropos* of the ' National,' what a capital leader that
is of dear Albert's, on ' Popular Pleasures'; a little too
circular and mundane, perhaps, but thoroughly able and
excellent. . . .

What bewitching weather this must be in England.
For two days even the Scottish air has been what in
Scotland may be called balmy, and the twilights have
been as tender as if thrushes were to be heard. How it
makes us look forward more than ever to the dear spring
and the long hope of the visit to home! As the time
draws nearer, we strain our eyes towards it, as it were, to
see if it really can have so blessed a face, and with a kind
of yearning incredulity.

To M——.

Have you read ' Aurora Leigh'? I am reading it
now with profound admiration. Not, however, that it is
a great poem, for it is not a poem, but a Saga, but because
it contains—blossoming up out of its green grass, and by
its dusty roads, or spouting up like geysers from its flats
—some of the finest poetry that has been written this
century : poetry such as Shakespeare's sister might have
written, if he had had a twin. The same voice with the
female difference in it—the Dian to that Apollo, as if the
sun were going through the changes and infirmities of the
moon.

I hold it to be no poem—for no woman (not even

such a 'large-brained woman and large-hearted man' as
Mrs. Browning, who has occurred but once since literature
began, and will not come again for a millennium or two)
can create one; but it is one of the most signal and
monumental books written in modern times. And it is
beautiful and touching to see the woman who, of all others,
might most rightfully claim exemption from her sex and
enter the masculine arena, giving us, as her ultimate
experience, this culminating moral: that woman is not
born to be the artist, that even when most strongly and
cosmically furnished, she is still not substantive, and that
the most glorious of Auroras must needs turn from her
best achievements as 'failure' and vanity, to find blessedness and success and content as housewife even to a
Romney Leigh. The more I live and study human nature,
the more I perceive all feminine literature to be an error
and anomaly. A necessary anomaly at present, and to be
dealt with as such; but always, under all circumstances,
to be recognized as an anomaly, and never suffered to
enter into the ideal of human society. 'I suffer not a
woman to speak in the Church' is of far wider application
than to the 'assembly of the saints,' and applicable for
*reasons not derogatory, but in the highest and divinest
degree honourable, to womanhood.* Meanwhile, we are
not yet in an 'ideal of human society,' and for 'the
present distress' the anomaly becomes often the temporary
and salutary *nomos.*

To his Father and Mother.

January 22.

I almost thought that for the first time in more than three years I was to miss my weekly letter to you altogether, such constant and unexpected matters these last few days have kept me so continually occupied.

Then follows a crowded list of engagements, social, literary and artistic : Noel Paton's poem-picture of ' The Guardsman's Return ' is described ; particulars are given of a controversy concerning the charges of plagiarism brought against Alexander Smith in some of the literary journals, and of the line he had adopted in defending Smith.

In regard to the approaching publication of the dying young poet's book, he says :

So the poor fellow will be able to feel before he dies that one thing in his life has really happened as he wished it.

February 18.

If nothing deranges our present hopes and plans, we leave Scotland early in April. . . . I stir towards the thought as the blind sap in a tree towards spring. You will see by the enclosed paragraph that I am again well enough to face night air. I enclose the scrap, because it will explain something else that is to take place, which you will be interested to hear. At the party it mentions

I was asked, by the family who give one of the others in the same series, to give a lecture to the company on the Theory of Poetry. I declined, on the ground that such a mixed evening-party audience were not likely to enter into anything so much below the surface.

He then explains how the arrangement, which ended in his delivering a 'Lecture on the Nature of Poetry' to the Philosophical Society, was made. And then goes on to speak of the death of the young poet B——, 'without seeing his book, but with a dying wish in his last letter to his sister, that it should appear.'

February 27.

I began this letter last night, tired with the day, but was obliged to lay it aside in favour of another letter on business that could not be postponed. I have been more than usually pressed lately, for, in addition to having my lecture to prepare, and the proofing of A——'s book to do, poor —— has been hindered by illness from some critical work he had engaged to get done, and I have been obliged to help him. And as, besides, this is the very heyday of Edinburgh fullness and activity, you may imagine there is sufficient tax just now upon energies not over healthy.

My anxiety concerning E—— has also been increasing. . . . I tell you these things that you—and I mean totally and individually—may understand any silence and

brevity, and comprehend that it is merely silence of the
hand, not of the heart.

To his eldest Sister.

. . . I hope dear W—— saw that I acknowledged his
witty letter in a paragraph of one of the family despatches.
If it were not for constant experience of how difficult
even the best people find it to believe anything that is
beyond their actual eyesight and earshot, I should think it
unnecessary to say he may be assured the delay (in answering it) has neither been for want of love, or interest,
or inclination, or remembrance.   I know you may be apt
to conclude that one like me, unoccupied, just now, in
what is called a 'business,' can have little to do; but I
could readily show you that had I two or three businesses
to look after, I should not have so much tax on my head
and hands as in this that seems to you an idle life.   A
tax unavoidable and necessary in the performance of important duties and the main objects of the work so evidently set before me. . . . I mention this because it not
only bears on my occasional apparent neglect of your
letters, but may help also to explain such things in my
family epistles as are open to misconstruction. . . .

. . . If I speak of any small portion of what I am
doing, recollect that it is not from any vanity or self-
consciousness of mine, but from an idea that it must be
interesting to the dear ones far away to be able to realise
how things are going with us here. . . .

I was very glad to hear (*à propos* of 'Politics') that

Mr. —— [the father-in-law of the sister to whom he writes] is taking so prominent a part in the affairs of ——. My own belief as to my own duties regarding politics is in no way altered; but all principles of that kind depend for their value upon their consistency with other principles of some harmonious system. And for anyone who does not hold such opinions, regarding Church Government, and the general scheme of Revelation, as make an abstinence from politics a logical consequence, to keep apart from those great public activities (when more imperative duties permit him to take a share in them) is a kind of social sin. And it is due to their own family superiority, and to the great principle that men of business can be and ought to be also something higher and better, that the ——s should publicly show themselves to be what they are. Every time a successful man of business gives evidence to the world at large that business is not inconsistent with the highest cultivation of the nobler qualities, he is doing a public benefit which will ramify in a thousand ways he hardly dreams of.

After speaking of the arrangements in regard to the lecture he was to deliver—which lecture he says, in a letter home, now it is written, seems to him 'good of its kind;' and of the manner of audience to whom it would be addressed, he wrote :

My mother says she should be pleased if she heard I was preaching *Religion* anywhere, but that to lecture on the *Nature of Poetry* seems to her mere vanity, in which she can take no interest. She forgets that the nature of poetry is precisely the question that underlies the most difficult and serious questions that concern the human mind, and those human thoughts and feelings with which religion has to do, and that he who should answer it more satisfactorily than it has yet been answered would do more than could be done by any other single act to alter and influence the whole system of human opinion. The lecture is, I believe, to be given early in the week after next. . . . We propose to stay with the Blackies while I give the lecture and for a few days afterwards; and then to go for a week, for rest and recruiting, to Bridge of Allan, before embarking on the long longed-for journey southwards. . . . How quietly I write all this—for it is as yet but ink and paper, and plans have been so often, on this subject, nothing more, that they have lost the power to stir me.

Edinburgh: April 9.

I know you will be anxious to know how yesterday evening went off, and I therefore scribble a despatch by the first post this morning. God be thanked—for it would not only have been personally unpleasant if the thing had been less than a success, but things more important than the personal would have been compromised by an appearance of failure—all was better than I dared to expect. I had been so ill for a week past with an aggravation of rheumatism, and my throat had got into so bad a state, that I felt uncertain of being able to speak for half an

hour even at the pitch of ordinary conversation. . . . .
The hall was creditably filled, without being full, and the
audience was of precisely the kind I could have chosen.
. . . The lecture lasted nearly two hours, and, so far as I
can judge, was very well received. I don't think I ever
saw so unceasingly attentive an audience. Those of my
critical friends, whom I spoke to afterwards, spoke highly
of the lecture. . . . The only complaint I heard was, that
it was 'too deep.' I was happy to find that I made everyone hear with ease, and—being so well prepared—was
able to read without losing the eyes of the audience—a
great matter—and that I really, after the first instant,
didn't feel less comfortable than if I had been talking to
a single auditor. I tell you all these little particulars
because I know you will all wish to realise the thing as
far as may be. . . . I trust to write within a day or two,
and tell you the day we propose to leave for the dear
southward journey.

The delivery of this lecture proved too great
a strain on throat and lungs already irritated by
the over-harsh Scotch climate, and on a generally
exhausted and over-taxed nervous system. An
eminent physician, consulted in deference to his
wife's anxieties, recommended an immediate return
to the South, and gave such a verdict on the state
of his chest as precluded the idea of any renewed
residence in Scotland.

. The homeward journey was undertaken almost

directly, and they reached Detmore towards the
end of April.

His father's note-book records that ' he looks
very thin and ill, is very deaf, and has a very bad
cough ;' adding, that he is ' very unaffected, the
same dear fellow as ever, but very serious.'

Weeks of illness followed, during which conflicting medical opinions were given as to the state
of the lungs, while there was no difference of
opinion as to the extreme nervous prostration.

Any return to Edinburgh was forbidden ; the
mild climate of the Isle of Wight prescribed for
the next winter.

Among the pleasant incidents of his residence
in Scotland had been the many warm friendships
formed. Of some of these, of indeed the larger
proportion, it happens that little or no record is
to be found in the letters in our hands. In many
cases personal intercourse was never again possible,
correspondence almost as impossible. A few of
his Scotch friends were, by and by, from time to
time, his guests in England, but for others, whom
he never again met, his friendship remained as
real, and his interest in them as lively, as on the
day he had bidden them good-bye.

Among those with whom he had enjoyed
pleasant association, and whose names hardly occur
in these pages, were the well-known and eminent
artists, the Brothers Paton, and James Archer.

Studies of his head, for pictures they were
painting, were made both by Mr. Archer and by
Sir Noel Paton, and of the hours spent in their
studios, and the talks that took place during those
hours, he afterwards spoke with lively interest.

Mr. Archer's subsequent removal to London
made the interchange of visits in his case feasible ;
but in the case of Sir Noel Paton, with the exception of one solitary interview some ten years later,
all communication ceased when Mr. Dobell left
Scotland ; and this, his wife says, was with him a
matter of no common regret.

At this period when—spite of all the hopeful
confidence to the contrary which never deserted
him—power of sustained effort and consecutive
literary work was lost, it does not seem out of
place to give the following letter from Dr. Westland Marston to Mrs. Dobell ; furnishing, as it does,
a sort of summary of what, in Mr. Marston's estimation, is the value of the work that had been
accomplished.

Westland Marston, Esq. LL.D. to Mrs. Sydney Dobell.

Notting Hill, London : December 1877.

Your letter on the Memorials you have in preparation
would naturally recall to me (were recall needed) the ever-
valued subject of them.   Often do I live again in that
long passed time, when he first called on me and brought
me a copy of ' The Roman,' which, with its noble fervour
of tone and wealth of illustration, proved that we had
amongst us a new poet, whose genius was dedicated, not
chiefly to the expression of personal feelings or to the
treatment of domestic themes, but to the worship of liberty
and the defence of a glorious but enslaved country.   The
sympathy which, in this first poem, he showed with the
larger interests of human life, is indeed discernible in all
the more important works that subsequently proceeded
from his pen.   His patriotism and love of orderly freedom
are, of course, obvious in ' England in Time of War,' and
in his ' Sonnets on the War.'   In both, while they present
many phases of the experience of individuals, the love of
country and the hatred of oppression may be recognized
as pervading motives.   In ' Balder' the ethical purpose
of the poet is less immediately apparent.   Its influence,
however, is not the less real.   Primarily, the poem was
designed to show the egotism of the intellect as contrasted
with that of the heart. Besides this purpose, however, there
was one deeper and more latent, which would probably have
been fully developed had the second division of ' Balder'
ever been completed.   A believer in the Millennial reign

of our Lord, the writer desired to suggest the necessity
for Divine Rule upon earth. Thus, in the First Part of his
drama he strove to exhibit the inevitable fallibility of
human judgment, to show how the higher motives of our
nature may at times occasion the very results which flow
from the worst motives, and thence to deduce the need for
an Omniscient Judge upon earth, who should pronounce
upon human actions in accordance with their moral origin.
I am here stating—not discussing—the poet's theological
aim.　It has been objected by some critics, that his purpose in ' Balder ' was developed through morbid agencies,
and that the tragedy resulting from the mental relations
between Balder and his wife could not have arisen from
the interaction of healthy minds.　If I can trust my
recollection, I ventured upon a similar comment, and
received from the author an avowal that the moral disease
in question was part of his plan ; but that, nevertheless,
the sin of a nature like Balder's, which, in pursuit of its
ideal, ignored domestic ties and obligations, and the error
of Amy in seeking to limit the world-wide aims of her
husband by the exactions of an individual love, were
relatively noble, while they led precisely to the same issue
which might have accrued from the basest and most selfish
passions.　Art, no doubt, sets limits to morbid delineation,
for the simple reason that in the degree in which motives
and characters are exceptional, the conclusions to be drawn
from them are limited in their application.　On the other
hand, were we to exclude from imaginative treatment all
that is in some degree morbid, the exhibition of human

feelings and the lessons to be drawn from them would
have to be confined within very narrow bounds.   Pride,
ambition, revenge, the selfishness of love itself—in a word,
all the forms of human egoism which, from the first, have
supplied subjects of dramatic illustration, would at once
have to be abandoned.

I will not attempt to draw the line beyond which
analysis of human disease ceases to be desirable in poetry.
Of this poem of ' Balder ' it may, at all events, be affirmed,
that it enters into and reveals states of being and suffering
which, however rare, are still real, and such as may in a
large measure consist with noble qualities in the persons
delineated.   Even those who protest most strongly against
the analysis of diseased conditions of mind might surely
find the highest claims to admiration in the number of
separate poems which the plan of Balder allows it to enclose
as in a frame.   Just, as in dealing with thoughts and
emotions, it was perhaps the speciality of the writer to
seize in them what is most subtle and latent, catch their
most delicate *nuances*—so, in his treatment of external
nature, nothing seems to me so individual as his power to
arrest and retain those aspects which are the most elusive
and difficult of definition.   Grandeur and breadth of utterance, as all his readers know, lay easily within his grasp
whenever occasion called for them, but exquisite fineness
of perception and expression was probably his most characteristic faculty.   How often is it exemplified in the series
of poems which ' Balder ' includes !   How purely imaginative, how far beyond the correctness of mere literal painting, for instance, is his description of Winter !   How weird

are the touches that give to the stern season an almost
supernatural personality :

> More and more the observance
> Of the astonished year is turned and turned
> Upon the solitary, and the leaves
> Grow wan with conscience, and a-sudden fall
> Leige at his feet, and all the naked trees
> Mourn audibly, lifting appealing arms.
> Which, when he knew, as a pale smoke that grows
> Keeping its shape, he rose into the air
> And froze it, and the broad land blanched with fear
> And every breathless stream and river stopped,
> And through him, walking white and like a ghost
> With grim unfurnished limbs, the cold light passed
> And cast no shade.

The exquisite description of the fairies is in the vein of
Shakespeare's description of 'Queen Mab' : and it is hardly
too much to say, that it may mate well with that triumph
of delicate imagination.   The power of language to define
the minute can scarcely have a better illustration than the
lines :

> The emerald wing
> Of summer beetle is a barge of state ;
> Her cock-boat, red and black, the painted scale
> Of lady-fly aft in the fairy wake,
> Towed by a film, and tossed perchance in storm,
> When airy martlet, sipping of the pool,
> Touches it to a ripple that stirs not
> The lilies.
>
> .   .   .   .
>
> Neither have fear
> To scare them drawing nigh, nor with thy voice
> To roll their thunder.   Thy wide utterance

> Is silence to the ears it enters not,
> Raising the attestation of a wind,
> No more.

Of bolder but not less profound conception is the image that embodies the awfulness and the immemorial existence of the Alps, and informs the murmurs of Nature with a human burden :

> Round whose feet
> Are wrapped the shaggy forests, and whose beards
> Down from the great height unapproachable
> Descend upon their breasts. There, being old,
> All days and years they maunder on their thrones
> Mountainous mutterings, or thro' the vale
> Roll the long roar from startled side to side,
> When who so, lifting up his sudden voice,
> A moment speaketh of his meditation
> And thinks again.

Fine is the whole of this passage—wonderfully fine the use of the word 'sudden,' so expressive of the abrupt 'roar' which disturbs the subdued murmurs or the awful silence of Nature

Of the writer's tendency, at times, to avoid set and substantial description and to furnish, in preference, hints to the imagination, many other proofs might be cited. No poet, perhaps, has ever shown more of that subtle instinct which teaches us that at certain intense points of feeling (whether they relate to external beauty or to human experience) to realise strictly is to limit, to define sharply is to degrade. Of work full of the highest suggestion, but in some degree purposely indefinite, 'Dead Maid's Pool' may be named as a special example. The

story of terror is not actually told, but the germ from
which it is to be derived, with the climate and atmosphere
—so to speak—under which it must inevitably, though
gradually, shape itself, is so presented to the mind as to
lead irresistibly to a ghastly inference far more powerful to
the imagination than would have been circumstantial detail.   With a mind that on certain occasions recoiled even
to a fault from realistic precision of statement, it is not
surprising that the poet should have relied unusually upon
implication to indicate designs which he forbade himself
to mark out with formal directness.   It is probably for
this reason that he depended at times almost exclusively
upon rhythm and other forms of sound to convey his in-
tentions.   Thus, in the lyrics, entitled respectively 'Wind'
and 'Farewell,' the iteration of sound in the former case,
and the iteration of sound, combined with fluctuations of
metre, in the second, are relied upon far more than the
words employed ; experiments these which show how far
the poetical explorer may venture in quest of expression
into the region of auricular symbolism, and at what extreme
point of his adventure he may find himself arrested
rather than assisted by the laws of another art, which,
though, to a great extent, the ally of verbal utterance, is
still independent of it and distinct from it.

That the author of ' Balder ' could not only be realistic,
but that in his realism he could make tune serve his
purpose to the utmost, will hardly be doubted by those who
have read his poems on familiar subjects.   The song of
' The Betsey-Jane,' for instance, moves in a rhythm that

has in it the whistle of the wind and the buoyancy of the
wave; while the 'Song of the Chasseur,' in its appropriate
variety of metre, is a wonderful identification of sentiment
with melody.   The description of battle in 'An Evening
Dream,' though in a yet higher strain, is equally successful as an example of emotion conveyed by rhythm.   The
poems included in the title 'England in Time of War'
express almost every legitimate feeling which war can
arouse—patriotism, heroism, exultation and suffering, while
the expression of those feelings is dramatically modified
by the individualities of the persons represented and even
by their positions in life.   Of the far greater number of
these lays it may, I think, be affirmed, that they are not
more remarkable for their dramatic character, their passion,
and their felicity of expression, than for a rhythm happily
conformed to their leading ideas and sentiments. . . .

In my brief and imperfect remarks I have spoken of
my friend with the same admiration, yet also with the
same candour, which I showed him in the happy days of
our intercourse.   The recollection of those days, though
it cannot escape the pain that belongs to all past and irre-
coverable joys, is yet attended with the solace that belongs
to all joys that are elevated and pure.   As I write to you,
I seem again to renew my communion with one whose
daily talk (with its charm of frank, almost child-like
simplicity) was ever rich in suggestion when Art or Poetry
was the theme, and practical in all its bearings when the
interests of common life were in question.   How many
high qualities—rarely indeed combined, were united in his

generous nature : the nicest taste and judgment, with the widest appreciation of what is best in various forms of Art; earnestness of purpose, with spontaneous humour; firm adherence to convictions, with the sweetest courtesy to opponents ; exquisite refinement, with a sympathy that was never checked by fastidious scruples.   Prompt to recognise genius in his contemporaries, liberal to all men, it is not too much to say that he carried into letters the chivalry that is the glory of arms.   With an almost religious reverence for the vocation of the Poet, the sentiment *Noblesse oblige* seemed to influence his entire conduct and to make his life the illustration of his ideal.   True poet, high-minded gentleman, dear friend—to have known him is to feel life brighter and nobler, and to love human nature better for the sake of a single man.

BOOK V.

CHAPTER I.

1857.

THIS phase of Sydney Dobell's life must have been one of peculiar trial.

As yet not fully recognising what, in a letter to an intimate friend much later, he describes as,

the dispensation which has now been for some years upon me—wherein the keen perception of all that should be done, and that so bitterly cries for doing, accompanies the consciousness of all I might, but cannot, do :—

he was continually testing the reality and the extent of his strange powerlessness to use his powers, essaying the strength of his fetters, doubting whether, by some supreme effort of will, they might not be broken—thus exercising and harassing the very faculties that needed unbroken rest.

Later came the long strain of patient waiting, watching, hoping, for the healing of the mysterious hurt and the return of working power.

Those few words quoted above—and the words

written or spoken in which he alluded to any
sorrow of his own were indeed few—touch the
core of his trial.

There was never any general failure or decay
of mental power : his keen perceptions seemed to
grow keener, his views clearer and wider, his
opinions firmer and stronger; in fact, his whole
nature intensified, while the motive power, the
physical force to work himself out in the work
of life, was wanting.

Dr. Johnson says :

A man's mind grows narrow in a narrow place, whose
mind is enlarged only because he has lived in a large
place ; but what is got by books and thinking is preserved
in a narrow place as well as in a large place ;

and there was no narrowing of Sydney Dobell's
mind, as the life he was obliged to live narrowed.

But it cannot be hard to imagine what a
crucial test this time must have been of the
faithful love, which, while 'led by a resistless
Hand,' could say :

> Enough, enough, if Thou wilt lead
>   To know Thou knowest : enough to know
>   That darkling at Thy side I go,
> And this strong Hand is Thine indeed.

The summer of 1857 was spent in unsettled wanderings, unfavourable to any literary work—which, indeed, was stringently forbidden. He tried to give himself up to the recruiting of his health, as the best preparation for future labours.

After a couple of months at Detmore, and a visit to a married sister, sea-air being recommended, the two invalids started for North Wales, and stayed some time at Beaumaris.

From his sister's house he wrote, to his father and mother:

I will not let the sight of the familiar invocation persuade me to believe that we are again really separated. I rather choose to fancy that, having gone up to Cheltenham, I have forgotten something, and shall send this scrap to Detmore by a messenger. A thing *in posse* is almost *in esse*, and the power of being with you in two hours is so like the actual presence, that exile loses all its solemnity.

Speaking of his sister's children, he says of the eldest:

The favourite amusement is for him and me—he on my knee—to go out, in imagination, with Maida on the mountains, looking for deer. I say what we see, and Paul, his eyes fixed on the air, follows with heart and soul. And not only so, but afterwards he evidently continues the whole thing as a truth in his mind—coming up to me a

quarter of an hour hence, perhaps, and saying, 'Did you
see what became of the she-deer and the fawn that we
saw lying under the shadow of the rock before we killed
the old stag?' with a gravity of enquiry that there is no
mistaking.

From Beaumaris :

I don't wonder you were not more surprised at Arran,
for the line of mountains I see before me is hardly to be
surpassed in Scotland. I had no idea they grouped so
marvellously, and that the absence of height is so much
compensated by this grouping and by multitude. . . .

. . . I can't tell you what an unexpected treat your
news [that his family were proposing to come to Beaumaris]
was. . . . If you have these lodgings, we shall be as near
you as the first white gate to Detmore. . . . We found
a glorious place about three miles from Beaumaris—the
old farm-house of Clenog—but it was impracticable, unless
we had a servant of our own. What I said with regard
to the change in Beaumaris since you were here, had
reference to lodgings and prices. You spoke of it as a
cheap rustic place. . . . We are not at all disposed to be
'penny wise and pound foolish,' and it was precisely on
the principle you mention, of being 'at rest,' that I was
anxious to get reasonable lodgings. I could not be 'at
rest' if we were living over our income. It is quite true
that, as you say, it would be wise to spend even a hundred
pounds of our 'capital' to make me well and strong; but
what if we spent it without making me well and strong?

Suppose this is the beginning of a long and very expensive descent. I don't say it is so; I hope and think it is not so; but I have so often during the last few months had it 'borne in upon me,' as the Scotch say, that I shall not get well—the feeling of illness is often so poisonous and central—that I cannot lose sight of that alternative: nor ought I.

From one so persistently hopeful, the foregoing expression meant much.

To his Father and Mother (in London).

Beaumaris: July 17.

I will scribble my weekly letter to-day, in case we should be out so much to-morrow as to leave me no spare energy. I shall, however, post it so that it may reach Detmore on Sunday. God indeed grant that it may find you there safe and well! . . . We shall be very much interested to hear, when you have again leisure, what you have seen and done. . . .

I hope you like Archer's 'Time of War'. ——'s criticism was grossly unjust. He was in too great a hurry, to perceive more than the mere surface. . . .

. . . Speaking of pictures, we had a wonderful study of colour to-day. A—— sent us a present of fruit—among it a splendid melon. You should have seen it when cut open. There was the sunshine it had grown in, all stored up and turned to substance. I never saw before, out of the sky, the exact colour which you may see in a cloudless summer morning before sunrise. . . . My hearing

is a great deal better, but I feel very used-up. The
church bells happened to be chiming the first day I heard
better, and ever since they have continued to chime in
my ears—so distinctly and musically, often, that I can
hardly believe it is a delusion. But I must confess that
such constant music teaches me great sympathy with the
old lady of Banbury Cross !

I had a strange experience last Sunday. Standing by
the roadside near the sea, I saw a shabby carriage with
two horses and postillion approaching. It passed close by
me, so that I looked clearly in at the open window and
saw— what the men saw of forty-two years ago : Napoleon
flying from Waterloo. Fat, yellow, dirty, dust-covered,
but the same unmistakeable, incommunicable face. For a
moment the world seemed to roll back, like a watch that
runs down. Walking into the village, I found it all agog
with the unexpected arrival of ' Prince Napoleon.' . . .

August.

It is a pleasure not to begin a ' Sunday letter ' with a
notification of a new address. You will be glad to hear
that these lodgings answer admirably. They are dry,
airy, sunny, sea-ey, and comfortable, and clean as a milk-
pail. The last quality is no trifle in the catalogue of
Welsh desiderata, for even the best rooms often have a
smell—half-kitcheny, half carpet-broomy—most unpleas-
antly suggestive of ' dust and hashes.' . . .

We have found the Castle inestimable. For a shilling
a week we get admittance as often as we like to the
quadrangle, and lie and read there, protected from the

wind by those most noble walls. Of all the many castles I have seen, I think this is the most satisfactory, in its union of the colossal order of strength with an unexpected and feminine beauty. . . .

I am ashamed to send such letters of unmitigated egotism. . . . You may easily guess that my head is full of things going on abroad.[1] If anything important occurs in any of your papers, would you kindly send it; for I only see the 'Morning Star,'—a very unsatisfactory affair. The blockheads that will write and speak about India—in Parliament and out! Oh for a month of health and strength! Every year astounds me more at men's ignorance of human nature.

To the Rev. J. B. Paton.

Beaumaris.

Herewith you will receive two copies of a new work by a very dear and much valued friend of mine. The book will interest you by its intrinsic merits; and when I tell you that its author is one of the noblest young men I know, and pledged to that new and great movement in Christian literature which you and I feel to be one of the dearest hopes of the time, I need say no more to ensure your deepest concern in its success. . . . You will find admirable passages throughout the book, and some of the smaller poems are wonderfully good. The tragedy seems to me bad in construction; but affords, like everything

[1] This it will be remembered was the time of the Indian Mutiny.

else in the volume, evidence in its materials that the author is a poet. . . .

The mistake is that these passages, good, true, and beautiful *per se*, are out of place where they stand. . . .

G. M—— intends, this winter, to give a course of Lectures, through England and Scotland, and has sent me his prospectus. If you have influence with any of the Sheffield Institutions, I know you will be glad to get him an engagement, and so have an opportunity of making his personal acquaintance. I am anxious that he should get as many fixtures as possible, because the profession of lecturer would be so much more favourable to his poetical studies than that incessant newspaper and magazine writing which now exhausts his time and brains.

To M——.

Beaumaris.

My first memorandum shall be devoted to your question concerning our lodging and landscape—or land-and-seascape. And since the view from this place is almost beyond the power of prose, and I have no poetry at command, I shall invest sixpence sterling in the ' sister art,' and send you visibly what we see from our window. As to the window itself, the Beaumarisians are slow in awaking to a sense of their honours, and I regret to say that, though we have been here nearly a week, no print, daguerreotype, or other graphic representation yet exists of it ! Of course, it will come in due time; but as that word ' due ' is supposed, in some connections, to be a playful abbreviation of ' deuced,'

—and, when taken in construction with 'time,' to signify
the chronic interval of that Californian gentleman who is
familiarly known to have waited for a porter—I think,
perhaps, my little M——, you may prefer to anticipate?
The window, then, is of course—being destined to such
laurels—a bay-window, and you, knowing who lies so
many hours a day within it, will only need me to remind you
that *para* is the Greek particle for the idea of parallelism,
to be certain that it is surmounted by a para*pet*.

And now, the elephant of my heaviness having capered
a little, as you see, doggedly refuses for the rest of the
journey to lift his foot an inch more than needful; so I
must finish the description at the equallest pace of the
most even solemnity. The bay window, which is very
quaint and pretty (the cottage is the oldest house in this
part of the village), and full of flowers in pots, is sanctu-
aried off from the rest of the little room by the cleanest
of muslin curtains. In this sunny and infinitesimal
boudoir is an arm-chair of the old-fashioned *nobbly* make
(as old Witts would say), partly covered with chintz. A
red, round ottoman, set on a four-legged footstool, forms,
in conjunction with this arm-chair, E——'s window-sofa.
Three other chintz-covered seats and a wee table, fill up,
as you may guess, this tiny *camaretta*, and hardly leave
one room to get in. I have described it so much in detail,
because, when not out of doors, we sit here during the
bright part of the day – I on a chair in one window corner,
whence I can see, through the other, the Glydr and several
other mountains, and E——, on her arm-chair-sofa drawn

across the vast apartment, just within the muslin curtains.
Beyond these curtains lies the remainder of the sitting-
room—about the size of the parlour at Amberley.   Chintz
furniture, a blue-covered dining-table, and an old strange
black cheffonier with buhl edgings, are the chief things to
be seen.   Over this room, and looking the same way, is
our bedroom—large (for a cottage), airy, and comfortable.
The cottage itself is cream-coloured stucco externally, and
is noticeable for the parapet before mentioned, which is
repeated round the roof.   Here my description must end,
for it is time to go to the Castle.   A magniloquent phrase,
which is key to a lovely bit of our life here.   The old
Castle, in many respects the loveliest ruin of all the many
Castles I have seen, has a courtyard of the greenest sward
—a little lake of sunshine on fine days.   Here we go (I
could hit it with my rifle from this house), and read or
dream.   I am especially glad, now, when getting slowly
into key for my mediæval drama, to be thus growing into
such a life of round tower, quadrangle, and every Gothic
type.   Not merely knowing it as a theory, but living it
as a daily and unconscious, or unintentional, practice.

To the same.

Beaumaris : September.

So no Ovid this morning.   A queer-looking beginning
for a letter to you ; but since it was the unwritten ejaculation with which I took up the sheet of paper, it seemed
natural to set it down.   I'll try and make it look a little

less outlandish by giving you that order of the day of
which you reminded me in your last letter.

We get up at seven: but between cleanliness and
godliness are not down till nearly nine. (Salt water
ablutions and flesh-brushing being added to the usual
routine.)   At nine o'clock, while E. rests on the sofa
in the little sitting-room, I stroll up to Menai Place, and
look in on the dear ones who are sitting down to breakfast; returning to our quarters by the time the cocoa is
cool.   About half-past ten Cyrus, Clarence and I go down to
the pier, quiz the tourists on the Caernarvon-Liverpool
steamer which calls here, scrutinise the yachts and other
craft with a care and profundity which, if the right men
were necessarily in the right place, would secure us commissions in the Navy—I was going to say Lordships in
the Admiralty, but we know too much for that—and enjoy
the breeze and sea.   During this time E. is still resting . . . Clarence now goes to the Castle to draw; Cyrus
wanders about in a desperate hope of sighting a porpoise—
on view of which he has promise of a boat and my rifle;
and I go in to rest : *i.e.*, to lie on the sofa and read Ovid
till dinner-time.

And why—ask you—why, in reach of that Protean Sea,
and of the metempsychosis of the seasons, and of the
evolutions and involutions of those mutable mountains,
are you bothering over those lying old ' Metamorphoses'?
You remember I told you the scene of my next book is
laid in the Middle Ages, and that, in preparation, I had
been *reading*, and am going to read, the Middle Ages—

not about them, but *them*.   Now it happens that all their
utterances are in Latin : and, as I found that such a large
familiarity as is desirable would require a more intimate
Latinity than I possessed, I resolved—during these invalid
times when I can't do real work—to read Latin till I find
it as easy as English.   I'm getting on well, and hope before long to turn again to those glorious old Churchmen
on equal terms.   Of course there are many translations
available, but in my case they would be useless.   The
character of an age, as of a man, is often rather in the
voice than in the words.   Now you understand : ' So no
Ovid this morning.'   After dinner (we dine at half-past
one) there is, on fine days, what a certain little person
here, rather given to *patois*, calls a '*scurse*; when the
whole family embark in a rowing-boat or a two-horse
break.   Sometimes the ' fellows' of the clan take the
rifle and a sailing craft, and tack in and out along the
other-side shore in pursuit of herons; but on these occasions we leave most of the ladies behind, E. being the
only one, as yet, who has been ' brick ' enough to venture
under canvas.

To his Father and Mother (after their return home).

Beaumaris : September 11.

. . . So many miles of incessant change must effec-
tually have shaken away the sentimentalities of parting,
and I daresay you all fitted into your old places as com-
fortably as if you had never been out of them.   Here we
had no such rough regimen, and you were missed as much

as you could wish to be. The first day I felt so burdened with a vague consciousness of some great affliction that I was obliged to be constantly waking myself up, as it were, to the real extent of the case. By the next day I had slept a little of it off, but it was still very bad. The third day found the symptoms still remaining, but reduced to a kind of tragi-comic pathos. I did not care for the pier ; couldn't get my heart up to go to the Liverpool boat ; hadn't spirit so much as to criticise a tourist of any sex whatever! . . . Finally, having to write a letter on poor ——'s business, my deafness returned, which explained some of the previous blue devils by showing I am more out of health than usual. It seemed so familiar strange to be deaf again. . . .

The sense of indefinite evil was partly also caused by the fact that I kept forgetting we should see you again before the winter. And I look to winter with somewhat the same feeling that a culprit bestows on judge and jury.

The probability that his physicians would recommend a foreign climate for the winter was, in part, the reason of this feeling. Much as he enjoyed new experiences, the exile from home and friends, and the indefinite postponement of work, were things to be dreaded. But, doubtless, the chief source of dread arose from his wife's unfitness for the fatigues and anxieties of travel.

When Mr. and Mrs. Dobell, soon after the

departure of 'the family,' left Beaumaris, their
first move was to Bowden, near Manchester, where
they stayed to have the opportunity of studying
the Fine Art Exhibition held at Manchester that
year.   Many readers may now, after the expiration
of more than twenty years, have forgotten the
nature of that Exhibition—at which were brought
together, chiefly from private collections, most of
the finest pictures in this country.

'This Exhibition,' he writes:

is such a very College of Art that I find the whole of my
energy for the fortnight we are to be here will not be
enough to learn all I wish to gain from it. . . . The
comparison of the North and South Walls is marvellously
interesting.   Perfection would be to combine the qualities
of both. . . . Of the Italians, Titian and Tintoretto have
had most of my time.   They change places every day, like
horses in a race, but always agree in leaving 'the ruck'
'nowhere.'   But, except Giotto and his friends, they
are a set of Godless, Christless infidels, all of them, and
their works are like them.   I am speaking now of those
that are represented here.   Michael Angelo does not appear,
and Raphael is only misrepresented. . . . The only picture
I have yet seen of anybody's that (irrespective of subject),
as a picture, a whole, an organised association of things,
seems to me perfect, and leaves nothing to be desired, is
Titian's Rape of Proserpine.   But if I begin these matters,
this letter will be long after all.   How I should have en-

joyed to have C—— with me, and to talk them over as they arose.

In answer to a home letter of remonstrance, at his giving so much time and strength to the study of secular, and comparatively unimportant, subjects, he wrote :—

You mistake me in supposing that the study of pictures makes me 'deaf.' . . . Anxiety, mental pain, or an effort to do a certain mental thing in a certain time—as to write a letter, or remember something forgotten—are the mental exertions that make me deaf. . . .

. . . And then went on to say that he must 'put on paper for the hundredth time,' his confidence that, in advancing 'the true faith,' 'no argument, or exposition, or definite "preaching" will avail anything *per se*,' unsupported by personal character and culture. That the only way is to strive to become great in other departments of thought, in order to be listened to, as an authority, when saying 'I believe so and so.'

He then continued :

The writer concerning whom you inquire is ——. He gave up Unitarianism and all kind of Christianity, I believe, and has been writing queer essays in sundry places ever since. He is a man of a good deal of talent, but

dreadfully one-sided and one-eyed, and very unfair in
using words in meanings which are misunderstood by the
reader. He would smile at your notions, and you would
be horrified at his, if you saw them naked. Indeed, I
couldn't help smiling myself to remember how fiercely I
have been attacked at Detmore for putting in plainer
language the same doctrine as this particular essay, which
you admire so much, really contains.

We expect to leave for Odsey on Monday. E. wanted
to write to you, but I would not let her, because, between fatigue and anxiety, she has too much strain on her
strength already. My cough is almost gone. . . . It is
curious what magic power irritation in that region has.
As soon as it began I felt that deadly sense of weakness,
as if struck by a poisoned arrow, which I felt last
spring. . . .

From Manchester they went on a visit to his
wife's mother in Cambridgeshire.

Odsey House: September 29, 1857.

As some one will be going to the post almost directly,
I send but one line that you may know we arrived here last
evening in safety. We passed over the terrible havoc of
the late great accident, which made that blessing of 'safety'
wonderfully visible and glorified. . . . Everybody here is
very kind. Even —— —— has sent to put one of his
carriages at our disposal during our stay. The non-
appearance of Maida was a great disappointment.

[Suggesting that his artist-brother, who about that time

would be returning to London, should run down with the
dog, and stay a night or two, he adds] : I should so keenly
enjoy showing him all the beloved places of which this
region is full ; and I may never have another chance.

I hope you are having the glorious autumn weather
that is making the dewy stubble so splendid at this
moment. Whether because I have been getting better
in it, or not, I don't know—but I never thought Odsey so
beautiful. Its fair lawns, noble trees, long garden paths
—one nearly half-a-mile—in a straight line—quaint
serpentines and leafy cloisters, with high close-clipped
hedges, are really very fine. . . . What use and enjoyment to how many might be made of these ample rooms
and empty walks ; situated half way between the University and the Metropolis, with a railway station from each
in its very grounds. Talking of 'grounds' reminds me of
dear Pater's question as to his spectacles. The day after
you left Beaumaris, I beat the paths you mentioned, like a
pointer. I found all manner of curiosities, in the way of
mice, feathers, dead birds, and odds and ends, that even a
quick eye would not notice except in such a systematic
search, but no spectacles. Speaking of things you requested me to look *for* reminds me of those you asked me
to look *at*. I paid particular attention at the Exhibition
to my mother's favourite Ary Scheffers. There is no
doubt they are very fine, but I confess they don't at all
satisfy me—there is a feeling of mannerism—almost of

trick—in the treatment. Almost his whole secret seems
to be in a mode of painting female flesh as if it were not
flesh at all, or flesh drained and gelatined by exhausting
illness. But I suppose there is something in his pictures
particularly touching to the heart of woman, for they
were my darling's favourites, I think, of the whole Exhibition. I looked at her, as she was some distance from me
once, and saw her eyes full of tears, and her whole face
pinked with emotion, and coming up quickly to see what
had caused it, found her before 'St. Augustine and his
Mother.' You will think it odd, perhaps, but the work
that seemed to me most poetical of the whole Exhibition,
ancient and modern (in the sense of a picture that
expresses something invisible by something visible), was
Millais' 'Autumn Leaves.' . . .

. . . We have enjoyed very much a visit to the cottages at Sandon. It was very touching to find the fond
remembrance with which, among all their hardships and
troubles, several of the villagers lay aside every year a
little store of woodnuts for 'Miss Em'ly,' as they still call
her. The accumulation, in our long absence, had become
enough to stock a fruit-stall. . . . We leave on Monday,
if all goes well, though we could have enjoyed to stay
longer. But E. is getting anxious that I should be
settled in some mild place before the cold comes on. . . .
We shan't stay in London, since we could not do so without being overwhelmed with visitors, and losing the little
good the country air has done. We go to dear M——.
We intend to get the verdict of some good doctor as to
what we ought to do for the winter.

Writing to his father, about this time, in answer to suggestions with regard to advertising his works, he said :

I think the best course is to leave the matter to time. I have just sufficient position in literature now for time necessarily to do all that is desirable. Till that position is obtained every active exertion is necessary, because otherwise one's works are buried in the overwhelming mass of nothings into which no future critic will be hardy enough to dig. There is no fear now of that interment for mine. No one who, a few years hence, looks back to the poetical literature of the past seven years can avoid seeing my name and examining my books. And that examination being inevitable, I have no fear of the result. I found 'Balder'—the principal parts of which I had quite forgotten—on the table at Odsey; and, dipping into it, was thankful to feel perfectly satisfied in leaving it to the first great poetical critic who shall arise in this country.

CHAPTER II

ABOUT the middle of November, in accordance
with the advice of the London physician, whom
his brother Dr. Horace had wished him to consult,
Mr. Dobell and his wife left London for the Isle of
Wight.

From St. Catherine's House, Niton, he wrote
home:

'The Undercliff' is, in fact, the ruins of many ancient
landslips, which are now grown over with all manner of
picturesque boscage (I saw this morning a little wood of
thorn-trees so covered with white lichen that the whole
copse looked like a colossal bottle-tit's nest), and is fine
and beautiful in a sort of scene-painting beauty, and a
kind of cockney-sublime. . . . We have too large airy
rooms. . . . The sitting-room has a south and a west
window, and the sea-view is marvellous. The unbounded
sea that seems to stretch, ocean beyond ocean, as it were,
before and on one side of us, is one of the most solemn
things I have seen.

We were much struck in our journey yesterday

by the evidences of the mildness of this side of the
island. Campions, crane's-bill, the yellow snap-dragon,
and violets, were in the hedges, and the gorse was in
flower. To-day has been cloudless, mistless, and brilliant,
but rather keen.

To his Father and Mother.

St. Catherine's House, Niton : November 22, 1857.

You wish for a description of the country hereabouts.
. . . This house stands on the top of a rugged and very
steep down, about a quarter of a mile above the sea.
Backward from us the down becomes a beautiful and
smiling little table-land of pastures and gardens, dotted
with a few cottages, and bearing one or two considerable
houses. This table-land is shut off from the interior of
the island, and consequently from the north winds, by a
semicircle of cliffs (very fine and varied colours, between
sand and grey, and wonderfully worn with ancient seas and
modern winds, *i.e.*, ' modern ' in the sense of post-diluvian)
—and contains, out of sight among the ups and downs,
the village of Niton. . . . The cliffs stretch eastward along
the whole southern sea-board of the island, and the
' Undercliff ' is threaded with warm lanes (not the true
English elmy lanes, but lanes with tall walls of ivy-covered
rock, rolled down from the cliffs in some of the innumerable landslips of which the whole region is the ruin).

. . . I should certainly have liked to live in a house
that looked less town-built than this ; but I expect we
must set the useful against the picturesque, or rather the

physically against the mentally useful, for there is utility in both. . . .

I suspect the superiority of this coast is not so much in difference of thermometer, as in the very peculiar character of the climate. The wonderful steadiness of temperature, and the indescribable clearness of the utterly dry air, which seems incapable of mist, is the essential distinction from every other English climate I have seen. Most of the days since we have been here have been cloudless, sunny, and genial, as June. I don't mean they were like June, for there is an idiosyncrasy in winter sunshine. . . .

In answer to something said about 'equal appreciation':

The very idea of appreciation, ap-pricement, appraisement, implies the likelihood of inequality. If my mother means the mutual appreciation, *i.e.*, the estimation of each by the other at his correct value, I can understand it, or the over-estimate of each by the other, which is a still more desirable state of things. But the notion of equality among human creatures is one of the most injurious pestilences that ever sapped the core of social welfare.

Many years later, 1871, he wrote to a political friend :

It will be as much as we shall do by the most desperate gallantry and opportune Leadership to carry the day for 'Christ (unencumbered by orthodox or heterodox defini-

tions), England, and *Inequality.*' That is my war-cry,
though, like all practical cries, its objectivity requires a
great deal of explanation that I must not enter on here.

To his brother Clarence.

St. Catherine's House, Niton : December 9.

This short note is to tell you, my dear old fellow, of
a favourite wish of ours which I should have expressed
before, but that I felt bound, before writing you, to see
what they would say at home. . . . We want you very
much to come and spend the Christmas recess down here
with us. . . . You would lose nothing artistically by the
trip, for this is a coast which you ought to know, and our
position here is admirable for knowing it. Apart from
the fact, that the central situation gives the opportunity of
easily reconnoitring the distances on either hand, we have
noble views within eyeshot, and ' bits ' of small beauty and
quaint character more interesting still.   It is a smuggling
coast, you know, and there is a little cove, seen from our
room, called Puckester (the very name suggesting moonlight mischief), where three fishermen profess to catch
lobsters, but where ten times three, ' in the season of the
year,' take their ' delight ' in something very different, I
suspect. A field off from our window the coast guard
stalks up and down, and on every sea-board hill you
may see a tall man against the sky, like a stork on
a Dutch housetop. How curious and beautiful the ivy-
coloured greensand stratifications of the cliffs are I have
described in my family letters. The sea alone is worth

ten times the length of journey. On two sides and in
front of us, either way as far as eye can reach, lies out the
wide omnipotent Evil. The roll of the waves, under a
sou'-wester, is so long and high, that standing on the beach
you involuntarily hold your breath as the vast arch of
black-brown marble poises a moment before breaking.
Very strange things it shows us sometimes. The other
day there was a great wind twenty or thirty miles at sea,
but it was comparatively calm here. From the shore to
the offing the sky was leaden clouds, and the water dark
—darkening with distance till the furthest verge was a
black line, as it might be the rim of Avernus. Meanwhile, beyond this rim there was a narrow horizon of clear
sky, and into this light the great waves of an unseen ocean
reared up as out of a gulph, like the heads of divine white
horses in some tumult and battle of the gods. Another
day there was what the papers called a thick fog. 'Thick
fog at Southampton,' I saw in the 'Times.'

The real fact was, that the clouds came down bodily
and lay upon the sea, leaving a spotless sky and clearest
atmosphere above them. From this house, not two
hundred feet above the level, we looked upon precisely
what such intelligences must see as pass by our globe, or
what they beheld who came into lower regions before
' God divided the waters from the waters.' But these are
only a few of the phenomena of the ocean—for the mass
seems to lie back, sea behind sea.

I understand, more than ever, why women love the sea,
and manly men are almost disposed to hate it. By a

beautiful dispensation it is in the nature of women that the idea of the *great* should suggest that of the *good*. Minus any flagrant evidence to the contrary, greatness with them presupposes goodness, and 'the great good sea' is the spontaneous logic of their natures. With men, on the other hand—that is, masculine men—the fact of Power, unless *accompanied with extraneous evidence of goodness*, naturally stimulates the instinct of *resistance*. At the same time their inherent chivalry dignifies even an evil power so long as it seems conquerable. That it is your enemy makes it, *de facto*, respectable, while there is anything like equality in the contest. But when a Power is manifestly bad and demonstrably invincible, there is, so far as the dictates of Nature are concerned, nothing for it but hatred. But I hope we shall talk these things over by the seashore. Meantime I have not been praising the scenery to tempt you here. You know well enough that if I did not believe you would come to see us, I would not do you or ourselves the injustice to say 'come' at all. But what I have said is to excuse myself from seeking my own gratification at the expense of the dear ones at home.

In the dear hope that we shall soon spend some days together, you know I am always your very loving Brother,
SYDNEY.

To his Father and Mother.

St. Catherine's House, Niton: December 19, 1857.

I hope you are approaching the shortest day of the year in something like the wonderful sunshine we have here this morning. Though I hardly ought to hope it, for the fogs and clouds and darkness of an English winter solstice are so essential a part of the great congruity and poem of a year, that one ought not to wish them absent, even for the temporary luxury of such unnatural light as this. We have had many cloudy days lately, but even they have been almost equally abnormal—soft shady days, with south-west winds, as tender often as spring, and with thrushes singing in all the hedges in a way that, at another season, would be so exquisite, but now, in the very death and funeral of the year, is sad enough, because unnatural. I hardly think Tennyson has done well, as a poet, in fixing his house in such exceptional conditions. He lives, you know, about twenty miles from us along the same coast. The country people are much amused at his bad hat and unusual ways, and believe devoutly that he writes his poetry while mowing his lawn. However, they hold him in great respect, from a perception of the honour in which he is held by their ' betters.' Our housewife here is a friend of his servant, and she entertained us with an account of how said servant had lately been awed. Opening to a ring at the door, when the Tennysons were out, she saw a ' tall handsome gentleman ' standing there, who on learning they were not at home turned to go. ' What message shall I give?' quoth the maid. ' Merely say Prince Albert called.'

. . . Christmas-day will be here before my next home-letter. How tenderly we shall see, with inward eyes, the well-known Christmas-morning scene. . . . We have been

much disappointed at not having dear C——, but can
quite enter into the reasons he gives for going home.

'Many thanks for your suggestion,' he wrote
from St. Catherine's House, Niton, to Dr. Horace
Dobell :

as to whether my fatigue in letter-writing may not be
due to writing 'too advisedly.' I don't think that can be
the cause ; and for this reason, that if you came to me
unexpectedly, and asked precisely the question to which
the fatiguing letter is an answer, I should reply, without
the slightest fatigue, in *exactly the same ideas and words.*

I think the fatigue is a mere nervous phenomenon,
depending on the facts that for several years I have, day
after day, obliged myself to write letters, with a brain so
fagged and ill that the commonest movement was an
injury, and that now the mere act of taking a pen and a
sheet of paper throws the mind involuntarily into an
attitude of weariness.

The following short passages are extracted
from correspondence, of about this time, with Mr.
W. S. Williams, of the firm of Messrs. Smith, Elder,
and Co. :

Kind thanks for your friendly wishes as to the popularity of my next book ; but I believe I may prophesy
that—in the sense in which they were uttered—there is
no chance of their fulfilment. . . .

After asking as to the possibility of employ-

ment, in the firm to which Mr. Williams belonged,
for a young man in whom he was interested, he
continued :

In ordinary cases, I should not think of asking the
question : for four-fifths of those who apply to me, in this
manner, are fit for nothing but literature, and unfit for
that ; but from what I saw of ——, I believe he is an exception to the 'ne'er-do-well' rule of literary aspirants.
He was in the University when I was at Edinburgh, and
sent me some of his MSS., with an inquiry if I would
recommend him to adopt authorship as a profession. I
gave my usual answer—'Not while you can buy a broom
and sweep a crossing,'—but the manner in which the
answer was received showed me that the lad had unusual
qualities. . . . From what I saw of him (the thing only
occurred just as I left Scotland), I feel sure he has remarkable abilities for his age, and I think they are of a
much more applicable kind than is usual with incipient
literaries, of whom, I need hardly tell you, I have had
enough experience. . . .

. . . I am right glad we agree so well about 'Esmond.'
What you say as to the 'pedestal ' is, I think, thoroughly
true. The Germans say, 'Time spares nothing that he
hasn't a hand in,' and that book gives me more the notion
of the laborious Patience which 'rocks ' the river of Life
for the grains of gold, and slowly adds them, one by one,
to the mass—determined that, whatever else it be, it shall
at least be *only* golden—than anything in modern prose
literature. It is a grand lesson, in this respect, to our

careless hasty young fellows—male and female—who seem
unable to learn that if they want *monumentum are*
perennis they cannot (forgive the pun) expect it to be
made with *œs.*

After speaking, in a letter home (of December
29), about the climate, and the wild-flowers still
blooming in the hedges, he said :

I am teaching little Katie [1] botany, and therefore find
this state of things very convenient. She is a nice interesting girl of eight years, and so quick in apprehension
that, if we are to go on as we have gone thus far, she will
be able, by the time she goes, to pass an examination in
systematic botany ' with honours.' She rummages the
hedges for leaves, as we walk, and brings them to me for
a technical description of their shapes, and as, already, in a
few days she will have thus learned the scientific names of
every variety of leaf, you may have some notion of the
child's celerity and apprehensiveness. Poor dear —— is
recovering her spirits wonderfully, though, of course, all
her light shines, as it were, ' through a glass darkly.' She
spends every evening with us, except a few, on which
E. goes to her instead, and no one could prize more
than we do the happiness of feeling that she is happier for
it. . . .

Some of his letters to his mother at this time
were chiefly filled with anecdotes, such as he knew

[1] The daughter of a widowed friend who was staying near him.

would interest her, of this 'little Katie' and her younger brother; both these children had—as children and young people almost invariably did— attached themselves to him with a passionate sort of attachment.

'If she lives,' he wrote of the little girl, 'she will be a girl of unusual abilities. She absorbs like blotting-paper, you have but to touch her with an idea, and it is sucked in.'

These letters speak also of daily horse exercise, 'on a good old horse, hired, for eighteenpence an hour, of a man who had not sufficient work for him,' and comment on the fact that he can always bear so much more riding than any other exertion.

Of some relatives, whose acquaintance he just then first made, he remarked :

She and her sisters seem to have a good many of the good qualities of our family, without the constitutional 'conceit' that gives an air of stuck-upness to our virtues. I was much pleased, in both of them, with an unconscious humility and simple-mindedness.

At the beginning of the year 1858 he wrote, in acknowledgment of good news from home :

God indeed be thanked for another season of welfare. We had imagined, on Christmas-day, the morning and dinner-time scene, and calculated by precedent very nearly

aright ; except that I hazarded a percentage of increase
on the number of children which brought them up to nearly
five hundred.[1]

To a young Sister.

St. Catherine's House, Niton : January 12, 1858.

I was going to write home to-day, and as your letter
has just come in, mine shall be to you.   And first let me
say very earnestly, dear, never suppress that 'want to write'
to me, of which you speak, by any fears as to your manner
of fulfilling it.   Be quite sure that, even if your style
deserved all the hard names you use to it, I should manage
to see something in your letters much better than the style.
Don't be afraid of writing 'catalogues'; a good catalogue
may be the best 'premier pas' to all manner of excellent
writing.   Merely try and make it a *good* catalogue, *i.e.*, a
list of facts in congruous language—language that conveys
them—such language as if you read it would make you
feel as you would feel at the facts themselves.   Facts of
the mind, facts of the body, facts of the external world.
To do this requires, first, that you should perceive clearly,
and feel unmistakeably ; and why, probably, you find it
difficult to write such a catalogue in a letter is that you
undertake a letter when you are neither, at the moment,
feeling nor perceiving in any high degree.   And from
getting a habit of letter-writing under such circumstances,
the mere act of taking up the pen throws the mind into
that dull condition.   As a remedy for this, I would try

[1] The children of Charlton village.

writing letters piece-meal—setting down a feeling at the
moment it happens to come upon you, and an external
fact at the instant your senses are vibrating with it.   If
you think this would make your letters too violently
heterogeneous, you might scribble the things down in pencil,
and transfer them by-and-by to their proper places with
pen and ink.   This of course would not do for a permanent mode of letter-writing, but I would prescribe a
temporary course of it, as a cure for what you complain of,
and a method of giving you confidence that you *can*
express your better self.   We were very much interested
in what you say of the Christmas stories ; but to speak the
truth, I don't regret your want of success : on the contrary,
except for any disappointment it may be to you, I must
rejoice at it.   The passion for writing, especially among
ladies, is the mental and spiritual nuisance of this age.
What the young people of the day want to learn is, that
Authorship, unless it is of the very best—the best and most
competent minds expressed in the very best ways— is worse
than useless.   What we want is a number of young people
of talent and character who should resolve to make themselves thoroughly competent not to *write*, but to *read*.   To
pen a crude essay or story is, as every magazine bears
evidence, an achievement that requires but little brains or
culture ; but so to cultivate the mind as to make it a
competent reader of the best books, so to elevate the taste
as to give it discernment of the rarest truths of the rarest
intellects, is a business of quite another order.   And the
difference between the results of the two students is, that
while the first is merely lowering the tone of general

literature, the second is adding to that public of worthy readers which, as it increases in number, will not only lead the popular opinion but stimulate the few real Authors which a nation ever produces at one time to yet higher efforts of genius.

Make up your mind, N——, dear, not to write stories, but to *read* them in a manner worthy to be called reading. When you do write don't attempt fiction (which is, so far as writing is concerned, no culture or help to the abilities, but rather the contrary); but, as a mere piece of mental gymnastics, do something of this sort :—Read a chapter of some first-rate Historian, or his account of some single historic action, making memoranda of the barest *facts,* if necessary.

Then, after some hours or days, when the *words* of the author have gone out of your head, write down an account of the same event, or events, as well and vividly as you can; and compare your work with the Historian. There will be real culture in such literary practice; but to write without some such standard is as useless as to write exercises without a key to refer them to. And in all such cases what is evidently useless is really worse than useless. . . .

To his eldest Sister.

Niton, Isle of Wight.

. . . Having made so long an explanation of why these congratulations on your first literary achievement did not come sooner, you will perhaps expect, when you

do get at my verdict, to find it proportionately elaborate.
But the fact is, the story was done too nicely to give
opportunity for criticism. I was very much pleased with
it, and thought it successful both as to matter and
manner. . . .

Now, I daresay you will say I am very unreasonable
when I confess that, much as I liked the performance,
I was sorry to see it. But to show you the higher
ratio of the apparent unreason I will explain why. I
never doubted that you could if you liked accomplish a
thing of this kind—and better even than this—and take
your place among the hourly aggregating troop of
authoresses, who are the pleasant vices and brilliant misfortunes of recent English literature. But I always
hoped you would be content with the *potentiality*, and
would set the much-required example of resisting a temptation which bids fair to stain with ink the sweetest
sanctuaries of life, and taint with the inevitable evils of
every unnatural and abnormal gratification three-fourths
of the 'women of England.'

It is precisely those women who could do otherwise
if they chose that should be careful to set the example of
reminding the sisterhood that there are nobler vocations
in this world than writing books, and a truer womanhood
than that which wears its heart upon its sleeve. All
honour and sympathy to those women for whom *res
angusta domi* make this self-immolation an unescapeable
necessity (and the best of them confess how sorely they
feel the profanation and all the defeminising influences
of their profession), but whenever no irresistible duty de-

mands the sacrifice, I think, and every year strengthens the conviction, it ceases to be justifiable. . . .

Later, on this same subject of female authorship, he wrote :

In speaking of the evils of any occupation one thinks, of course, of those representative occupants in whom each special ill has become extreme and demonstrative. It is not the comparatively fair fingers of apprenticeship, but 'the dyer's hand subdued to what it works in' that warns us of the dangers of the work.

When I spoke strongly of the moral and intellectual dangers of female authorship, I was probably thinking of poor Miss Martineau, who seems to me typical of the female intellect—even though hers be the most manly of her sex—when adventuring upon those heights of speculation where strong men grow humble, because they get high enough to see the hopeless Alps beyond, but where the mind of woman, reaching no further than what *seems* the shoulder of the summit, is apt to grow blasphemously proud. Or of ——, in whom the histrionic element of the novelist has so absorbed the rest that, after some years of intimacy, I could not find in her one inch of terra firma, and came to disbelieve alike her loves and hates, likes and dislikes, faults and virtues. Or of —— and her school who, carrying out logically the principle which many others have not enough courage to follow to conclusions, have brought themselves, most of them, and are bringing themselves, all of them, to a state of hybrid abnormal hermaphrodite humanity. . . .

The following passages are extracted from
Memoranda made by Mr. Dobell about this time
on a novel, called 'Caste':

I would suggest that you have put your theory at a
disadvantage by drawing your heroine so very far from
the ideal of a lady. She has not one of the qualities that
differentiate the lady from the mere female-with-an-
education. Her very 'pride' is not the pride of ladyhood
(which, when unhappily it exists at all, should be always
like Hegel's 'all' which seemed 'nothing'), but a veno-
mous arrogance. I am sure you feel that a true lady
should be—whatever else she be—the very opposite of
this: as unconscious as a flower, as sweet-blooded as a
child, as inoffensive and undefensive as the sunshine
that comes everywhere in its simplicity of universal welcome. And what we should theoretically demand of
perfect ladyhood happens to be also what is, even conven-
tionally speaking, most truly distinguished and 'aristo-
cratic,' what is found in the very best specimens of the
highest conventional ranks.

I think, too, you do injustice to your argument by so
thoroughly ignoring what is to be said on the other side.
There is no doubt that there are many things in trade
which are inharmonious with the finest qualities of a true
gentleman. What we have to do is to show that, if inharmonious, they are not *incompatible*; that in many
respects they can be modified, and in all they can be over-
come and dominated. And, in the spirit of 'lead us not
into temptation,' which applies to every department of

education as well as to the graver morals, the modifica-
tion is as much a duty as the domination.   When there
are many true gentlemen in business they will show us
the fact by so far idealising trade (and in every true
idealisation the *useful* element is not lessened, but rather
increased, by its efflorescence into beauty) that it shall
cease to be incongruous with them, or at all events lose
all its harsher incongruities.   Skill and wit, in natures
whose gentle-hood is over-mastering, will devise unthought
of means.   I think, therefore, it was unadvisable to obtrude
the *unæsthetics* of 'shop-keeping' so violently as you
have occasionally done, and to show so little sympathy
with the very natural, and, to a high degree, justifiable,
prejudices of the non-trading portions of society.   While
'shopkeepers' remain what the majority of them at this
moment are, those prejudices are personally justified; the
intolerable and absurd injustice is in directing those
prejudices not against the individual men who are really
obnoxious to them, but against an arbitrary 'class'—a
class formed upon no 'natural system,' but on mere accidental signs! . . .

.   .   .   .

In old times gentlehood, the one comprehensive *caste*,
depended solely on blood.   Given the blood, and nothing
within the wide limits of virtue and honour could degrade
the Gentleman.   To believe otherwise he would have
resented as mortal insult to the noble liberty of gentle
birth.   To be made or unmade by external circumstances
(of moral indifference) was the characteristic and villain-
ous condition of the serf.   'Gentleman,' therefore, came

to be the social standard, and we find 'gentlemen' employed in the free and various manner that might be
expected from the liberal consciousness of inalienable
rank. We never went so far in England as abroad, where
nobles, without loss of caste, might be found as grooms
and menials, but the difference was not in the principle,
but in the degrees of application. . . .

. . . It is time in these nobler days to restore that
grand old principle, but in a manner as much higher and
more spiritual than the ancient application as these days
are more illuminated than those. And the first necessity
in this restoration is the utter scout of that base cant-
word ('tradesman'), by which a mean, gross, atheistical
society endeavoured to perpetuate a social theory as contemptible as itself.

To a Sister (the wife of a 'man of business').

. . . A great deal has been written and talked lately
about the possibility of *gentlemen in business*, but what
would do more for the subject than a library of books
would be one really complete, thoroughly furnished, unmistakeable *illustration*. When I saw you—or thought
of you rather—and your dear husband, settled for fourteen
years in your beautiful 'Moorlands,' it seemed to me
'here is precisely the golden opportunity: here are the
husband and wife, father and mother, just fitted by
original qualities and education (for if either element is
absent, the experiment can't be perfect) to realise, if they
try, the ideal home and family of a gentleman, and just

so placed by the fortune of life as to make such a realisation under such a combination of circumstances the very
Q. E. D. for which we are all looking.' I don't say it is
to be done without difficulty; but I do say, and believe,
that you have the power to do this thing, if you set yourselves to it, and resolve that morally, intellectually, and
æsthetically you will be content with nothing short of the
highest you can attain. And to make this illustration
perfect, it is almost necessary that it should be representative, *i.e.*, that it should depend for its beauty on things
that are not in their nature exceptional, but can be shared,
more or less, by every well-organised, well-educated
member of the great middle class. A husband and
father carrying on successfully the practical affairs of
work-a-day life, and depending for his nobility of station
simply on the ideal degree of excellence to which he carries his duties, occupations, tastes, and pleasures. A wife
and mother content in the same manner with simply
trying to live out Christian ladyhood to its fairest and
noblest possible. These are the two heads of such a household as I want to see; such a household as may enable
me to answer the incredulous—' Ah, my dear poet, a very
pretty dream indeed!' with . . . an introduction to my
brother and sister at ——.

I must not pursue this most interesting subject, for a
pleading voice has already interceded too often against
this long letter. . . .

The following extract and letter will speak for
themselves:

I have been sick at heart [he wrote on February 19] with the drivel with which our press has been beslobbering Louis Napoleon, and at the cruel perversion of truth which seemed likely to let those four unfortunates [1] go to their graves without so much as hearing a word of justice; and at last I felt the duty of speaking—not so much with any view to the general political question, as to the special character of the men, and the much-abused enterprise—to be so strong that I could resist no longer.   So I have written a letter to the 'Times' on the subject of Assassination, and if they decline to insert it, shall send it somewhere else.

The political friend by whom this 'Letter on Assassination' was to have been communicated to 'The Times,' declined to be its introducer, holding that its publication would be impolitic.

Illness, no doubt, prevented any further effort concerning it, till the time when its appearance would have been seasonable had slipped by.   It is now printed for the first time.

Those who have recently read Victor Hugo's 'Histoire d'un Crime,' may be, for that reading, more inclined to sympathise with the tenor of this paper.

[1] Orsini and his associates.

Of Assassination.

St. Catherine's House, Niton, Isle of Wight : February 1858.

To the Editor of ———.

Sir,—Travellers call us a matter-of-fact nation, and certainly, when we catch up a formula of any kind, we can be guilty of notable eccentricities.

More than a month ago, at a report of an 'attempted assassination' in Paris, a cry was raised here that 'Englishmen abhor assassination,' and the country has rung with it from that time to this. Whether, after all, we are a wildly speculative people, or whether our genius is so essentially operative, so purely material, so wholly independent of all but 'the concrete reason,' that we are compelled, by some law of extremes, to seize on an occasional theory and carry it to heights that transcend the most imaginative nations, is, I suppose, a question for 'the intelligent foreigner.'

'Howsoever these things be,' it must be confessed we are too apt to play King Charles and the Royal Society. Given a fish in a basin, and we seldom make mistakes about it; but given a creed concerning a fish in a basin, and we are sometimes a spectacle for gods and men. It was never more necessary to bear our popular peculiarities in mind than when listening to this clamour on the subject of assassins, a clamour that might otherwise be unfavourably suggestive—like the 'gentleman' who takes you by the button to asseverate his hatred of a lie, or the lady who remarks 'What a good book the Bible is!'

Sir, as an Englishman—English of the English—I ' abhor assassination,' but I really think we islanders are too thoroughly incapable of the crime for any great excitement on the matter to be either natural or wise. I feel no such nervousness, and am sure we may afford to look at it from a very easy distance. The more alien the monster, the more calmly one may dissect and describe. It is in the anatomy of things near akin that the eye grows too impassioned for science. It seems to me, therefore, ungenerous and undignified—unjust to that judicial temper which, on such a subject, we, of all the world, have a right to claim as our national privilege—to spend our breath to-day in execrating the ' assassination ' in the Rue Lepelletier, and to leave some historian, five years hence, when the scenes are changed, the actors beheaded, and the act itself diminished by some larger catastrophe, to ask for the first time, whether any ' attempt at assassination ' has taken place?

What is Assassination? It would be easy to answer negatively—to say, for instance, it is not the act of killing a man, witness all kinds of justifiable homicide ; nor of killing him unexpectedly, witness sharp-shooting, ambuscades, &c. ; nor of killing him in the dark, witness night-attacks, from Abraham downwards: nor of killing him without danger to yourself, witness bombardments at long-range, &c.—and so on to the end of the induction.

But I prefer a more positive and popular reply, because, for one thing, our public thought is unused to subtleties ; and because, for another, one does not care to surround a great crime with the hairsbreadth rubicon of a definition.

I shall therefore take a *sine quâ non*, on which we can all agree, and lay down that assassination is, *quidquid ultra, a breach of the peace*: *i.e.*, can only take place between parties who are rightfully bound to be peaceable.

While we hold Charles XII. to be killed by a ball from Frederieshall his death is the fortune of war, but when we find it fired by his own party the act is assassination. The slaughter of Colonel Fraser in the war with America was not assassination, because in time of war. Had Gustavus been hit in front, we should have called it a soldier's death; killed from behind, we suspect his friends, and believe him assassinated. But the reader may multiply instances at pleasure. It is the peculiarity of the assassin that *clam ferro incautum superat*. It is because he is *impius ante aras*, because he strikes not only his victim, but the sweet sanctities of national and social confidence, that he is *scelere ante alios immanior omnes*.

There can, therefore, be no assassination between belligerents; there may be ambush, surprises, forlorn hopes, reprisals, cutting-off-of-stragglers, &c., &c., but not assassination.

(Hence every attempt on the life of a constitutional sovereign is in the nature of assassination; because, being irresponsible, he can never, whatever the national attitude, be otherwise than personally at peace).

Now, sir, I might point out that a political refugee, a subject of a fallen but once legitimate government, proscribed by the dynasty that has forcibly overturned the power to which he swore allegiance, must be held, with regard to that dynasty, as in a state of open and declared war; and that, therefore, if the attempt of the fourteenth of January had been made by Frenchmen, it need not come into the category of assassinations. But the case is stronger still. The actors in that deed were Italians. They had been, as we all know, defeated, after a hard resistance, by an overwhelming French army; their capital city is actually at this moment in the possession of that army; and they, driven from home and country by irresistible numbers, are, in fact, *the remnant of a retreating force.*

This, then, is no affair of private individuals, commencing, on their own authority, an attack upon a foreign power. The war was declared by Louis Napoleon, was prosecuted by Louis Napoleon, and is still, by the forcible occupation of the conquered country, practically maintained by Louis Napoleon.

The position of these men is that of the subaltern and his small following who retire to the hills on the dispersion of the main army, and carry on, as occasion serves, a guerilla warfare under the original flag. Such warfare remains legal till a treaty of peace has been concluded by their recognised leaders, and, whether continuing for months or years, retains all the rights and honours of war. Therefore, at any time since 1849, Napoleon and these refugees have been at open war —war as unmistakable and legitimate as in the day when Oudinot's guns first opened on the walls of Rome. Is an outraged people to call it 'Peace' because the aggressor, with his heel on the neck of Italy, chooses to cry *L'Empire, c'est la paix* '?

Sir, we are at all events a commercial nation, and we know what a contract is worth that has only one hand to it.   Doubtless the robber cries 'peace' when his pockets are full, but does that prevent you from your remedy?   Napoleon and these men are at open war, and whatever is lawful to belligerents is lawful to them. Neither party has an excuse for misconception.   They— God help them—can hardly mistake expatriation; and he is not 'Incautus' who pays twenty thousand spies, and whose 'Cave!' is blown by every French trumpeter in Italy.

Now, sir, if the enemy's army lies yonder, and I send a corps of rifles into those trees, half a mile thence, out of sight and out of reach, and tell them to pick off the Russians with those new Enfields, is that assassination? If so, our best regiments were bands of assassins.   Or stay: on that hill beyond the lines, reconnoitring, in fancied security, the Prince-General is surrounded by a brilliant staff.   I send a shell into them at long range, and knock the campaign on the head.   Is that assassination?   If so the old tag, 'one murder &c.,' is something more than a sarcasm.   Or look you: that midnight city, there, is Sebastopol; four grenadiers volunteer on the forlorn hope, creep through the sentries into the sleeping town, and blow up the magazine.   Are these assassins? Though five hundred non-combatants are buried in the ruins —aye, though two thousand wounded are roasted alive in the hospital hard by ?   We should give them medals if they

lived, and pension their children's children if they fell.
But when four men land in a hostile country of thirty
millions, enter the chief city of the enemy, and, at the
door of his most public edifice, in an artificial day of
gaslight, walk up to him, through the drawn swords of
his ranks of soldiers, and the Argus eyes of his crowded
police, and do what they know to be certain death to
themselves—death as inevitable as if they jumped off the
Monument—we lift up our hands, and cry ' Assassination ! '

Sir, I appreciate the present master of the French
as one who, having spent a life in preparing for a foreseen
conjuncture, has proved, when 'the hour' arrived, that he
had not miscalculated 'the Man.' I can, in a certain
sense, sympathise with him on his own standpoint, and
understand his view of the situation. But because I
comprehend Cæsar, must I needs undervalue Brutus?

I lament the adventure of these unhappy patriots—
this *coup d'état* attempted last January (at the cost of a
hundred and fifty persons), against the hero of a previous
coup d'état accomplished on a certain second of December
(at the cost of uncounted lives and of exiles in tens of
thousands). I believe these enterprises to be usually unwise, and that in state-craft to be unwise is to be crimi-
nal; but to call this devoted piece of warfare ' assassination,' is one of those cruel and passionate perversions of
language which distinguish annals from history.

If our ' fourth estate ' were content to be merely the
annalist of Europe, I should not send you these remarks.
But because it aspires to be the public voice of England,
and because that function is incomplete unless, while

uttering the national impulse of the hour—the roar of the ranks and the ' noise of the captains and the shouting '— you also express those of us who, standing, as it were, on the knolls and hillocks of the battle-field of politics (at once in and out of the conflict), anticipate, in some sort, the verdict of a calmer Future, you will probably give a place in your columns to

Yours &c.,

'Επίσκοπος.

CHAPTER III.

APRIL 1858 TO APRIL 1860.

On his 34th birthday he was at Detmore. The benefit to his general health of the winter spent at Niton could not have been very apparent—for his father reports him as looking very thin and ill, and suffering greatly from deafness—but the symptoms of chest-irritation had been allayed by the soft and yet dry climate of the Island.

During the stay at Detmore, a wide area of the neighbouring hill-country was explored, in search for a suitable home, and, at length, a small house, known as Cleeve Tower, was taken.

The pure and bracing air of the hills about this new home invigorated him; he spent many hours of each day on horseback, and during this summer his health considerably improved.

At the urgent recommendation of his medical advisers, he was prevailed upon to try the effect of allowing his brain a prolonged rest from all purely literary work and effort, and with the happiest promise.

About this time he wrote, from Cleeve Tower, to his brother Dr. Horace Dobell:

The misfortune of us younger men is, that we have not the *physiques* of our grandfathers; and that one defect may be fatal to us as a generation.

Meantime, such of us as would redeem the general character, by deeds fit to live, must do our best to get flesh and blood enough to carry us to the necessary maturity. And I fear you won't do that—nor I —without more care than has been compatible with your late occupations.

His life was more outwardly active during these months. Having lately taken a new business-house at Gloucester, he was organising there a business on a much larger scale. Three days, at least, in the week he rode to Cheltenham—a distance of some miles—thence to take rail to Gloucester.

His abilities as a man of business were considerable, and his energy, tact, and far-sightedness, combined with a chivalrously punctilious honour, ensured the success of all he undertook, as long as he had sufficient physical health to retain the reins of government.

On this head his brother writes :

Whatever he did, he did *well* : in business he was practical and shrewd ; and while he had time and strength to direct, his affairs prospered. I fully believe that for many years he was well and faithfully served by those who managed for him ; and that he might have been so served to the last had he not trusted too much, and expected more than was reasonable to expect from ordinary human nature. . . . Characteristic of him were his simplicity and courage in carrying out the daily round of business duties that must, of course, have been uncongenial, and, even, sometimes, antagonistic, to his personal tastes and feelings. . . He worked on in accordance with a code of principles which he applied to the acts necessary to gaining daily bread. His opinions upon the art of gaining a living will be found in his Letters ; he held, that the first business and profession of every man is to be a Christian Gentleman ; and that the acts and processes by which he gains money should always be a secondary part of his life and character ; that, consequently, so long as the occupation is honest, it does not much signify what that occupation happens to be, it can be made mean or dignified according to the personal character of the man who pursues it. He, therefore, did not attempt to escape from the business he had been brought up to pursue. He was strictly abstemious in his habits ; but he considered the use of wines and spirits to be a ' legitimate luxury,' and that to condemn that use for fear of its abuse might accord with Mahometan or Buddhist morality, but was inconsistent with the whole tenour of Christian philosophy. He held, moreover, that what was allowed to the rich should not be withheld from the poor, that the more difficult and dangerous the traffic might be, the more important was it that men of character and courage should undertake and conduct it; and, in this spirit, he worked simply and fearlessly.

He was fully conscious of the ludicrous and disparaging view of 'trade' and 'tradesmen' that is common in some circles; having lived in a district where caste prejudices are exhibited in their most unreasonable and grotesque forms. And yet we find him, after four or five years of literary life and society, setting to work to remodel and enlarge his business, and adapting himself to the necessities of business life, without hesitation or regret.

The letters of this period are few. He was within easy riding and driving distance of his family, and was, therefore, relieved from that constant and voluminous correspondence. His wife now, as far as her strength allowed, often acted as his secretary.

During this summer a good many friends visited him in his little hillside home: to feel the heart-warming and potent charm his affectionate hospitality could give to somewhat primitive quarters and limited accommodation.

The winter of 1858 to 1859 was exceptionally mild, and permitted him to carry out his wish of wintering at the Tower, and thence continuing his superintendence of his Gloucester affairs.

The hill, Cleeve Cloud, which rose immediately behind his house, was rich in Roman remains, excavating in search of these was one of his relaxations, and he made two or three curious discoveries, concerning which he corresponded with Sir David Brewster.

During the summer of 1859, Mr. Fields, of Boston, and his interesting and accomplished wife, were for a few days guests at Cleeve Tower. Mr. Fields was desirous of arranging for the publication of an American edition of Sydney Dobell's Poems ; which appeared in the following year, introduced by a brief biographical sketch, to the last sentence of which Mr. Dobell in later life appended—in giving a copy of the book to any of his friends— a sentence of protest.

The little sketch concludes in the following manner :

Though by constitution and habit pre-eminently a thinker, Mr. Dobell's private life is sufficiently practical. An excellent man of business, an expert rider and driver, accustomed to the gun, the rifle, the rod and the oar, he is singularly unlike the fancy portraits of a metaphysical

poet in which his adverse critics indulge. And the charge
of anti-Christian speculation, which has occasionally been
brought against him by hasty readers of ' Balder,' is yet
more curiously infelicitous. Mr. Dobell is neither a bigot
nor an enthusiast; but it is known to his friends that the
great object of his life is the introduction, in due season,
of a new and nobler organisation of Christianity.

' This last sentence,' Sydney Dobell wrote,
' contains a signal mistake. One may desire a
reform, without the egotism of desiring to intro-
duce it.'

The feeling which led him to write this protest,
signally marked an enlargement of views and
maturing character; for there can be little doubt
but that in youth and first manhood he had regarded himself as one of the probable organizers
of a new Christian Church, embodying the principles set forth by his grandfather, but founded on
a yet more comprehensive basis.

Professor and Mrs. Blackie were also visitors
at the ' Balder-Tower,' as the Professor called it,
and much interesting word warfare, and argu-
mentative tourneying, took place between the
friends (whose opinions on many subjects differed
widely and radically), both indoors and out, with-

out the slightest disturbance of the cordiality of
their mutual affection.

An excursion made from the Tower to Tintern
by the four friends—Mr. and Mrs. Blackie, Mr.
and Mrs. Dobell—was the occasion of a Sonnet,
printed in the collected edition of Sydney Dobell's
Poems, beginning :

> If Time that feeds love dies to die no more,
> Immortal hours, dear friends, were yours and mine.

From the few letters of this period, but few
extracts can be made.

To Mrs. Samuel Brown (in answer to a request for letters
from her husband).

Cleeve Tower, near Cheltenham : May 16, 1859.

My dear friend,—How pleasant it is to feel that you
have crossed the Border and are really within fifty miles of
us. This seems a ' cruel kindness,' considering the affliction [1]
that has caused your English advent. . . . The root of
many a flower would disenchant it, but that we see the one
at six months' distance from the other. Therefore, a
heartiest welcome to ' merry England,' though, alas ! it
can hardly seem ' merry ' to you—except in that lovely
and oldest meaning of the word, wherein I wish to think
our country first won the title — the sense in which
Canute said :—

Merrie sungen the Muneehs binnen Ely.

[1] The illness of one of Mrs. Brown's children.

. . . I left off to search for the letters. Unhappily I can find but three. The rest of what he wrote to me must be buried somewhere—and in consecrated ground, for I never treated anything of his carelessly—but I know not where to dig for them. We filled a very cemetery of sacred graves when we left Coxhorne, but they have no epitaphs, and after six years of absence one green mound is like another. I found these letters side by side with some of Currer Bell's; with one from that strange Hungarian, Madame von Beck, who died in the cell at Birmingham; with another from a brother-in-law, whom I last saw, young, handsome, and vigorous, and who lies among the unknown corals of the Pacific; and with others tragical in less degree, that yet when they were stowed away in this innocent looking desk were, also, no tragedies at all. You will readily understand that after reading such things as I found in them I was in no mood to write. I don't think a visible audible ghost could affect one with so solemn a perplexity as the paper life of letters like these.

I know you will restore them to me, some time hence, —if I am here to claim them, and whenever (in turning up the dust that lies—in no figurative sense—upon the remains of dear old Coxhorne) I disinter more treasures, you shall have them.

At this time, during the holiday of his manager, he wrote to his brother-in-law, Mr. A. J. Mott:

Counting-house, Gloucester: August.

I fear I've been getting credit for more generosity in the case of W——'s holiday than I can lawfully lay claim

to. It is true that, after being accustomed for some years
to the reverent *je ne sais quoi* of those in whose eyes a
poet is ‘ greater than a king,’ the voice of sudden and un-
respective persons demanding a dozen of porter for Mr.
Smith of Blank Street, seemed at first a little ‘ out of
fashion.’ But I’ve enjoyed the opportunity of seeing how
things worked here, and of setting right many small
details that a subaltern’s eye overlooks. Curiously enough
—but of course only by coincidence—the business during
this week has been greater, by a third, than usual.

We have a comfortable bedroom in the Museum,[1] next
door to a particular friend of Pharoah, and I am inclined
to think we sleep more soundly than he. Whether the
Christian air has a kind of chronic resurrection in it, and
the poor heathen—sleeping lightly—snore in a dry rattling
mummified manner, or whether—having been ‘ Captain of
the Barge to the King ’—he was such a dissipated leisure-
eaten courtier, that he still plays pitch and toss o’nights, I
don’t know, but the noises in the house might puzzle a score
of philosophers. However, as E ——’s little dog, whom
I would back against all the philosophers for detecting
varmint, takes no notice of them, they do not disturb us.

Mr. Dobell’s relations with the ‘ W—— ’ of the
preceding letter were of an exceptional, what the

---

[1] A fine suite of rooms—the first floor of his new house of business—
had been lent by Mr. Dobell to the citizens of Gloucester, for use as
Museum and Reading Rooms, and continued to be so lent for a
number of years, till a suitable building had been erected for these
purposes.

ordinary man of business would consider a poetical
rather than a business-like, kind and origin.

W—— was one among the many young men
attracted to Mr. Dobell during his residence in
Scotland. A certain power of chivalrous devotion
shown by him in his intercourse with a common
friend, drew upon him Mr. Dobell's special regard,
and made him resolve, if the opportunity ever
offered, to do him good service. At the time Mr.
Dobell first knew him, W—— was a medical
student; but, by and by, family misfortunes made
it impossible for him to continue his University
education, and imperative on him to seek a more
directly bread-earning employment.

On taking his new house of business, Mr.
Dobell's thoughts turned to W——, perceiving
now the opportunity of carrying out his wish.
W——, being entirely ignorant of the business he
was to conduct, was first allowed the opportunity
of learning something of it at Cheltenham, and
then received a good deal of drilling and training
—personal and by letter—from Mr. Dobell himself,
by whom he was always treated with singular
confidence and affection.

To his Father and Mother.

What a lovely calm autumn day it is—hardly autumn
but September, which is a season *sui generis*—just like
the same day five years ago. That never-to-be-forgotten
day of Alma, never to be forgotten at least by that young
world that fought its first great battle in that poetry of
weather, and found that ' the old days' were indeed no
' better than these.' No battle, I think, can ever be again
to us what that first victory was—what with the cause, and
the season, and the equipment, and the sunny day, and the
character of those who were to die or live, and the marrow-
deep excitement of that first trial of young strength by
the old historic standard—war was so transfigured that we
did not wonder when the ' Times' reported that the very
dead were smiling. . . .

I must tell dear A—— [1] of an awful adventure.
Walking with Maida on the hill-top, I saw her suddenly
dart behind a rubble-heap, but supposed it was only a
rabbit. A moment after some sheep scudding and then
returning with that strange look of curiosity which always
indicates something in the wind, roused me to the top of
the rubble heap. On the other side behold Maida, tearing
at a live sheep's leg as if her life depended on making
rags of it. . . .

Maida herself—her master's in-door as well as
out-door companion—soon became too gentle and

---

[1] A little sister.

civilised a member of society to indulge in amuse-
ments so costly to her owner; but she was the
mother of a family, and her descendants, before
they got fully trained, generally went through
sundry similar adventures.

On the receipt of some Poems.

Cleeve Tower: December 1, 1859.

. . . From ordinary friends and acquaintances I take,
as those who blame me for it complain, any amount of
over-estimate and 'make no sign.' If the estimators
believe the estimate true, they do but common duty in
speaking truth; if it is false, the fault and the loss are
theirs. Therefore, except for a kindly feeling towards the
good-will in which such things originate— and a little
sadness, perhaps, whose source I don't exactly know,—I
usually receive quite passively any amount of praise.
But this is when it comes from the general world. Coming
from you I should have to meet it by confession. And
confession *in propriâ personâ* goes hard with me, you
might as well try to screw wine out of this oak table on
which I write. And, if I could make it, it would hardly
please you, such a discontented face and hung-down head
as I should have to draw, such eyes that seem so blind,
straining for more than twilight, such hands, groping out
into vacuity. . . .

. . . I would point out a defect in the picture of your
last Sonnet, which, with larger experience of the original

VOL. II.   L

[his wife], you will perceive more and more. It is impossible that the greater portion of her light can be *reflected*—however transfigured and made exquisite by the purer nature of the reflecting medium—because some of its most priceless elements are not constituents of any human light she receives. . . .

. . . You know I am not attempting here to paint her portrait—I tried that once—but merely making a brief memorandum of one mistake in your beautiful sketch. Keep it, and see how it agrees with the teaching of time.

The winter of 1859–60 proved unusually severe, the attempt to weather it at the Tower was unsuccessful and unfortunate, and produced a return of the symptoms of chest-irritation.

They went early in the new year for a short time to Detmore ; and then, after a couple of days in Gloucester (during which he left 'directions down to every smallest matter of detail,' for the management of his business), to the Isle of Wight, for ten weeks.

February 25, 1860.

We had a curious surprise, in crossing from Southampton to Cowes. About half way across I saw a steamer lying at anchor, whose shape seemed familiar, and whose extremely commercial looking cut and Yankee leanness gave an uncomfortable feeling of being too narrow and slight for its length. . . . Our little steamer bore about the relation to it [the Great Eastern] that an ordinary boat bears to a common Clyde or coast steamer, but I confess the whole appearance of the 'colossal ship' is anything but that of a Colossus. There is an undignified outrigger look about it, and an abnegation of all qualities but stowage and speed.

To his Father and Mother.

Niton : February 27, 1860.

We have had till yesterday gentle days, with slight frosts at night, hardly perceptible in the morning, and south-west winds. Crocuses are (scantily) out in the garden and daffodils in large bud; yesterday was rain and sleet, but still not severe. To-day and last night it has been blowing great guns from the nor'-west, and, if that hideous Pagan be right, who says the top of human happiness is to stand safe on shore and see a shipwreck, we ought to be enjoying a frightful Elysium. One little ship was blown ashore just now, and two or three—small and great—are battling within sight. The sea is like a flat world of green marble. How I hate it! A brave man can hate nothing that there is a chance of conquering, but this blind, senseless, woman-drowning, child-freezing, man-choking god—I stand and look at it here till every drop of blood in my body is black.

To ——.

One should not desist from speaking out one's perceptions because those who hear may not also be able to

perceive. As, in the great world, it is precisely by the
calm assertion and repetition of a truth, before mankind
are ready for it, that the great human instrument at last
comes round to the tuning-fork, so, in the smaller world
of each individual, it is by a brave open unmistakeable
enouncement (in words and deeds) of what we feel and
know—however incredible, for the time, to the audience—
that the tone of those we live among is imperceptibly and
unconsciously raised.   The very act of disagreeing has
often a re-actionary effect on the dissentient that is
vitalizing; and the bracing result to our own moral constitution of quietly doing what is not 'the way o' the
world' about us is invaluable.

Controversy is seldom useful to either side, but un-
subdued witness-bearing is (as our word 'martyr'-witness
indicates) among the most heroic disciplines of the
soul.

Extract from criticism.

I think the idea of 'supplement' is not accurately true
to the fact.   It seems to me that man and woman should
be two versions of the same truth.   That the qualities in
each should be the same, but in different proportions and
of—so to speak—different material.   If each had not the
same qualities it could not understand them in the other.
The exquisiteness of the relation seems to be that what is
less in one can coalesce with what is more in the other;
that what is coarse in one can be conscious of the other's
ineffable fineness; that woman's intellect uniting itself to

man's can feel, by consciousness of her own change, with
what greatness she has become identified; that man's
moral qualities—not all, but many—recognising the cor-
responding qualities in woman, should know in them such
difference of grain, texture, *substans*, as between a blue
pigment and the blue of heaven, or the light of a red fire
and the subtlest rose of dawn.

To his Father and Mother.

Niton: April 5, 1860.

I fear from W——'s account of his *reconnaissance* at
the dear little Tower last Sunday, and from L——'s description of the Odsey wild flowers, that the April you are
having is very different from what is making the starry
hill-sides hereabouts fuller of constellations than skies in
winter. The primroses are almost like the sand of the
shore, they overhang for multitude, but somehow they are
not quite like the primroses of home. There is a popular
look about them, like the faces of a crowd, and there is
greater difficulty in finding, among all those millions, a
handful of perfections than there would be on any simple
bank in our hills. But the abundance is testimony to
that general blunting of the edge of winter whereby,
rather than from any absence of the knife itself, this place
is distinguished from the mainland.

During these weeks at Niton, he had a good
deal of pleasant intercourse, frequent walks and
talks, both with old friends staying near, and

with some interesting new acquaintance, one of
whom jestingly reported that the search for a
perfect primrose—for the typical ideal blossom
—was 'the serious occupation of Sydney Dobell's
days.'

As soon as the spring was far enough advanced, Mr. Dobell returned to the Tower.

He wrote this summer a Poem, 'The Youth of England to Garibaldi's Legion,' which was first published in the August number of 'Macmillan's Magazine.' Speaking of it, at the end of a long business letter, to his brother-in-law, Mr. A. J. Mott, he said :

I think you will see that with the living deeds speaking for themselves in the ears of Europe, there would be only bathos in the kind of poem you thought I should write. At such moments it is for the poet not to express Garibaldi, but to write what might make Garibaldis. And this must be done not by stimulus, but *ab initio.*

To M——. (In answer to a letter on the subject of 'the Position of Women.')

Cleeve Tower: August 1860.

I am at a loss to tell you what a relief and what an abiding comfort your letter was and will be to me. If

you knew how deeply—solemnly—I feel on the subject of
which it speaks, and how each new experience adds depth
and seriousness to feeling,—how each fresh day that whets
perception, and heightens the standpoint over the enlarg-
ing plain of life, shows me a landscape everywhere vital
with new forms of the old, old story, and everywhere
repeating the old proofs already so familiar, till I come to
see that what was once regarded as a tea-table question of
domestic regimen is really one phenomenon of those great
abstract evils which make themselves visible in the direst
sorrows of our time, and that whoever shall either destroy
it by destroying these principles, or mortally wound these
principles through the body of this their most seductive
concrete, will do the greatest good for mankind that the
age admits of—if you knew how, seeing all this, I feel
every year of growth add iron to my convictions, and if
you knew all the proud love and joy with which I see one
whom I love as I love you, taking her part in what I know
is not only for the blessing of others, but must a thou-
sand-fold react in beauty and blessing on herself—if you
knew these things, I might use them to express that 'unknown quantity' which now is past my algebra.

. . . Perhaps, however, you may find it a little assistance in your labour, a little solace in difficulty and dis-
satisfaction, to remember that, under the dispensation
which has now been for some years upon me—wherein the
keen perception of all that should be done, and that so
bitterly cries for doing, accompanies the consciousness of
all I might *but cannot* do—one of the most intimate
consolations I can taste is to see the work go on by hands

that are dear to me,—to witness, either in the incarnation
of a life or the demonstration of apostleship, the progress
of those truths which I am but permitted—from this
Pisgah of mere eyesight—so helplessly to perceive.

But though I shall say nothing of what I feel, either
concerning your loyalty to the Ideal, or the spirit in
which you are endeavouring to do your loyal service, I
may write a word or two on that portion of your letter,
because it has regard not to feeling but intellect. You
contrast your own sensations of doubt and self-distrust
with the working joy of those women who are advancing
the opposite cause, and confess to a respect for their
successful support and illustration of their 'principles.'

An examination of the women, the work, and the
'principles' would leave no cause for wonder and little—on
this ground—for respect. The secret of *pleasure* in life
—as distinct from its greatest triumphs of transcendant
joy—is to live in a series of small, legitimate successes.
By legitimate I mean, such as are not accompanied by
self-condemnation. If these successes can be achieved in
such fields as the nature of the agent makes most congenial, the pleasure is enhanced. If they can be advanced
from the negative virtue of non-condemnation to the
positive of Duty performed, it is still further increased.
And if the conceit and vanity, which of all selfish *sensoria*
are the most readily touched and the most acutely
pleasurable, can be titillated by a personal possession in
the 'Duty'—the ownership of discovery, or patronage, or
any kind of special relation—the total pleasure is still
further raised. Now this, in a greater or less degree, is

the case of the women you speak of. But their application of these principles, and performance of these duties is—with some rare exceptions—no just ground for respect (except in so far as the duties be admirable *per se*), because in reality there is no genuine application at all. These women are self-deceived.

They do not act to fulfil principles; their principles are invented in justification of actions *which more irresistible motives* impel. The happiness they find in applying those principles and defending them is therefore made up of two elements both eminently gratifying—the free and unrestrained exercise of their own constitutional idiosyncrasies (the full-swing play of those dominating faculties to which, like all functions, free action is its own reward), and the approval of a conscience which has been already brought down (by a theorem of ‘principles’) to the actions it is required to approve. To such natures there is no difficulty in this tuning of the conscience, because the fact that the principles, being new, are their own special property, is the most exquisite stimulus to that egotism which is their centre, and they mistake the vibration of this stimulus, and the blind thrill of foreseen liberty which the license such principles will give to some other qualities produces in those qualities, for the emotions of satisfied reason.

Ask yourself, in the case of any ‘strong-minded’ woman, whether, if there were no such thing as theories or principles in the world, her actions and life, in type and character, would have been other than they are?

Ask yourself also whether, in these merely human days,

the activity of the best and greatest of us is, or has been,
of this self-confident, self-rewarding order?   When our
race, under a Millennial dispensation, reaches its happiest
development, the certainty of assured duty and the confidence of an unquestionable right may be among the
choicest blessings of a Divine kingdom, where Infallible
Authority can issue to each enquirer his modicum of truth ;
but in our present state of things, to see far, to feel subtly,
to know widely, is the guarantee of that ' trembling ' in
which all salvation must be wrought, and which assails
him most who learns most supremely the infinite variety,
complexity and *per*plexity of this universe.   Our greatest
heroisms are done unconsciously and with sickness of
heart : our greatest truths are handled as one touches
something cold in the dark : our truest course is steered
as he who, over seas beneath and under clouds above,
catches, glimmer by glimmer, through wind and tempest,
a sight, just visible by eyes strained to bursting, of the
unerring guide within the binnacle.

Remembering these things, take comfort in any
amount of humility and discontent ; and fear only, and
terribly, when you find yourself approaching the state of
those spanking benefactors of their species, whose jovial
welfare almost moves your envy.

About this time the question, ' Why are early
marriages more and more rare ? ' was mooted
in the ' Times.' The various attempts made to
answer it, by those who seemed to Mr. Dobell

incompetent to fathom the depths under the ice which they had broken, provoked him to essay a reply. The letter begun would, if finished, have been of considerable length ; from the rough draft of it before us we may give. to indicate its tenor, a few extracts.

In ' the increasing selfishness of young men and the decreasing loveliness of young women,' he thought the true answer might be found.

Is there (he asked) any among your readers who doubts that selfishness is incompatible with love ? If so, I will ask his definition of love, and shall probably find from the answer a sufficient explanation of the doubt. . . .

. . . There are in ancient and modern literature many fine things on the subject of love ; and though there is none that fully defines it as a whole, there is one that consummates all that can be thought or said on the love of man for woman : ' Husbands, love your wives, even as Christ also loved the Church.' There is nothing in history, philosophy, poetry, or romance that for depth, tenderness, and comprehension surpasses this formula ; and there is nothing, also, within the resources of human language that could so utterly express an unconditional self-oblivion. . . . It is not often, of course, that we can expect to meet with this highest manifestation of love ; but in proportion as the passion called by that name approaches the standard, it deserves the sacred title, and is capable of yielding that subtle, enduring, and imperturbable bliss which the greatest thinkers of all ages have united to attribute to love alone, and which, of all that we are privileged to feel on earth, must, since it results from the divinest exercise of our nature, be nearest to what eye hath not seen, nor ear heard, neither hath it entered into the heart of man to conceive. . . .

Concerning the 'decreasing loveliness of young women,' after observing:

'Lovely' is an unsatisfactory word, but it is the best available. . . . A lovely thing is a thing which is loveable, and it is more or less lovely as it is more or less adapted to be loved:

he wrote:

While the great object of their care and ambition seems to be the exercise of those functions wherein we surpass, and must always surpass them; the attributes by which, in their own sphere, they would be irresistible, and whereto our noblest must look up with that 'divine despair' which a devotee may feel towards the shape and substance of angels, are shrinking by disuse, withering of inanition, soiled by aspersion. . . .

I never knew a man of more than moderate stature who felt undersized by the side of the loftiest female intellect; but I know that the strongest and proudest men have often felt ready to sink, in sackcloth and ashes, upon knees no human force could bend, before the humility, the purity, the unconsciousness, the self-oblivion of the simplest woman in the world. . . .

The subject of what is called strong-mindedness in women is one on which it is easy for many persons, as their tempers vary, to indulge in a light contempt, a virulent scorn, a careless levity, or an emasculate adulation, but wherein it is difficult for an ordinary writer to maintain that sweet-blooded strength with which a noble man, whose nature, and whose respect for women, alike forbid him to tamper with truth in their behalf, dispenses, when called to pronounce on female error, the firm amenities of a gentle justice. . . .

I put it to any man of large acquaintance, whether among the majority of his young-women-friends, self-consciousness, self-esteem, self-righteousness, self-defence, and self-assertion have not been, for some years past, on the increase?   And I ask the consciences of three young ladies out of five, whether they would feel more complimented to be thought as modest as Lucretia, as humble as the Sidonian,[1] as patient as Burd Helen, as meek and obedient as Enid, (or any other shining illustrations of these adjectives), or as talented, or independent, or plucky, or learned, or indefatigable as . . . , or as any other milder or stronger exponents of the same special abilities, who may happen, in their particular, to be the representative woman. . . .

Will that noble rebuke, begun by our great Laureate

---

[1] The allusion here is, probably, to the woman, 'out of the coasts of Tyre and Sidon,' whose humility of faith our Lord tested by the words: 'It is not meet to take the children's bread, and to cast it to the dogs.'

in 'The Princess,' continued in the Idylls, and echoed more or less audibly by nearly every strong man of our day, repeat in every Penthesilea the miracle of that prototype,

> Whose falser self slipped from her like a robe
> And left her woman?

Writing, from Cleeve Tower, to his father and mother, October 8, he said :

. . . Poor Gray's book (I had such a letter of delight from him, which you shall see) is already a certainty.

And then went on to explain how the funds for the publication of this book had been raised.

Of very many of Sydney Dobell's beneficent deeds, no record, of course, remains; but the kindness shown by him to David Gray, the author of 'The Luggie,' was not only recognised, but, as he thought, exaggerated.

What I was able, at any time, to do for David Gray, consisted chiefly of unpalatable advice, and of introductions to friends who had more cash and leisure than I : [was his own version of the matter.[1]]

It is to be regretted that of his letters—to the number and the nature of which we have David

---

[1] David Gray's own letters, and other evidences, show how much Mr. Dobell, as was his wont, under-estimated the amount of assistance, of various kinds, rendered in this, as in similar cases.

Gray's answers to testify—the Editors of these
Memorials have been able to obtain only the part
of one, which is given on the following pages.   The
'unpalateable advice' addressed to poor young
Gray, and to his friend and companion in the fight
for literary distinction, might have been of service
to others similarly situated, and would have been
interestingly illustrative of their writer's own views.

In the letter in which the young poet speaks
of the 'sudden happiness' of hearing that his book
would be printed; would be 'a book' which 'my
dear mother would read on Sunday—the only day
she ever reads—and my father would show to
every person who came into the house,' he also
says :

'Not that I troubled myself about it while I was well ;
but when death looked on me the desire to behold it
grew horribly keen. . . . But now I shall see it.   I think
of it by night and day, and cannot look over the MSS.
for anticipating my pleasure.'

The MSS. were, accordingly, sent to Mr. Dobell,
with a note from the dying lad's father, saying :

'You will have to look over them, as he was not able
to finish them as they should be.'

The same letter of young Gray's from which
we have quoted, concludes thus :

Your Christianity gave me comfort indeed ; it was that long indefinite 'purposeless torment' from which my soul shrunk in horror and despair.   I am too far through, from want of breath, just now, to write more, or I should have asked one or two questions concerning the Resurrection and Ascension.   You may unriddle them for me yet, however. Good bye.   'I wish [sic] it were night, and all well, Hal!'

Some weeks later, as was written to Sydney Dobell by one who had been a true friend to David Gray :

He took the specimen page in his hand as soon as the post arrived (the day before his death), and a smile passed over his pale countenance.   In the evening, when alone with his mother, he requested her a second time to bring out the page of his 'Luggie,' and to hold it up before him, for he was now too feeble to hold it himself; by the means of the lamp he was able to read it, with the aid of his mother, and said, 'This is a real pleasure—all is right now—good news.'

The letter alluded to by David Gray in the words, 'Your Christianity gave me comfort indeed,' was evidently the one of which the following part has been preserved :

. . . And now having attended a little to things on the hither bank, let us look a moment across the dark river. I have seen by your letters that you are in a state of doubt

and unhappiness as to received creeds and formulæ, which
happens at your age to almost every man who has mind
enough to think, and soul enough for spirituality.   For
such men, to believe the 'orthodoxy' of the day, or to
remain contented in a general disbelief, is equally impossible; and the dark interval between the conventions
we leave behind and such truths as are possible to us in
this imperfect condition of all human eyesight, is not often
passed through till a later time of life than yours.

Seeing, then, that you are likely to proceed to those
regions which are the subject of Religious Knowledge at a
time when, in the usual process of growth, you have not
attained to the functions of seeing clearly what can here
be known of them, you will forgive me for suggesting (in
a matter so intimately affecting your peace while you remain with us) one or two things, that the various friends
and advisers who surround you are in all probability too
'orthodox' to agree with, but which, I think, your own
instincts and receptivities will, when proposed, dispose you
to accept.

Let me recommend you, then, that putting aside
resolutely the various theological subtleties that may be
pressed upon you, you take up the New Testament and
yourself seek for Christ.   Not the Christ of Trinitarian or
Unitarian, but that historical Personage whose appearance
in this world no sane sceptic can deny, and who left, I
believe, *no such explanation of His precise nature* as
may justify us in dogmatising thereon.

Sufficient for you that One has appeared in our shape,
and spoken our language, Who was unquestionably beyond

us in every virtue and in every wisdom, and Who showed
by what He lived, taught and performed, an *intimacy
with God* which has appertained to none of us before or
since.   From such a Teacher, whatever His nature, every
wise man will be only too glad to receive whatever a
knowledge thus demonstrated may please to deliver upon
subjects on which he knows himself to be, alas! so helplessly in the dark.   Whatever Christ's essence *per se,*
there can be no doubt that He was nearer the Centre of all
Truth than ourselves, and than any human being of whom
history makes record.

Having thus received your Teacher, and those whom
He specially made the depositaries of His wisdom, let me
advise you, when questioning them of that God before
Whom you expect so soon to appear, to leave all minor,
and, as it were, accidental details and possess yourself,
with all the grasp of your soul, of such central and essential
declarations respecting Him as are simple in form, unmistakeable in phrase, and of *analogies so far human* as to
admit, with safety, the test of human reason.

Foremost among all such declarations, and fulfilling all
the foregoing conditions, is that cardinal truth of Christianity—*God is Love.*

Nothing can be simpler, or more absolute, in expression, nothing can be more safely within the province of
human experience and the legitimate exercise of a reverent logic.

If God had *not* pleased to reveal Himself in the
likeness of any human faculty, we should have no right to

wonder or complain; but we should, also, have no right to employ our finite reason upon His attributes. But when He has vouchsafed an analogy, and has put the analogy, in the strictest shape possible,—has made it, in fact, rather *homological* than analogical—we are justified in using, with a brave and thankful alacrity, the premises which His condescension has given to our use.

Take, therefore, confidently this great premise of Love, and believe nothing—however speciously supported by the appearance of isolated texts (I say 'appearance,' for they all dissolve before the touch of strong sense and scholarship)—which is inconsistent with the conclusions it justifies.

I need not point out to you how every 'orthodox' theory of damnation—every theory of punishment which does not include the *amendment of the punished*—disappears before these conclusions, and how infinitely consoling are those nobler, purer and wider beliefs that they substitute. A brave man can look humbly forward to a period of discipline, however long and terrible, which has *perfection for its object and eternal peace beyond it.* It is only from the prospect of hopeless, endless, purposeless torment that the soul recoils in horror, rebellion, and despair.

I will not attempt here to go into the various departments of those great kingdoms of thought which I have ventured to enter in this letter, for your own strong powers will, doubtless, in your enforced leisure, explore them again and again; but I could not resist taking you to the two metropolitan ideas which, as it seems to me, you will find to be the centre of their geography and the *foci* of their organisation. How much I wish you were near enough for that word-of-mouth communication by which alone, in these difficult subjects, we can really interchange ideas.

I dare feel confident that there are no objections, to such a Christianity as I would fain see you accept, which a few words of such communication would not suffice to clear away. I have forced time for this long letter. If in future I write briefly and seldom, be certain no less of the continuing interest and deep sympathy of yours heartily,

SYDNEY DOBELL.

CHAPTER V.

AUTUMN OF 1860 TO AUTUMN OF 1862.

THIS summer had been a time of weaker than average health, and the Tower was to have been left for a milder district early in October, but illness postponed the move.

Both as to situation, and as to the house itself, the romantic little place was unfit for an invalid's home; and, after holding it for three years, Mr. Dobell reluctantly decided to give it up. He had great power of attachment to places, associations took deep hold of him, and he felt the serious and crippling sort of inconvenience of a manner of existence which necessitated the packing away in inaccessible places of the great bulk of books, and various papers, which a student and man of letters loves to have always at hand. But these minor troubles of life he always took lightly and equably; partly from intrinsic sweetness of nature, but partly, also, it may be, because there was so

much heavier pressure upon him as made trifles
seem really nothing.

To his Father and Mother.

. . . I hope you think me an ungracious dog to fall
ill just at the wrong time—when we were half-packed for
moving, and had no regular household . . . But I have
been nursed as well, day and night, as if I had fifty
nurses ; and now I sleep so much better there will be less
to do. You know how naturally we turn to the dear
mother in times of unusual sickness, but we were anxious
that what promised to be a temporary affair should not
maim the middle of your excursion.

After a long passage of suggestion in regard
to something he was anxious should be done for
the benefit of one of his brothers, he adds, ' I
would gladly scribble on, but really can't sit up.'

The house, known as the Victoria Baths, near
Niton, at which Mr. and Mrs. Dobell spent this
and the ensuing winter, was built almost upon
the shore, only so far raised above it as by the
moderate flight of steps that led up from the
beach to the garden. In heavy storms the waves
often broke over the garden-wall, washed the
garden, and lashed the windows with spray. The

roll of the winter-sea, in sunlight or moonlight,
was a magnificent study from this house, and suggested many fragments of song and ballad. The
house which, sheltered from any but south winds,
and with its large sunny exposure, was well adapted
for a winter sanitorium, now no longer exists,
having been so much damaged in a great storm
as to be pulled down.

To his Mother (after speaking of the horse-exercise the
good weather had allowed of his taking).

Victoria Baths, Niton : December 6, 1860.

. . . Therefore, as I know E. gives you with more
satisfying care and accuracy than I should, where myself
is concerned, just what you want to know, I have waited
from day to day for such compulsory inaction of the body
as may spare me a little mental superfluity, and it has
come at last. How long the imprisonment may be,
though, is very uncertain, for one of the rare advantages
of this undercliff, and especially of this peculiar nook
thereof, is the feminine rapidity of its smiles and tears.
Till the last week there has not been a day, I think, that
however wildly it began was not summer-fair before night,
and the reverse of that order is not unfrequent. The
wettest and most hopeless tempest will change in an hour
to the happiest calmest sunshine—the disorganised mist-
clouds, that hang 'without form and void' over the sea,
furling into form like so many flags at a signal. . . .

I have walked on the shore by twilight, because the
silent softness was so spring-like, within an hour of such a
storm as sent the waves as near that maximum height, of
twenty-seven feet, to which science has reduced the old
image of 'mountain-high,' as waves in-shore often go.

Looking up, I see the sea covered with a fleet of dark
sea-birds, rising and falling. We have had strange ap-
paritions of birds lately—migrations, I suppose, before the
deadly time of winter. A week ago there passed, every
morning for an hour, at a distance of about half a mile
from shore, innumerable armies, all flying from west to
east. Most of them dark, but officered by large white
gulls with black tips to the wings. The rank and file
flew in companies of from ten to fifteen, but the succession of such companies was bewildering. . . .

The rain comes from the south to-day. Usually when
we have rain here we look across the sea, southward, to
the edge of the gay French day which is so visibly shining
beyond the 'insular cloud.' But this morning an English
mist is (I hope) choking the people at Cherbourg, and the
sea runs thence to tell us the good news, leaping, like a
mad Caliban, cataract behind cataract. . . .

After a long account, for his mother's amusement, of the other inmates of the large house, he
adds:

After such specimens, you may fancy what a pair of
quiet proper people we appear to the good folks here.
The housekeeper says, she shall remember us as the couple

that 'ate the least and had the most letters' of any she
has seen in twelve years!

Niton: December 24, 1860.

I am not going to say anything of our Christmas feelings and wishes, because they can't be expressed, and
because, by the law of contrast, the stronger the inexpres-
sible the more painfully feeble looks all attempted expression. . . .

. . . I would give a great deal that dear C—— could
pass some days with us here, on this wonderful promontory,
in the midst of this strange new winter life.

Apart from personal considerations, the whole natural
and human environment is full of new and invaluable
experience. No artist could really paint the sea—that
veritable thing, *the sea*, with its whole being and specific
difference, as distinct from those *bulks of water* which go
by its name in ordinary pictures—who had not either lived
some time on shipboard, or lived, as we live here, on something that looks equally *down into* the ocean, and down
into it not for some particular hour, or in some unusual
season, but continually, under every change of night and
day. The mere *skin* of the sea—the endlessly reticulated
implication and complication of natty surface—has never,
to my knowledge, been represented. Then the strange,
wild, lawless life of the solemn, lawful-seeming people is
an inexhaustible study. We have here, on St. Catherine's
Point, the most southern nose of Great Britain; and the
whole population therefore are smugglers. Everybody
has an ostensible occupation, but nobody gets his money
by it or cares to work in it.

Here are fishermen who never fish, but always have pockets full of money; and farmers whose farming consists in 'ploughing the deep' by night, and whose daily time is spent in standing, like herons, on look-out posts. Nearly the whole village lives in masquerade, even to the names of the villagers. Hardly a man is known by his lawful surname; and we had been here weeks before I suspected that the nomenclature in use was no more real than a play, and the mere protection of confederates always amenable to the law and in danger of eavesdroppers. Everything suggests the abnormal sort of bandit or clan life of the place. Here we are on this desolate shore, shut out by a hill from such other human life as the place affords; but living safely in a house which has not, even on its ground-floor, a single shutter, and where the front door is often unlocked all night, with a 'certainty' against molestation.

But I must not go on with this description, or this letter will not go by this post. I meant to have spoken of other things; and that I have been betrayed into another expatiation on a subject which I must have dealt in during our former stays, you must set down to a strong desire to tempt C—— hitherward.

At the end of this year Mr. Dobell had the great enjoyment of a visit from Mr. Nichol.

During a week spent together, an intimacy, before only slight, ripened into an affectionate friendship. Of this visit Mr. Nichol speaks, at some length, in the following reminiscences, addressed to the Editors, which, for this reason, seem most fitly to find place here.

I was first introduced to Mr. Sydney Dobell at Trinity, in the autumn of 1854, by Alexander Smith. I came to him with an almost embarrassing sense of the courtesy with which he had received the criticisms of a novice in literature,[1] a sense which all our after intercourse only served to deepen. On this occasion he spoke of some juvenile efforts I had ventured to submit to him with a kindness doubly encouraging from the fact that it did not consist in vague commendation but, as was his invariable wont, in discriminating advice. On recent popular works, especially 'The Scarlet Letter,' 'Uncle Tom's Cabin,' and 'Esmond,' he made some comments which seemed to me almost excessively minute. I can recall his contending that Hawthorne's imagination was not always accurate, citing an alleged reflection in the water in the forest scene where none could have been. Of Mrs. Stowe, he thought she had shown real creative power in a few passages, till he found them all referred to in the 'Key' as incidents of real life. These indications, slight as they are, of the scrupulous attention he gave to everything on which he expressed an opinion, are characteristic of his whole career as a critic. For the rest, all I remember is his passing some acute remark on a line of Smith's, a good-natured allusion to Aytoun's 'Firmilian,' and his objecting to the use of

[1] See Vol. i, page 359.

tobacco, on the ground that a cigar was apt to be used as a pocket conscience-soother. I left him with the feeling of having been brought into the presence of a mind of rare beauty, whose weakness lay in intellectual over-refinement.

We again met, in Edinburgh, later on ; and, towards the close of December 1860, I accepted an invitation to visit Mr. and Mrs. Dobell, at Niton in the Isle of Wight ; and can never forget the cordiality of the reception he gave me, nor the charms of his entertainment during that week of soft southern weather by a quiet sea. I had come from a term of hard work at college to rest, and change, and influences that remain among the healthiest memories of my life. I found Mr. Dobell con-siderably aged, the effect of frequent illness, but con-spicuously grown in mental strength or rather breadth of view. He seemed during the years since we had met to have known and mastered much of the world ; and the frequent look of weariness in his face was overspread by a spiritual gleam which called up the thought of ' one of the shining ones.' Of the graces (in his mind always identified with the charities) of his hospitality it is impossible adequately to speak. No man, under guise of receiving favours, ever took more trouble about making other people happy, or with so little seeming effort took so much care of little things. An almost unique combination of man-liness and delicacy, he could sympathise with every phase of nervous or physical weakness, while his example was a living exhortation to surmount them. During this week, at meals, or walking, or driving, we talked at large on a

variety of themes, religious, political, artistic. I have
never known anyone who could speak so suggestively on
so many subjects. In his presence, as in that of the late
Mr. Luke of Christ Church, whom he in many ways resembled, you could ' utter nothing base ; ' and essentially
mean or vulgar persons, poetasters among the chief, may
have resented his unasserted but commanding superiority.
Otherwise nothing was tabooed ; there was perfect freedom,
and a perpetual stimulus as of mountain air. I never
discussed any question without learning something from
him, nor thought seriously on any public matter without
wishing to know what he would have felt about it. At
this period I was fresh from the ferment of the somewhat
inconsistent Radicalism fashionable with the ' reading '
young men of our time at the University—where the tide
has an ebb and flow of some half dozen years—and I had
many differences with Mr. Dobell. Enthusiastic about
the American Constitution, the Extension of the Suffrage,
Woman's Rights, &c., I remember assailing with youthful
vehemence the ideal of character, then recently reproduced
from Chaucer's Griselda, in Tennyson's ' Enid.' ' Depend
on it,' said my companion, ' the stronger minds of the age
find more to attract them and more to respect in that
type of character than in the female men whom you now
profess to admire ; but you will altogether alter your mind.'
In this, as on many other points, I have since recognised
the riper judgment of one who was himself ready to admit
the change that had passed over his own politics. Sydney
Dobell was the antithesis of the democratic tyrant—he
never wavered in his detestation of Louis Napoleon, nor of

the tyrannical democrat of which we have so many examples
nearer home; he had grown to have an utter distrust of
impracticable doctrines of Equality, to esteem Order as
much as he loved Freedom—he was equally steadfast in his
advocacy of Italian unity—to have a reasonable regard for
ancient use and the real distinctions of rank; but every
inferior in station with whom he came into personal
contact cherishes the memory of his benevolence. As
regards his religious beliefs, I can add nothing to what has
been indicated in the published 'Thoughts,' and made
plainer in the narrative of his life. His views of this
period have been generally but correctly defined as those
of a Broad Churchman, modified by a Quaker-like disregard
of ceremonial. I never heard him engage in dogmatic
controversy; his conversation being rather that of an
artist saturated with devotional sentiment than that of one
who had passed through the intense and peculiar religious
experiences referred to in his early letters. His faith in an
earthly Millennium seemed to have been already refined
into something more ideal. He had a strong aversion to
Scotch Calvinism; but he never spoke with anger of any.
form of orthodoxy or heterodoxy. Mr. Dobell was invariably generous in his estimates of his literary compeers,
and considerate even towards those whom he might well
have charged with ingratitude for services to which he
never alluded. He lived with open heart and hand, but
his kindest deeds were done as it were by stealth. He
constantly disclaimed the position of a patron, and recoiled
from the *rôle* of a 'beneficent faery.' Tolerant of differences of belief he was, within wide limits, almost equally

tolerant of differences of character.   His appreciation of
the greatness and the defects, so far apart from his own, of
the poet Byron was especially conspicuous.   His conversation evinced a more genuine sense of humour than is, I
think, anywhere apparent in his works ; but he had little
reticent irony, and insisted on exhausting his subject even
at the risk of exhausting himself and his hearer ; a result,
however, rarely felt till the close, so many winged words
and bright illustrations beguiled the way.   These illustrations seemed all the more vivid that the limitations of his
scholarship led him to seek them in life rather than in
books.   His persistency, as far as my experience goes, never
hardened into dogmatism ; and though he was unwilling
to yield his positions, he never defended them by main
force.   A keen opponent, he was a good listener, and no
older friend could have been disposed to entertain more
graciously or with less shadow of condescension, the half-
formed opinions of a younger.

The same welcome greeted me when, in the October of
1868, I rode from Gloucester to spend a day at Noke
Place.   On this occasion our conversation turned on travel
and foreign architecture ; in the course of it I remember
quoting Browning's verse in reference to a photograph of
Giotto's tower, ‘ the great Campanile is still to finish,’ and
Dobell's expressing a belief that the structure was perfect.
In our walk round the house and garden, I was more than
ever impressed with the minute observation and knowledge
of animals (we were inspecting his magnificent dogs), birds,
plants, and flowers, exhibited in his ‘ Sketches from Nature,’
and attested by all who have been privileged with even a

few hours of his company.   Like the American Thoreau,
he found sermons in stones and theories of life in every
tint of cloud or scent of blossom.   A yellow primrose was
to him at once a subject of botanical analysis and a basis
for a metaphysical system.

In June 1872 and May 1873 I found Sydney Dobell
settled at Barton-End.

We again compared reminiscences of the Continent, and
he dwelt at considerable length on his experiences of Spain,
and his perhaps over-sanguine hopes for her people, with
whose stately manners his own had a sort of natural affinity.
Mr. Dobell maintained that the Spanish idea of equality
was levelling up ; that of the Americans levelling down.
He hardly seemed to me to recognise the higher qualities
and more promising aspects of American civilisation ; but
one of his messages on this occasion was a most courteous
invitation to Mr. Emerson, whom I was about to meet.
Among my other scattered recollections is that of keen
arguments, with no ruffling of temper, but from opposite
sides—he from the Latin, I from the Teutonic—about
the Franco-German War, Euthanasia, and the power of
external Nature to soothe the mind.   In all which and
other matters Dobell stood out for the ordinary Stoic and
Christian views.   About Poetry we were more at one.   I
remember especially our agreement in preferring Camp-
bell's war Lyrics to the luscious and effeminate verses
then so belauded by the young Oxford school of criticism.

I must break off these fragmentary notes with the stale
regret at their utter inadequacy to convey any proximate

idea of the social charms of the bright intelligence to whom they refer.

> Quis desiderio sit pudor aut modus
> Tam cari capitis ?

To have known the genial companionship of Sydney Dobell is one of the things that have to all his friends made life better worth having : to have lost him, is to have lost

> a gentle tone
> Amid rude voices, a beloved light.

A letter of January 23, 1861, to his father, speaks of a brief stay at Freshwater, and of an evening spent at Farringford.

We found, (he says,) the glorious old god as godlike as ever. . . . Nothing could be kinder than both Mr. and Mrs. Tennyson—he in his great blind superhuman manner, like a colossal child—and his often repeated disappointment that we could not stay longer near them was evidently as unfeigned and straight-spoken as everything, large and little, that comes out of that mouth, with which he rather seems to think aloud than, in the ordinary acceptation, to speak. When E—— told him, in the morning, that we were going to bring an authoress, his horror at 'writing women' was grotesque to behold. . . .

To ——.   *On Moral Courage.*

. . . You have mistaken what I said about moral courage. No one is happier to believe that where unmis-

takeable duty points the way, you will go, without a doubt
or a falter, to any danger, and through any difficulty : and
God indeed be humbly praised for the testimony you are
able to bear as to the extent in which this belief has been
already justified by experience.   Few things can gladden
me more deeply than any such evidence to your moral
victories.   But this power of following duty is not moral
courage.   Moral courage is to the *morale* very much what
physical courage is to the *physique.*   A man is not physically courageous because, under certain stimuli, he can
endure great physical pain or confront great physical
danger : and a man is not morally courageous because,
under sufficient moral motives, he is equal to deeds of
moral heroism.

A man of great physical courage does not *conquer*
fear : he has not the feeling.   And a man of great moral
courage can not only use his noblest qualities manfully
when the positive voice of duty commands, but give them
at all times their free and natural exercise.   They are
active, full-shaped, and free, whatever their surroundings,
not because the definite, written Law makes it wrong to be
asleep, but because it is not in their nature to slouch,
shrink, shirk, make excuses, or be anything but themselves.   They may not be able when brought to the scratch
to do more, in actual dynamics, than those of the man who
lacks moral courage ; but they don't want bringing to the
scratch, because they don't, comparatively speaking, dislike
difficulty and danger.   It was in this sense of moral
courage that I have always noticed you to be deficient

therein—deficient, that is, when compared with your other functions. You are very much affected by all the smaller difficulties and obstructions of life, and are likely, therefore, to be less than a match for anyone who is skilful to know them or dexterous to place. You are—for the same reasons, doubtless, considering the substantive nature of your mind—much affected by the atmosphere you breathe. . . .

In February, Mr. and Mrs. Dobell left the Isle of Wight for the neighbourhood of London. The spring and summer were spent in different spots near Gloucester and Cheltenham, on Leckhampton Hill, and at the little old-fashioned Inn at Birdlip. After much reconnoitring of the upland country, a small house then being built on Crickley Hill, seven miles from Gloucester, about the same distance from Cheltenham, was taken for a summer home. Its chief attraction was the glorious situation. A beautiful undulating stretch of thymy down rises behind it; the near views of woodland and pasture are of specially sweet and rich loveliness, while beyond and below stretches the whole wide extent of the vale of Gloucester, bounded by the Malvern and the Welsh hills.

The winter of 1861-2 was again passed at the Isle of Wight. The irritability of the lungs, shown

by a constant and wearing cough by day, and by
night attacks of asthma, was so considerable, that,
by his physician's advice, he used a respirator
even in moving from room to room, and was only
on the most favourable days able to leave the
house.   The state of general exhaustion was such
that he owned to feeling, when writing, 'as if the
ink had to come out of my veins.'

You say, (wrote his physician), that you have not
strength to write more than one letter a day, but that one
letter you sent to me contains a portrait that photography
itself cannot rival, and though I never saw the original, I
have him in my mind's eye and realise all his ways.   One
such portrait is enough for any man to draw in one day.

Public events called from him characteristic
expression of his sentiments concerning them.   A
series of Sonnets, 'On the Death of Prince Albert,'
and 'To 1862,' were written this winter.

In regard to the prospect of war with America
—which seemed imminent in the early part of this
year—he wrote, in one of his home letters, January
1862 :

I will only say a word— from the intellectual side—on
the American war, and your horror at me, and my inferred
'change' of nature, because I believe it just and necessary. . . .

With the war you speak of—' a cruel and un-Christian war merely to revenge a personal insult '—I have nothing to do. There is no danger, I am quite sure, in modern England, of any such war. . . . Neither insult nor revenge has anything to do with the present dispute, or with its warlike issue, however likely such things are to supervene when the sword is once drawn. But a duty is not to be neglected because if ill-done it may produce evil: the obligation is to do it so well that evil may not accrue. The war, if war is to be, is what all moralists who have justified war at all have held to be not only justifiable, but sacred—a war of defence. An English ship is English soil: an invasion of that ship is as much invasion of the soil of England as if the French landed in Hampshire. So long as the benefits of invasion are retained by the invaders, the invasion itself is still in force; and till the men taken violently out of the ship are restored to England, the Americans are as much upon the English soil as if a regiment of them at this moment refused to leave Southampton. And the government which should permit an invading regiment or army to hold an English parish, after having had notice to quit, would be less treasonable to all its best duties than the Government of a state, whose ships are in every sea, which should permit the violation of that dearest and most privileged of every portion of its territory—the floating England that sails under our flag. Nothing, to my mind, can be clearer than this; and nothing, upon a Government that fights at all, more peremptory than the duty to fight under such circumstances. I only wonder the

'Times' or some of the Government leaders have not put
the case before the world on this footing, instead of resting it on grounds which, though sufficient, are less unmistakeable terra firma. . . .

. . . Brilliant beyond description though the sunshine
is and has lately been, a keen east wind for ten days past
has swept along the shore with a subtle electrical kind of
swift continuance, that, with none of the usual uproar of
the wind, has kept the finer sand streaming like a flame
before it. . . . We are meditating an escape from the
sea, and are at present looking towards Clifton.

A stay of some length was made at Clifton ;
and he there formed a pleasant intimacy, which
on later occasions grew to friendship, with Dr.
Symonds. well known and eminent, not alone in
medical science, and with his accomplished son.

There is an almost complete absence of available letters at this time. A business correspondence was obligatory. With this exception, almost
all letters that had to be written were written by
his wife or by some intimate friend.

Two or three notes, dated from York Crescent,
Clifton, and Hill House, Leckhampton, to Professor Nichol, seem to comprise the whole friendly
correspondence, from his own hand. of many
months.

In the first of these he says, in regard to some
' Testimonials ' :

I can't speak of them without an ejaculation of pain,
that the meagre thing I wrote when I knew you so much
less adequately should misrepresent—or, at all events, so
far *sub*-represent—my present estimate and knowledge.
Believe how keenly I shall enjoy to hear of your success
at Glasgow, how heartily we, shall expect you in our
Gloucestershire home this summer.

To the same correspondent, a couple of months
later :

The brave news came this morning. When your friends
are giving you hands of congratulation, imagine a shake
that sums them all up, and give me credit for it.   Because
I presumptuously assess my friendship at the total of
theirs ? By no means ; but they will supplement action
by looks and speech ; while, I, being absent, and, as you
know, dumb, can signify no otherwise the hearty sympathy
of yours, most sincerely,   SYDNEY DOBELL.

' All these things and many more,' he wrote
at the end of a letter of urgent invitation to his
temporary quarters, the new home not yet being
habitable,

we are soon to talk over. I can't wait even for that
' soon,' however, to tell you that I read your poems with
an eye for faults which is keen in proportion to friendship ;
and found, as I believe, an advance on your previous poetry

precisely where that was backward. It seems to me that some passages of what you sent were as well as could be done.

To the Same.

Crickley Hill.

At last we are in our new home; not thoroughly settled yet, but able, at least, to welcome you to a place where you may be tolerably comfortable and weather-proof even on this violent hill-side. When may we look for you? . . .

A few summer months were spent in the new home, the situation of which was beautiful and romantic in the extreme, but, in other respects, not very fortunate.

'The violent hillside' proved too violent, and the hill air too tonic and stimulating for his wife's health. The difficulties of daily life were formidable, but many friends were entertained at Crickley during the three summers spent there; and Mr. Dobell frequently rode or drove thence into Gloucester.

A Poem entitled 'Love,' and addressed to a little girl growing up in his wife's old home, was written during this year, and shows, as any intelligent reader turning to it must own, no sign of decay of poetic power, but abounds in delicate subtleties of poetic insight.

BOOK V.

CHAPTER I.

FINDING that the indoor existence which now, in England, seemed a winter necessity, greatly weakened her husband's general health, Mrs. Dobell was anxious to try the experiment of wintering in a climate sufficiently warm to make this imprisonment unnecessary. The summer quarters at Crickley were left this year early in October; and, after a brief rest in town, Mr. and Mrs. Dobell, accompanied by a friend, spoken of in his letters as 'our daughter,' started for the South of France.

To his Mother.

Hyères : October 18.

. . . The heat in Burgundy was so great that on arriving at Dijon, I took fresh tickets while the train halted, and so had the advantage of the long cool evening, at the end of which we were in Lyons. Waiting Thursday in that strange memorable city, where the South and North seem to meet in sight of the great bronze Madonna, that shines over head three or four hundred feet above us, and driving to the hill of Fourvières, on which her church stands, to see a view which, except one or two continental features of it, is not a bit more remarkable or admirable than the scene from Crickley, we arrived here in Hyères, at nine last night, after fourteen hours through a glorious landscape, in which Arran, North Wales, and the West Highlands are, as you get southward, first touched over and then painted in with the peculiarities of Italian vegetation. The change is so gradual that when, some time before dark, olives, almonds, cypresses and figs, had come into full possession of the whole scene, the eye hardly recognised them as new. The first sight of Marseilles at sunset was something to be remembered ; but, so far as the main skeleton of it is concerned, I have seen things very like it in the Highland seas about Oban.

It is the combination and intensification of elements, raising the sum-total just to that *beyond* which is so seldom reached, that—as far as the difference between prose and poetry—makes the differentia of these celebrated landscapes. . . . There is something so magical in the intensely dry air of inland France, and in the sun-soaked air of these more southern regions. In Burgundy, for instance, I felt as I feel on our hills, but without the bronchial irritation. . . . Fond English love (incessantly hearing, speaking and seeing French, even for a week, raises that dear adjective to a new eloquence,) from us both to all the dear ones.

P.S.—Opposite this window is a garden full of cypresses, bananas, and palms, and a country of Olivets.

After a brief rest at Hyères, the travellers

proceeded to Cannes, then a comparatively quiet and rural place, somewhat deficient in good accommodation.

A little house—which has since been pulled down, and a grand mansion built on the site—was taken on the Cannet road. For the first few weeks Mr. Dobell seemed to benefit signally from the Southern climate. But the winter of 1862–3 was in the South unusually tempestuous; and the favourable influences of the first few weeks were soon exchanged for singularly unfavourable conditions.

To his youngest Sister.

Maison Dubreuil, Cannes : October 29.

. . . I should have written more from Hyères, but that it was Sunday morning, and on Sunday the life of these southern places seems to effloresce. The whole week breaks into flower, something not different from the week days, but in every way more characteristic. You should have seen the *allées* opposite our hotel at Cannes last Sunday—*allées* of acacias growing parallel to the Mediterranean, and closed at the further end by a small mount and a couple of castles. The music, the singing, the *causeries*, the incessant to and fro of groups in every costume, were just like an opera-scene, except that the half-seers who write operas usually make the men and women in pairs; while what strikes the observer in the

South of France, is the utter indifference of the two sexes
in their outward relations, the men talk to the men, the
women to the women, in groups that never seem to mix.
We particularly noticed this at Hyères, which is a much
more primitive place than Cannes, on the Sunday I began
to speak of just now, when in the afternoon all the town
promenaded, laughed, and sang, up and down the little
street before our windows.   But what kept me from letter-
writing was the bear-baiting.   This is evidently the grand
treat of the Hyères Sunday.   The roars of the bear and
the baying of the dogs drew me out to enquire, and finding
the spot was too far-off up the street for E. to get within
range, —— and I started forth to the outskirts of the
crowd.   The bear, a brown bear, about as high as a Newfoundland dog, was muzzled, but had his four great paws
at liberty ; the dogs were the best bred bull-dogs I have
ever seen, even in England—Tumbler himself would
knock under to them—and higher on the legs than the
usual English bull-dog.   The bear-leader, a tall moun-
taineer, with a keen adventurous face, very high narrow
head, and exceedingly fluent tongue, began by describing
a bear-hunt, and making the bear enact it, even to the
final death-wound and death.   Then, when the admiring
ring had thrown many centimes and sous into the bear-
master's hat, which was set down beside the dead bear, the
' Ourse ' suddenly came to life, and the baiting began.   As
the pence continued to come into the hat, the man walked
round and round it discoursing vehemently to the dogs,
on the great wealth contained therein, and exhorting them
to have courage and dispute possession with the bear.   At

last, after ' ayez courage,' and as many sous as the crowd
seemed likely to yield, had roused the dogs to competition,
one of them, at a sign, I suppose, but apparently for love
of halfpence, went in suddenly at the bear, who stood up
roaring to receive him, fighting like a boxer with his
paws, and dealt such head-flaying blows, right-and-lefters,
that the dog was glad to retire for a moment ; but came
back to the scratch (very literally, for both dogs were
seamed all over with past encounters) at once ; and, after
several attempts, got the bear by the throat, who thereupon, roaring furiously, (to the delighted horror of a ring
of shrieking women) hugged him, and rolling down upon
him, brought the round (for the dog's sake) to a conclusion.   The bear-master (by a little chain passing
through the bear's upper lip) dragged the bear off, and
somebody else drew the dog away.

Then the other dog tried his luck, and so the game—
as far as one could judge by the noise—went on all day.   I
pitied the bear, who looked very used up, and, to say the
truth, had sometimes to be dragged up to the fight, but
though he evidently fought unwillingly, the energy with
which he went at it when escape was impossible was good
to see.   I have scribbled this as fast as possible in the
hope to tell you as much as time would allow, but find I
must put off any more to another day. . . .

Our *bonne* is a fine-faced Provençale of forty, who is
to do the whole work of this little house, marketing—a
very important business here, done at seven in the morning,—included. . . .

I hope to-morrow to send a line to my mother. . . .

Afternoon. I am glad the bad weather—the first of the 'winter'—prevented me from going to the post, so that I can add a word or two. You would hardly have a fair notion of the bear-baiting at Hyères, unless you pictured to yourself the scene of action. Fancy, therefore, an oblong square of tall, old, flat-roofed houses, all with green jalousies to every window, backed by a conical hill, rising precipitously within two hundred yards of the *place*, with four ruined castles on its outline. The very hill, if it had more wood, for that picture of mediaeval romance of which I have sometimes spoken to dear C——. How much we have wished for him at every phase of the journey hither and the experience here! I believe nothing can equal the North for subtlety and delicacy of colour—for complexity and *finesse* in the interplications of shade and hue, which raises seeing with the outward eye to the dignity of the most difficult and metaphysical of inward experiences ; but the South gives lessons in colouring with a broader brush, which must be invaluable to an artist, if only by teaching him to value the northern idiosyncrasy.

When I say, for instance, that this cottage stands in a little vineyard on a little hill of olives, in the midst of yet greater Olivets ; that a little orchard of flowering orange trees (that make the sitting-room almost deadly sweet) is at the back and round one side ; that the country between us and Cannes is almost everywhere bearing at once its fourfold crop, of wheat, olives, vines, and mulberries, the wheat springing between the lines of trees and patches of vines—you can hardly realize what it means

unless you saw the colours of these several objects. The
olive is of a grey difficult to describe, like the under-side
of willow-leaves, of the evergreen oak at Coxhorne, or of
rosemary leaves. This grey gives the whole country the
appearance of a wood of pollard willows in a wind; and
yet that does not describe it, because the trunk of the
olive branches low down, like an aged shrub. Then the
orange tree has above its black-green leaves a crop of large
young leaves something like the young leaves of laurel,
only more exquisite in delicacy (more like the first spring
leaves of a Malvern Hill pear); and, *en masse*, the effect
of these is different from the same tint in a shrub. The
wheat is yet another tint of green, which you can better
understand. There is a kind of pine which masses itself
among the olives, of a green I have seen nowhere in
England (I think); and then we get a glimpse of the blue
Mediterranean. . . .

It may be well to mention that, in sending the
foregoing highly coloured description of the ' bear-
baiting ' to the correspondent to whom it was
written, he had a humorous consciousness of the
horror and reprobation with which the account
would be read.

November 8th, he wrote, in a very long letter
to his mother, devoted to a detailed statement of
the difficulties and dangers of the journey south
for a very delicate invalid, in whom his family
were at the time deeply interested :

As I see more of the marvellous dryness of the air and the perennial summer of the climate, I feel that a very high price may well be paid for such immunity from the worst external conditions of English winter life. . . . The reason I have written this letter in two mornings instead of one will almost sum up enough of contrast to the English November you are doubtless feeling, to balance, for anyone in tolerable health, the merely material items I have set down on the other side. From breakfast-time till the heat became too intolerable, I have been these two mornings catching (for my good friend M——, the Gloucester entomologist, to whom I promised some Provençal specimens) brilliant butterflies, and crickets, in and round a little wood (ten minutes hence), where the ground is rough with myrtle, lavender, lemon-thyme, and many other of our garden-plants which I know by sight, but not yet by name—all wild, of course,—and to which I go through vineyards and olive-grounds, where beans are in blossom and young peas are half-way up the stick. . . .

. . . Marie—our *bonne*—who deserves the French title, for she certainly does her best to be *bonne* to us, and from the humblest matter to the most exquisite foreign dish (or a lesson in the 'Romance' language, which is the *patois* she speaks), is always ready with her whole good will—has just announced dinner, and there will be no more time for writing afterwards. . . .

To a Sister.

I shall better thank you for your pleasant letter by telling you of some fresh facts of interest than by commenting on those you already know. . . .

I will begin (lest what I have said of perennial summer influence the plans for poor ——) by telling you of our new meteorological experiences. 'Winter' set in with us, a few days after my last despatch, in a manner worthy of southern passions.

First, the weather sat down, as it were, in a whole day of 'strong crying'—incessant great rain of rapid violent drops for twenty-four hours. Then it rose up in a fury. At dinner we were roused by Marie—our *bonne*—crying out that something was to be seen, and by a great cackling of peasants running together in the vineyard. Going to the door, which commands the sea, there was no doubt what they were all looking at. From the edge of a long straight line of black clouds a water-spout was beating up the Mediterranean into smoke. As it passed slowly along, at about two or three miles from shore, the spray, rising into the air about twice the height of a schooner's masts, looked like the steam of a submarine volcano. The water-spout itself was in shape like a tap-root, with the wavy deviations from the exact straight which you see in such roots. Indeed, it so closely resembled a species that we continually have for dinner here, that one could imagine an old psalmist or prophet saying that 'The Lord smote

the water with a root of salsify.' As the sun gleamed on
it you could plainly see the passage of those millions of
tuns of water, now in greater, now in somewhat smaller
bulk, swelling, as it were, the tube of air through which it
fell, or suffering it momentarily to contract. The fall
was so perceptible that it produced somewhat of that disposition to hold your breath with which you might see a
man fall from a house. This, however, was not the most
remarkable sensation connected with the sight. After
watching it for some time, one began, for the first time in
life, to recognize by what an instinctive faith we remain at
ease *under the clouds.*

For the first time one looked up with a slight uneasiness
as to how far they were certain to come down in nothing
heavier than rain. This infraction of an unconscious and
constitutional belief, though soon disappearing, gave a new
and interesting illustration of that happy blindness wherein
all living things walk among and beneath wonders and
dangers which, but for that merciful deficiency, would be
distraction. The feeling with which, while those falling
clouds were hitting the sea with a force that would have
flattened a city, one glanced up at the hills of similar
water overhead would, if it were general, put a stop to the
whole process of the world.

The water-spout had hardly spent itself, and after
diminishing to a drip (altogether it reminded one of
nothing more closely than that leather hose with which
they water engines at railway stations, and which drops a
little after the full flow is over), and then to a mere
lowering angle of cloud, had disappeared altogether, than

a hailstorm, of stones as large as rifle-balls, swept in a
furious wind across the country, and at the end of half an
hour left the orange-leaves riddled to rags (that is to say,
the upper and younger leaves), half the crop of olives
fallen, and the earth covered four and six inches deep
with white marbles, above which an exquisite green
suffusion showed where the tatters of vine and orange
leaves lay far and wide.   When the hail melted, the young
peas and beans cut to shreds, and every garden-leaf of
this salad-eating nation ripped to shreds, justified Marie's
report, when she returned from market—'les pauvres
paysans s'écrient partout.'   These paysans are a curious
and interesting race, and, according to development theories,
ought, at no distant date, to furnish a new variety of mankind.   For the three or four months during which the
olives are slowly ripening and falling, they are a squatting
people, on an inexhaustible 'Tom Tiddler's ground,' and
the unnatural attitude, maintained for so many hours a
day, has already distorted the old men and women, and
seriously affected the anatomy of all ages.

It is a very rare thing during these months to see a
peasant standing, except when travelling on a highway.
Everywhere you see groups of squatters and crawlers,
picking, picking, picking up the millions of green, purple,
and green-and-purple fruit.   There is Italian blood in
most of the families, and some of them are pure Italians :
not the olive gatherers, who are permanent *fermiers*,
cultivators who get half the crop for their labour.   The
bergère who supplies us with milk and butter comes every
winter hither from Italy, driving her cows before her, and

the *fille*, who occasionally helps Marie in house-cleaning,
descends with her family every season from Italian
mountains, to take her chance of 'charing' in Cannes.

Marie's husband is an Italian, and she herself, though
French, is Italian by sympathies. . . . Like all the
peasants, she speaks two languages: one *patois*, par
excellence, the old Provençal, a kind of Hunnish or
Vandalized Latin: the other, *patois* French, very intel-
ligible when acquaintance has enabled you to discover the
principles of its transmutations. . . . With all their Italian
blood, the people here are, for the most part, very French
in their policy and prejudices.   I was chatting the other
day with a very intelligent mason who, with his men, is
building a cistern in this vineyard.   He asked me why I
did not go to Italy, as it was still warmer there ; and on
my replying, that I was afraid of an Italian outbreak so
long as the Italians were kept out of Rome, he answered
eagerly and with mischief in his eyes, 'Jamais, jamais,
nous ne céderons Rome.'   'But,' I said, 'Rome belongs to
the Italians; it is only just they should possess their
capital.'   'Oh, oui, juste,' said he, 'c'est assez juste,
mais' (with a twinkle of delight), 'jamais, jamais, nous
ne la céderons!'

This mason gave occasion the other day to a curious
illustration of the country of *chansons* and Troubadours.
All his work, by a slip of earth, fell down, about a week
ago, nearly burying him, and destroying, what was of deep
importance to so poor a man, a week's work and a good
deal of material.   The proprietor of the vineyard and I
agreed to pay the loss.   Yesterday Marie came in, chant-

ing, in the queerest voice, a tune which the old mother of the mason had 'made and sung' in praise of the English monsieur.

The peasants are like the skies hereabouts, very quick and emotional in temper; but like the skies also—we have had glorious weather since the storm—true to an underlying principle of good humour. Marie came back from town the other day looking as yellow as a queen's head on a sovereign. *I*: 'Qu'est ce que c'est, Marie, vous ne vous portez pas bien?' *Marie*: 'Jaune, Monsieur?' 'Jaune comme un citron, Marie.' 'Oh, ce n'est rien, ça. Ce n'est que j'ai frappé Victorine (her little girl); toujours la colère me fait jaune!'

A little while since as —— and I were walking in Cannes a man sat so far out on the path (when the workpeople are not busy they sit on the footpath, tilting their chairs lazily, and slowly roasting chestnuts in a little machine that turns like an iron hurdy-gurdy), that there was hardly room for her to pass. 'Pardon, Monsieur,' everybody is Monsieur in this land of "Égalité,"' 'mais vous ne donnez pas place aux dames.' He looked round, and surlily got up, moving his chair the least possible. As we returned, he saw us a little way off, jumped up with a smile, and, bowing, moved his chair to the wall. A few days afterwards we chanced to meet the same man in a lane. When he perceived who we were, he came quickly up to me, and putting into my hand a bunch of sweet basil he was carrying said, pulling off his hat, that I should find it smell very good, and was off again before I could answer. One might wait a long

while in England for so delicate an apology for a black
look.   But these little illustrations of the mental facility
that distinguishes the southern peasant from the northern
are continually occurring.   The other day an old peasan-
tess who was chatting with me as we walked said, pointing
to —— 'Madame?' 'Oh non,' said I, 'ce n'est pas
Madame.   Madame est malade : c'est mon enfant-ci.'
'Votre enfant,' answered she, measuring —— with her
eyes. 'Eh! mais elle est assez grande.'   Mark the delicacy of the 'assez'—an Englishwoman would have
said 'too.' . . .

You will see that I am getting a considerable circle
of low company.   Already Marie declares that she must
warn Madame how much I gossip with the market-
women.   If she knew my private opinion of their looks . . .
Up to fifteen they are sometimes pretty, but thence, till
they are quite old women, painfully the contrary.   The
men, on the other hand, are singularly characteristic,
handsome and historic.   I am wishing for C—— every day,
and a dozen times a day.   It certainly is waste of time
for a young history-painter to begin his studies in England.   England must furnish the subjects of his work
and the finishing lessons to his study of character; but
with these southern races you have in every street and
lane more typical illustrations of *soul by body* than you
would find at home by a week's journey. . . .

The weather prevented me from taking this to post
after all.   What do you suppose we are using just now
for nosegays?   Ripe oranges, with leaves and long stems.
What do you suppose are among our cooked vegetables at

dinner?   Sorrel, goatsbeard, chicory and thistles.   How
many flies do you think sit at once on this small table?
Ninety.   How many mosquito-bites do you guess I had
at once on my forehead?   Forty.   What do you fancy I
ate for breakfast?   Four lamb chops and a loaf!   I do
you to wit, however, that a leg of lamb here is not bigger
than an English leg of turkey, and that the 'loaves' are
the size of my fist.

Monday.   The bad weather continues.   To a northern
the despair of these poor southerns at bad weather is almost ludicrous.

The Church bells are ringing all the world to prayers
—for good weather.   They look upon the slushy roads as
impassible morasses, that justify the stoppage of all communication.

Tuesday.   The wild weather has been as wild as ever
I saw it at home.   This morning the peasants report a
deluge in Italy . . . *and*—we are to have no vegetables
to-day because when Marie had fought her way to market,
the terrified people were not there!

To his Mother.

December 20.

I should have written to you some days before this,
but that I waited to tell you that I had got rid of a cold
which befell me in the late abnormal weather.   The
severe winter of which all reports speak has, of course,
extended hither; and though the wet weather, which had
begun when I sent my last long letter, has been followed
by clear days, the nights are cold; and, before the cloudless

skies had radiated the accumulated moisture, the daily
vapours raised by the intense sun were noxious, and the
dews, of course, even unusually evil. All the natives
have been suffering, and our Marie among them. Either
the violent cold she brought into the house was contagious, or I got chilled in crossing from sun to shade while
walking, and for some days was a good deal out of sorts.
Everything in this climate is tempestuous, you know, and
if one is soon ill, the change back again is proportionately
unEnglish. I am now almost right again, though I find
by the experiment of writing these few lines that my
strength is less than I believed when I took up the
pen . . . I have had no asthma and no bronchial
cough. . . .

. . . No ' oldest inhabitant ' ever saw such a Provençal
season. Eight inches of rain in two days and fifteen
inches in nine days. Two water-spouts, and an earthquake, which, unfortunately, happened when we were
asleep.

As the early spring came on, and the winds
which afflict the Riviera at that season made themselves felt, and the snow lying on the mountains
chilled the nights, and gave a pernicious keenness
to the air even by day, the old symptoms of
bronchial irritation several times recurred, with
more or less severity.

All favourable intervals of indoor leisure were
eagerly seized for working at the accumulated

materials of the projected book. But business, which was, of course, from so great a distance conducted at a disadvantage, and the necessary letter-writing, were often as much as he could get through.

On March 6, he wrote to his father :

My late illness so disabled me, that the little daily strength I have had to spare since progress began, has only sufficed to clear away such inevitable matters as had accumulated during inaction. . . . We poor foreigners you know, [he had made use of some unusual form of expression], are likely to use words in their etymological, rather than their conversational, acceptation. Seriously I can detect an influence thitherward, even after no more than four or five months of foreign atmosphere. I caught myself trying to recollect this morning in what phrases we speak to servants at home. Not having since the beginning of last October, said a word to any 'inferior person' in English, I had quite a momentary perplexity. All the more, perhaps, from the fact that the lower classes here are so strangely intelligent, in some mental functions, that one finds oneself in a somewhat different attitude respecting them than would be natural towards the correlative classes in England. This morning, for instance, our cook came to me with a grave case of conscience. A Protestant young girl, a friend of hers, was 'engaged' to marry a Catholic. The Protestant 'pasteur' (an evangelical, of a sect something like the Free Church in Scotland), refused to perform the marriage ceremony unless she would take an oath never to change her religion. What would I advise her to do?

It is curious to see the bitterness of the two antagonistic creeds in these advanced pickets of either camp. The place is, of course, as a colony of English, a stronghold of Protestantism-militant-and-propagandist. . . . As one might expect, the passions of the armies face to face are stronger than the intellects; and the furious exaltation of means over ends is instructive to see. When our cook refuses to be cheated by the Catholic market people, they call her 'maudite Protestante.' If you asked a Protestant pastor to leave dogmas a little while and preach against lying, he would shrug his shoulders, and think you were daft. To fail in an iota of the creed, that is mortal sin; but to lie, morning, noon and night, as every French man, woman, and child is accustomed to do, till the habit has become almost a fine art, that is as necessarily human as thinking and feeling, and therefore cannot be immoral. To teach every little ragamuffin, who can be coaxed into a free school, to read, in order that he may use his 'private judgment' on the Bible, that is the first of sacred duties; but to teach the little creatures, who are to live by their hands, how to sew and knit, that is one of those contemptible and material trifles, which are always drawing unworthy eyes from the majesty of eternal Truth. . . .

. . . I was interrupted yesterday, and must finish quickly. I thought you would be interested to hear something of theology *à la Française*, but must leave other details to some other opportunity. Indeed, you can well

afford to spare French polemics, while the Jowett controversy is furnishing so much of the English article.
Did you see ——'s voluble claptrap in the 'Times'?   I
confess I was not sorry to see, on a subject less local and
partial than those on which we used to hear him, such
complete confirmation of his character for facile and con-
ceited commonplace.   To say the truth, however, the
noted men who have yet figured in the controversy seem
to have shown but shabbily.   Newman's was the only
letter (how strange it looked dated from a 'Birmingham
Monastery'!) that gave any evidence of a powerful and
accomplished thinker.

Pleasant times, of fine weather and of fair
health, came between the sundry attacks of illness.
During these, excursions, in which Mrs. Dobell
could join were made, and Marie, while serving
al-fresco repasts, would amuse those she served
with her fund of racy talk, and her graphic recital
of both comic and tragic anecdotes of South French
peasant life.   Marie herself was a constant interest.
A letter which recounts an interview with her a
couple of years later, shows how she attached
herself to her employers.   She was proud of the
manner in which her master's graciousness kindled
the enthusiasm of those with whom he came into
contact, and her quick intelligence delighted in
every evidence of the goodness of heart which—

as she boasted to her acquaintance in town and market—had so much '*amitié*' even for little birds as to forbid their purchase for his table.

Towards the end of April, the homeward journey was begun, rather earlier than had been planned, because, as the season advanced, the intensity of the southern light proved too trying both for eyes and brain.

The following notes of one or two natural facts of the Provençal spring, are taken from his memorandum-book :

From the middle of January the anemones in flower, a flower here and there at first ; by the last week constellations in fortunate places. By the end of February the oblongs of land between the rows of vine-stems, (each stem in two arms, like goat's horns, runes, or bi-truncate satyrs or fauns), are ribbons of purple and mauve ; the flower-stems, straight and stiff, not more than an inch asunder. The Mediterranean-blue come earliest, soon followed by the reddish-purple, which are followed by the red.

The first week in April, or last in March, the vines begin to weep; by the second week the young shoots and leaves are out, pale downy grey-green with plum-coloured tips, (like a forethought of the wine), the young vines commencing, and the old slowly following at intervals proportionate to age and soil.

The candelabra of the fig-tree hold up, by the first week (of April), small green lamps.

The olives (April 18) are showing flower-buds. The young leaves have appeared, and there is a constant clicking rain of the falling old. The orange-flower buds are white on early trees, and will open in a few days.

The most considerable pause on the homeward journey was at Avignon,—a place which in many ways peculiarly interested him, and where he made many notes, then and on later visits, of the antiquities of the city, and the salient features of the neighbourhood. Minutely detailed descriptions of baldaquins, marriage coffers, ancient coins, of the Seal of the Vice-legate, and other objects preserved in the Museum, occur in his memorandum-books. Also of ancient frescoes in other buildings, and of ' the vast artificial rock with windows in it ' —the Palace of the Popes.

These things were chiefly studied with a view to the correct elaboration of minor matters in the mediæval drama, health to work persistently at which he was hopefully waiting and watching for.

On May 7th, he wrote from Hampstead, to his mother :

You shall ' abuse ' me as much as you please just now. I am so glad to be within only a day's post of your ill-

usage! When I am still nearer, however, I may be able
to show you that the forced marches you speak of as so
rash and unreasonable are really the best and wisest mode
of campaigning. The secret of success, with such travellers as we, is to make the halts as few and as long, and the
intervening distances got over at once as great, as possible.
When an *invalide* to whom any journey is certain to bring
suffering is well settled in a good place in an express
train, three hundred miles at a stroke are much less injurious than three separate hundreds are likely to be, with
all the attendant triple chances of discomfort, and the
three-fold fatigue of the extra halts. . . . We stayed no
longer than unavoidable in Paris, because, as the state of
the weather made it no desirable grade of acclimatisation,
we really could not stand the expense of the Parisian
hotels. We remained, however, long enough to let me
make some investigations in the Louvre that I wanted for
my book. We should have seen the Emperor on Sunday, if
he had not driven about in a style of such zigzaggy cross-
purposes that to get near the carriage was impossible.

. . . Whatever English climate may be—I feel the
cold a good deal in spite of the bright weather—don't
give me another pang by apologising for English beauties.
I have seen nothing in the South so beautiful as the road
between Birdlip and Crickley, for example, or as one or
two other rare spots near home that I could point out.
And as for the 'sunshine,' be it cold or warm, an hour of
the golden English light is worth a lifetime of the white
electricity of Provence.

Odsey House : May 23, 1863.

How lovely this place is—I have never so much appreciated its gracious elegance as this year.   Partly perhaps because I have never before seen it at this exact season. The nightingales are singing, even by day, in the beechen walks, and blackbirds and thrushes are never silent round the lawn.

Our plan is on Friday to reach Gloucester. . . . In so much hope of seeing you so soon, I will give no history of what we have been doing.

CHAPTER II.

THERE seems to be no available record of the summer of 1863. It was passed at Crickley ; and in his little study there, commanding what he considered one of the most magnificent views to be found in England, he was sometimes able to work.

Friends came to visit him, and, two or three times a week, he drove to and from Gloucester. Meanwhile, nothing in the state of his health seemed to indicate much gain from the winter at Cannes ; and his wife, believing that a yet warmer, and, above all, more equable temperature was required, after much study of guide-books, and books on various European climates, turned her thoughts towards the South of Spain. It was finally decided that Malaga should be the chief resting-place for the next winter.

On the eve of starting from Crickley, he wrote :

To his Father and Mother, (then in France).

Crickley Hill, near Gloucester.

We think of leaving on Monday. . . . We knew, of course, by the signs of the times that you were in Paris! When E—— woke me, at 3.25 the night before last, and said—'We have just had an earthquake,' I replied —'you see how it is, those two friends in Paris are going to meet to-morrow, and Somebody himself has come up to stand by.'[1]

You will have seen by the papers all about the English shock, so I need not occupy this short time with details. This house was shaken like a pepper-box, and W——'s caged birds in Gloucester wakened him, by their screaming, to find them lying with their wings open and beaks agape on the aviary-floor. I wish I had been awake. This is the second earthquake I have stupidly slept through in the last nine months.

I need not tell you this joking does not show I am merry. The near approach of the winter journey is always a sombre matter, and this time it has special reason to be serious and sad.

A poem, entitled 'An Autumn Mood,' written at this time, breathes, what in a boyish composition on the same season he had called 'the wordless

---

[1] An allusion to what was a frequent subject, sometimes of mirthful, sometimes of serious, discussion between father and son—the admiration of Mr. Dobell, senior, for Louis Napoleon.

fragrance of farewells,' the indescribable yearning and 'pathos of gentle September.'

It significantly indicates the sad seriousness that occasionally characterised his thoughts at this epoch, when he felt as if more than the old year were well nigh 'dead and done,' and asked :

> Where is the Nevermore and the land of the Yesterdays ?
> Where are Youth and Joy, the dew and the honey-dew,
> The day of the rose, and the night of the nightingale ?

A few lines pencilled on an old envelope, speak his sense of the contrast between a time when existence seemed :

> Behind,
> A sea of sunlit memory ; around,
> All flowers of life on Home's enchanted ground :
> Before, a Heaven of hope, where star by star
> Great glories rose —

and this later time of 'mirk eclipse.' But the hope that the change was only eclipse and temporary never left him.

The journey began unprosperously ; he wrote from Nismes :

The day, which had been stormy, since Avignon showed signs of a regular French tempest. It caught us a few miles beyond Nismes ; and, at a specially unpropitious place, about ten miles from any large town, the train stopped. We were in a curious predicament. In front of us the swollen torrent had torn down the railway-bridge; on the left hand a small lake was rapidly rising to the level of the line, from which only a foot of bank divided it; on the right hand the torrent that had carried away the bridge forced its way between the carriages and a perpendicular wall of rock, hiding the rails and threatening soon to reach the carriage-floors; behind us the waters of the *étang*, having broken its banks, had moved the rails, and cut off our retreat; overhead the rain was already dripping through the carriage-roofs : on all sides stretched a dreary plain of marsh (the little wall of rock was artificial and due to a short cutting), and the enormous rain of these abominably passionate climates made it almost impossible for the guards to stir from the train.

Having ascertained that they had sent to the nearest telegraph-station, to stop the other trains and to order horse-carriages from Nismes, I felt that nothing more could be done, and we therefore sat and watched the water slowly rising round us. By a great Blessing, however, the rain ceased in about half-an-hour, and the danger that we should either be carried away in the train by the water, or have to wade through it to the nearest land, was over. The officials then went back on the line to see if it could be so far mended as to allow the train to be pushed back to Nismes.

At first this was reported impossible; and as no carriages arrived, and the night and the fogs of the marsh began to rise on all sides, I need not speak of the anxiety with which one of us was counting the minutes and watching the thickening darkness. . . . After sitting for four hours in this perplexity (during which lightning,

showing the vast flats, and the slow lamps of country
chaises, from time to time, along a road on the other side
of the *étang*, made our stationary darkness more perceptible), we had the welcome news that the rail was enough
mended to allow of a return to Nismes : which we reached
about nine at night, having left Lyons at half-past seven
in the morning. . . . As the same storm (with others
preceding) has destroyed the Spanish line of railroad
by which we were to reach Barcelona, and the diligence
road from Perpignan, we are forced to change the plan of
the campaign ; and now think of going hence to Marseilles,
and from Marseilles, on a good day, by sea to Barcelona.
But we must rest here for some days, before encountering
fresh difficulties.

Nismes is a good resting-place, inasmuch as it is both
a Roman and a modern city ; second only to some of the
chief Italian remains in classical monuments, and the
centre of all manner of characteristic French life.   From
my window you may look across to a Roman arena, more
perfect than the Coliseum (though not so large), and in
the square near may see a couple of charlatans—travelling
doctors—one male, one female, on painted cars, harangu-
ing, to the sound of the kettle-drum, a many-coloured
country crowd, and handing to dupe after dupe his box of
pills.

The weather is hot (70° in the shade).   I won't enlarge
my letter, for fear I lose post. . . . and for fear of your
being made anxious before any direct news come from us.

On November 5, he wrote from Marseilles :

To-morrow, if the sea is still tolerable, we are to sail in
a fine steamer, the Paris, which should reach Barcelona in
eighteen hours, but probably won't be there for twenty-
four. . . . I should like to have seen more of this
Marseilles, which seems in itself the Hotel of the whole
world.

Hôtel de las Cuadra Naciones, Barcelona.

We left Marseilles on Friday—the morning being
cloudless and with little wind. . . . At eleven o'clock we
began to leave that wonderful forest of leafless trees—the
merchant fleet in the docks of Marseilles—that seems as
if the intolerable sun had made a kind of burning winter
along a shore of volcanic mountains. Our one ship was
no more than a single beech-tree in Witcombe Wood.
For a little while E——— was able to keep on deck and
enjoy the wonderful picture of Eastern-looking Marseilles,
with its background of mountains, and the French shore
along which we coasted—very much like the coast of
Scotland beyond Oban.

In an hour, however, a sudden wind began, which was
evidently Mistral, and which therefore threatened mischief. . . .

. . . We were hardly three hours from Marseilles
before it had become furious; at dusk it increased to a
serious storm; and by midnight we were in one of the
most violent affairs of the Gulf of Lions. The great
arm of the main-mast was blown away; and the captain
said in the morning that if the vessel had been of ordi-

nary size we must have gone back to Marseilles, or have been lost.

For seven or eight hours the crashing of glass and crockery, the clashing of furniture, the bang of gang-ways, the thump and squash of waves into the saloon, the enormous blows of cross-waves that struck the ship till she staggered, the groaning of over-strained timbers, the roll of the heavy goods on deck, and every now and then the great cry of the deck passengers who thought they were lost, were elements in an experience that will not soon be forgotten. Once, when, the ship swing-ing over with a lurch even greater than usual, all the cargo of merchandise, with an immense noise, shifted to that side, and the creature seemed for a few moments unable to right herself, I thought there was little human likelihood she could struggle through.

The rest of the letter tells a dreary story of his wife's suffering.

After a short rest at Barcelona, the travellers proceeded to Valencia, where they remained about ten days.

Of the mass of memoranda made while in Spain, a great portion, jotted down in pencil and on the spot, are not decipherable, and among the remainder there is not much of general interest; they consist chiefly of brief notes, merely meant to help the writer's own memory.

He set down, for instance, long catalogues of things exposed for sale in the markets of Valencia; commenting upon the small peculiarities of likeness and of difference between these and similar things at home.

Sometimes, a picture is suggested by the facts named in such catalogues: as the girl day-dreaming by her melons, piled up like oval cannon-balls; or the twenty yards of baskets, full of grapes, pomegranates and apples, with the great matting baskets of chestnuts and maize on the ground; or the narrow straight street of shops—for the sale of guitars, votive images, fleeces, carpets, shawls, sweetmeats—covered over with a coloured awning, making a street booth, a quarter of a mile long, and with a picture of some saint or sacred personage hanging over each shop door.

There occur, too, descriptions of the houses of Spanish grandees—entered by large open arches into a vestibule court, from which another arch and a larger court lead to the unseen domicile; with trim and quaint gardens, crypts adorned with frescoes or gilding, 'The whole effect grotto-esque for coolness and cathedral-like for weighty dignity.'

Of a marble sculpture, of two colossal Indians, over the principal door of one of these houses, he wrote:

The marble seems alive with muscle and the adaptive apprehensive consciousness and force of living members.

The journey from Valencia to Malaga had, at that time, to be made by diligence, and was a terrible affair as to fatigue, but splendid as to the scenery and the wild excitement of the manner of travelling.

The arable plains of Murcia were described as

A fieldy Sahara of dusty furrows, where the immeasurable sands seem always submerging the land-marks of human industry, and the vague tillage of the vast half-indicated farms looks as if some compelling power had taken the Arabian desert and was forcing it into the temporary concession of a savage and reluctant fertility.

In La Mancha, in November, he noted :

On the immeasurable undulated plains, the nations of dead thistles (all nearly the same height and with arms near the end of a stem), like kingdoms of ghosts, of a colour emptier than white.

And of La Mancha, he spoke as

The kingdom of horseman and horsemanship, the native soil of the Caballero, where the absence of limit, either of local authority or provincial horizon, gives the sense of inexhaustible liberty, and the upward roll and down-ward sweep of the green moors involuntarily suggest the exhilaration of full-gallop across turf as free and an

expanse as endless as if all the heaths and commons of
Europe had come together as the natural practice-ground
for the cavalry of the world.

What follows is a fragmentary memorandum of
the diligence start for descending the mountains, to
Malaga :

With a great shout the demon swings up to his perch.
Every horse and mule makes a frantic push at the collar,
the great machine hesitates a moment, pivots over to the
descent, begins to roll headlong, and down dashes the
wild herd, like a charge of Bashi-bazouks, with a train
tied to it ; the two mad leaders neck and neck together,
the rest in every plane and line, racing, kicking, biting,
plunging, with bells ringing, horn blowing, chains clashing, springs banging, wheels screeching, harness in wind,
and a rushing cloud of dust and sweat almost hiding
this living torrent of lumber and agony of hullabaloo.

To his Mother (acknowledging news, awaiting him at
    Malaga, of his father having had a serious attack of
    illness).

                      Hôtel Victoria, Malaga : December 1.

We arrived here this morning about seven o'clock,
having had no letters for many days . . . At present my
chief consciousness, after the sense of a blow, is of the
immeasurable, intolerable width of seas and lands. I
humbly hope that another post will soon bring confirmation of the better news in the second of your two dear

and touching letters . . . E. is indeed exhausted, but that she is alive after so many and such vicissitudes is a fresh testimony to the atmospheric elixir of this climate. . . .

Some day I hope to tell you something of so wonderful an experience as such a diligence journey through the Switzerland of Spain . . . I have seen nothing more desirable to be seen than this most magnificent of European lands.

To the same.

December 10, 1863.

Now that the letters which immediately succeeded the news of my father's illness have so far confirmed the hopes which your second letter suggested that I may turn the key upon the first state of things, I will take the earliest leisure (I found two large packets awaiting me from Gloucester), to write some of the things which I am sure you are wishing to know. I can't leave those letters of yours, however, without saying, if you must write so philosophically of your possible departure from this world, don't forget the passionate difference between those who go and those who remain. Philosophical as I ought to be, I confess that in this matter I have not reached—and I think I shall never reach—'philosophy.' . . . But if I enter further this region of thought and feeling, I shall be unable to talk about those external details for which I know you are waiting; and I will, therefore, strike at once from the inner to the outer world.

That world, as seen from these windows, is not especially

interesting. After some trouble, we have secured a pleasant
cheerful sitting-room, with a bed-' alcove ' opening out of
it, looking towards the south, and therefore on to the
promenade of the town. This promenade is, like all the
' Alamedas,' or public walks, in Spain, a triple road, the
middle for foot-passengers, the two outer ways for carriages—with acacias and other southern trees, for shade,
and on fête-days a military band or two for amusement.
This Hotel is near the marine end of the Alameda, and
we therefore have a glimpse of the pier and the Mediterranean. Still, for a Spanish city, the view is singularly
uncharacteristic. From the upper stories of the hotel it
is much finer, as, above the opposite houses, the magnificent mountain ranges that guard the district give you on
one hand the Highlands and on the other Switzerland . . .
The manner in which we have rallied from the exertions
of the journey hither is but a new illustration of the ' old
old story.' . . . By the time we were at Lyons I was
feeling ill and used up . . . Yet we were hardly past
Marseilles when we began to revive . . . I tell you these
things as counteracting considerations of those ' moving '
incidents by ' flood and field ' which I have been so often
obliged to send. And, after all these difficulties, at last I
believe I may report that we have found the finest
climate in Europe—indeed, almost the perfect climate.

Barcelona and Valencia had serious disadvantages, and
E. therefore could not be content without trying the only
better that remained. And she certainly has her reward,
in finding by how much and how various a superiority
this place has gained its good name. Instead of the

white electric light of Cannes, Nice, and Barcelona, we have here a large, substantial, generous sunshine, like English August; and instead of the super-subtle ether that takes the place of air in those districts, an atmosphere more like English summer than anything I have found abroad . . . Instead of the deadly Provençal nights, we have here a temperature that allows us to sleep with the window open. It has not yet been lower than 60° at the coldest part of the night.

We have a queer committee of nationalities at dinner —made up, to a great extent, by the representatives of foreign merchants in Malaga: Germans, Italians, Spaniards, French, Portuguese and—as I found when denouncing Russia to somebody across the table—a Russian. The American friends I told you about have also joined us here, so that nearly all Europe and Trans-atlantica (for a Peruvian, now and then, is not impossi-ble—I breakfasted for some time beside one), feed together. Besides these accidental opportunities of national study, we shall soon have as many as we choose of the Malaga notabilities. The Spanish friends who were so kind at Valencia, wrote to their uncle and cousins here, and the family have already been behaving, like their relations in Valencia, with as much hearty kindness as if they had known us for twenty years. I am glad to find Spanish the easiest language I ever encountered, and hope, instead of learning it just a little, to really master it. Already I can read the Spanish newspaper pretty easily. It will be an immense comfort in travelling home to be able to speak. During all our long hundreds of miles through the kingdoms of Valencia, Murcia, La Mancha, Granada, and Andalusia, I don't think there was a single official who spoke French. I had to pick out travellers in a train, diligence, or hotel, who looked as if they were likely to speak it, and after finding one, if fortunately one was to be found, to get him to be my interpreter. I never thought I should come to feel that the mere fact of being or seeming a Frenchman (of all men on earth!) would make me welcome 'a man and a brother.' You may fancy some of the difficulties of three days and three nights of incessant travelling, with many changes, in a case of this kind. Some of the more obvious physical difficulties of that journey I must try to give you in another letter. I should like you to have (now it is over) some idea of diligence travelling in a kingdom of mountains.

During the time spent at Malaga, Mr. Dobell occupied himself in studying the people, the country, and the language. It was not long before he was able to converse in Spanish with tolerable facility. He received the kindest and most constant attention from the family of a Spanish merchant to whom he had brought an introduction: one or other of the sons visited him almost every evening, and through them he learnt more of Spanish social manners and customs, politics and religion, than it would otherwise have been easy for him to learn in even a longer time.

The temperate winter climate allowed him to be much out-doors, and the streets and market-places offered endless objects of interest, suggestion, and enquiry. At Christmas he accompanied his young Spanish friends to the houses of some of the artisans, and witnessed the characteristic festivities of the time ; and thus, in one way and another he learned a good deal of the national life and character.

He also, during this winter, enjoyed a good deal of pleasant intercourse with some interesting Germans and Americans, who were staying at the same hotel.

His note-book in use while at Malaga contains an amusing instance of the patiently minute manner of his observations. Some chameleons had been given to his wife by his Spanish friends, and he filled several pages with the results of his study, during odd minutes of leisure, of the curious little creatures, noting their changes of colour through a marvellous variety of gradations. Nor was he content with merely noting these changes, but, having specified and numbered them, recorded the different circumstances, external or emotional, which produced them. As, for instance :

January 25.—Sunny day, with light wind from S.E.
Morning: Large chameleon, awaking in shade, No. 1,
[a black grey, somewhat like rough iron, more like the
blacker bronzes]. On feeling the sun, No. 2 and 10.
Twelve o'clock, Nos. 3, 4, 5, 6, 7, 8, 9, and 10. Soon after
quarrelled with small chameleon for a patch of sunshine :
after mutual threats with open mouths and breath-squirts,
both became No. 4 and remained so.

The changes of form in their patches, spots,
and lines, the effect upon them of different kinds
of food, their various attitudes and actions, are also
noted.

At the beginning of March the travellers left
Malaga. With advancing spring, and the setting
in of the ' wind from Africa,' the climate was less
desirable than it had been during the winter, and
Mr. Dobell wished to see more of the interior of
Spain, and to visit the great wine-growing districts,
before returning to England.

En route he noted, beside the railway, in the
sand-flats between Cadiz and Port St. Mary's, fields
of white gladiolus in flower ; and, in a wood of
stone pines, multitudes of the Provençal white
jonquil.

To his Father and Mother.

I must leave till another time a more detailed account of our journey and of the unlimited kindness which—as on former occasions in Spain—did so much to alleviate what could be alleviated of its hardships. I must use the introductions I have, for learning something of the sherry trade in this district (which extends over more than twenty miles), where wine is almost the only growth that enriches the great plain of sandy salt 'lagunas.' These lagunas, or salt-ponds, with their pyramids of salt, and a few woods of stone-pines (white below just now, and deadly sweet, with flowering jonquils—how different a 'white' from the salt-white!)—are all that is to be seen as you look from this window (across the finger of that arm of the Atlantic which connects this 'port' with the great sea) over the 'Marina,' or salt-plain, towards the distant hills of Sherry. All day the butts of sherry are going by on *geleras* (rough waggons), drawn by oxen and mules, or in the sailing barges (with lateen sails) that take them from this little quay, nearly opposite the hotel, to the ships at anchor.

Please send us a line, when you get this, addressed '*poste restante*, Cordova, Spain.' We hope to be in Granada, to rest there a fortnight, by about the twenty-third. . . . Not a soul in this hotel understands a word of anything but Spanish, which makes matters rather more fatiguing.

The effect of the Giralda, at Seville, is thus suggested, by a memorandum hastily scribbled in his note-book :

It blossoms, takes fire, disembodies, dissolves, flies, alights, unfurls, furls, as you begin first above or below. The mystery of the arch. Here this root becomes its flower. There that fuel takes fire into its flame and smoke : that body sublimes from its matter to its spirit. Here the practice exhaling the principles : there the hovering cloud of the half-discerned Posse descending in shape.

Along the rail between Seville and Cordova he noted :

Orchards of flowering apple, pear, and orange. In the fields, a flower like ‘ Virginian stock ’ abundant, other flowers blue and yellow, and the delicate Spanish gorse. Along the banks of the Guadalquivir the most exquisite grey-greens in the spring leaves of a silver-barked tree.

At Cordova :

Alcazar-ruin, with Caliph’s garden. Orange-tree 1,000 years old. Tower, apart from the rest, where was the Inquisitorial chamber ; now a dove-house swarming with doves. View from the garden-wall along the river very characteristic. The garden a wild confusion of flowers and herbs and trees. . . .

In the Cathedral, ‘ some columns like the trees in the forest of Hamilton ’ are mentioned, and

'the waving connecting quasi-arch in the "vestibule," which destroys entirely the sense of weight
—like a serpent swimming through water.'

Between Cordova and Montilla (March 25), hedges of
aloes, figs, and chestnuts, abundance of small blue iris-like
flowers, fields of red-purple clover-like flower . . ., a
Provençal coloured[1] small quasi-crane's bill.

Between Lucena and Anteguera, March 26, abundance
of this crane's bill, of spurge, of dwarf mallow, and
of pale bluish lavender. After entering red mountains,
lavender, gladiolus, rose des Alpes, yellow broom, larkspur,
borage, flowering pink pea, dragon's mouth, marigold, a
yellow star-like flower with thin stem, a flesh-coloured
flower in thin spikes, a globular white flower with spidery
stems, profusion of saffron. Large purple orchid. Dog
rose. Reached Anteguera—through provinces of olive-
woods, without house or passenger for ten miles at a
stretch.

Burgos: from the site of the Cid's house, the treeless,
shrubless near hills as hard, flat-round as his steel fist, and
with almost the glint of it. Approaching—the Cathedral
looks like shafts of spears; more near, like flames of
fourteen candles; still nearer, like spikes of Cid's mace or
helmet.

---

[1] Some peculiar and delicate shades of red—not scarlet, rose, pink,
carmine, crimson, or vermilion—found in a small kind of Provençal
anemone, and used by some of the old masters, notably by Fra Angelico
and Fra Bartolomeo, were so named by Mr. Doboll.

Of the Basques he wrote as reminding him of
' the Jura, Wye, West Highlands and Scotch border.
The vegetation being English and Scotch, and the
oak forests like those of Hamilton.'

At Loja, he noted the ' Moorish-looking village ;
the bridge over the green-grey turbid water ; and,
in the distance, the snows of the Sierra Nevada.'

Then, miles before reaching Granada (from
Malaga), ' the Alhambra looking large and heavy
on its hill.'

To his Father and Mother.

Fonda de las Siete Suelos, Alhambra, Granada :
April 4, 1864.

You see by the date of my letter that we are at an
inn nominally within the Alhambra walls (really it is just
under them—they bound the garden), but you will hardly
guess the route by which we came there, or that, since I
wrote, we have been nearly a week at Malaga.

There are two great roads by which one can go from
Cordova to Granada—one by Bailen, the other by Malaga.
In either case the mountains make the route a triangle,
but the Bailen triangle is the smaller.   Just as we were
deciding which to take, news came that the father of the
Spanish family with whom we have been intimate during
our Malaga stay had unexpectedly broken a blood-vessel.
This decided us to go round by Malaga, notwithstanding

the ten hours' greater length of route. You will hardly
understand this, unless I give you some account of the
family in question, for which, as I think press of other
matter has always prevented me from speaking of them
more than incidentally, this is a good place. They are
seven ; but those we know best are five—father, mother,
two sons, and a daughter. The father is of an intensely
Spanish stock, from the Basque provinces. He is fifty-
five, and something like Lord Palmerston in face. He is
kindly, sagacious, and—though a little soured by untoward
events—an experience of every country in Europe, and of
some beyond it, has so far enlarged his sympathies that,
for a Spaniard, he is almost impartial, and therefore an
invaluable referee on the matters of difference between
his own country and creed and those farther north. He
is uncle to a wealthy marquis at Malaga, and for years
was leading partner in one of the greatest firms there (in
foreign trade), but speaks English with so careful and
critical a knowledge and so abundant a vocabulary that,
meeting him in a railway, you would mistake him for an
Englishman. It would be difficult to overstate the indefatigable and considerate kindness he has, in the midst of
much pressing business, shown us during our whole stay ;
and he finished it characteristically (if that can be called
a ' finish ') by insisting, when I left, on giving me a
letter of credit for two hundred pounds, ' in case ' I ' might
want them,' and leaving me to use as much as I might
require, and repay him when and how I pleased. His wife
—daughter of an Italian count, but Spanish by the mother's
side—is an admirable example of the Southern mother of

a family.   Healthy, indefatigable, inexhaustible, all heart
and feeling, but with her whole life in the house and
family, talking (with the natural wit and gusto so notable
in Andalusia) at a hundred miles a minute, and incessantly
looking after one thing or another, from almost dawn till
the son that comes home latest is safe in his room.   She
has been nurse and mother in the most extreme Spanish
fashion, and is still hardly less so than when the family
were babies.   You should have seen the bouquets she used
to send us, and the profusion of sweetmeats, made with
her own hands, with which she provisioned us when leaving
Malaga.   That we could not touch them seemed no argument against this sort of active expression and visible
good-bye.

The eldest son, Juan, is eight-and-twenty, strong-
bodied, warm-hearted, simple-minded, a devoted son and
brother, and not a bad man of business—in the easy,
pleasure-loving Spanish fashion.   He speaks English
fluently, and French well, and has been the most brotherly
sort of friend you can well fancy, almost from our first
arrival.

Jorge, his next brother, four years younger than Juan,
is a curious specimen of that boy-man who is so frequent
in Spain.   He is much more meditative and enquiring
than his brother; has, though a Catholic, a good deal of
inner life that will some day or other trouble him, but
is, in many functions of the mind, as youthful as an English boy of ten.   He speaks English moderately, French
fluently, German ditto, has very good general abilities;
but never does to-day what he can put off till to-morrow,

nor himself what any one can do for him— and formularises this Andalusian practice into a principle. The only exception he makes to its application (and that is an involuntary inconsistency) is in the case of some friendly kindness, for which he is always ready and would, I believe, get up early in the morning or forego a turn or two on the Alameda! For both Juan and Jorge I have a real affection. The daughter, Maraquita, is one of the beauties of Malaga, and far too interesting for such short time and space as I alone have left. . . .

I should not have tried, at any leisure, to say anything about Granada, or our mountain journey from Cordova to Malaga. Fifty copies of Wales, a dozen Highlands, a Switzerland or too, ' rich and rough ' all over with old Arabian cities and villages, are not to be meddled with in a letter. My heart in the midst of them has been continually wishing for C——. It does feel provoking that he is in London when he might have been here.

We hope to start for Madrid on Monday next, and to remain there three or four days.

In travelling from Granada towards Madrid, he noted ' the wonder of colour, made by a succession of Cadiz-like sand-hills, between mountains of (Loch Ech-like) grey or lavender stone, which, by and by, open into a " vega " of sand within such mountains.'

Between Alcira and Xatura ' the Hesperides of orange-shrub-trees, and the beginning of the mountain, castle and convent-crowned, region.' Then a region where 'shrub-olives are like a green sky over great tracts of heath and lavender.'

The country between Dax and Pau he likened to the poetry of England with a background of Pyrenees.

To his Mother.

Bayonne : April 24, 1864.

Your welcome birthday letter, by some postal accident, arrived a good while after date, and we have therefore been *en route* almost from the time of receiving it.   It reached us at Granada, where we had arrived the last day of March, after about twenty-four hours' 'correo' from Malaga, through mountains by night, mountains by dawn (with the 'tremolar' of the Mediterranean through the gorges), mountains by Spanish day, and afterwards the 'vega' (plain among mountains), which the Moors made the richest in the world, and across whose flowering orchards and almost flowering corn we drew towards the snowy Alps, at foot of which—on its promontory of hills—stands the Alhambra.

I should explain that a 'correo' is the diligence which carries the letters, and which, instead of conveying many passengers, like the ordinary diligence, is limited to *two*.   It therefore goes faster and is supposed to be more comfortable.   It has, as we found on experience, however, this disadvantage—that whereas when, in racing down mountain-sides as fast as ten mules or horses, tortured to their maddest energy, can go, the ordinary diligence comes to a bit of rock or heap of wood in the road, its enormous weight *ploughs* through the obstacle, while the lighter 'correo' *leaps* it. E. found the slam-bang-blunder landing from these leaps excessively trying. . . .

Spain, glorious as it is above all other countries in Europe, epitomising as it does the glories and the wonders of all other temperate—and of many tropical—lands, is a murderous place for a delicate traveller ; and though E. declares that if she could have foreknown all, she would still have encountered it, I was deadly weary, long before we passed the frontier, with seeing her suffer. The distances that must be done at once (' must,' because there is not any inn, capable of even the roughest accommo-dation that civilisation requires, between one point and the other) are so enormous that only steam-travelling can make them safely practicable to any but the toughest ; and the ways are so often through and over mountains, where the best road is necessarily full of the strangest vicissitudes, that the amount of what may be called acci-dental exertion would alone be far more than would suffice for the whole effort of the same number of English hours. Even the trial to the nerves has to be counted in the general wear and tear of vitality, though it is astonishing how soon use relaxes the tension in this respect. Fancy charging down places as steep as the Leckhampton road, at its steepest part, at the full gallop of a wild team, kick-ing, squining, biting, (being first goaded desperate by a separate flogging, administered to each as you turned the hill-top, in order that the sting might last till the next pitch) mad with pain and pace, and turning, in the same fashion and gallop, round the edge of the road, within a foot of the precipice, where a wheel off or a snapped pole — almost a snapped strap—must launch you over.

Or passing through wastes of olive-forests or of moorland at midnight, and through 'the small hours;' where for ten miles at a time you see not a house, and the wilderness extends, through the moonlight on each side, to the far horizon. Or through mountain passes, league after league, where the sheep-folds are little fortresses and the sheep-dogs (mastiffs) wear spike collars, each spike a foot long, like one prong of a pitchfork, to defend them from the wolves and bears . . . Often and often in tearing down these mountain roads I have had to hold E. with my whole force to keep her in her place ; and in the 'correo' this was necessary not only to keep her off the floor, but to prevent her from a shuttlecock jerk towards the ceiling. It was happy, however, that we chose the 'correo' that night. The choice had lain between it and a diligence (some of those things so often called 'chances' had decided the preference) which we passed in the mountains, at the edge of a precipice, with its wheel off and its luggage strewing the ground.

It is difficult to estimate the slow process by which this kind of physical danger loses its impression on the mind. One can notice the difference at two points of time, without detecting the gradations. I remember, for instance, we felt a little nervous last November, in our first night on the Granada road. In returning from Cordova lately, we passed through one of the wildest regions in Spain by night. There was only one passenger

in the diligence besides ourselves, and therefore the wild
fellows in charge of it outnumbered us, and the two
soldiers, who, as the country is specially unsafe, ought,
according to rule, to ride in the diligence, often for a stage
were absent; often for leagues and leagues we did not pass
a house, small or large. Yet we slept, as well as the
bouncing would allow, and really did not feel the circumstances more remarkable than an ordinary night-ride in a
country where the machinery of civilisation brings out,
by contrast with its smoothness, every little asperity of
perilous possibility.

Again last week in the Basque provinces—those touch-
ingly interesting provinces that unite the mountains and
vegetation of Scotland and Wales—the regular inn of the
little town, where fatigue obliged us to stop (Irun, so
terribly notorious in the Carlist war, you remember), being
full, we had to search through the strange moonlight
streets for some 'posada' that might be endurable for
the night. Finding one, after several trials—(I wish C.
could have given you the wild long cow-cavern on the
ground-floor, and the suggestive corridors upstairs, and
that you could have heard the picturesque, or dramatic,
song-singing from half-seen rooms, and the clatter of unseen heavy feet along the shining hard old-oak floors)—
I really felt that in such a romantic place for 'Spanish'
adventure one ought to be watchful; but we were so tired
that we both slept profoundly till morning. In justice to
myself, I ought to say, however, that the faces of the good
people had filled me with confidence; or, tired or not, I
should have watched. From Irun to Bayonne was our

last diligence journey. What journeys they have been! From Cordova to Malaga twenty-six hours' diligence; from Malaga to Granada twenty-four hours' diligence; from Granada to Santa Cruz twenty-four hours' diligence, followed immediately by ten hours' railway. . . . It was well that no one who loved us much saw our arrival at Madrid—she half-dead with exhaustion, and both of us coughing with severe colds. The moment these were enough abated to let us dare move, we left the hideous climate of Madrid ; and, struggling for three days through Castille, reached the mild Basques, through which we passed to the curing warmth and much-needed rest of this place, at the foot of the Pyrenees.

. . . We propose to continue northward to-morrow (stopping for two days with Mrs. Stuart Menteath at Pau, *en passant*), and reaching Paris, I trust, by the beginning of next week . . . .
How in looking back along the road of life, one almost shuts the mental eyes at spots that were passed with hardly the thought of danger!

I wish I had time after all these lugubrious details— and I have left the greatest weight of them, after all, for word of mouth—to amuse you with any of our lighter adventures. I have often wanted to make you laugh with the Spanish language—I know you would get so impatient over it. Think of a tongue with no ' you ' in it, and whose simplest sentence can only be on the principles of stately leisure. You are obliged, whether you like it or not, to speak in the third person, and say ' your grace ' on all

occasions. You wish to call out to the cabman 'Stop!'
Not a bit of it; he is of noble blood (he believes), and can't
so much as understand an idiom that comes so im-
pertinently near him. You can only say, at the shortest,
'Let your grace stop himself.' So with the waiter at the
table d'hôte, and every beggar in the street.

The language just suits me, because it is so impossible to *hurry* in it: and in five months I learned to
feel more at home with it, than I ever shall feel in this
chattering French. However, notwithstanding your vex-
ation with its slow-coaching, I am sure when you hear
Spanish spoken, you will acknowledge the fascination of
its noble and gracious manliness.

But I must leave this and all other matters till you
do indeed 'hear it spoken;' for it is getting late, and
we start in good time to-morrow. It still seems incredible
that England is so near, though this day last year we left
Cannes, and in ten days were in London.

While at Madrid he had managed to spend
some time in the picture-galleries, to visit which
had been the object of the halt there. He studied
the works of Velasquez with special interest, and
often afterwards spoke of the powerful impression
made upon him by this most masterly of painters,
and of the vivid reality of his productions—which
made one feel, when entering a gallery of portraits
by his hand, as if coming into an assemblage of
living personages.

Among his memoranda occurs the following passage, contrasting the effect produced by the work of Murillo and of Velasquez :

One floats his figures in dusky air, like fish *in* black water, the water more or less drowning the fish, in proportion to its depth (Murillo); the other floats them *on* the yielding water, which cuts them as water cuts a round floating body, so that a man's face stands out one third *beyond* the canvas.

The few days spent at Pau. under the kind care of a warm-hearted and valued friend of Edinburgh days, Mrs. Stuart Menteath,—was a bright and restful incident in the homeward journey.

After leaving Pau, pauses were made at Bordeaux and at Angoulême. The travellers reached England in May.

CHAPTER III

THE summer of 1864 was the last of the three summers spent at Crickley.

Returning to England in May, the travellers had hardly, at the beginning of June, established themselves in the hill-home, when Mr. Dobell was prostrated by rheumatic fever. The illness was long and dangerous. Confined to his sick-room great part of the summer, he had not regained his previous average of strength, when, with autumn, came the necessity of seeking a milder climate.

This time they left Crickley with no idea of returning to it; the place did not appear to suit his wife's health, and, from the exposed situation of the house, the portion of each year which could be spent at it was inconveniently short.

At Crickley, as at all other places where he ever had a home, he will be long remembered in many a cottage for his generous kindness, and for

the genial pleasantness of his words and ways.
For many years after he had left the neighbourhood, he had several old and infirm pensioners in
it, and at Christmas each little household received
some sign of his remembrance. One fine old
woman among his neighbours there, always spoke
of him as of 'a good king who had reigned over
them, and whose like they would never see again.'

After a brief stay in town, Mr. and Mrs. Dobell,
in October, left England for the South; Mrs.
Dobell taking with her, this year, a French servant
accustomed to travel.

From Avignon, after giving his mother the
always eagerly craved information as to his health
—not a bright account; cold weather had set in
unusually early, and the incidents of the journey
had been unpropitious—he wrote:

I had not overlooked the considerations my mother
indicates with regard to the new capital of Italy and the
excitement attending the change. . . . We propose to
stay here till Monday, and then, after resting a few days
at Cannes, to go on to Mentone, the last French town
towards Italy.

This Avignon is a wonderfully interesting place; and,
if the advancing season allowed it, I could gladly stay a
good while here, for it is, in fact, to live in the middle ages.

A hundred yards from the hotel you stand in the fourteenth
century.   There, on this bank of the Rhone, you have the
machicolated city walls, with their gates and watch-
towers. Beside you, a bridge *built by miracle.*   Opposite,
on the other bank of the Rhone, two of the finest remains
of feudal times at present in existence.   A castle of the
largest class, almost exactly as it was built, the keep of
another of gigantic size; and a little town of feudal
building between them.   Indeed, in looking over the
Rhone, you seem looking across the centuries into the full
strength and reality of feudal life.   Behind you, on the
Avignon shore, but hidden by the city walls, is the enormous
palace of the Popes —more like a hill than a human building—where Petrarch used to visit, where Giotto painted,
and where Rienzi was long a prisoner.   Not far off is the
church where Petrarch first met Laura ; and under the
distant hills, you can see his favourite retreat of Vaucluse.

Cannes : October 30, 1864.

[After speaking of a drive taken 'along the old road
towards our cottage of two years ago.'] . . . But for the
absence of ——, with whom every turn, every cottage,
every old wall and special tree is immemorially associated,
I could have believed that the world had rolled back and
that this was another October.

It has been very pleasant to see the kindness with
which those who knew us here have welcomed our return,
from the good Rector and his wife (whose evidently genuine
and cordial pleasure was, considering our heterodox be-

haviour, singularly to the credit of their heads and hearts)
to the mason who worked in the field near our house, and
who meeting me by chance in the street, the other day,
almost shook my hands off.

Marie (our old servant) says that the cottagers near
where we lived still come to her, from time to time, to
ask for news of us.

Marie's meeting with us might (as the newspapers
would say) have touched the sternest heart. She flew at
E.—her grand old face in a passion of tears and smiles—
threw her arms round her neck, kissed her rapturously,
held her at arms' length to see how she looked, hugged her
again, more passionately than ever ; and then, turning upon
me, she seized me by both hands, shook them again and
again, then caught me by the arms to get a firmer grip,
all the while, through her tears, crying out ' Oh, madame !
Oh, monsieur ! que c'est bon, que c'est bon.'

I was a good deal amused, as well as a good deal
pleased, by the kindly confidence of the banker with whom
I used to deal. Meeting him, at his door, yesterday, I
asked him to give me fifty pounds, which the kind
little man, with evident pleasure at showing in any way
his friendly remembrance, paid down almost before I
could finish my request. As I had no letter of credit
he had no means whatever of knowing I have not gone
to the dogs since two years ago. We have received a good
deal of kindness, too, from some new friends made by
accident. . . . Part of the family of Prosper Mérimée,
the French author and senator, whom I had long wished
to know.

Mentone: November 5, 1864.

We arrived here from Cannes last Monday, by rail as far as Nice, and thence by diligence, arriving at this Mediterranean Switzerland (the Alps of Savoy with the olive, lemon and orange-woods of Italy) about eight o'clock in the evening.

Except in the Tête Noire, I have never seen anything better than the mountains at foot—really at foot, like Llanberis at foot of Snowdon—of which Mentone stands. The air seems in many respects far finer—as regards English invalids—than that of Cannes; but as, unluckily, the little town is almost in the sea, and the sea air, especially of the Mediterranean, is always singularly trying to E., we intend going on some miles farther, to San Remo . . . farther from the sea, and which has, in addition, the great charm of being in Italy. . . .

It is very pathetic to hear the good Mentonians protest against their mechanical transformation into Frenchmen. They need not take it to heart, however, for a thousand Emperors could not *un-Savoy* their Alps. If I had awakened up among them, I should have identified them at a glance. . . .

From the middle of November 1864, to the beginning of February 1865, the travellers remained at San Remo. During these weeks, Mr. Dobell made friends in various ranks of life, and enjoyed pleasant intercourse with interesting men of different nations; among them Ruffini, the author of 'Dr. Antonio.'

He took part in the social movements of the little town, then a much more primitive place than it has since become, and was elected an honorary member of the San Remo Artizans' Mutual Aid Society.

The following letter relates to one of the humbler friends of this time—a waiter at the hotel where he was staying.

To the Rev. R. Glover (at Dover).

Hôtel de Londres, San Remo: February 1, 1865.

This note will, I hope, be given to you in England by Giacomo Ferrari, who had the rare fortune (I know how keenly you will appreciate it) not only to be one of the little Garibaldian army that liberated Naples, and to be wounded in the campaign, but to take his turn of personal service in the very tent of Garibaldi. After saying this, it almost looks like presumption to add that for the last three months he has waited on me; but unless I do so, you will hardly understand the manner in which I have learned his good qualities, or the right I have to judge of their substantivity. It is impossible to talk with him about his campaign days without remarking the true, quiet, modest signs of soldierly pluck and unconscious heroism, and of that unostentatious passion for country and liberty which

separates—as sharply, suddenly, and irrevocably as if
some new miracle of Babel (with the differentia of order)
had cut the communications—the young Italians of the
' Kingdom of Italy ' from the fathers and grandfathers who,
at this moment, can understand nothing of it, and would
take the youngsters back to the profitable Austrians : and,
during the three months I have daily observed him, I have
seen nothing to contravene the good opinion these ' signs '
create, and a good deal to confirm my belief in the things
they should stand for.   His business in England is an indirect illustration of some of them.   He is paying his own
expenses thither (I write, you see, as if you were already
reading) with the intention of taking place for six months,
without pay, in some English hotel, in order that by learning the language he may return to his country better qualified for his occupation (a ' sommelier ' in an Italian hotel
gets very much higher wages if he can speak a little
English).   I am so desirous that he should take his
' premier pas ' well, that, in my anxiety to secure him
against the dangers which beset a foreigner on first landing at Dover, I take the friendly freedom of giving him
this line to you.   Whether or not you can give him the
advantage of spending his first English night under your
roof, I am certain your kind advice and surveillance will be
invaluable.

   If, by any chance, a situation of the kind he seeks
may be open at Dover, I think there are many reasons
which would make it preferable to a place in London ; but,
at any rate, the advantage of a kindly and efficient interest

in his first hours of English experience may be important
to a degree difficult of calculation.

I know, my dear fellow, how thoroughly the word
'Garibaldian' will be the young man's passport to your
good wishes; and I hope the frankness with which I am
asking such a practical demonstration of them will seem
to you, as indeed it is, an evidence of the feelings with
which I am always

Yours affectionately,
SYDNEY DOBELL.

On February 5, having been joined by the
'adopted daughter,' who had spent the Cannes
winter with them, they left San Remo for Rome,
which they reached ten days afterwards, travelling
by Genoa and Spezia to Leghorn.

Two or three of the memoranda made *en route*
may be interesting.

Of the peculiarities of Genoese architecture,
'taking the small Church of Saint John the Baptist
at Finale Marina as a strongly illustrative type,'
he noted 'the marine speciality — *atque unda
impellitur unda*—so permeating as to produce a
qualm of sea-sickness. Out of all available forms
the same undulatory predisposition extracts and
interplicates the water-lines.'

After leaving Genoa, in mounting the Bracco—

one of the Apennines—he described a district like
the Sierra Morena, and then the unsurpassed view
from near the summit: 'In front, the near gorges;
to the N. W., a Switzerland of snow-mountains; to
the West, Mediterranean bays and distant Riviera;
between them an Andalusia of Spanish form and
colour.'

Further on : 'A Sierra of grey rock, with lower
slopes of pale grey and yellow sands.'

The summit past, and descent begun:

A view across nine or ten mountain ridges to snow-
summits; the lower ridges everywhere sand-coloured and
with sea-ripple outline, the higher more massive and amor-
phous. . . . Everywhere on the sand-slopes the mulberry,
with old vines basketing the inside of the few-branched
tree. Over the sand-hills a rosy heath in full flower ; a
white heath in bud ; hellebore and gorse in flower. Among
the yellow sand much lead-coloured sulphurous-looking
rock.

In the pass, after leaving Borghetto, the sand-hills—
tawny, long and narrow, with a deep ravine between each
body, and all the heads against the main transverse ridge
of higher mountains—like stalled lions.

Lago, a village on the summit of a mamelonesque
hill—chestnuts everywhere—peasants with trusses of dry

chestnut-leaves. Villages the colour of ruins. Primroses on the torrent-side banks. Road-side hedges, sometimes myrtle, sometimes blackberry.

Standing on the sea-line at Spezia and looking south-south-east—to sea—across the gulf made by the east and west mountains—the east shore a line of sand-hills; beyond them, and running behind them, a ridge of Welsh-coast hills; beyond these a Sierra of dark grey crocodile-(chameleon)-backed mountains; above these the snow ridge. On the west shore a mass of elephant-faced mountain, with old-looking villages of black grey. . . . The higher mountains near here seem generally crocodile-backed, *i.e.* crocodiles rampant, with heads meeting at the upper ridge. These are the Carrara mountains.

The journey from Leghorn to Rome was then a fatiguing one, the great part having to be performed by diligence. The weather, which at San Remo had been of a pleasant spring temperature, became, when the Riviera was left, extremely cold.

He often afterwards related, with much amusement, how, on this occasion of their arrival in Rome, he held the Papal sbirri in interested conversation, and so hindered any enquiry as to what he had in his hand—a case containing a revolver—the carrying of fire-arms by foreigners being then strictly prohibited.

The first stay at Rome was very brief—not
much more than a month ; and the severity of the
weather hindered the seeing and doing of much he
desired to see and to do.   But his memorandum-
books contain a considerable bulk of notes and
observations, from which a few likely to be of
interest may be selected.

‘ Laocoon ’—*non causa pro causa*?   But the details,
not considered in relation to general design, alive with
truth.   The marble often soft, warm, almost fibrous with
organism, giving the idea of through-and-through organic
complexity as distinct from surface texture upon un-
organised stone.   Are the children enough affected ?   Do
they not put off the snake as they might their stockings ?
Is not the one who is so admirably carried off his feet,
so carried rather by a friendly arm than by a deadly
master ?

‘ Cupid ’ of Praxiteles.—A feeling, or some feeling, dis-
sected away from all other facts—such as intelligence,
ability, but not inconsistent with them.   The rightness of
the complete beauty of the same kind as the rightness of
an absolutely fine manner.   The whole thing the quotient
of Possible, after deducting each form of mistake that
each kind of faulty taste would be guilty of.   The
melancholy in face and attitude, the melancholy of feeling
without a *moyennant*, or of beauty that has no more to
attain.

‘ The Faun ’ of Praxiteles.—What would remain of a

fine human being, after subtracting every quality that
would be inconsistent with an eternity of mirthful (non-
passionate) indulgence.

'Dying Gladiator.'—No sentiment, no sorrow, anger,
shame, disappointment—entirely given up to dying.   The
first experience by habitual strength and health of the
difficulty of physical weakness.

'Bust of Young Augustus.'—Large, equal, harmonious
intellect, with the moral qualities that put it in motion,
and a face to correspond.   No passion or heroism.

'Bust of Aged Augustus.'—Taste, ability, *sagesse* ;
the pose of mind produced by years of unquestioned
supremacy on one so naturally superior to vulgar errors
as to keep the habit while losing the consciousness of
command ; a mouth of kindly and tolerant scepticism ; the
twinkle of an old man's good-humoured indulgence of
human follies.   The face of an ideal English nobleman.

'Bust of Nero.'—All the qualities necessary to
enormous self-indulgence, without those which bring, in
the necessary manner of their exercise, physical retribu-
tion. The good-humour of entire selfishness, conscious of
infinite meat and infinite stomach.

'Sitting Statue of Tiberius as Pont. Max.'—What would
be the splendid fulness of glorious and admirable welfare,
if there were no such things in the world as human duty
and obligation ; no such desirable qualities as fidelity,
sympathy, persistence, self-sacrifice ; no human suffering,
labour, or society—if man were a pagan God, and not a
developing nescio-quid-Christ-simile.

'Caracalla.'—An ordinary choleric man, whose

enormity was due to the machine of which he held the
handle.   A common anger that found itself master of the
world.

'Pompey.'—Nail of the second (longest) finger, holding the globe, *bitten* straight.   Sword under left arm;
pommel of it fish-scaled.   Eyes bolted, with very deep
recess next nose, and over nose two deep vertical wrinkles
in forehead.   Mouth soft and Indian-bowed, as with latent
humour; but side lines very strong and deep.   Face
introspective, though with such great machinery for outer
perception, like the introspection of an opium-eater.
Character either wanting in decision, or carrying out a
large predetermined course irrespective of circumstances.

With Domenichino, especially as a colourist, he
was greatly impressed; the notes made on his
pictures show how closely they were studied.
The following are among the shorter of these
notes; those on the 'Communion of Saint Jerome'
would occupy several pages.

Domenichino's 'Chase of Diana.'—Best illustration of
true unity, and unconsciousness in expression I have seen.
The gravitating force being on left side of picture, and
hardly any figures on right, the violent dog straining across
from left to right, and shown to strain by restraining
nymph, puts force of motion on other side. . . . Best
example I have seen of potential motion.

'Cumaean Sibyl.'—In the Cumaean Sibyl the reddish
autumn grape-leaves, and even the idea of wine, seem to

have flashed out in the red and gold drapery; the dark
olive-leaves and stone-work into the green and faded
yellow head-dress; the dull yellow of the lute-handle, and
thence through golden hair, sunlit forehead, and flesh tints,
into high light of breast and arm and hand and paper of
music.

'Guardian Angel.' [Among Neapolitan notes.]—
Memorandum.—The dominance of the angel, with whom,
by lateral arrangement, and windy side-flow of drapery,
the whole picture is suffused. Only three figures in
picture—angel, child, and crouching observant demon,
whose *observation* puts him in unity with them, and whose
ugly contrast brings them out. As usual the colours of
the principal figures, yellow, claret-stain, and shady blue,
got out of the ground colours—greenish, house-top-reds,
stone colour, grey blue, and the venous-blood tint of the
demon.

Of Raphael's celebrated 'Entombment' he
wrote :

The figure meant to be supporting the main weight of
the body in an attitude of violent exertion; but the sheet
beneath the body which he holds, and by which the whole
gravitation must be supported, shows *no sign of strain.*

The travellers left Rome for Naples towards
the end of March. 'Even the very Latin *land*,' he
wrote, 'contains the idea of rhythmic quantity,

the Latian and Volscian Apennines being a rhythm
of undulation, each *unda* rippled into *subunda* of
longs and shorts.'

The rooms occupied in the Chiaja, at Naples,
commanded splendid views of the Bay, and he was
never weary of watching the beauty of sea, and
sky, and distant mountain, by sunlight and by
moonlight, 'when the full moon, near the horizon,
diagonalises the sea-ripple—an effect as of a
rushing Indian-file of birds down the light path,
whipping the water with wings.'

While at Naples, a great part of many days
was spent at the Museum. Of his notes on things
studied there, a few cannot fail to be interesting.

Luca di Leyden.—' The Tryptich '—Crucifixion—in
centre, with a noble, kneeling, in one wing ; a noble lady in
the other, scutcheons over head. Beside the lady, head of
stag-horned satyr in open-mouthed smiling admiration, the
human animalism so diffused as to be inseparable. The
round brute eyes fuller of humanity than most human
portraits. The lady, her lady of honour, and her two little
girl attendants entirely unconscious. Beside the noble a
lion holds the mass-book, and observes him with half-shut
eyes of concentrated *absorption*. He is entirely given up

to a docile desire to learn humanity, and seems *growing* a man as you look at him. A cherub climbing the cross and catching the blood in a chalice, so round that it comes out of the picture, and so metallic that it glistens. A flying cherub, catching the blood from the left hand, in position and buoyant life perfect. Background equal to Titian's ' Sacred and Profane Love.'

Matteo da Siena's ' Massacre of the Innocents.'— Herod on throne, in a niche of judgment-hall, crowded with mothers and babes. A picture of confusion should be confused, but with elements that *necessarily* lead the mind to perceive (by long looking) the organism of art. This attained here by a broken fire of red, running diagonally across the picture, from right-hand corner of crowd to Herod's red stocking. If Herod's robe had been red also he would have unbalanced and broken the picture, but his dull-gold robe puts him in dominant relation with the crowd of faces and baby-flesh, and with the warm grey of the basilica. The variety in the reds used, the carriage of the black of the door downwards, in the blue-black armour of a soldier, and from side to side by a purple dress in right-hand corner, by Herod's black-blue cape, and by a similar dress in the left-hand corner, and the *rapport* of these blacks to red, by a purple robe over a red in a woman near the blue-black soldier, show more sense and mastery of colour-composition than frequent at that time.

If Herod had been in the centre he would have impaired the confusion. Being at the side, but elevated, he gives unity, when the latent guides have conducted the sense to

him, without destroying confusion. The faces looking,
through grating over door, out of the hubbub and tragedy,
and the sight of quiet outside Temple through open arch
over side-door, increase by sense of contrast the confusion
within. *Memorandum.*—The smashed child (trodden), and
the child lifted above the heads of all, in mad hope to be
out of reach, and the hand grasping the *blade* of a sword.
But why not more of such incidents, and less of mere
running away or condoling?

Memorandum.—In torso of Psyche, from Capua, the
breasts flattened (in the idea of giving more spirituality by
less beauty): bad art, because bad imagination and bad
philosophy. Nothing good but the attitude, and the good
of that borrowed from the Cupid of Praxiteles.

Memorandum.—In Farnese Bacchus the support of
the toes (not entirely on tip) sufficient to give sense of
momentary stability, but (since momentary) of necessary
subsequent motion.

On an excursion made, early in April, from
Naples to Baiæ, Mr. Dobell met with a seemingly
unimportant accident, to which, however, disastrous
results were subsequently traced. On the way to
Baiæ a pause was made at Puteoli, to visit the
ruins of the ancient Temple of Serapis. But
Puteoli was still more interesting to him, as the
landing-place of St. Paul.[1] Leaving the carriage,

----

[1] Here is his description of 'St. Paul's landing-place': 'Walls
of white sand-rock (height of Crickley rocks above our road): to the

in which were his wife and her friend, under the
care of the guide who had accompanied it from
Naples, to wind down the road to the site of the
temple, he descended the rough and broken hillside towards the sea, on foot.

By and by, trying to realize exactly what St.
Paul saw on landing, he walked some paces backwards, entirely absorbed in what he looked at, and
taking no heed of the nature of the ground under
foot. Coming in this way to the open mouth of an
old Roman drain, or other subterranean passage,
he fell through to a depth of eight or nine feet.
The smallness of the aperture through which he
fell—while bruising the back of the neck and upper
part of the spine against the edge of the opening—
probably broke the force of the fall. He found
himself in darkness, but upon his feet, and with
no consciousness of having sustained any injury.
The smoothness of the masonry—offering no hold

left, sudden-shaped hill above the sand-rock. The sand-rock wall
extending round Baiæ—descending almost to sea-line after Baiæ, and
rising to the mount of Capo di Miseno. The double head of Ischia
behind the right horn of Baiæ. The buildings of Procida, visible
over the lowest point of the promontory towards Miseno. Puteoli
running out to sea on right of landing-place. Capri visible in the sea-
interval between Puteoli and Miseno. Turning to right, under the
white rock wall for the Temple of Serapis, St. Paul ascended by
the Via Consularis.'

in climbing upwards—made escape difficult. His
hat, stuck on the top of his sun-umbrella, thrust
through the hole, by and by attracted the notice
of a herd-boy, who, after satisfying himself what
the appearance meant, called a man, with whose
help the prisoner was extricated.

He joined his wife at the ruined temple within
half an hour of having left the carriage. His coat
was whitened with lime-dust, his hat battered, and
he looked pale, but he laughed at the adventure,
and would not yield to his wife's wish that the
excursion should be given up and they should
return to Naples.

Next day he felt bruised about the spine,
especially at the back of the neck, and a good
deal shaken ; he experienced, also, qualms of a
peculiar kind of sickness, with which he was subsequently to become only too familiar. By the
advice of a medical man staying in the same house,
he took a couple of days' rest ; after which he
did just as before, and thought little more of the
affair—except as a cause of thankfulness for such
an escape from serious hurt, and as furnishing a
good story to be told at his own expense.

But the blow at the back of the neck received
at Puteoli was afterwards considered as probably

the provoking cause of the disease which struck him down in the following year.

After a good many days chiefly spent at the Museum, and a visit to Pompeii, the travellers left Naples for Rome, just before Easter, which fell late that year.

Miss Cushman, then living in the Via Gregoriana, insisted with generous warmth of hospitality that they should occupy a suite of rooms in her house, instead of seeking accommodation at an hotel during this crowded season.

The rooms so kindly placed at their disposal commanded magnificent views over the city; and, owing to a sharp attack of bronchitis, Mr. Dobell was chiefly confined to them during this second stay at Rome. He had especially wished to study the gorgeous Easter ceremonials of the Romish Church; but was disabled from doing more than witnessing 'the Benediction' on Easter Sunday. The effect of this he thus suggests :—

The balcony hung with crimson (?) coagulated-blood-colour, and in the middle an oblong of cream, with flatted-gold embroidery. Before midday the balcony filled with priests (?) in white; towards the benediction filled with men wearing *white* mitres. A stir among these, and then a silver cross and other silver insignia come to the front. Then appear, moving frontwards, two great white fans, each with a central eye, and between the fans the Pope, borne high in a chair, and robed in soft cream-white, with flatted-gold apron; below him an official in red. Half-hidden in the mystery of the fans, and appearing greatly larger than the officials in front, (are they intentionally boys?) he reads, and is afterwards borne through the fans to the front of the balcony. Gives the benediction, and is drawn slowly back, after the Bull has been read by the officials and thrown down to the crowd.

The same illness also interfered with his mixing as 'such a social creature' (so his hostess called him) would otherwise have done, in the interesting society which congregated at Miss Cushman's house.

The two American sculptors, Miss Stebbins and Miss Hosmer, had their home, at this time, under their countrywoman's roof. Gibson was a frequent visitor there, and with him Mr. Dobell had more than one animated discussion on the observance of those 'rules of Art' for which Gibson was so punctilious, while the poet, as has been shown, held that all artists should rather—

Trust the spirit,
As sovran Nature does, to make the form—[1]

[1] Mrs. Browning.

than bind and fetter themselves by traditions and conventions.

When, on April 29, he finally quitted Rome, it was with the hope of a long future sojourn there. He always afterwards spoke of it as ‘ the only place out of England for an Englishman to live and to die in.’

On the homeward journey a considerable pause was made at Siena, where the heavy fragrance of flowering acacias, blown in warm gusts about the streets, was noted as a peculiarity of its May atmosphere. This city had much to interest him in a special manner, and he closely studied its pictures, wood-carvings and architecture : so much here belonging to the period in which he had laid the scene of the drama that he now hoped shortly to be able to finish.

In a letter, written from Siena, May 9, of congratulation to his brother Clarence, on a bit of artistic good fortune, he dates from ‘ within a stone’s throw of Guido da Siena’s “ Madonna,” painted twenty years before the “ Saint Cecilia ” of Cimabue.’

But where is the good of holding out open hands across the Val d’Arno ? And, by the way, the Val d’Arno—an undulating, mountain-fenced plain of girlish

May-green young elms, hardly higher than girls, every
one with a yet more girlish vine clinging about it, with
green corn or buttercup-grass, knee-high, at their feet—
is but a small strath of the thousand miles between us.
. . . (For perfection, in each kind, I would choose a
Ligurian January, a Provençal February, an Andalusian
March, a Roman April, a Tuscan May, an English June.)

Of Cimabue's Saint Cecilia he wrote, after
very minutely describing the series of pictures :

The face at once more modern and more Grecian than
Duccio's or Guido's (da Siena), but still the long Byzantine
almond-eyes.

In side-scenes much attempt at character-painting
and still more at painting from models—*i.e.* evident
portraits. . . . The crude science—*e.g.* the vertical plates
on which the fowls are (impossibly) brought to supper of
the Virgin. . . . In boiling Saint Cecilia the man blowing
the fire, who not only turns away his face to avoid the
flame, but *mispoints* the bellows in consequence, is notable.

Of Giotto's ' Christ in the Garden ' :

The face a great advance in character-painting—*i.e.*
in soaking the material with character.   Trees conventional ;—one [would seem to be] from a Japan screen, one
from a Nürnberg toy, one from a feather dusting-brush,
one from seed-grasses.

In the ' Betrayal ' and ' Calvary ' still greater imagination.   *Memorandum.*—The man hammering the cross (of

which the lowest part alone is visible) and the interest of the Roman soldiers in that operation, though Christ is at their elbows. The Virgin's face, hardly obscured by the robe she lifts to it, nobly fine in effect ; and the sympathy of the Apostle who addresses Christ given with quiet intensity. But there seems little imagination for fine faces *per se*—*i.e.* apart from expression.

Of Simone Memmi's 'Salutation' he says: 'Simone having painted Laura, seems unable to lose her image.'

The gradual growth out of, and divergence from, the Byzantine manner, in the Madonnas and Bambinos of Simone and Lippo Memmi, Guido da Siena, Duccio, Sodoma, Taddeo di Bartoli, Spinello, Aretino, and many others, is elaborately traced, and many of their pictures are minutely described.

The 'Torre della Mangia,' at Siena, he compared with the 'Giralda' at Seville, detailing the points of likeness and of difference :

The whole effect lily-like, especially seen rising from the crowded roofs of the city. The myriads of swifts round the Torre della Mangia only equalled in effect by the hawks round the Giralda.

The pulpit of the Cathedral—by Nicolò da Pisa —is here described :

Its marble pillars, resting on backs of lions and lionesses, some of whom suckle cubs, some kill beasts, as if to increase the sense of instability. The bowl of the pulpit alive with crowding Scripture—birth of Virgin, Salutation, Nativity, arrival and adoration of Kings, Presentation in Temple, transition, Crucifixion, Heaven and Hell—all in high relief, and the subjects not separated except by their nature—*i.e.* not by the ordinary means. It seems as if Nicolò had intended so to charge the marble with motion and, at the same time, to subtract all guarantees of stability, as to make us half expect it to roll off in cloud or incense. The outside of the Duomo, where marble is lost in history, philosophy, vegetation, and animal life, seems in the same idea.

Much study was given to the house of Santa Caterina da Siena. Some readers may be interested in this somewhat elaborate description of it, extracted from his note-book :

In a narrow street on a sharp hill. Her father's (the fuller's) shop, now a chapel, containing pictures of her life and a hundred shields of powerful families, 'protectors' of her shrine. Mounting the stair, since widened, by which the saint used to ascend when a child—kneeling to say prayers on each step—on the left her *camera* and *camera di letto.* The bedroom, a very small alcove, arched, paved with ordinary tiles, on which she lay, with a rough jaggy stone for a pillow. The alcove now hung over with offerings, flower-crowns, and symbolic mementos. In the room, on

the altar, her lantern, rather elegant, in flower-stem metal,
with which she visited the sick by night, the handle
(round-knobbed) of her walking-stick, and the scent-bottle,
with silver top and grating, whereby she guarded herself
from infection in those visits. A silver-looking string
hung it to her arm. Also a small piece of her flannel
chemise—the threads very coarse—since ornamented with
pearls. In another part of the house the room where she
was born, and at the under end of which was the kitchen.
Lifting the rich drapery of the altar, you find the original
kitchen chimney. The room soon after her death tiled
with azulejo—or something similar ; the roof coffered in
blue and gold squares, and the walls enriched with
Corinthian pilasters of blue and gold, the lower halves of
which have the delicate Sienese wood-carving in flower-
tracery. In a chapel beyond the house the cross, from
which she received the stigmata, in a locked pyx. A
painted portrait of it seems, in the dim light, to be about
three feet high—a stone-white Saviour, with gold carved
draperies on either side the cross-stem, which leans forward.
In the house a list of wonderful things done therein by
the young saint. *Memorandum.*—The precocity and
strength of matrimonial ideas indicated by vowing, at
scarcely seven years, ' consacrare a Dio la sua verginità : '
ergo, the vision of the Bride of Christ. At twelve, her
parents being very anxious that she should marry, she, to
ensure celibacy, at the advice of a frate Domenicano, who
had taken upon himself to persuade her to comply with
their wish (but only with the purpose of proving the
strength of her resolution), cut off her beautiful hair. As

a punishment for this, she was deprived of her little room, in which she had been accustomed to pass much time in prayer.

In consequence of this, 'nacque in lei il sublime pensiero di fare una secreta ed interiore cella nel suo cuore.' A legend narrates that her father found her praying in the room of her brother Stefano—a white dove resting upon her head. Being asked by him what dove that was, she answered, 'Nulla saper di colombo, ma soltanto intendere alla preghiera.' After this, being convinced of her holiness, her parents ceased to persecute her. At fourteen, while meditating in what way to establish her vow of consecrating herself to God, she has a vision in which San Domenico offers her 'il suo abito delle Suore della penitenza.' This it becomes her desire to assume, but she cannot get the consent of her mother till she is lying ill with small-pox —then her entreaties (and the threat 'altrimenti potrebbe Iddio voler di me tal cosa che voi non mi avreste più nè in questo nè in altro abito che sià') prevail. She was the first virgin who assumed this habit; all the other sisters being 'widows or mature women.' In 1362 she received the dress in the Church de' frati Predicatori, in Siena. *Memorandum.*—It was at seven years old that, being with her brother Stefano in the 'contrada' called Valle-piatta, she raised her head towards the Church of San Domenico, which was opposite, and saw Christ appear, seated on an imperial throne, wearing pontifical vestments. She felt 'una poderosa voluttà scendere dentro al cuore.' Christ raised his hand and blessed her.

The following catalogue of natural facts noted between Siena, (left on May 11), and Empoli, calls up a picture of a flowery and pleasant land :

The many acacia trees, full through and through with flower. The corn in flower. The country—where not cornfield, vine, elm, and olive lands—a wooded up and down, sometimes of lavender and Spanish broom, sometimes of oak—chiefly saplings or young trees. Wild rose in flower : hedges of China-roses in crowding flower. A tree like quince, but whiter, in blossom (wild medlar?), yellow cytisus in thick flower. Cistus has been in flower for some weeks. Flowery thyme banks (oolitesque breakings up of stone and gravel?) wherever the ground is barren. Small woods of acacia with golden underwood of cytisus. Poppy-flowers among the corn. The white-stemmed poplars by shallow streamlets. The vines sometimes trained on maple-trees, sometimes on acacia and cropped poplars, sometimes mountain-ash, but principally maples. Almonds, cherries, white mulberries, olives, but not used for training vines. Flowering bean-fields. A few walnut trees.

Certaldo, half-way between Siena and Empoli, the birthplace of Boccaccio, ... a most mediæval-looking little *città* on a Crickley-high hill, like the mound of a fortress. Behind it, towards Empoli, three or four smaller hills, precisely like artificial mounds, and behind them many mounts of an unusual greyish sandstone (?) in fortified appearance like downs near Winchester. . . .

Nearer Empoli hills of quasi-volcanic mud, scored everywhere deep with torrents (dry). *Memorandum.*— The beautiful Campanile of Empoli.

The travellers spent a night at Empoli; and next day proceeded to Pistoja, passing through Florence, and remaining there a few hours. The first impressions of that city were received at a time when it indeed seemed worthy of its name— the City of Flowers—standing in so fertile and flowery a land, flowers selling in glorious profusion in the streets. The Uffizi Gallery was visited, and a few pictures carefully studied.

At Pistoja he was struck by ' the fine character of the Tuscan face—intelligent, courteous, refined, and proportionate : Southern aptitude and Northern stability.'

Near Pistoja, towards Milan :

Hills of Ligurian character—woody with oak, chestnut, flowering acacia, a few olives, and pines. Cytisus in flower : the grass crowded with pink gladiolus : ragged robin, a pretty small yellow heath-like plant ; flowering Spanish broom, flowering laburnums and wild thyme. The hills often tilled to the top (or green with pasture) by terraces.

After two hours, chiefly through tunnels, the conical, precipitous, woody. torrenty mountains remind of Loch

Katrine and the Basque Provinces, but the trees are less noble than the Basque trees.

After Bologna—*en route* for Piacenza—a Belgium (without dykes) of elms and vines—with distant mountain line to the left. The elms older than in South Tuscany, the vines growing more at will.

At Milan another considerable halt was made.

Of the view from the roof of Milan Cathedral he wrote as resembling ' many vales of Gloucester, with even taller and thicker trees, out of which stand forth church-campaniles. While in the distance lies the is, has-been, will-be of Switzerland, which in Monte Rosa looks out of, and in Mont Blanc has entered permanently into, the cloud.'

Of the exterior of the Cathedral he wrote as suggesting :

The pathetic struggle in the mind towards the past and the dead.—As though the music made by a vibrating string strained, like a flapping bird, to escape from the string that made it—as though, in another moment, another wing-beat, it would be gone, and the string dead and silent, and the music—where ?

And the following is another attempt to describe the impression made :

The vast white incense petrified,
Spiral, or globed, or undulous, enwrought
All of an act but motion, and remained
For ever done and doing : a stone flame,
Lambent or lambit, framed in stirless flames
That never stirred nor shall stir : the seen sound
Of everlasting anthems, made and made
By thousand thousand voices, each as pure
As snow : a frost of stone, as if one cloud,
Alpine, a sudden spiked and pinnacled
Into innumerous number, and betrayed
Its freight, not Moses only or Elias,
But Heaven mainprized, and every standing saint
Astonied into marble.

Of a picture of Domenichino's in the Brera
Gallery :

It has the usual means of colour-unity, but the form-
unity is less obvious than usual—being on the principle
of an arrow, the angle being of flesh colours (cherubs, angels,
St. John's face, neck, leg, &c.), the point the two cherubs
playing with the mitre. *Memorandum.*—The *humour* of
this upsets the mind from dwelling on it as an important
part, and sends it, therefore, upwards towards the Madonna.
Above the head of Madonna three bodiless cherubs. So
that there is double unity—that of planetary circulation
around her as well as the other. . . . There is yet another
principle of unity more mechanical than the others, inasmuch as the two principal angels sit one on each side the
Madonna, on seats supported by the same stone dais,
and therefore manifestly accessory to hers. There is yet

another principle, more metaphysical, inasmuch as all eyes below her, angelic and mortal, look towards her, except the two cherubs with the mitre—whose relation to the saint puts them, through him, in relation to her—and the piping angel whose temporary look-away is so manifestly temporary as to be a better *rapport* than positive attention.

Of a picture of Paul Veronese :

The green shadow of the green book which the green page supports on his head, greening even the face to unity with the general effect. *Memorandum.*—How Veronese has got the green and yellow out of the mottled green marble pillars on each side the Pope, and made them leaf and flower, through the greens and yellows of his robe and those of the others, till they become blue in the high lights of the page's green velvet, and produce the necessity for the faded peony-colour of the abbot's outer robe.

Among many other, more elaborate, memoranda, note is made of 'St. Peter, carrying solid keys,' by Crevelli, as 'in face, the representation of all that has been strong and crafty in the Papacy.'

At the Biblioteca Ambrogiana, he studied many curious manuscripts, and, with special interest, as belonging to the period of the projected drama, the pictures of Luca di Leyden. Noting, in that artist's 'Saul and David,' 'the muscular grip with

which David's fingers really *twang* the strong harp-
strings—and the heavy cud-chewing hopeless contemplation of him who can command every wish.'

In his 'Temptation,' the face of Satan, 'able
with the ability of *ça m'est égal*, and an equal
curiosity and interest in all things.'

In his pastoral scenes, 'the eager questioning
look of the would-be-milked cow, and the comparatively heavy intelligence of the peasant.'

An excursion was made from Milan to Linterno
—Petrarch's house. Through ' a willowy flat of
dykes full of streaming weeds, like drowned hair,'
bordered by willows, poplars and alders; with,
to the northward, 'the Alps, like stone thunder-
clouds, with edges of petrified ripple, like those
that show coming deluges of rain.' The poet's
house, chapel, bedroom, and study were minutely
described.

Of ' The Cenacolo ' of Leonardo he wrote, among
other memoranda concerning it :—

Though the Twelve divide into two great sets, each
subdividing into two subsets, there is no loss of unity,
because the torrent of interest, enfilading the centre
from each side, produces a unity greater than that of contact. . . .

This picture, which peculiarly impressed him,

and which he studied with especial minuteness, seems to have been the last thing seen and noted at Milan, which was left on May 25, for Turin.

Milan to Turin, May 25.—A green villagy flat of mulberries, corn (in flower and ear), flax, vines and acacias. Switzerland and the Tyrol looking on. The hay being carted. The corn full of wild pink dianthus (?) and of blue flowers, tinging it to morning or to midday sun.

Magenta.—A little brown-roofed town, with square tall bell-towers emerging from tall trees. On all sides a rich flat of poplars, mulberries, and vines, with pasture and corn. North-westward, Switzerland dominating. North-eastward, the Tyrol. The battle began at the Ticino, which runs southward from the point in the land-scape where Tyrol ends and Switzerland begins.

Novara.—On a little rising ground among rice-fields, corn-fields, upright willows and poplars, with massive forest-tree avenues round and in the town. The snows of the high Alps turning even the clouds to storm and shadow.

After entering Piedmont, nearing the Alps, the walnut-trees give an Alpine character to the Lombard vegetation. The mulberry trees look older.

At Turin he wrote of the balmy air, ‘as if some *inner* nature gave out a scent of hay-fields,’ and of nightingales singing, all night and part of the day, among the lamps in the piazza before the hotel.

May 28 they left Turin for Susa; nearing the
mountains he noted the *dryer* luxuriance of the
herbage as renewing the feeling of Tuscany; and

the green-yellow-grey of the ripening corn, surrounding
the living, shining, succulent green of the mulberry, and
the various tints of the other trees—the hedges of flowering wild-roses—the keen, subtle intensity of effect in the
youngest green of the new vine-shoots, in the lower Alpine
slopes, among the corn and grass.

Crossing Mont Cenis, on the 29th, ' The chame-
leon-backed, but green, mountains of the lower
Alps, near Susa,' are remarked, ' and the growth,
in the lower slopes of the pass, of walnuts, chestnuts and acacias.'

Above the walnuts and chestnuts—*i.e.* 2,000 feet above
the valley—the beeches and ashes begin, together with
hazel, birch, service, wild cherry, and a few firs. Cowslip,
small polystellar yellow flower. Soon after, blue gentian,
large wild equifoil pansy, rhododendron, and a small
polystellar hepatica-pink flower begin, and firs supersede
the other trees. Near point of road, about 3,500 feet,
wild auricula begins. Soon after, in a depression, king-
cups and a flush of tall polystellar pink flowers.

Ospizio di Monte Cenisio.—*Memorandum*. The tenderness with which the long-robed nereids in the waterfall
throw themselves upon the rock.

Wild auriculas abundant. Above and around the

midway Albergo, king-cups, gentianella, large yellow
pansy, and a flush of the pink polystellar. Double yellow buttercup.

Beyond the Ospizio, the Lake. Crowds of large white
downy-stemmed anemones, with yellow bosses and woolly
leaves. Many coltsfoot. White, light yellow, and blue
pansies. *Memorandum.*—In mountain torrents the sur-
face-waves often *run up-hill*, by reaction from boulders
beneath, and this in the ratio of their real downward
tendency.

After passing St. Michel, in French Savoy, he
comments on the wild fashion in which the vines
are grown, by 'fieldsful, nearly close to the ground,
and the fresh note they furnish in the harmony of
Savoyard colours;' and compares the beautiful
small cattle of Alpine Piedmont, like 'Alderney,
but nobler,' with 'the great cinereous ox of Tuscany, Rome, and South Italy, and the antediluvian
mammothesque buffalo of the Campagna.'

After resting at Chambéry, the travellers proceeded *viâ* Paris to England, which they reached
early in June.

CHAPTER IV

1865—1866.

On returning to England in June of this year, 1865, Mr. and Mrs. Dobell, after brief visits to friends, a short stay at and near Detmore, and much exploring of the district, took, for the summer, a well-situated, but ugly and ill-built, house on the lower slopes of Chosen Hill, three or four miles from Gloucester; not far from Lark Hay, where they had lived for a short time in 1848.

During this summer Mr. Dobell wrote a 'Letter on Parliamentary Reform,'—the result of long and thoughtful study of the subject. Great part of this pamphlet has been reprinted in the volume entitled 'Thoughts on Art, Philosophy and Religion.' It attracted a good deal of attention and comment, and a second edition was issued.

He wrote to a friend, in answer to some objections :—

Its political proposals are merely subordinate inferences from certain other things immeasurably more
important, and the exposition of which was the main
purpose of the essay.

Those things are:

I. The claim to treat Morals as a department of
   Embryology.

II. The theory on the relation of majorities to minorities, and the yet more difficult and important
    theory from which it is an inference.

III. The definition of Liberty.

IV. The formulæ for the best conditions of human
    development.

*Questions to be asked of those pronouncing upon the
scheme proposed by the pamphlet.*

What do you know of the science of Embryology—
of its present state and recognised principles—the peculiarities by which it differs from the other 'ologies'—the
specialities which make the claim to range Morals under
it one of the most important (perhaps of the most dangerous, perhaps of the most useful) ventures that could
happen to practical philosophy?

Have you truly and conscientiously considered the
difficulty of finding, *according to any democratic or constitutional principles*, the right of majorities to rule
over minorities?

Do you know that to find or prove such a right is one
of the most difficult problems in all ethics?

Have you plumbed the difficulty and sought for its
solution in the foundations of Right and Wrong?

Have you carefully examined those foundations?

Do you know the present state of the best thinking in
regard to them?

Do you know the special difficulties where other men
have stopped?

The special faults that have invalidated previous
theories?

The special ins and outs that have, in any new theory,
to be specially provided for?

The special changes that, whether apparently large
or small, may, like the small-looking changes which Watt
made in the old steam-engine, give to a theory the real
novelty of a thing practically new? . . .

With autumn, again came the necessity for
going abroad. During this summer he had constantly required medical treatment. In various
ways he had overtaxed himself; and had besides
been subjected to a good deal of mental pain and
harass, of a kind that always reacted disastrously
on his physical health. In addition to which, if
the subsequent verdict, as to the injury received
at Puteoli, was correct, that injury must have been
at work as a source of accumulating mischief.

The portrait of him engraved in the Frontis-

piece, the most successful of any attempt of the
kind, was painted at this time, by the brother who
contributes the following note.   It shows something of the worn and suffering expression his
face, so bright when animated, was apt to betray
in repose.

I have tried to paint his portrait [his brother writes],
and have compared notes with three well-known artists who
have made a similar attempt. We all agreed that we
never had a subject to whom it was more difficult to do
justice, and the portraits were all more or less failures.
The general effect of our model was so extremely beautiful and impressive, though the features when examined
and drawn in detail were not regular; and the expression
was so subtle and peculiar, that it was never caught on
paper or canvas, so that the effect we wished to reproduce was marred, and unsatisfactory when compared with
the original.   He belonged to no type, for I have never
seen another man at all like him : those who knew Lord
Byron personally, said that Sydney's face recalled his. . . .
Castelar says that Byron was 'a typical Scandinavian, true
descendant of the Norse sea-kings.'   The type is certainly neither Celtic nor German, and it is probably Scandinavian.   Byron's features were more symmetrical and more
perfectly moulded than Sydney's, but both had straight
Greek features, curly dark brown hair, and remarkable
blue eyes: in both the face was the long oval, belonging
to the long and rather narrow as distinguished from the

short and broad. But Byron's head, though of similar proportions, was small, while Sydney's was exceptionally large, some three inches larger in circumference than the ordinary full-sized man's head, and the height was even more remarkable than the length. His eyes were the bluest violet I have ever tried to paint ; no colour could quite match their liquid ultramarine hues, and no lines convey their varying expression, sometimes tender and sympathetic, at others stern and commanding ; but usually, when in repose, they had a curious searching gaze, as though for ever trying to read and solve some unknown problem. The nose was straight, the upper lip rather long, but the mouth, even in middle age, was fresh, full and expressive as a boy's.

Some of his mental characteristics seem to me to throw a light on things that are difficult to account for in the attributes and works of some great men whose personal history has been lost to us ; notably of Shakespeare. Sydney had not the artistic faculties of Shakespeare, but he had many gifts and peculiarities similar to those which must have belonged to Shakespeare, and which alone can account for those elements in his work which have astonished and perplexed the world. Shakespeare's familiarity with the habits, customs and modes of thought of all classes, all professions, all nations, might, perhaps, be better understood by studying the manner in which Sydney's imagination absorbed all the elements of knowledge which were necessary for its growth and expansion. . . . He was equally at home in the cottage or the palace, for there was no chamber so secret or so guarded but that he had been there in imagination.

He possessed a similar power of realising the atmosphere and topography of unseen countries. He wrote 'The Roman' before he had been out of England, and in after life, when he had spent two or three years in Italy, he had no cause to alter the local colouring of the background.

His brother goes on to ask whether 'Sydney's keen and wide appreciation of affection and love—love purely fraternal, whether from man or woman —might not arise from that same yearning which fills the Sonnets of Shakespeare, and has been so often and so grossly misunderstood? . . . . Doubtless his clear vision perceived the actual loneliness of life to a degree happily rare in duller natures.'

It is probable that Sydney Dobell must often have suffered intellectual loneliness, ill-health cutting him off from more than occasional intercourse with intellects of his own calibre; but it will already have been seen that, even apart from the chief love of his life, the tie between him and his mother was exceptionally intense and strong, and indeed, that affection of all kinds was so bountifully given to him, while his charity and sympathy with all humanity were so full and wide, that he can hardly have felt 'loneliness' of the kind that would account for his unusual appreciation of love and friendship.

Florence and its neighbourhood were chosen as the resting-places of this winter, 1865–6.

Pausing at Milan, *en route*, he received an unexpected pleasure in the enthusiastic welcome of the patriotic proprietor of the Albergo Reale, to whom his Italian sympathies had become known.

As the author of ' The Roman '—the first book written by an Englishman to advocate the cause of Italian unity—he was made the object of something approaching an ovation. Afterwards, much to his own amusement, he found himself described, by the book-keeper of the hotel, proud of his English, as ' the man of large heart and extensive sensibilities.'

Some one has said that the world is for each of us pretty much what we make it for ourselves; and truly the world he made for himself was always full of interest and incident.

The following letter, written at Milan, at this time, though its subject is only the homely one of Inns, seems worth reproducing :—

Spanish Inns.

Albergo Reale, Milan: November, 1865.

Since your entertaining correspondent, F. W. C. [a
writer in the ' Athenæum '], has evidently been misdirected
in respect to the hotels of Burgos, and lest his discourag-
ing hints as to Spanish accommodation may deter some
of your readers from (as I think) one of the most glo-
riously remunerative tours in Europe, you will, perhaps,
accept a short list, taken from my memorandum-book, of
places in Spain wherein an Englishman, and even an
English lady, may rest, without being reminded of the
traveller's useful proverb, ' Quand à la guerre, comme à
la guerre.'   I merely offer it as a contribution towards
such a complete list as I have no doubt might be easily
made up from the note-books and memories of any two or
three experienced Spanish travellers, and which I as little
doubt might include, either as regards hotels, or certain
rooms in them, the names of almost all the important
towns of Spain.

At Burgos, for example, the scene of your correspondent's complaint, you may find at the Fonda del Norte
as good food and lodging as even an invalid is likely
to require.   Indeed, I do not remember to have had,
during many months in Spain, or to have met with anywhere in France, Italy, or Germany, a more blameless
petit salon, or a cleaner bedroom, than in that little
hotel ; and as for breakfast, dinner, &c., I do not think
that even in this comfortable and well-conducted Albergo

Reale of Milan (which should be called, by the way, '*Al-bergo patriottico*,' since when Garibaldi set up his standard for Naples, the waiters volunteered almost *en masse*, and some of them—Giacomo Ferrario, for instance—behaved with notable gallantry), the *comida* (as the Spanish say) is more satisfactory.   At Granada you should go to the little 'Fonda de las Siete Suelos,' actually within the precincts of the Alhambra, where any of the front bedrooms are creditably clean and pleasantly warm. The cooking is careful, the food good, and (I mention this for the sake of F. W. C., who has evidently a chivalrous interest in the feminine staff) the landlady a fine specimen, mentally and bodily, of that people whose cardinal social dogma is the born nobility of every Spaniard.   If you prefer to be in the town, and to see from your window every morning and evening (when the Sierra Nevada sends its snows up in incense, and receives them back in manna) one of the sublimest sights in the world, the hotel (I forget the name) opposite the 'Street of the Genii' will please you; but the climb to the Alhambra, thence, is a fatigue (or a tax) which you escape at the 'Siete Suelos.'   At Cordoba, the Fonda de Rizzi, kept by an Italian, Maulini, is good in all respects.   At Seville you should go to the Fonda Europa, in the Calle de Gallegos, and ask for the three little rooms numbered 14, opening into the canopied balcony of this fine old Moorish palace.   The central *patio*, with orange-trees that reach their fruit to you through the marble balustrades of the roof-garden (the in-door garden of the

harem), the grand staircase, with its ceiling of rare
Moorish work, so high overhead that many travellers
miss it, the windows looking into the narrow 'Calle,'
across which, in the saloon of your *vis-à-vis*, you may
see how Velasquez learned to drown his backgrounds
in pellucid shadow, to steep his figures in various
depths of that limpid darkness, and to bring at the
top (so to speak) of the dark-clear water, his foremost
faces and half-faces naked into the sun, would be sufficient to compensate for hard living. But the accommodation and food are admirable, and the charges are
moderate. At Port-St.-Mary's, the small Fonda, Vista
Alegre, is good and pleasant. At Malaga, the Victoria
and Alameda hotels have some clean and comfortable
rooms; but when I was in Andalucia, two years ago,
the food was not sufficiently good for the palate of most
Englishmen. I understand, however, that they have
improved in this respect. The landlord of the Victoria
is very obliging; and an English merchant in Malaga,
Mr. Hodgson, has opened a place adjoining the Alameda,
where such English 'comestibles' as are not good in the
hotels can readily be bought. At Valencia you should
go to the 'Fonda Paris,'—not, however, to the most expensive apartments (which are very cold in winter), but
to some southern rooms near the house-top, commanding
the Moresque roofs of the city, or to a southern flat, lower
down, which looks into a back street, full of Spanish life.
The cooking (by a Frenchman) and provisions are good.
At Barcelona, the 'Fonda de las Cuatro Naciones' is

clean and fairly conducted, and has—or had when I was
there—the best bread in the South of Europe.   At Irun,
you should go, if you want *couleur locale*, to the 'Posada
de Francisco Ystueta, Calle Mayor, No. 7,' rather than
to the regular inn.   The place looks fit for brigandage
and Carlist romance, but is (or was, two years ago) full
of the cleanliest and most genial hospitality.   It would be
well, however, before quartering yourself there, to ascer-
tain that the family of Ystueta is still in possession.
Here I am sorry to end my list; but I believe an experi-
mental traveller might lengthen it, even on his first
Spanish invasion, by changing our native haste for the
unhurried and tentative manners of the people.   The
sentence by which Spaniards like to teach us slow-coaching is an amusing curriculum to the English mind and
mouth, and (at all events, till you are pretty well up in
it) a good illustration of the pace that befits the country.
If I remember rightly, it goes somewhat thus:—'El
arcobispo di Constantinopla, quere desarcobispoconstan-
tinopolitanisarse; si el arcobispo di Constantinopla se
desarcobispoconstantinopolitanisarà, bueno desarcobispo-
constantinopolitanisador sarà.'   I add my name to these
bare details, since anonymous recommendations are open
to suspicion.

SYDNEY DOBELL.

From Milan the travellers, by and by, proceeded
to Pistoja, and thence to Florence—which place
being unusually crowded at that time, they took

a house for the season at Fiesole. The air of
Fiesole proved too stimulating for his wife's health,
and the villa had to be abandoned for several
weeks, which were spent in Florence. The few
memoranda jotted down at this time concerning
pictures and statues in the churches and galleries
are merely fragmentary. While in Florence he
made some interesting friends, and much regretted
that want of health precluded the possibility of
more than a very little social intercourse.

Of the external life of this winter there is
hardly any written record.

For a long time past, his mind had been much
occupied with the politics, not only of England
but of Europe. With declining health, his tendency
to abstract and abstruse modes of thought seemed
to increase. The memorandum-books in use at
this period are full of notes for a work he con-
templated, which would have been entitled ' The
Physiology of Nations ; ' but any adequate key to
the arrangement of these notes is wanting.

He studied Italian, of which, before this his
knowledge had been slight, with a master, and,
before leaving Florence, was able to converse in
that language, even on political and philosophical
subjects, with tolerable ease.

The one thing chiefly prescribed for him by his physicians at all times of his life—rest—seemed always unattainable. Rest of brain, rest of heart, were alike impossible. The more difficult all effort became, the more resolved he seemed to persevere in it; the more a duty cost him in personal suffering, the more indomitably determined was he not to give up the doing of it. Education, early habit, and natural disposition, combined to produce an over-conscientiousness which, as far as earthly results went, defeated its own end. To try and follow from his memoranda, and from other records, his inner life of this time, is to wonder that nerves and brain so long endured such tension, that the blow which soon struck him down did not fall sooner.

To light upon any bit of objective observation is a refreshment.

A few such were made at Fiesole, to which he returned for the softer spring weather.

A morning sky is described as 'full of great wings of shadowy butterflies—each wing many acres. The exquisitely rare cirri conforming in this manner.'

The horizon-clouds of another morning are likened in colour to the purple of the unripe but nearly ripe olive. While the sky of another dawn is said to be of the green-yellow of the yellow egg-plum.

Tuscan peculiarities in the training and dressing of the vines are remarked on.

March 18 he wrote:

> One of the whinchats among the most frequent pipers just now—the species with the black head, white collar, and red-ochreous tippet.
>
> April 20.—Between Milan and Turin. The butter-cups tall, cherry and pear trees in full bloom, poplars in full leaf, willow with grey-yellow catkins among the grey-green leaves, corn half-high. *Memorandum.*—The Lombards and Piedmontese train the vine from tree to tree, but in oblongs of three or four branches on the same plane, instead of the Tuscan single-twisted 'swing.'

At Milan, and again at Turin, on the homeward journey, he had seizures of alarming illness; but with change from the hot and steamy atmosphere of those places, at that season, to mountain air, the threatening symptoms cleared off.

BOOK VII.

CHAPTER I.

1866–1867.

THROUGHOUT the past winter and spring, Mrs. Dobell's health had caused her husband increasing anxiety. On their return to England, at the end of April, there had been some hope that they might be able to meet Sir James Simpson in London; but this hope failing, after a few days' rest, during which they were joined by the friend who had twice been with them abroad, they started for Edinburgh.

This revisiting of old scenes under the renewed pressure of the old apprehensions, no doubt considerably taxed his already over-worn heart and brain. Moreover, the political events of the time—especially the war of Italy with Austria—excited his sympathies so keenly that he felt compelled to struggle, under unfavourable conditions and amidst crowding engagements, to finish a paper on the subject, for the immediate publication of which he was extremely anxious.

The struggle was a vain one: the gathering
mischief came to a climax and struck him down
before the paper was completed. A few of its
more finished fragments will show its scheme and
purport.

I love Peace, but I think Christianity in saying, not
Pax, but *Pax vobis*, may have bequeathed the blessing with
limitations: that there are times when peace on earth
and good will to men may be best forwarded by the
destruction of those systems built of men, and those
ideas concrete in flesh and blood, which are the great
hindrances of that benevolent pacification; times when
I may best do to others as I would have them do to me,
by fighting against them that strong battle of indomitable
but chivalrous antagonism which, seeing as I see, I would
devoutly pray they might have strength to hurl upon my
own head if I were ranged, as they are ranged, under
the banner of what I believe to be intolerable wrong:
times when we may better love our enemies with beneficent grape-shot than with the cakes and caudle of
conventional philanthropy.

I shall not readily forget the day on which this year
[1866] I crossed from Calais to Dover. To those who
have lived rather than travelled abroad, that short *trajet* is
always suggestive and touching, but this spring I found it
particularly memorable.

I had come through Italy almost in front of the marching
armies; the country had not yet sprung up, but already

every town, hamlet, and '*paese*,' was thrilling and scald-
ing with that passion of glorious blood wherewith, a little
later, she started to her feet ; Austria, Prussia, and all their
satrapies, were already stirring; Roumania was in acute,
Spain in chronic, Greece in intermittent, revolution ;
Russia, lean and large, seemed by her yelp and teeth to
have the prescient nose of the hyena; France, grinding
her knife and grinning with expectation, looked like the
Aretino of the Uffizi.

The day was quiet and bright ; behind, were French
rocks and sandbanks clear and coloured ; before us, was
the great mist that hid the English coasts.   But there was
artillery practice at Dover Castle, and we had hardly
passed mid-channel when the white silence began to shake
with the distant cannonade; a few knots nearer and the
half-understood vibration began to throb itself into rhythm
of gun and gun ; yet a few more, and the heavy boom of
the 98-pounders filled and swelled the great obscurity and
lined the well-known but unseen shore with a rampart of
audible defence—as though slow-billowed thunder dis-
tributed its undulations upon the counter-heavings of the
reciprocal sea.

In defending the present war of Italy against Austria
I am unhappily relieved from the necessity of arguing the
great general subjects of War and Peace.

Whether war of man against man—especially of
Christian against Christian—can ever be justifiable, is a

question so profound . . . the arguments on either side are so innumerable. . . . I could fancy the controversy continuing down the ages . . . and illogically finished after all, by the advent of that time when wars shall be no more.

But the general belief among Christian nations of the present day is, that wars of a certain species are entirely justifiable. I believe there are very few Christians, how peaceable soever, who would not agree that there are occasions when he who has no sword might sell his coat to buy one ; and I do not envy the Christianity of that man who, having received the right to wear the sword, can wear it only in self-defence. For myself, I might hesitate on the question if a Christian may fight ; but of this I am as certain as of the law of love, that if he may fight to save himself he may lawfully fight to save his neighbour.

Is the present conduct of Italy lawful and right? As this question has come more than once from men whose honesty and great capacity were beyond doubt, it seems to me that the first duty of those Englishmen to whom Italy is dear, but to whom the rightness of English judgment and English action are yet dearer, to answer it at the very beginning of the great European struggle ; and to answer it in such sort that the intellectual verdict of Britain on the merits of the Italian cause may be entirely in harmony with that enthusiastic sympathy for Italy which is the natural sentiment of the British people.

It is said, that for Italy to invade Austria to liberate Venice is an infraction of that non-intervention which is in these days the great doctrine of international jurisprudence.

Let us examine a little this doctrine of non-intervention.

Non-intervention would send the Good Samaritan past on the other side, for fear there might be another thief in ambush; would keep Dives away from Lazarus, lest his sores should be contagious; nay, might justify Peter for preserving a wise neutrality. . . .

It is the privilege of the highest forms of organic life to combine the multiplicity into unity. . . . Descend in the scale of vitality, and you come upon the phenomena of ganglionic life. . . .

. . . In morals, the modern Pharisee who has lost the oneness of the law of love, breaks up into a thousand agonising atomies, to which wood, hay and stubble are similes of too respectable a utility.

In politics, if a nation falls below a certain point of national health, you will soon see it take on the diagnostics not of disease only, but of ontological degradation. The political brain and heart cease to dominate the social system—provinces and cities set up their own nervous centres, and what was a throbbing, feeling, working, fighting man, enfeebles to the disbanded force and dishevelled consciousness of a worm or a zoophyte.

You have an example, at this moment, in Spain. Spain, for special reasons, may be, for the moment, safe ; but, let the Italian people sink into the physiological condition of Spain, and not that famous cloud of crows and vultures which even blackens the moonlight desert above the dying camel, could worthily represent that shrieking night of harpies that would swoop from the four winds upon the living carcass of Italy.

A sonnet entitled ' Perhaps,'[1] written at this time, expresses something of his consciousness of over-strain and low ebb of nervous power.

The constant reception and visiting of old friends, and the wellnigh incessant conversations thereupon ensuing, though a great delight, was also a great exhaustion.

He had many pleasant and happy experiences, in finding the hearts of those friends as warm towards him, and as open to him, as his had remained for them. But even the pleasantest and happiest experiences involved undue expenditure.

In one way and another, his life was filled with such conflicting elements that he was torn this way and that by different claims, to each of which he felt as if he owed his whole attention.

[1] Vol. II., p. 366, of collected edition.

His worst immediate anxieties as to his wife's
state were relieved, but a suspended opinion as to
her health hung over him like a dark cloud.

The spring was exceptionally cold and bitter,
and, no doubt, the change of climate, from Italy
to Edinburgh, was injurious. But what was most
injurious of all, was the constant, yet seemingly
unavoidable, wear and tear of every feeling and
faculty that most needed rest.

The following must have been written just
before the blow fell that was to make rest compulsory :—

To John Nichol, Esq.

No. 39 Melville Street, Edinburgh.

By an accident, your right pleasant and welcome letter
did not reach me yesterday till too late for 'return of
post.' Many cordial thanks, from both of us, for the
charming plan your friendship has sketched in it, and of
which I can well foresee that the execution—physical and
metaphysical—would be more charming still.

But the charm of a plan like that is so substantive
and *per se* that it is really independent of fulfilment :
though it never blossom into performance, one has the
flower in the bud : as the French papers said of Thiers'
speech, and as somebody else has said of a much earlier bit
of 'cookery' (I remember your translation of Plato) 'Ce
n'est pas une ovation, c'est un acte.' . . .

We are here for my wife's ill-health (is that bad English?—but I got into the habit of saying *para* in Spain, and the Italian *per* keeps up the same kind of thinking), and it would be more weeks than you are likely to remain in Braemar, before so serious an additional journey as thither could be other than injurious to her. As a little bye-proof, however, of how really I want to shake hands with you again, I hope before Friday to run over to Glasgow, literally to do that and return—and if you don't see me on that errand you may be sure that no every-day cause has cut me off from it. . . .

That ' run over to Glasgow ' was never made. A sudden change of temperature, bringing in a stifling hot fog, seemed to give the *coup de grâce* to his shaken health. One morning the inexplicably deadly sensations he had, now and then, before experienced, kept recurring, but in greater force. He applied himself as usual to his writing, striving by a strong effort of will to dominate his mysterious enemy—perhaps the suspicion of approaching overthrow made him the more keenly desirous to finish the work in hand.

When called from his writing-table, at the early dinner-hour, he rose, walked across the room, put his hand to his head, as if to ward off a blow, and fell, full length, senseless on the floor.[1]

---

[1] This swoon was at the time pronounced to be epileptic, but there was afterwards considerable difference of medical opinion on the

Weeks of absolute prostration, then of slow recovery, checked by constant relapse, followed. So great was the physical weakness, after mental power seemed re-established, that had not his physician insisted on his removal to the country, while he still seemed utterly unfit for any such effort, it appears probable that he would not have rallied at all.

A little house was taken at Morningside, and, in the fresher air, he immediately began to revive, and was soon able to ride a quiet pony, with the usual happy results from that manner of exercise.

The veto laid for the present upon brain-work of any kind was imperative, and what had passed proved even to himself that it was now his duty, as he valued all chances of future usefulness, to relax the strain he had always put upon himself, and to try to rest. The certain assurance of this brought some sense of ease and repose. He felt the blow that had felled him to have been 'the Hand of the Lord' upon him, and therefore his submission was absolute and cheerful.

That he was ' to do anything he was inclined to do, and nothing towards which he felt disin-

point—some of the most painful features of epilepsy never characterising any of his attacks.

clined,' was the advice of his wise and genial
physician, who knew him well enough to know
how sorely such a prescription was needed. In-
activity being, however, the thing to which he
was always most disinclined, he supplied himself
with grammar and dictionary, and began to study
German during this time of disablement.

But, just as recovery seemed well advanced, a
chill taken by pausing too long in the hill-air on
one of his rides, on a bleak autumn morning,
brought on a second attack of his malady.

As soon as travelling was possible, he was
taken to Clifton—to winter in a milder climate
than that of Scotland, to be near home-friends,
and in the medical care of Dr. Symonds. Here,
too, he was able to take daily horse-exercise, and
during the next few months gradually regained a
considerable amount of vigour.

From his long prostration he seemed to rise
with brain and all mental powers (except to a
slight extent, memory) unimpaired, and yet with
fetters laid upon him as to their use. So long
as anything was done spontaneously, it was done
without injury, and without more than a natural
amount of fatigue. 'Talking,' he used to say,
when those about him feared he was over-tiring

himself, ' is as easy as thinking,' and thinking, the most subtle and profound, he believed to be, as long as it was involuntary, as easy as breathing. But if he were obliged to force himself to do some special mental thing in a given time, or to turn from one subject to another—not, as it were, of his own free will, and by natural sequence, but on compulsion—the result was a dangerous amount of exhaustion.

While he could talk for hours with keenest interest and animation, and with clearness and vigour, on subjects called difficult, and be conscious of no more than moderate and easily recoverable fatigue, to be obliged at a certain time to write even a short and unimportant note on a definite subject would appear to be an almost insurmountable difficulty. The note would be written and re-written, the very pen, ink, and paper all seeming as if under some baleful influence, some hindering bewitchment.

'The pity of' this state of practical incapacity was all the greater because a peculiar clarification, which appeared in the expression of his face, was from this time apparent in all the spontaneous workings of his mind.

That 'grand power of indignation,' which

nothing ever quenched in him, just now found
occasion for manifesting itself. On the death of
his old friend Alexander Smith he was stirred to
anger by what he considered the injustice of the
manner in which the dead was spoken of. During
the recent stay in Edinburgh they had renewed
their personal intercourse, and now neither his
sense of justice nor that ' fidelity to friendship,'
which has been commented upon as of unusual
strength in him, would allow him to be silent.

What he wrote was considered too strong for
the readers of the journal to which it was sent,
and the editor declined its publication.

After explaining the disabled condition which
made it impossible for him even to dictate a letter
without incurring the danger of an attack of
illness, he said : ' But I should be untrue to the
friend I have just lost if I did not, at any risk,
make some sign of my disgust at that paragraph
concerning Alexander Smith, which disfigured the
——— of last Saturday.'

That paragraph he then described as ' a scalp-
dance upon the new grave of a poet who, whatever
the value of his poetical labours, had but just lain
back into the night where no man can work.'

If Alexander Smith [he went on], whose great hope

and ambition was to write poetry, had really been proved
to have mistaken his vocation, the act of triumphantly
shouting his mistake within a week of his untimely death
was that of a coward and a savage. . . . I speak freely
because I have been pretty well hit by criticism in my
time, but, so far as I know, have never felt either pain
at the hit or ill-will at the hitter. I am sure, therefore,
you will sympathize with me in those very different feelings with which I see my friends ill-used.

As showing that the comparative prostration
of this time in no way dulled or narrowed his
intellectual sympathies, we may also quote something from letters dictated from Clifton during the
spring of 1867, addressed to an eminent politician
whose career he at that time watched with keen
interest.

The letters are on the subject of Parliamentary
Reform—supplementing some of the suggestions of
the pamphlet he had published eighteen months
before :—

Since the Resolutions, as presented on Monday, seem
capable of attaining many of the ends which I would have
liked to bring about by a more consistent system of means,
I should be a bigot not to wish them every success . . . .
but a question has occurred to me, when considering the
debate, which, I think, may be practically valuable. . . .
Would not apprenticeship-franchise in towns, and a good-

conduct franchise in counties (to be claimed by holders of prize-medals only) be the legitimate application, in other ranks of society, of the principle recognised by your Government in the educational franchises they have already proposed?

It seems to me that an apprenticeship-franchise (the vote gained by it to be used cumulatively with any vote or votes possessed by the same voter) and other fancy franchises among the labouring classes, would make the measure of your Government much more popular than it is at present. They would also accomplish what, as seems to me, should be a great object of every true English statesman just now—*i.e.*, to divide the inorganic or semi-organic unity of the 'masses' into a sort of secondary aristocracy of many grades, each capable, if necessary, of being used against the other, and as much less easy as an army is less easy than a mob, to be led hither and thither by illegitimate adventurers.

Not long after he wrote again, having found 'one or two more notions on the all-important subject of the hour.'

I. In redistributing seats would it not be well to measure the claim of any town or district to an extra member, not by its number of *inhabitants*, but (since rumour says the Government is about to recognize the principle of plural votes) by the total number of its votes?

II. Would it not be well to reward towns and districts

that had given exceptional proofs of present or exceptional guarantees of future enlightenment (such, *e.g.*, as the adoption of Ewart's Act), by adding a vote to every voter therein, so, *e.g.*, that he who would have otherwise had one should have two, he who would have had two should have three?

You will see in what a peculiar way this would change the relation of forces between the classes, in the given district, by elevating the proportional power of the lower precisely in the place where it had best deserved; and how it would in other ways assist in that dislocation of strata which I indicated in my former letter, as, according to my view, one of the greatest duties of a modern English statesman in his action on the immense unity of the masses.

In May 1867 he returned from Clifton to the neighbourhood of Gloucester, having again hired the house at which he had passed the summer of 1865.

His health was now too uncertain for foreign travel, with an invalid wife, to be safe or desirable; something of a permanent home was, therefore, requisite. Not having been able, after much enquiry and search, to find anything that, on the whole, seemed more eligible, he took Noke Place on a short lease, and, at different times, had a good deal done to alter and to improve it. But it required, as he used to say, so far as the house was concerned, to be improved out of existence before the front it presented could be other than an eyesore.

In situation it was a pleasant place, with a green and quiet environment of its own meadows and orchards. It had an open and sunny south aspect, commanding fine views of the beautifully wooded hill-district, which was within reach of a drive or a ride; while a sheltering hill rising at its back kept off unfriendly winds.

'It was always a pleasant place,'—said an old beggar-man, with meditative pathos, pausing to look up at it one sunny morning, after his necessities had been relieved at its door. And this was felt to be its appropriate description.

In spring-time, the time of orchard blooms and blossoms, till the early midsummer, the hay-time, when it stood 'deep in dew, and green, and nightingales,' and when the tall hedges of its elm-shadowed lanes were flushed with wild roses, this pleasantness culminated to some ideality of beauty.

'Always a pleasant place,' and how pleasant he made life for all those who lived within his immediate influence! 'Sunshine was he in the winter day, and in the midsummer, coolness and shade.' No one ever took to him their troubles and perplexities of heart, or of brain, or of fortune in life, without finding some peace, some rest; feeling as if they had entered a region of halcyon weather.

It seems the more needful to say this, because it has been felt difficult to avoid leaving on the

reader's mind an unduly sombre impression of
many periods of Sydney Dobell's life. The truth
is, that few of his days were without intervals of
keen enjoyment of various kinds ; new glimpses
of either mental or material beauty would delight
him ; touches of humour and at times of almost
boyish fun would enliven what might otherwise
have been the tedious hours of an invalid's existence.

Very worthy of remembrance [his brother writes] was
the practical result of his conviction that a man should
fix his thoughts on the great things of existence, both
seen and unseen. This principle had become so much a
part of himself, that although he felt acutely all pain, disappointment and misfortune, either happening to himself
or to others, yet these, however severe, rarely shook his
cheerful serenity of manner. Within a few minutes of
receiving some serious blow to his hopes, I have known
him ready to hear the story of another person in distress,
and able to give careful and thoughtful attention and
counsel concerning it ; or have heard him dilate with tender
appreciation on the beauties of a landscape, or flower, or
any beautiful object shown by the world around him.

That almost invariable calm, often commented
on by comparative strangers, as signally characteristic of him, and which, among some of his
Edinburgh friends, won for him the name of ' the

Imperturbable,' arose not only from the largeness of view commented on in the foregoing note, combined with sweetness of nature and strength both of character and conviction, but also from his habit of holding himself prepared—as he was at times with some impatience told—not merely for probable, but even for most improbable, emergencies.

Yet though, as a rule, he was as deliberate and temperate as resolute, he could also on occasion be prompt and fiery. If he saw too clearly and keenly for his own ease and comfort, suffered too acutely and resented too indignantly, this was greatly due to that habit of his mind by which his thoughts were constantly projecting themselves beyond ' this life.'

Just as, in art [1] and in nature, he was pronounced, by many, to see more than existed, because he saw more than existed *for them*, so, in

[1] In regard to his seeing more than existed in works of art he used to tell a story, with keen enjoyment of its humour, though it was at his own expense, of his having discoursed at length and with much elaboration to a lady, at an Edinburgh dinner-party, concerning some pictures which had impressed him at the Exhibition of the Royal Scottish Academy. ' Do you always see so much in the pictures you admire, Mr. Dobell?' his passive listener had inquired, languidly. ' If not,' he answered, ' I should not care for them.' On which his fair interlocutor asked, yet more languidly, ' Don't you find it a great bore, Mr. Dobell?' This latter phrase—which he, of course, interpreted to mean, ' I find you a great bore, Mr. Dobell'—became a household word.

the moral and spiritual world, he saw more than existed for most of us, perceiving in people and in actions, potential good and evil, things before and after.   For this reason it would sometimes seem as if—considering the generally wide tolerance of his charity—his indignation at some special wrong was out of proportion to that which provoked it.   This, when he judged the wrong to be of a kind that must have had its birth in things worse than itself, and that, if unchecked, must lead to things worse than those in which it had its birth.   That we may judge the character of all, but the criminality of none, was one of his axioms.   And in some species of wrongdoing, in themselves comparatively trifling, he, of course, found indications of character more hopelessly alien from good and akin to evil than in other sins of greater apparent magnitude and importance.

He himself wrote as follows, in a New Year letter, not dated, but judged by the handwriting to belong to a much earlier period of his life than this, and expressing views that were no less distinctly his to the last day of consciousness :—

I am no gloomy ogre or straightlaced ascetic.   I have no sympathy with those who despise 'this life.'   I know of no such thing as 'this life.'   I see that every man born on this earth has commenced a life which no thought can measure, and should think as confidently of this time a billion years hence, as of this time next year. I know of no difference of rule for living here and living hereafter, and I look upon life, therefore, as a glorious, a happy, an inestimable thing. To him or her who has objects as glorious as such a life deserves, I say, you cannot love this life too well; you cannot make it too high, too noble, too lovely, you cannot prize it too much. . . . It is that unnatural and unscriptural plan of degrading our earthly existence—of breaking our immortality into patchwork —which is the source of an incalculable quantity of our follies, fripperies, affectations, unworthinesses, and sins. Men do here what they would be ashamed to do in heaven, and occupy their minds with paltry objects which they think are 'good enough for this world.' If they saw the true dignity and nobility of this world, if they felt as they ought to feel, that they are living in the very presence of God, and with the eyes of angels upon them, and have begun here, or ought to have begun, the same sort of life which, under happier circumstances, and with still purer souls, they are to live hereafter, how many men and women, do you think, would be content with their present style of acting, thinking, and feeling? But there has been so much cant on the subject of religion that men have been taught to think it another word for gloom.

Does the earth look gloomy, and is it likely while the work is full of sunshine that the Word is all shade? Are we not to be perpetually with God in heaven, where the very atmosphere we breathe will be Religion, and are we to

be gloomy there? Let us be quite sure that it is religious
to be happy; but let us see that our happiness be worthy
of our natures, springing from high sources, occupying
itself with great and wide or beautiful and true things,
and looking forward to elevated objects. Let us see that
it be pure and unselfish, and we cannot be too happy. I
have said all this—more than I meant to say—lest you
should misunderstand the meditative mood in which I
spoke of the New Year.

––––––––

It would be omitting a considerable element of
external interest in his life at this time, not to
speak of his dogs; for, now that he led a more
stationary life, he had them under his own care,
and made them his constant outdoor companions.

The beautiful deerhound, 'Maida,' who was the
mother of the race, has been mentioned in some
of his letters from Scotland. At Cleeve Tower, at
Crickley, and during some of the Isle of Wight
winters, Maida had been a beloved and much-con-
sidered member of the family. In 1864 she won
the first prize—a silver cup, in which her master
took proud pleasure—at the Birmingham Dog
Show. The news of her triumph reached him at
San Remo: some of the friends he made there
may remember the almost boyish pleasure with
which he announced to them Maida's success.

In 1866, at the time of her owner's severe illness, Maida died, leaving children and grandchildren.

While he lived at Noke Place, one, two, often three, of these beautiful creatures were always with him when he went out. Their movements—the perfect grace of perfect strength—when they chased each other about the large field in front of the house, it was a real delight to him to watch.

A present of one of Maida's descendants was always a sign of special esteem or regard. Their owner never allowed any of them to be sold, and if any such sale took place it was without his knowledge and against his most stringent command to the contrary.[1]

Thor, promised from his birth to Miss Cushman, and kept for that lady till her arrangements allowed her to receive him, was for two or three years one of the goodly company: ultimately he went to America, was for a few months an object of universal admiration, and then died.

Torrum, another prize-winner, a noble deerhound of the 'white species, and of most perfect

---

[1] A question of disputed pedigree, raised since Mr. Dobell's death, in respect to a dog *presented* to the Prince of Wales (the keeper of whose kennels had requested to be allowed to *purchase*), furnishes a reason for making this statement.

disposition for sweetness and bravery, was, at one time, destined as a present for Victor Emmanuel, and some preliminary correspondence with regard to the manner of his transport had taken place, between Mr. Dobell and a friendly acquaintance occupying an official position at Florence; but, by the imprisonment of Garibaldi, Victor Emmanuel forfeited something of the esteem of which Torrum was to have been a sign, and Torrum remained at home, the household favourite. He did not long survive his master; seeming to pine from the time he no longer heard his voice or step, or even saw his face at a window, he died in the spring of 1875.

During this summer of 1867, and the following summer, Mr. Dobell could spend some hours daily on horseback, taking vigorous exertion in that way with only beneficial results. He was able to exercise some supervision of his Gloucester business, and felt a lively interest in all Gloucester affairs, gladly helping any good work in that city, for which he always had a hearty affection.

On his daily rides he made himself acquainted with his cottage neighbours, and was often the bearer of some special help needed in some special distress.

It was not, in any of his charities, the money's

worth of his gifts which best proved the love for
his neighbour of which they were the expression,
but the trouble he would take and think no trouble.
He did not now, any more than formerly, give
from the superfluity of a large income. He seldom
indulged himself by the purchase even of desired
books, maps, or photographs, or anything that
could be done without. His largest personal expenses were those made necessary by his own and
by his wife's ill-health.

To give pleasure to poor children was one of
his daily pleasures : he never liked to ride along
his usual route without a supply of sugarplums,
of pennies, or of small silver coin, to be administered
to the little ones who would run out into the road
at the sound of his horse's feet. But there was
wisdom in this ' extravagance,' for he always tried
by his gifts to stimulate some good thing—care of
the baby-brother or sister, helpfulness to the mother,
kindness to animals, regular attendance and good
conduct at school, cleanliness, and so on.

There are some yet living on the two or three
miles of the straight old Roman road along which
the beginning of his rides and drives while he lived
at Noke Place generally took him, who, long
after he had left the neighbourhood, still looked up

at the trot of horses' feet with a momentary expectation of his friendly recognition.

'We shall never see another like him,' was said
of him in this as in other neighbourhoods where
he had lived. To leave a neighbourhood, and to
undertake a new set of charitable pleasures and
duties in another, was never allowed to be a reason
for any abrupt breaking-off of the old.

A little weekly allowance from him secured
extra comforts to aged, or sick, or crippled creatures:
in cases of special poverty or distress, where the
mother was a widow or the father invalided, he
paid for the 'schooling' of children, and followed
them with help further on in life, when the time of
schooling was past: to village reading-rooms, out-
of-the-world hillside cottages, or to some chronic
sufferer, he supplied newspapers or magazines.
Kindly deeds kept his memory green.

The then almost invariable companion of his
rides, writing of them years after, recalling frequent
impatience at constant interruptions, and sometimes justifiable anxiety at the pauses made, to
listen to some long story of misfortune, says how
those rides, looked back on now, seem something
too delightful and beautiful to have belonged to
everyday life, and dwells upon the way in which

his intense recognition of all natural beauty—whether of grand and broad effects of cloud and sun over the wide valley, or some subtle loveliness of light on tree or grass or flower—added a new depth of charm to all things. 'Sermons in stones and good in everything' he certainly had the fine faculty for finding.

One secret of his being always so interesting a companion was, doubtless, that he was always an interested one; giving cordial sympathy, and not the mere surface attention demanded by courtesy, whether to young people who delighted to hear and to tell little anecdotes about the habits of bird or beast, or to older and more experienced interlocutors.

However monotonous his outward life might seem, he never suffered from *ennui* himself, or let it be possible for those living with him to do so. He had no dull and no taciturn moods. His wife, all her life more or less a prisoner, had every outward experience of his so vividly reproduced for her that she could recount his adventures as if they had been her own.

Towards the autumn of this year, 1867, a short time was spent on the hills above Gloucester, for the benefit of more bracing air.

Literary work was still, and was, indeed, always to the end, forbidden.   Brain-rest and out-door life and exercise were insisted on.

As far as he could, he lived in accordance with prescribed rules, in cheerful hope of restoration to sufficient health to make the continuation of the long-planned book practicable.   But in all the questions of the day—religious, social, political, or literary—his interest was so keen and eager that he could not refrain from, now and then, breaking a lance in some chivalrous cause.   This was done with the more difficulty, as he was able to make but little use of his own eyes in reading or writing ; and, either from spinal injury sustained in the Puteoli accident, or some other reason, could only think easily when lying down.

The affairs of Italy were always near his heart :

> That Italy, who, though she hath been hewn
> In pieces,—as when the demons hew
> An angel, whose immortal substance, true
> To his Eternal Image, is not slain,
> But from a thousand falchions rears again—
> Still undivided by division,—
> His everlasting beauty, whole and one—
> When sounds the trump whereat the nations rise
> Shall lift her unseamed body to the skies
> And in her flesh see God.

The following letter, published under the heading 'A Speech for a King,' was written at this time :—

To the Editor of the 'Pall Mall Gazette.'

Noke Place, near Gloucester : December 5, 1867.

Sir,—Since the telegrams seem to show that the Italian 'Cabinet of humiliation' would authorise no such speech from the throne as an honest king could read to a noble nation, one cannot help fancying what a '*Rè Galantuomo*' must be saying, in his heart, to the people who put their honour in his keeping. I send you my fancy, because I believe—and, as having lived in many parts of Italy, and conversed much and cordially with nearly all classes of its inhabitants, I have taken some pains to believe rightly—that a few weeks ago (when a timid Cabinet drew from the King's mouth that drivel which damped so much good gunpowder) even so simple an appeal as what follows would—from the lips of a King whom his subjects still trusted—have smelted the red-hot kingdom into unity, settled, at a blow, the temporalities of the 'Roman question,' and shown, by a crucial experiment, the inherent weakness of the Napoleonism that at present assumes to be arbiter of Europe.

'You, 25,000,000, who stand upon the ground where once stood that nation whose capital was Rome, you also may well indeed claim to be Romans, for how many times has a more insolent Gaul than Brennus flung his sword at you through the Roman Gate ? But observe this difference between ancient and modern Rome, that in the one, the

Gaul found chastisement, and in the other impunity. Yet
who may doubt that you are Romans? This your Italy was
their Italy. Your language is the natural posterity of
theirs. Your flesh and blood are made from wheat and
wine that sucked, from fields you call by the names they
gave them, the very dust and ashes of those old heroes.

' Yet I remark another difference between them and us :
that whereas once or twice their armies succumbed to the
invader, we are expected to yield at the mere threat of
invasion. Invasion! What invader in the history of the
world conquered a great nation wholly and honestly in
arms? But then, your modern invader is French, and the
Frenchman has a Chassepot. Chassepot, forsooth! When
army is to meet army, and the question is, shall so many
be killed by so many, one may well indeed be curious in
weapons ; but what matter if your enemy load this wise
or that wise, when rifle and rifleman are to be drowned
together in the millions on millions of a nation unanimous?

' Oh, you Italians, I say to you again, why should
Frenchmen be your masters? Nay, what race upon earth
should dare to hold itself above you?

' Send up your thoughts above the Apennines, and see
your Italy, from her stem of the Alps to her stern in
Taranto, so loaded by your fathers with great and fair cities
that, starboard and larboard, her bulwarks ship the sea!

' You know what those cities contain! You know the
monuments of genius and valour which draw, and will for
ever draw, the pilgrimage of the world! And you are the

children of those fathers, and you let a chess-player in
Paris sit at the end of a long wire and juggle you—you,
with your fine armies on foot, your great reserves of trained
men, only waiting for the trumpet-call ; your innumerable
youth, so born to warfare that, while the boys of France
are still at bat-and-ball, they play with bayonets and at
victory !

'Flash back his telegrams into his face, and bid him
send at you as many of his legions as he can spare from
the domestic glory of keeping down their brethren at
home ; as he can spare from the proud privilege of waiting
on Count Bismarck ; as he can spare from the myriads
of that swarming North which is already on the march
to avenge Sebastopol.

'Oh, you immortal people, on whom tyrants and priests,
those who kill the body and the soul, have done their worst
for age after age, only to prove you indestructible, what is
a French army to a family of Bourbons ?   What are ten
French armies to ten centuries of Popes ?

'Knaves may sneer at you ; priests may gibber at you ;
many brave men may say you are mad, and many wise
men may say you are fools. Fight ! you mad, magnificent,
foolish nation, and show them that your folly is of that
Apostolic kind which is destined to confound the wisdom
of the wise !'

I am, Sir, your obedient servant,

SYDNEY DOBELL.

He also sketched a much longer letter on ' The

Roman Question,' to have been called ' On Preaching Patience to those under Murder.' But it was
now an almost invariable experience that the con-
centration of thought in a definite direction, and
the effort to complete anything in a given time,
induced an attack of illness, which disabled him
from all mental work, before he had effected his
purpose. It was so in this instance, and the
letter, of which the following are a few fragments,
was never finished :—

. . . Certain journalists and public men are preaching patience to Italy, and assuring her from this, that,
and the other English safety-ground that she can afford
to wait for Rome. Allow me, I pray you, to say as
earnestly as I can, and to back the saying with what
demonstration I am able, that patience *in statu quo* is for
Italy politically impossible, and that she can no more
afford to postpone the possession of Rome than you can
afford to postpone the wish of your heart. Excuse me for
dragging you so brusquely and personally into the argument,
but though some of those journalists and publicists to
whose opinions I have alluded are doubtless good men and
true, who, if they were near enough the facts to see them
clearly, would come to very different conclusions, there are
others to whom I could not address a metaphor drawn from
a heart without fearing to do them the discourtesy of
speaking beyond their experience. But we must remember
that Paris is pre-eminently the city of vivisection : and

that, from the theatre of the veterinary school to the arena
of political and social action, never in any city that is, or
has been, has what we may call the objective heart—the
heart considered as an organ of somebody else—so terribly,
with such ruthless fidelity of investigation, such an
elaborate anatomy of torture, been laid bare, bedeviled,
chronicled, and defined.

And the fact is, that the Italian question is, and has
been (I speak not sentimentally, but physiologically), pre-
eminently a question of hearts.

He then goes on to point out the error of supposing that the question, Shall Rome be the Capital
of Italy? was a question still to be asked, instead
of considering it a question already and for ever
answered in the existence of Italy as a Kingdom. . . .

. . . 'This cry for Rome being the cry of a
starving nation for bread.'

From Emperors and Ministers of State who know too
much about her, to stay-at-home politicians, who know too
little; from the ridiculous 'Never' of an evanescent
dynasty to that 'Patience and water-gruel' which has
become so stereotyped a British recipe (for everyone's
maladies but our own) that La Marmora has taken the
trouble to translate it for the benefit of his countrymen—
everyone has had his psalm, his tongue, his interpretation
for Italy. . . . All this confident advice, which would be

hideous insult to any one man in the pangs of starvation
or the grip of an assassin, is actually addressed to a great
people under murder, to a nation struggling in the folds
of that political boa-constrictor which is slowly tightening
round the neck and head of Italy that monstrous living
knot which (unless the glorious victim can maintain, till
some Perseus or St. George shall come, the spasmodic life
that convulses the fair body and galvanises the exquisite
limbs) must surely throttle it to stupor, congestion and
death.

The winter of 1867–8 was passed at Clifton,
while alterations were carried on at Noke Place.

During this winter his health was sufficiently
good to allow him to enjoy some little social intercourse, and the visits of his physician were
always occasions for interesting talk on a wide
range of subjects.

In May 1868 he returned to the neighbourhood of Gloucester. The alterations at Noke
Place had been completed, and it was seen then
at its most favourable time, embowered in snow-
white and rosy-pink pear and apple blossom.

During this summer and autumn, Professor
Blackie, Professor Nichol, and several other intimate friends visited him, and he was well enough
keenly to enjoy intellectual encounter.

Something of the impression made upon one of

these friends—Professor Blackie, perhaps his most energetic antagonist in such intellectual encounters —may be gathered from the following letter :—

24 Hill Street, Edinburgh : November 12, 1877.

My dear Mrs. Dobell,—I am delighted to hear you are contemplating the publication of some of your dear husband's epistolary and other memorials ; and it is a matter of no common sorrow to me that I am not able to make any contributions to such a work. I have never been in the habit of keeping my correspondence, a neglect which I sometimes regret now ; but the fact is I live so entirely in the present and the future, that I have no time to make use of past records of my life, even if I possessed them. Not the less vividly, however, remains the impression stamped on my mind by those noble specimens of human nature with whom it has been my special good fortune during a long life to have enjoyed familiar acquaintance ; and among these there is none who occupies a more prominent place in my Pantheon than Sydney Dobell. A man so purely, and yet not proudly, placed above the platform of what the Scriptures call ' the world ' I have never met with. Indeed, I always felt when living under your roof as if I had left the world behind me altogether, and was privileged to hold communion with angels for a season. In our views of Literature and Poetry there was no doubt a sort of marked antagonism. I had been knocked about a great deal more amongst men, and hence, perhaps, had acquired a tendency to practical compromise in regions where he stood stout and stoical. In Art also, if I might think him sometimes over-subtle and overstrained, he might with more reason complain that I took things too easily, and sacrificed artistic finish to popular breadth. But whatever antagonism of this nature in regard to literary matters existed betwixt us, and however frequent the hostile encounters of wit were, of which you were witness, I never felt anything but the most perfect harmony of soul when in the company of Sydney Dobell.

In him there was a combination of solid thinking and large reading with what Matthew Arnold calls 'reasonable sweetness,' general human graciousness, and chivalry of sentiment and manner, which to me was a sort of living poetry, which I place far above anything written in books. It is a greater, because a more difficult thing to live a poetic life than to write a good poem. The mere quick sensibility and vivid impression of the moment may produce a poem : only the careful culture of a life can create character. There was a central atmosphere of large intelligence and gracious love in your dwelling which I nowhere enjoyed to such an extent, unless, perhaps, when in the company of my dearly beloved and much honoured friend, the late Baron Bunsen ; and if I should ever be tempted to do anything unbecoming a Christian or a gentleman, I should pray for nothing so much as that the image of Sydney Dobell might rise up to remind me with whose friendship I had been honoured, and by whose example I had been inspired.

Believe me, my dear Mrs. Dobell, yours with sincere esteem and warm affection,

JOHN S. BLACKIE.

It must have been during this summer of 1868 that an election took place in Gloucester, his interest in which led him to write the following letter to the Editor of the ' Gloucester Journal ' : —

. . . As I had intended not to vote in the forthcoming election, and had mentioned the intention in several quarters, and as I now intend to vote, you will, perhaps, allow me space in your columns for a few explanatory words.

I am going to vote for Messrs Price and Monk ; not because a single vote can have any perceptible effect on the election, but because a vote is the strongest protest I can devise against an electioneering practice which, I see, is gaining frequency just now, and which, baneful at any time, and before any set of electors, will be, if it should become a political habit, especially dangerous to the enlarged constituencies which have henceforth to be addressed. I mean the practice of sending to a distance for unknown candidates, and expecting that boroughs or counties, to which they are personally strangers, shall elect them, on the evidence of their spoken professions, and of certificates of character from this or that member of their party.

There are few things more difficult to all sorts of minds than to judge accurately of human character, and to judge it with anything like accuracy apart from much personal intercourse is a feat that the highest abilities can, as we all know, seldom achieve. Therefore the offer

of unknown or little-known candidates to a popular electoral body that must judge them purely by an intellectual
process, is an injustice to which no constituency should be
exposed, and which any constituency has a right to resent
by the notable defeat of those who are concerned in it.

But if this be true at any time and of any popular
election, it must be true a thousandfold of that great
choice which is to be made next Monday. Concerning
men who have lived long among them, whose outgoings and
incomings they have seen for years, and whose daily activities have left on their perceptions a sum-total of many
small impressions, the English millions have, by slow, but
pretty sure, mental processes, a tolerable chance of coming
to a sufficiently true idea ; but to ask the new, untried
majorities in our cities and boroughs, who come to the
poll for the first time, and to whom very humble mental
efforts are a novelty, to go through such a logical *tour
de force* as might overtax any philosopher, and discover
by the talking and writing that has been going on lately
whether, for example, Mr. Brennan and Major Lees are,
in any honest sense, their true representatives, is an absur-
dity so cruel that, irrespective of party, men of all shades
should surely unite in its reprobation.

If any of the capable members of the Conservative
party in Gloucester, who might worthily represent such
citizens as belong to that party, had come forward in can-
didature on the present occasion, I should have voted
with neither of the contending sides, because, in political
theories, I could agree heartily with neither. I think

our Disraeli-Bright-Gladstone Reform Bill, by which, on
the most difficult and serious of questions, the foreman is
to be outvoted by his labourers, the skilled artisan by his
hodmen, the clerk by his porters, the head of a household by his grooms; by which, in short, the electoral power
is increased in proportion to the unfitness of those who
are to use it, and which seems to answer the fine old
question that was at the head of our first franchise-laws,
' What sort of men should be chosen, and who should be
choosers?' by 'The choosers should always be those least
capable to choose, and they may choose whom they will:'—
I think a Bill which attempts to establish a political order
of things in diametric opposition to that system of social
order which, as the result of the first principles of human
life and co-operation must, Reform Bill or no Reform
Bill, continue, for a long time hence, to exist among us,
would be one of the most ridiculous, if it were not likely
to be one of the most disastrous, illustrations of human
folly of which good men have ever been guilty in this
world.

Whether I be right or wrong in this opinion of the
new electoral machine, you will admit that, while I hold
it with hearty conviction, I may well decline to be an
active portion of anything that seems to me so monstrous,
and may well prefer to wait and work for the more reasonable system which, if we rightly believe in progress, must
supersede, and at no distant date, a statute of topsy-turvy
and cart-before-the-horse. But whatever electoral system
had been at work in the coming election, I should, except

for reasons just now stated, have abstained from voting next Tuesday, because I cannot conscientiously enlist under either of the three chiefs who lead the parties that are to contend for mastery.

It seems to me, after long and careful observation, that Mr. Disraeli is the most adroit and audacious acrobat that ever turned somersaults at Westminster; that Mr. Gladstone is a political talkee-talkee, with neither the eye nor the hand for government; and that Mr. Bright is a forcible rather than a powerful man, in whom talents, originally fitter for the stump than the council room, have been so stimulated and biassed by the life of a professional agitator, that he can perceive no subtler organisation than that of a mass-meeting, and is incapable of any nobler public duty than the vulgar work of demolition.

Whether I be right or wrong in these opinions, I might well decline, while I hold them, to consent, even by a single 'Yes,' that either of these Parliamentary captains should, especially in these days, and in those more difficult days that are near, direct the councils and wield the strength of our country.

But it seems to me that the question to be decided at Gloucester on Tuesday is one at once more general and more local than the political creeds of parties, and more important even than the differences which divide them, because it is vital to the first principles of all true representation everywhere; I mean the question between known and unknown candidates, between native worth and foreign invasion (no matter whether that invasion be instigated by Mr. Mill, the Carlton Club, or individual adventure); between Mr. Brennan and Major Lees, of whom two-thirds of Gloucester voters have not the slightest chance of forming any right opinion whatever, and Messrs Price and Monk, who have so long been known to every man, rich and poor, among you, who have shown in so many ways, sometimes even at the risk of popular displeasure, their deep interest in the truest welfare of the humblest of your citizens, and who have so won the respect of all classes and parties, that until a few weeks ago the most eminent of their political opponents in Gloucester considered that to contest the city with them was something too hopeless to be attempted. Therefore, Sir, I hope to be early at the poll on Tuesday, and to poll for Price and Monk.

I am, faithfully yours,

SYDNEY DOBELL.

In the autumn, a few weeks were again spent on the hills, to which horses and dogs accompanied the family. The hill-air invigorated him, after the exhausting influences of an unusually hot summer, and he returned to Noke Place in rather stronger health than of late, and hoped to be able to pass the winter there. But, after Christmas, change seemed desirable, and Clifton was again resorted to—this time for only a short sojourn.

On returning from Clifton to Noke Place, in the spring of 1869, Mr. Dobell was taken ill, and, almost before he had time to recover, events occurred which caused him an amount of anxiety and necessitated a strain of mental effort for which he was, just then, peculiarly unfit.

He struggled through the early and mid summer, always more or less ill ; and, at the beginning of August, more bracing air seeming requisite, he took, for a month, a house on the edge of Hampton Common, above Stroud ; the district, in which, · before first going to Edinburgh, in 1853, he had finished ' Balder : Part I.'

He had only been there a week when, while trying a recently purchased horse, an accident befell him, so light to what it might have been that he considered it a merciful escape ; the indirect consequences of which, however, no doubt shortened his life.

Not feeling full confidence in the docility of the new purchase, he wished to give it a thorough trial before it should be ridden by the lady for whose use it had been intended, and took it out upon the turf of the common ; where, for a time, it behaved admirably.   But, by and by, desiring to have both hands free during a good gallop, he threw away his heavy hunting-whip—heavy because, after an adventure in the Noke Place lanes, it had been loaded, to serve, in case of need, as a weapon of defence.

On seeing him without the means of punishing her, the mare immediately began a series of efforts to unseat him, rearing, buck-jumping, and, finally, throwing herself backwards with, and on, her rider.

The whole affair occupied so brief a space that the witness of the accident—sitting on the turf to see the mare exercised, and with a confidence in Mr. Dobell's horsemanship which prevented any anxiety—had not had time for a pang of alarm when she saw him lying on the ground and the mare disappearing in the distance.

He found himself unable to move, beyond leaning up on one elbow, and at once faced the probability that he was dangerously, perhaps mortally injured.

All this happened not half a mile from the gate of the house he was occupying.

A farmer, passing by just after the accident, refused to drive five minutes out of his road to leave a message for the groom at the stables. But a little later, some ladies, who were driving across the common, immediately, on learning what had occurred, got out of their carriage and placed it at his service. It was brought close up to where he lay, and he was somehow got into it—got home, and carried up to his room. Medical aid was sent for and the news broken to his wife.

Nearly three months of helplessness and of much suffering followed. Though the injury proved to be, in some ways, less than could have been expected, the blow to the spine and the shock to the nervous system caused an amount of prostration that induced doubt as to whether he would recover the use of his limbs ; and the muscles of one hip were so far strained and weakened that he never again felt to have a good and safe hold of his horse. Riding, which all his life had been the one almost unfailing restorative, became from this time impossible.

During the many weeks before he regained

power to walk, or even to stand—while he was very incredulous of ever again being anything but a cripple—those about him were struck with his wonderful serenity and thankfulness.

In a sonnet written at this time—headed 'Under Especial Blessings'—a sonnet that for some of his friends was, and always remained, a psychological puzzle—he tried to express his sense of overpowering gratitude for the mercy which had spared him life.

Love of life was, indeed, always characteristic of him. It was not simply that he was 'resigned to live,' because such was God's will, and for the sake of those who loved him ; but that he rejoiced in life. Life, mere life, in 'the sweet air of this upper world,' he valued as a priceless blessing. Knowing how intrinsic was his faith in all that makes the hope of immortality most consoling and supporting; knowing, too, how the deepening pressure of sickness made most things men count 'worth living for' impossible to his later years, this joy in living was often, even to those most intimately near him, a marvel and a mystery.

As soon as Mr. Dobell could be moved, the family returned to Noke Place, and the winter was passed there.

Drives in a closed carriage were now the only possible winter exercise; the power of walking, except a very short distance, at a very slow pace, was only gradually regained.

In spite of physical drawbacks, during 1870 and 1871 the events of the time often stirred him to the attempt to express himself in regard to them. Friends who visited him, even those to whom he had been chiefly known in the first vigour of early manhood, were struck with the undiminished force of his conversation and the brilliancy of his intellectual power. Yet all literary work was invariably followed by injurious results, more or less marked.

Writing to a friend, about Midsummer 1870, he said,

I am still under medical command of *far niente*—I can't admit the usual *dolce*—mentally and bodily; but a heap of letters are lying unanswered—in spite of the dear activities that are always quarrying for me at that cumulus —and I cannot let another month begin without at least telling you how unwillingly and laboriously I have withheld my hand from a reply to yours.

Two of the 'Fragments' printed at the end of the collected edition of his Poems—'Mentana' and 'A Bayonet Song'—several sonnets, and the

Saga entitled 'England's Day,' published at the beginning of 1871, belong to this time.

About this poem, 'England's Day,' as much as about anything he ever wrote, opinions conflicted. This is saying a good deal, for, probably, the work of a man of genius has seldom been so variously estimated.

It is interesting to know what a distinguished and patriotic American woman—Miss Cushman—wrote about it, from America, to a friend of her own in England :—

A few days ago I received—addressed in your handwriting—a pamphlet, 'England's Day.' Even when I read it I did not guess the author; but I *enjoyed* it, really enjoyed it—if I were English, sailor, soldier, poet, or man or woman of any kind, I would say the same thing, if I were clever enough. I think it is just splendid, and when I read it to them at Mrs. C——'s the other night I wish you could have heard how delighted they were, and how they all said 'Splendid!' I do think there is a ring of contemptuous defiance in it, such as I don't know of *any* where else. Why have I been so out of the world as not to know of it? I think the authorship ought to have been given. Tell Mr. Dobell that I would like to grasp his hand upon it, for it is just glorious, and I like it, down deep I like it! And he is right- let them prick and stamp and goad and writhe as they will. The metal they are moulded of is 'Envy,' and I have enough of the old English blood in me to rise up against mean spite anywhere.

It will easily be understood that the correspondence of this time was very slight. Two notes to his friend Professor Nichol are among its few preserved and available traces. The first merely gives characteristically cordial welcome to the prospect of seeing his friend :—

I won't let a post go out without the unusual effort of writing with my own hand—or rather with my own *eyes*, for it is rather the optical than the manual in handwriting which, since that blow at Puteoli, I have not fully regained—to signalise that *benvenutissimo* of surprise and welcome with which I read your note of this morning.

The second requires a few words of explanation.

An anonymous letter reflecting on the Headmaster of the College for having, at a large public dinner, given expression—temperate though it was —to his sentiments in favour of Irish Disestablishment, had appeared in the 'Clifton Chronicle.'

This ungenerous, if not cowardly, attack having come before the notice of Mr. Dobell, called forth the following burst of indignation. The more significant as —the sentiments the expression

of which had elicited the anonymous letter in
question not being in accordance with his own
views on this subject—there could be no party-
feeling in the matter :—

My dear Nichol,—With this you will (?) receive a
copy of the 'Clifton Chronicle.' I take the paper, but
this week happen to have left it some days unopened.
Yesterday, therefore, too late for post, I saw for the first
time that letter about Percival, and, as you may guess,
fell to cursing and swearing in a manner St. Peter himself might have envied. That such a set of arrant snobs
should fancy they can confer honour on a man like Percival, that they should pass years of daily life with him
without suspicion that he has any English rank beyond
that of their nominee—these things are so naturally con-
vertible as not to be astonishing ; but when this kind of
logic is paraded in print and some sly devil entitling himself 'M.A.,' and who claims, therefore, the responsibilities
of education, stirs up the numskulls with the sight of
their own thoughts, it's time that something should be
done.

The first thing, as it seems to me, is to tomahawk that
letter. I would have done it myself, but I feel that, in a
thing of this kind, whatever iron is used should have the
professional stamp on it ; that no rank which is not also
academical is such as would be authoritative in the given
arena, and I hurry off the paper, therefore, that you may

catch sight of the enemy. Any axe you may have at liberty would do the business—the blunter and heavier the better.

I don't ask you to excuse me, my dear fellow, for this sudden inroad; I know where your heart will be and what a right arm it has; I only hope that other hard-hitting, in these combative times, is not fully taxing you nearer at home. Late as the day is I can't help sending off to you, because I should fear that Percival's friends at Clifton can hardly—in fear of collegiate schisms—do much on an occasion like this; and because it is precisely disgust and astonishment from a distance that will best startle wavering and dim-eyed people in his neighbourhood to a notion of whom they have among them.

In greatest haste, with our very kind remembrances to Mrs. Nichol, always yours affectionately,

SYDNEY DOBELL.

In answer to this Mr. Nichol wrote a letter which shortly appeared in the newspaper, and which was not answered. So the matter ended.

Towards the close of the summer of 1870 the hill-district was again resorted to, but not with the usual restorative results: after some weeks of extreme physical prostration, Mr. Dobell had—for the first time since 1866—a decided and severe epileptiform attack.

He was taken home to Noke Place as soon as

he could be moved, and rallied well; but a second attack occurred two or three months later.

To those about him it now seemed too certain that the only change to be looked for in his health was one to greater invalidism. He grew capable of less and less physical effort, and became increasingly sensitive to all atmospheric influences. For these reasons, his wife was anxious that as soon as possible they should move to a more suitable and substantial home. From the thinness of its brick walls, Noke Place was as stiflingly hot in summer as it was cold in winter.

Diligent inquiry and investigation at last resulted in the taking of Barton End House, near Nailsworth—to which the family removed in August 1871, and where the three remaining years of his life were uninterruptedly spent.

Early in 1871 Mr. Dobell wrote, from Noke Place, to a friend, of the way he felt the pressure of the time upon him: felt ' the want of proportion between demand and supply—demand from this many-voiced, over-interesting, or, rather, hyper-interesting, external world, and supply of time, brains, and *vis vivida.*

The political season just now impressed him as one of danger.

Dr. Johnson says that a *wise* Tory and a *wise* Whig will agree—their principles being the same, though their modes of thinking are different. A high Tory, he goes on to say, makes government unintelligible ; and a violent Whig makes it impracticable, because ' he is for allowing so much liberty to every man, that there is not power enough to govern any man.'

Sydney Dobell's political opinions will probably find sympathy from many enlightened and reasonable thinkers, whether calling themselves Liberal or Liberal-Conservative. The danger he now apprehended was, that by an injudicious and undiscriminating extension of suffrage, an undue proportion of power would be thrown into hands unprepared and unfit to use it, either for their own or others' good ; and thus ' so much liberty be allowed to every man that not power enough should remain to govern any man.'

Danger, also, lest laxity, falsely supposed to be Liberal, should confound religious liberty and popular self-government with the claims and pretensions of a Church which—

by nothing accidental in nature or in circumstances, but as the inevitable consequence of its primary dogmas and fundamental constitution, must—whether, in Ireland, in

Spain, or in Rome, and whether in sheep's clothing or the
natural hide—necessarily be a spiritual and moral despotism, under which there can be no true political freedom.
The existence of such a despotism in the midst of a free
people must always be a social misfortune; but when that
despotism has the skilful and infrangible organisation of
the Roman Catholic Church, and when the head of it is
a foreigner, and a foreign prince, it must be, not only a
popular misfortune, but, in proportion to its magnitude,
a more or less serious national danger.

'I could never,' he says in one of his latest
letters, 'trust a Jesuit, or feel other than an affectionate and sympathetic desire to have him shot.'

It will be as much as we shall do [he wrote, just at
this time, to a political correspondent], by the most desperate gallantry and opportune leadership, to carry the
day for 'Christ (unencumbered by orthodox or heterodox
definitions), England, and Inequality.' That is my war-
cry; though, like all practical cries, its objectivity requires
a great deal of explanation, that I must not enter on
here.

In the Franco-German war, his sympathies had
at the beginning been on the side of Germany;
but they were, after Sedan, transferred to the falling and failing cause of France.

His deep-rooted antagonism towards Louis
Napoleon will have appeared, as also the absence

of any enthusiastic Gallicanism, and the warmth
with which he felt and expressed himself in regard
to German oppression surprised many of his
friends. After the appearance, in the 'Times,' of
Colonel Hamley's 'catalogue of Prussian barbari-
ties,' he could not resist an effort to make his voice
heard on behalf of what he considered an outraged nationality, and he wrote, for publication in
a leading journal, two long letters 'On some recent
great Crimes.'

Near the beginning of the first he says :—

If Paris, the pest-house of sensualism, Communism,
and the other 'isms' of which Comte has been a principal
inoculator, and which are the diseases naturally resultant
from that great constitutional defect called Atheism—
whether that defect be hidden under the rags of priest-
craft or visible in its cavernous nakedness—had been
rubbed out, like an obscene scribble, from the tablet of
Europe, I should say that France and mankind were
gainers by the loss, if those moral and mental maladies
could be obliterated with the city. But the war of the
Prussian bloodhounds, whose fangs are yet in the arteries
of France, was not against creeds or vices, but against the
health and life of a people.

In the body of the same letter the following
passage occurs :—

We all know that skill, courage, excess of numbers, and an unparallelled *glück* enabled Germany to take from France, in the first weeks of belligerency, and almost on the common frontier of the belligerents, its civil and military head, and nearly all its generals, armies, artillery and munitions of war. We remember the France that was behind this unexampled cataclysm of misfortune. A France without troops, without cannon, without commanders, and, above all (as German leaders took care continually to proclaim), without a Government that had even the semblance of national authority. A France where, of thirty million human atoms of confusion, no one knew whom to obey or resist, whom to believe or distrust; to whom loyalty would be patriotism, and to whom it would be treason in disguise ; whose plan was the raving of folly, and whose the *grand incroyable* of genius; whose passion was madness, and whose the noble rage of indomitable honour. A France whose condition, indeed, so nullified all popular metaphors and phrases of helpless dislocation and distress, that, beside the chaotic misery of its unprotected nakedness, sheep without a shepherd is an image of order and defensive security, eagles in a swannery the picture of equal conflict, *disjecta membra* the definition of an organic whole, and *discordia semina* the very proverb of cosmos.

To see, in this decade of our century, a nation of nearly sixty millions send into such a France a greater army than our times have before witnessed, armed and equipped beyond all precedent, and supplemented with more and

greater artillery than had ever been assembled in the
world, with the avowed object of ravaging, starving,
bombarding, and slaughtering, till this helpless human
herd, in the wildness of its despair, should consent to the
most tremendous terms that the insolence of heathen
conquest ever imagined ; to watch these scientific hordes
of educated barbarians steadily, month after month, ac-
complishing this object—with a professional cruelty and
systematised rapacity as much beyond the wickedness of
ordinary war as crimes *prepense* are worse than the out-
bursts of passion, or the premeditative ruffian who lives by
strangling women for their purses, than the old-fashioned
Turpin of the road—and climaxing, at length, by an arrogance as much above the usual lust and swagger of conquest
as Anti-Christ transcends the peddling of common sinners—
might well make us turn, in the spirit of the old poets,
to demand from heaven and earth how these things are
possible.

Is our age the most savage in history ?   Are Germans
the race by which we join ' the ape and tiger ' ?

' Musa mihi causas memora !' Μήνιν ἄειδε θεά !
Unhappily the true answer is more serious than anything
so transient as Junonian hysterics or the sulks of the son
of Peleus ; for it is contained in one of the most important of those truths that continually shake the hopes of
philanthropy.   Woe to that people whose leaders embody
its besetting sins !

These things have happened, not because the German
race is immoral beyond all races on the earth, but be-

cause it happens to be led by men who possess individually, in an exorbitant degree, the worst ethical features of the people to which they belong; and because any race so led is certain to undergo a temporary distortion, analogous to the change in a human face when a sudden appeal to its ruling lust enrages it to the Caliban of itself. The union of the Jew and the Ceorl which characterises the Teutons since their first appearance in European history . . . . which shows itself at later dates in their favourite title of 'Deutsch,' and in a language unassisted and self-secerned, at once super-subtle and over-gross,—as if some sudden metempsychosis had filled a tribe of swineherds with Plato and the Muses—that curious mixture of spiritual and intellectual egotism with physical strength and moral rudeness, which was never more remarkable than when, in this last of his campaigns, toiling through the snowy roads of the worst of winters, we saw him dragging, with Brobdingnagian muscles, the iron monsters of his militant science after officers who could graduate with equal honours in the arts of slaughter and the philosophy of the Absolute,—seems to have been, in all times and changes, the specific difference of his race. This union of the worst extremes of selfishness, the egotism that, magnified by the presumption of being a sort of Vice-Providence, leaves no room for any rights but its own, and the other, which tramples on the rights of other men for the mere reason that they are the rights of others—and which we may fairly call, respectively, the Gulielmic and the Bismarckian—may, as the private life of Germany often demonstrates, be counteracted, in a nation at peace, by the possession of signally opposite virtues; and there are, of course, as English experience has shown in some illustrious instances, and as everyone personally acquainted with the people will testify, so many Germans who are individual exceptions to the characteristic German type, that a century might pass without throwing to the head of Germany such a monstrous dual of what is worst in her as we have just seen leading her military orgies in France. But when, as now, the cardinal vices of a people break out in its rulers as master-passions, when the forcible feebleness of a sentimental caricature of King David, helped by the gigantic abilities of that colossal *gamin*, the German 'Chancellor, offer in the name of patriotism and historical romance unbounded license to the national sins of which they are themselves the extravagant personal incarnation, human experience forbids us to believe that the offer should be nationally refused. It should, therefore, also forbid us to be astonished that even an invasion to which the achievements of Greek and Italian bandits on unarmed shepherds and defenceless travellers are, as Colonel Hamley well pointed out, deeds of heroic self-devotion, should seem honest and glorious to German army and Vaterland: it should explain the deification of Force after force had declared on the Prussian side, the ignorance of all but the rights of the peculiar people, which distinguishes the German press when discussing the Philistines, and the odd combination of military skill, civic adroitness, rural strength, and barbaric *génie de garotte* with which Prussian officers and soldiers, while chanting the songs of Zion in a strange land, discover and squeeze the larynx and jugular of Canaanitish city after city.

At the conclusion of his second letter, he wrote :—

If I have denounced a gigantic immorality which history will show to have been as stupid as ferocious, as injurious to the best interests of Germany and the wholesome growth of Europe, as it was cannibalish to the half-dead enemy in whom it left life enough for memory, recovery, and immortal revenge, it is from no wish to depreciate the German people or the part they ought to play in the drama of the world. It is not the German nation, however multitudinous, but that social system which puts nearly sixty millions of Germans in the controlling hands of a war-caste, numerically large but comparatively small ; a social system which enables the leaders of such a caste to unite at their will, for reasons of family or friendship, the enormous power of Germany with that of Russia, and thus, by destroying the moral freedom of other nations, to debase throughout Europe those national qualities which, in nations as in men, can only be developed by liberty; it is this system, and not the Germans who are its victims—though often, like other slaves, they seem callous to immemorial chains—that must henceforth be treated as enemy, not to this or that civilised country, but as the common foe of civilisation.

The editor, to whom these letters were sent for publication, declined to print them, pronouncing that they would be good things said out of season— the time when they might have been useful being, according to his judgment, past. No doubt this was correct; and moreover, it is probable that for the columns of a newspaper, they were too sweeping in denunciation of what the writer held to be injustice, only the more hateful because it was huge and successful.

Yet, fiery and impetuous as they were, at the time these letters were written, he might well have used these words of Milton's :—

I can boldly say, that I had neither words or arguments long to seek for the defence of so good a cause, if I had enjoyed such a measure of health as would have endured the fatigue of writing. Being but weak in body, I am forced to write piecemeal, and break off almost every hour, though the subject be such as requires an unintermitted study and intenseness of mind.

To his Mother.

Noke Place : January 29, 1871.

I have been longing to write a line to you for many weeks past, but every day that has been on the top, the rise, or the descent of the undulations which my health

performs has had such urgent claims upon it that pleasure
had to give way, and when I am in the bathos of the
up-and-down, you know I am neither fit for pleasure nor
work. . . . I feel all the more deeply for your isolation
because it has occurred at a season when external nature
offers the fewest of those things which have always been
as companions to you.

Not, however, that spring itself will be very visible
or audible this year. For the first time in my life I
have not cared to look for the first snowdrop, nor had an
inward consciousness of primroses to come. This Europe
of men seems as if it filled and over-filled every mechanism of thought and perception with things present, past,
and future, beside which the unvarying processes of
Nature have something almost of a cold impertinence. I
don't mean 'beside' such a comparative trifle as the fall
of Paris (for France would be a deuced deal better without her), but 'beside' those facts of which that fall merely
illustrates the commencement. I was asked, a few days
since, to join a London committee that is to press on our
Government to obtain good terms of peace for France,
but declined, for the reason that I should probably dis-
agree with every section of it, inasmuch as while I would
think almost any quantity of blood well spilt that should
destroy so hideously strong an engine of oppression as the
present German army, I would willingly shed a still
greater to put down Comtism abroad or ——ism at home.
You see, though we can't meet, the temptation to a little
skirmish with you is so irresistible that, like a naughty

boy, I am throwing a stone all the way hence to Detmore ; and I took up pen with the intention of merely one line of love. . . .

. . . Lest you think I make affectation of industry, I must tell you that, notwithstanding many illnesses lately, I have finished a long war-song throwing down the English gauntlet to Russians, Yankees, and Prussians: a sonnet doing ditto to the Papacy ; and am in the midst of a bayonet-song, to be sung by British troops, and a long letter, soon, if I can finish it, to come out, on the theory of British statesmanship in the East. . . .

You may fancy that certain guardian angels have had, and have, a nice time of it ! Briton [1] might make a moving picture of a horse with bit between his teeth, and a celestial straining at each rein. 'I hear a voice you cannot hear' which says that I have been much longer than according to promise, at this letter. It looks a terribly selfish letter, but I know is really less so than if I had spoken of matters with which you are already familiar.

The 'long letter on the theory of British statesmanship in the East,' alluded to above, was, as usual, planned on too comprehensive a scale to be written in any brief number of such days as were now his—days whose invalid routine afforded but scanty, and, because of his wife's anxieties, almost furtive, opportunities for such work.

[1] His brother-in-law, Mr. Briton Riviere.

Mr. Gladstone's 'Chapter of Autobiography,' published about this time, was the provoking cause of Mr. Dobell's attempt to expound a theory he had long held on the intellectual character of that eminent politician, of whom he speaks as—

A man of ambitions so noble, of an honour so candid, a conscience so urgent (a conscience not necessarily morbid, though made to seem so by the faults of its intellectual instruments), a heart so warm towards the public good, as almost to justify his friends in supposing that Nature when lavishing so many virtues would have emulated in her intellectual gifts the excellence of her moral work.

The fragments of this letter which were written—a considerable mass of MS.—give nothing of the 'Theory of British Statesmanship,' but are occupied in showing why, in the writer's judgment, Mr. Gladstone's intellectual peculiarities (the physical analogue of which the writer finds in 'colour-blindness') unfitted him to cope with the great conjunctions or sudden emergencies of the time—making him, in fact, resemble 'a machine elaborately constructed to go wrong.'

The following brief notes seem characteristic enough to be interesting :—

To the Rev. E. Harris, A.M., The College, Clifton.

Noke Place, near Gloucester : April 24, 1871.

For more than a week I have been daily intending myself the pleasure of thanking you for your kind and valuable care of my ward,[1] but every day some urgent work that could not be postponed has consumed the small quotidian of pen and ink which, as yet, is all the doctors allow me. To have enveloped the enclosed cheque with a merely formal word of compliment would have so maligned my notions on transactions of the present sort, that I preferred the more negative misrepresentation of delay.

I always think the monetary part of such matters to be rather—as in case of a physician's fee—the recognition of an insoluble debt, or the algebraic sign of an unknown quantity, than a mercantile correlation of value to value. Begging you to see my enclosure in this sense,

I am, yours faithfully, in haste,

SYDNEY DOBELL.

To the same.

Noke Place : June 28.

I especially wish to see Vaughan before he leaves England; and as I am particularly unable to forecast the future (and must, therefore, extend the moral on ' the night when no man can work' to those not-to-be-calendared *eclipses* which befall me), I should very much thank Dr. Percival

----

[1] The son of a dead friend.

if, consistently with routine (I scratched out 'routine,' but replaced it on the consideration that a route may have marginal deviations), he could give him a furlough next Sunday, or the Sunday after. Vaughan tells me that an application from me to the Rector is necessary in the matter; but, as I should regret to add a note—read or written—to his overcrowded day's work, and have been awaiting some occasion for a line to yourself, I am sure you will be good enough, during one of the daily opportunities, to act for me in the case, and I hope you will make Vaughan save you from a pen-and-ink reply.

Cordially reciprocating the friendly wishes in your letter—a reciprocation which, but for severe illness, would have been long since expressed—and hoping that their realisation may not be very distant, I am, dear Sir,

Very truly yours,

SYDNEY DOBELL.

Politics, if perhaps the keenest, was not the only interest which provoked him to write.

The 'Winchilsea Controversy,' in regard to the supposed discovery of a poem of Milton's, was then occupying attention in literary circles, and about this he wrote at some length—arriving at the conclusion that the poem was not Milton's. He wrote, also, on the subject of Strikes and Trades' Unions; suggestions for a fitting Albert Memorial,

and drew out an elaborate scheme for the revision
of the Poor Laws.

But, in these days of crowding and jostling
interests, the topics of newspaper excitement which
he touched had generally given place to others
before the shackled and intermittent use of his
brains (which, he said, danced, when they danced
at all, as if in chains or sacks), that was alone
possible to him, allowed him to complete letter or
article.

Friendship, also, stirred him to an attempt.

During his first residence in Scotland he had
had a good deal of friendly intercourse with Sir
George Sinclair, of Thurso. On the appearance
of a Biography of this gentleman he was anxious
to say a few words on some points of character to
which he thought the biographer, 'in spite of
laborious love and care' had not done justice ; and
had thus lost 'an opportunity of illustrating the
amount of unsectarian religiousness and genuine
liberality that in Sir George, as in some others of
his party, were stronger than the dogmata of his
creeds.'

If a true and thoroughly accomplished gentleman is
the consummate flower of Christianity, the best that his
ecclesiastical compeers can say of Sir George hardly

indicates so finely the noble order and special eminence of
his merit, as the testimony that could be borne by associates
who, however heartily they agreed with him in the ends
that all good men would accomplish, held scarcely one of
his opinions as to the means by which those ends should
be attained. . . .

It was precisely with these (liberals and heretics)
that his best self achieved its most characteristic efflorescence. . . .

As the faultless host—who outdid the classic notion of
Hospes without the *ratio quid*, and practised, without
saying them, the euphuisms of chivalrous romance—or
as the ever-interesting, ever-interested companion whose
wealth of sterling anecdote was, like his other wealth,
sometimes underrated, because he carried such things with
an ease which weaker men mistook, and because, with
something less conscious than modesty, he was always
ready to play his best gold against any honest coin of
current talk—or as the many-sided Humanitarian, who,
though the staunch *laudator temporis acti*, respected
To-day, and 'stood up and took the morning of' To-morrow
—the princely old man who lived, unawares, his friend
Carlyle's great axiom on 'good-breeding,' and was so
'high-bred' as to be above the satire with which the
philosopher has coupled it, must have left, in the remembrance of those whose memory is the best kind of fame,
such domestic and social portraits of himself as are more
likely to find place in future Valhallas than any statue to
him as hero-militant which the natural partiality of his
brethren-in-arms may set up.

To this same time belong the following translations and comment :—

Translations of ' Animula vagula blandula.'

> Little soul, little fluttering
>> Forsaking soul, that of this mortal breast
>> Hast been the friendly guest,
> Ah, whither dost thou wing?
> Little thing, little naked thing;
> Poor little naked, pallid, shuddering thing,
>> That hast forgotten even how to jest.

> Anima, animetta, animina,
>> L' ospite e l' amica, carezzante,
>> Di questo corpo amante,
> Da chi tu vai vagare
> Animinina.   Dove vorrest' andare?
>> Nuda, pallida, silente,
>> Ah, povera tremante!
> La beffardina non puo più beffare!

Neither of the foregoing translations conveys the
beauty of the original—the tender raillery of the parting
soul by the dying body : nor, I think, is there a word in
either language which expresses the reciprocity of relationship which the social habits of antiquity had given
to the notion of ' Hospes.'

He often amused odd quarters of an hour,
when resting on his sofa, or longer periods of his
unrestful nights, in making little *jeux d'esprit,*
sometimes in English, often in French, Italian,

or Spanish, which he afterwards scribbled down. He wrote, also at such waste times, two or three political and electioneering burlesques. His pleasure when a punning couplet, on a question of the day, sent to 'Punch,' was immediately inserted, was like a boy's.

There was unselfishness, as well as philosophy, in the sweet-blooded way in which he made the most of all the more mirthful and pleasant aspects of his life. Although his deeper thoughts must often have been serious and solemn enough, they were never touched with gloom.

BOOK VIII.

CHAPTER I.

In August 1871 the family removed from Noke Place to Barton End House.

It is pleasant for his friends to remember that Sydney Dobell's last years were spent in a place which delighted him—which made him feel, for the first time since he left Coxhorne, that he had a home—as he himself said—'a home to live and to die in.'

If any true idea of him has been gathered from the preceding pages, it is needless to say how great a part of the delight he derived from the roomy comfort of the substantial old house, and the beauty of its grounds and situation, was found in his hope of the benefit and the pleasure they would be to the friends, new and old, whom he looked forward to entertaining there.

The following letter was written during the first winter spent at Barton End :—

To the Rev. E. Harris [accompanied by a copy of the
American edition of Dobell's Poems].

Barton End: December 16, 1871.

As you have done me the pleasant honour to write
'Amicus,' I can't resist copying it into a place where it
may chance to have the good luck of being useful to you,
as well as the certainty of gratifying me. I lived for the
greater part of two years in Italy, and in any fix of any
kind I found ' Ho l' honore d' essere il primo Inglese chi
ha scritto un libro per l' unità d' Italia,' an irresistible
spell among all classes, except, of course, the Jesuits. My
friends, I believe, have found it an incantation that even
works at second-hand.

I don't doubt you go to Rome well armed with introductions ; but I am old enough traveller to know that one
can never be too well furnished, and that often the un-
looked-for adventure occurs precisely on the unforeseen
spot of your map.

The American pocket edition of my things which
should reach you by the post that brings this, may be useful not only among Italians but Americans, who are very
numerous and powerful in Italy. Should you need to
appeal to authority, don't forget my admirable friend the
American Ambassador (Mr. Marsh, the philologist), who is
very influential. He lived at Florence during the memorable kindness I received from him and his wife, but is
probably now in Rome.

I scratch this lest I lose a post and you be started. Had I not been in bed yesterday, and therefore under extra interdict, what could I not say to you, if this is your first visit to Rome!

Pray remember that I send the book on condition only that you do *not* write to acknowledge it, but come and tell me on your return, the last news from that city whither every Englishman should go to die ; but which I am little likely to see again. (I mean my travelling days are over.)

In haste, with all good hopes for your journey,

Yours very faithfully,

SYDNEY DOBELL.

In April 1872—his first spring at Barton End House—he wrote to a friend :—

Among the crowd of claims which an invalid has to bear about with him—numerous and often loud, as the rooks in yonder trees (congratulate me on the possession of a rookery—I had one for five years twenty years ago, and till I came hither have never ceased to miss it), I have continually been conscious of that unanswered but most welcome and heartily valued letter which I received from you long ago. Had I intended to treat it less well —to make the welcome less visible—it would not only have escaped ill-usage but, very likely, have got signs, of what I wished you to understand, that would have been just as expressive as any that time and leisure could produce. The more one lives and matures the more one

perceives (at all events I perceive) how really speechless
are those fatuous gesticulations of tongue and pen—and,
also, perhaps, how stupid as the fingers of Isaac that finer
sort of touch we call sight.

My first impulse, therefore, on reading anything I
wish to 'answer' is to lay it aside. So it comes to pass
that scores of men have been 'answered' while your letter
has lain in my despatch-box, as to its paper and ink, and,
as to the sense of it, has dug its claws of continually recurring reminder into my consciousness. I see by the date that
it came just when we were leaving Noke Place for this
lovely home—did I tell you I had, after much patient
waiting, found the home to live and to die in ?

After coming here, a continual fight with serious illness left me very short intervals for most needful mental
work, and when the long campaign of winter was nearly
over, the *faiblesse* of our Government about America stung
me to strike a blow in that quarrel.[1] I am amused to
recognise how the congratulations on the quality and
strength of my strokes usually include felicitations on the
recovery of that robust new health and strength of which
they are supposed to be proof positive. So few people
have experience enough of work under difficulties to know
that whether you load a ninety-eight-pounder, ounce by
ounce, or at a charge, it explodes—if rightly rammed—
with the same unity of roar . . . . So here we are in April ;
and though I have sent off the concluding letter about
indirect damages, and have time to work a little daily at

---

the solid heap that lies yonder—by which I mean, to
answer the letters that, like yours, have remained without reply—the fact that it is April, and that you are only
forty miles off, forbids me to do anything but that of
which (I suspect) the prescience has already helped to
keep me silent.

Pray come over here for a few days and read some
specimens of the poem, and let us discuss the subject *as* a
subject. . . . Perhaps a poet can make a poem of anything that can be assimilated to his own being, but that
is by a process of digestion that really exchanges the subject
for the poet and makes *him* the poem : which has been
very much the process with modern poetry, of which the
modern ear is getting tired. Had you not tried the
experiment and, therefore, probably, refuted me already, I
should have said *à priori*, that friendship was rather for
prose than for verse—except, perhaps, friendship in the
form of devotion to a leader—in so far as the entire unity
of love is only possible between different sexes—mental
and physical.

It seems to me that the office of prose is, to embody
all the things our knowledge (or quasi-knowledge) gives
us, from without or within, which have not yet reached the
highest phase we can imagine—and that to verse remains
the rest. . . . But perhaps you will convince me, either
argumentatively or practically, that I am wrong. Pray
come and do it. All that we thought of this place before
it was ours, is more than ratified by more than half-a-year's
life here.

To another friend he wrote :—

We have here the rare privilege of being in almost moun-
tain-air, with environments of such singular felicity as to
defend us from all the worst winds, and from that comparative sterility which usually makes residence at such a height
too severe an optical asceticism.   Barton End is an oasis
of romantic beauty ; and yet I have just sent a party of
friends to a neighbouring height from which they will
have a *coup d'œil* of eighty miles by fifty.

From correspondence of this time with a personally unknown friend we make a few extracts :—

It is very natural that, young as you are to your new
profession and to provincial experience, you should retain
that 'graceful infirmity of blushing' which Lord Chester-
field thought so diagnostic of good things ; but you will
soon find that, charming as the symptom is in regard to
your own idiosyncrasy, the virtue it indicates is thrown
away in the service of the goddess whose temple you speak
of with such tender reverence.

. . . You will find, too, that if you are to be a lecturer,
you must make the profession 'pay' by organising your
campaign with careful generalship—making every town
you visit not only a field of action but a basis of operations ; and you can't do this if you wait to be solicited.
There is no need to make your application too mercenary
or commercial in tone : an intimation that you purpose
during such and such months to give such and such

lectures, and that your route will pass through such and
such districts, is all that is needed (with a memorandum
of the fee for each lecture, which should not be higher
than that usually charged by popular lecturers, nor *much*
lower) to open the game. . . .

Later date :—

Had your letter been less profoundly interesting you
would, believe me, have long ago seen some sign of the
hearty and various feelings it aroused. But incessant
ups and downs of worse and better health—the ' downs '
drowning all capacity, the ' ups ' swelling together such a
climacteric of many claims that every one avoidable had
to be avoided—have stretched from the day I received it
till now.

And ' now ' I am not writing an answer to that welcome
(for such a letter, however pathetic, cannot but be welcome)
letter of yours, but merely to ask some favours—with an
invalid's cool confidence.

One is that you won't wait for your regular ' holidays '
before taking a peep at this ' earthly paradise,' but, when
a plunge into the Spring of springs would seem to be of
special value, remember that we can always meet you at
Stroud (six miles hence) on any Saturday night, whirl you
up here *for a spring Sunday,* and have you at Stroud
station on Monday morning in time for the early London
train. . . .

To the same.

May 7th,

. . . I can't resist the pleasure of telling you that the most exquisite phase of the Cotswold year is just expanding. The leafing of the beech, of which no one who has not lived among it can even imagine the superterrestrial ideality, is in mid-miracle, and in the grounds here we have every act of the Epiphany at once, from the first grey move of the bud to that perfect leaf which transfigures in a day, and thence—sometimes in a few hours—descends to that earthly level of merely material loveliness which those who only see the ' summer woods ' associate with the notion of ' sub tegmine fagi.' Can't you run down to feel this ? Or would it be safer to wait till the contrast with London is less strong ? I think, however, that one is best saved from bad music by taking every chance to pitch the ear aright.

The apple-orchards are, just now, blossoming in the valley, and there's no Cashmere of roses that can equal them : so that you would pass up through the richest notes of the optical range.

It must emphatically be said that Sydney Dobell never resigned himself to *mental* invalidism.

It has been stated that the important literary work of his life ended with the break-up of his health in 1857. The reader will, nevertheless, have

seen that he never could allow himself to desist, for
long together, from the effort to work, and that
the years since then, spite of increasing physical
drawbacks, were years of various and considerable
mental activity, of which the available literary
evidences form only a small proportion. This is
especially notable during these last years—1871
to 1874. Books were filled with philosophical
and religious, political and philological notes and
memoranda, set down hurriedly at odd moments,
but the outcome of long trains of thought; and
the drawers of his writing-table got crammed with
sheets and half-sheets of manuscript. The central
idea, concerning which the chief part of these
things were broken ejaculations, tentative utterances, always occupied the background of his
consciousness, and formed the under-current of
thought.[1]

His interest in politics was increasingly keen.
The situation of Europe, and schemes for the re-
distribution of territory, greatly occupied him.

He caused large maps to be hung on the walls
of his room, so that he could see them from his

---

[1] It is difficult to describe the exact nature of this 'central idea;'
but some clue to it may be found in a sentence written by him more
than five-and-twenty years earlier:—'Whatsoever things are true
for man the Immortal I call Religion, and, in this sense, Religion is
the only worthy object of human study.'

bed or sofa, and towards these his eyes were
continually turned.

'A political Utopia, based upon the reconstruc-
tion of European boundaries, by the expansion of
Switzerland over all the mountain centre of the
Continent,' was gathered, by one of his corre-
spondents, to be part of his dream of the future.

Through the first winter and early spring spent
at Barton End, some comparative health and vigour
were gained. The place seemed to suit his wife's
health better than any other they had lived in,
and this was, in itself, a source of great happiness.
Long drives and short walks were possible. He
soon made himself felt as a beneficent influence
in this new neighbourhood. It now seemed, as
sometimes before in his life, as if, could he only
have abstained from drawing off through the brain
every particle of newly-acquired strength, partial
recovery might have been possible. But he *could
not* spare himself. From one cause and another
he was taxed with a large amount of unavoidable
correspondence, not of a kind to be of general
interest, for which he was now often able to use
his own eyes and hand. Moreover, things that did
not come under the category of ' unavoidable ' were
often felt by him as equally imperative ; among

them, the writing of a series of letters on the
Alabama Claims, published as a pamphlet, entitled
' Consequential Damages.'   After the strain he put
upon himself to finish these by a given date his
health began again to decline.   The season was
singularly unpropitious, and he was now almost
preternaturally sensitive to atmospheric influences.
In May he wrote :—

. . . The revolutionary forces of external nature seem, this
year, to be in symbolical uproar against the sweet order
and progress of the seasons. We had, yesterday, a snow-
storm greater and blacker than I ever saw, except in the
high Alps.

During the early summer of 1872 he had the
pleasure of receiving some of his old friends in
the new home—among them Professor Blackie
and Professor Nichol—when the old combats were
carried on with the old spirit.

His keen enjoyment of all social intercourse,
his animated interest in everything, his almost gay
cheerfulness, the hearty peals of genuinely mirthful
laughter that welcomed any amusing anecdote or
incident, and the ready flow of eloquent speech—
all this gave an impression of fullness of life and
life-enjoying vigour that deceived his friends and,
to some extent, his medical adviser.   His wife was
considered over-anxious and over-careful.   Rela-

tives who came to see him took away such bright
impressions of mental vitality as could not be
made easily to harmonise with the reports of excessive weakness and exhaustion they frequently
received.   It was not that he kept his brightness
and strength for casual visitors.   He never complained or seemed depressed ; he was always the
source of household sunshine ; to pass into his sick-
room was always, even when things were physically
darkest with him, to pass into a fresher and more
vivid atmosphere than one breathed elsewhere.
Even his servants felt this, and the errand that
would take them there, the service that would keep
them there, was coveted and contended for as a
privilege.   But there were 'signs' enough for
close observers—in the frequent sleep of profound
exhaustion fallen into at intervals during the day,
in the look of the face during such sleep, and in
the profuse perspirations induced by slight efforts
of mind or of body.

And in July of this year, after a short time of
special weakness, came one of the dreaded attacks.
On recovery he yielded to his wife's passionate
entreaty for a consultation of physicians.

Concerning this, he wrote to his brother, Dr.
Horace Dobell, at the end of a long letter :—

July 28, 1872.

. . . I feel some additional delicacy at yielding to my
wife's very earnest, and long-felt anxiety to have the
great benefit of your general *reconnaissance* of my case
before deciding on an appeal (should you conclude such
necessary) to any specialist. The fact is, we don't know
enough about it—certainly not of its *fons et origo*—to be
competent to indicate a *spécialité*. . . . No doubt —— is
under some disadvantage from the nature of his practice
in this farming and manufacturing part of the country.
. . . Of course his potential faith—what Aristotle calls
πίστις—is confined to those symptoms with which his
experience is already familiar. . . . I think when you see
him you will recognise a man of as good scientific
abilities as we have any right to expect.

His brother came from London to meet his
usual medical adviser and an eminent local physician, and a consultation took place.

Certain rules of life strictly adhered to might,
it was thought, tend towards something like re-
establishment of health. Much sleep and much
nourishment were prescribed, and the necessity
for more exposure to open air was insisted on, as
well as complete abstinence from all brain-work.

For some years past, movement in an open
carriage through the air had induced symptoms

supposed to be rheumatic; but now, at the wish
of his medical friends, he again made the experiment, with the result after a few days, of another
seizure by his malady—as to the nature of which
some doubt had previously been felt.

Before this had taken place he wrote to his
brother :—

August 5.

I forgot to ask yesterday that in any of the valuable
arrangements your kindness makes for me it will remember, that though to attain a very important object I
can make some outlay, I am not so ' well off' as I give the
effect of. A fellow who lives in such a place as this, and
drives a pair of horses, can't put down very small sums in
subscription lists without making his 'good' (house and
horses) ' be evil spoken of ' in a very undutiful manner.
And as (many as are the local and other subscriptions in
which I have to take part), we, I am happy to say,
' communicate ' in many ways, and in cases that don't
appear in any lists, I find that, on an average, at least a
fifth of my income is yearly given away—*i.e.* all that does
not go in paying ' debts,' commonly so-called, goes to those
other *debita.* You will see, therefore, that I must not
leave expense entirely out of sight, though I am competent to such expenditure as duty may demand.

To the Same.

August 13, 1872.

Written thanks look so stale when often repeated, and
yet congruity demands so imperatively that my letters to
you begin with some thankful recognition of the valuable
time and mind you spend on my affairs, that I must
invent some short-hand sign by way of overture, that may
not increase my debt by occupying your minutes, and yet
may somewhat obey my sense of τὰ δέοντα. A great T
won't do, because our word 'thanks,' like much else in our
language, belongs to an ungrateful type of words. *Theta*
seldom comes from very deep : nearly all the originative
and *de profundis* words, in all languages, begin with a
hard guttural.

The Spanish word 'Gracias' seems to me the most
expressive in European tongues, because (the *c* before *i*
being pronounced *th*) it combines the gamma and the
theta. So I shall in each of my letters put ✗, as my
exordium, and proceed at once to business.

It has long seemed to me, as the almost involuntary
induction from innumerable facts of experience, that if
any portion of my head-machinery is wrong, it is that part
which connects Will with the effectuating functions. Not
Will itself, nor that result of 'Will' or desire on the
imagination which we call 'Purpose' (for neither will
nor purpose was, probably, ever clearer or more definite
than at present), nor the 'effectuating functions' themselves—for they seem all right—but whatever organism is

the electric conductor, so to speak. For instance, my devotional feelings, and originating religious powers, are quite healthy and strong, and my will is distinct enough on sacred matters; also my powers of speaking or reading on sacred subjects, *if taken unawares*, seem healthy; but for my will to *oblige* my powers of speech, of reading, or of thought, on such subjects, to act with the reverence, attention, and consecration with which I will them to act soaks me with sweat, and strains my whole mental machine. . . .

So my memory, when *accidental*, seems good, and my mental powers when brought to bear *on present objects*, by their own stimulus, seem as good as ever; but memory fails when will has to make the dogs hark back for the desiderata.

Even as regards physical efforts the same law seems to hold, more or less. Everywhere, in short, there is neither devigoration of will nor tubescence of purpose, nor frustration of will or purpose, by *malfaisance* of the external doing-machine; but there is profound fatigue, weakness, illness, or what not, of some mediatorial organ.

No good had resulted from the efforts made. He had hoped to be able to abandon the habitual use of a sedative medicine,[1] which he took always under protest, with a sense that it poisoned life and fettered the use of his brain, but which, during the last eight years, had been prescribed for him by every physician consulted.

[1] Bromide of potassium.

The result of medical experiment and observation now led to its being prescribed in larger quantities. This was a severe disappointment, as, during the few days of its discontinuance, he believed that his mind worked more freely and easily. From this time, too, his became a more and more indoor existence. He drove out occasionally in a closed carriage, but this manner of exercise, except when taken for some definite object, he always felt to be irksome. His carriage and horses were, however, a source of pleasure to him—when they were used by his friends. In getting out on foot he delighted, but very little of this was possible. Even a quarter of an hour of quiet sauntering about the grounds would often be followed by a terrible kind of exhaustion; and any exposure to a keen wind brought on an attack of illness.

On December 2 of this year (1872) he wrote to an old friend, the well-known George Dawson, with whom he had not for many years had any intercourse :—

To George Dawson, Esq., M.A.,

Barton End House, near Nailsworth.

Dear Mr. Dawson,—I see by the lecture-list of our gallant little Nailsworth Institute that you are about to favour it next week ; and I can't resist telling you that I am here, and claiming that—for sake of ' auld lang syne '— you will let me be your host while you are in the neighbour- hood.   I have long been attached to this district (I lived in it twenty years ago), and have always hoped to live and die there.   How near, perhaps, the latter part of my programme may be to fulfilment, you may guess by the fact that even so short a note as this is a serious infrac- tion of doctors' orders.

I am all the happier, therefore, in having secured the loveliest of homes in which to transact life or death.   My wife, who joins me in kindest remembrances to Mrs. Dawson and yourself, unites cordially in the hope that we may have the great pleasure of seeing you both here ; and I am, though with an invalid's enforced brevity of speech,

Yours heartily,

SYDNEY DOBELL.

CHAPTER II.

1873.

In looking over the records of these last years, the proportion of effort made for others is more than ever notable. As notable is the fact, that those who asked 'favours' were always so treated that, whether the request had to be refused or could be granted, the applicant was converted to a friend and left with warmly grateful feelings.

'The care with which the few minutes allowed me for writing are timed' (he wrote in one of his latest letters, when those about him,—having learnt by experience that every effort made beyond the inevitable routine was an irreparable expenditure, that, as it seemed to them, calculably shortened the period during which they might hope still to hear his living voice and feel the sunshine of his presence,—felt as if the price of every such effort had to be paid out of their hearts' blood), 'creates in me a desire for velocity that seems, in me who

have always acted on the German saying, "Time
spares nothing he has not a hand in," to paralyse
such brains as I retain.'

This, said as an apology for 'a bungling sentence,' is more like a complaint than anything that
occurs in the rest of his correspondence.   And these
minutes, so grudgingly tinned to him, were almost
invariably given to the affairs of some friend, some
acquaintance, sometimes even some stranger.   The
number and the variety of the claims made upon
him and the appeals made to him—of which almost
every morning's post-bag contained some example
—never wearied the charity of his will; but, of
course, made him more keenly conscious of the
weight of the fetters in which he lived and moved.

Most of his friends felt that the life he now led—
of self-denial, of suffering, of constant frustration
and chastisement, of gallant resurgence from prostration, only to be overwhelmed afresh by the
mysterious evil that sapped the powers of life—
could have had for them no beauty that they
should desire it.   Yet not one of them but felt,
when with him, the beauty of it as he lived it,
and even the happiness; and to some it must have
occurred to apply to Sydney Dobell the words of
St. Paul: 'As chastened, and not killed; as sor-

rowful, yet always rejoicing ; as poor, yet making
many rich ; as having nothing, and yet possessing
all things.'

Truly, he possessed many kinds of joy. No
one, his wife says, who had ever seen could ever
forget the rapt delight with which he would listen
to the matin-music of spring birds ; nor the illu-
mination of eyes and brow, of the whole face,
pallid from a restless night of suffering, but wearing ' reflex bright of joys that shall be,' with which
he would raise himself to look out

> When winds of morning lead between their wings
> Ambrosial odours and celestial airs,
> Warm with the voices of a better world.

And he certainly spoke from his own heart
when he said :—

> Dews to the early grass, light to the eyes,
> Brooks to the murmuring hills, spring to the earth,
> Sweet winds to opening flowers, morn to the heart !
> But more than dew to grass, or light to eyes,
> Or brooks to murmuring hills, or spring to earth,
> Or winds to opening flowers, morn to the heart !
> Once more to live is to be happy.

This pure joy in the exquisiteness of spring
and of morning made the very opening of his eyes
upon these aspects of nature, a feast of thankful

wonder. His keen joy in any noble deed stirred
him to an exaltation of generous enthusiasm that
hindered the possibility of mental stagnation.[1]
His loving joy in love, and in recognising any
ideality of love, gave warmth and colour to his
existence. His faithful joy in the 'deep things of
God,' as revealed to us by 'the mind of Christ,' and
his unwavering adherence to the central truths of
the religion thus revealed: these things combined,
made an atmosphere about him which it was a
spiritual, and even a physical, support and elevation
to breathe. Consciousness of the weakness of his
sick body was lost in the impression of wholesome
health made by the sound and strong spirit.

Early in this year 1873 occurred a little incident worth recording, because Mr. Dobell's pleasure
in it was characteristic of his affectionate interest
in Gloucester affairs, and his value for the esteem
and good-will of Gloucester citizens.

He received, in a letter from Mr. Gambier
Parry, of Highnam, Secretary of the 'Gloucester
Museum and School of Science and Art Building

---

[1] Almost his last attempt at poetry was in response to an act of
heroism, told in the newspapers, of a young soldier in the Ashantee
war. See Vol. II., p. 377, Collected Edition

Committee,' the following ' Resolution,' passed on
the opening of a new building :—

On the transfer of the original Museum to this
Institution the Committee desire to record their very high
estimation of Mr. Sydney Dobell's generous act in having,
for many years past, provided, entirely at his own cost, the
accommodation for all the purposes of the Museum ; and the
Secretary is requested to communicate to him the thanks
of this Committee, and to assure him of the great admiration that has been felt for that long-continued and
gratuitous provision made by him for the benefit of all
classes of the community.

In a letter written shortly after, to Professor
Nichol, he alludes to having sent him an extract
from a newspaper containing this vote of thanks,
and says :—

I knew that you, who know my favourite theory that a
poet, because he is a poet, should try to be signal in the
performance of all human duties . . . would be sure that
I valued that vote from no vulgar motives. . . .

But I took up this pen, which my enfeebled right hand
finds difficulty in forcing to work, to write on a very
different subject.

I see by the papers that Emerson (I can't call him
Mr.) is to be in Oxford this week. Several of his friends
have told me that he has often expressed a wish to meet
me. (Of my wish to meet him it would be pleonastic to

speak.)   If you, who know him well, really think that this
so-called 'wish' of his is of any such strength or sort
as will survive the strain and crush of competition with
which English society will contend for him, perhaps you
would let him know that Oxford is not far from Barton
End—is, probably, nearer than any other English town he
is likely to visit.

Oxford is close to the Great Western Railway, at the
Stroud station of which, as you know, we could meet him
and bring him hither.   Should this be to happen, could
you not, my dear fellow, so arrange that promised—*promised*, remember!—visit of Mrs. Nichol and yourself as
that you also should be here?   Surely this is not beyond
the generalship of Hannibal?   And the love between us
is capable of much more than even the trouble it would
cost you for, yours always affectionately,

SYDNEY DOBELL.

Months passed, during which, though all definite attacks were warded off, physical strength
declined.   During the spring and summer of 1873,
at his wish, his house was constantly filled by his
friends, with whom his intercourse could only be
limited and occasional.   His own life was chiefly
lived in his bedroom and in a pretty little up-stair
sitting-room, the view from which, towards the
rookery, delighted him, and where his friends came
to him, now and again, for an hour's talk.

To plan the day's enjoyment for his guests, and
to hear of their delight in excursions made in the
remarkably beautiful neighbourhood, was a vivid
gratification.

He gave up, with no feeling of giving up anything, his own few small varieties and distractions,
when the house was full, that the whole force of
his establishment might be devoted to the entertainment of others.

He was now quite unable to read to himself,
not from any physical failure of sight (which, on the
contrary, was piercingly keen), but from the condition of general nervous exhaustion. To be read to
was, therefore, one of his greatest pleasures, and
listening to the daily paper was often the chief
external interest, and always a very vivid one, of
his day ; but this, and the companionship of wife
and adopted daughter, were foregone more than
willingly for any possible advantage to his friends.

He would lie and gaze on the beauty of the
scene from his window, with a face of serene
tranquillity. He never seemed to find the lonely
hours tedious, but the entrance of a friendly or a
beloved visitor received a radiant welcome.

Scribbled on a bit of paper in his handwriting
occurs this sentence : one of those definitions he so

constantly attempted : 'He is selfish who is specially conscious of the differentiæ which mark self
from non-self.' If this definition hardly describes
the unselfishness of Sydney Dobell, it is that he
was, perhaps, conscious of self, as the thing to be
set aside and ignored.

During this summer of 1873—a time of excessive
physical weakness—there was no dulling of perceptions, or of any mental faculty. It seemed as
if everything were there in full measure, and only
the failure of some part of the physical machinery
hindered the innocuous use of the brain.

His interest in all questions of the day, whether
social, literary, political, or religious, was so keen
as to make all these things a fatigue to him. The
more the power to strike a blow in what he
thought the right cause failed him, the more cru-
cially he felt indignation, disgust, grief, or whatever emotion the special case called forth.

It was impossible to him to submit to be easily
and carelessly amused. When the paper was read,
if the topics were of importance he was roused and
stirred by them over-much ; if they were of little
interest, he minutely criticised the literary style,
noted flaws and faults of composition, the occur-
rence of unintentional rhymes and alliterations, or

the jingling concurrence of words of similar ter-
mination in close succession.

The same difficulty applied to reading novels
or stories to him, especially if they were the work of
friends or acquaintance.   If by anyone in whom his
interest was very great, his overstrained closeness
of attention often obliged the laying aside of the
book.   And in several instances, during his last
months, volumes presented to him elicited an
amount of critical remark, both as to detail and
general grasp of subject, immensely valuable to
their authors, but causing him an amount of expenditure he could now ill afford.

One of his friends writes :

I shall never cease to remember with mingled gratitude
and regret, the time and thought Mr. Dobell persisted in
expending, during a week of this period, in listening to
the reading of a long manuscript poem, which owed much
of its subsequent share of success to his verbal criticisms.

In intercourse with his friends the same difficulty occurred.   They tried to amuse him with
gay talk and anecdote, and he was amused ; but,
on the first opening, turned the conversation into
deeper channels, and soon plunged into some subtle
argument.

Even with music it was the same.   When his

drawing-room was again ' full of Beethoven,' as the
· M.' of early letters played to him on a fine-toned
piano, a new possession of his wife's, the enjoyment was too keen, and the attention too absorb-
ing, not to produce injurious results if long continued.

The last time, a year later, that he was thus
played to, it having been perceived that it was too
great a strain for him to follow the old beloved
movements from Symphony or Sonata, the player
chose simpler kinds of music, listening to which
seemed, for some time, to soothe and rest him.
But one special air, though not at all a sad one,
was of that rare order which seems never to have
been ' composed,' only to have grown naturally,
like a daisy or a primrose. And before this was
quite ended, he interrupted it, saying with an
expression of pain: ' No—I cannot bear *that*. . .
It goes deeper even than Beethoven.'

All emotion, of whatever kind, appeared visibly
to diminish the small residue of vital power.

It seemed in one sense impossible to him to
take life easily, while in another and a higher sense
he took all things easily. The burden which is
easy and the yoke which is light, of a complete
and unquestioning Faith and Love, he had so pro-

foundly made his own, and he seemed so constantly
conscious of the support of a Guiding Hand, that
he lost the sense of being weary and heavy
laden.

One of his friends wrote of him after his death :

Like one of the old heroes who suffered for the world,
he had to bear in this life such burden of disappointment
that the freeing of that chained spirit ought to be to us
the subject of the keenest joy. His patience was a living
lesson in all nobleness and gentleness and manly strength,
and nothing more beautiful can be imagined than the
serenity with which he bore that worst of all torments to
an ardent soul—its enforced inaction, apparent atrophy.

Inaction emphatically enforced, atrophy not real—for
we know that he has carried with him to the ' abode where
the immortals are ' a spark of Divine fire so keen and pure
and triply refined by suffering here that, even while we
are now mourning by the grave-side, he is already
serving God with plenitude of power undreamed of, un-
imagined. . . .

In a letter written at the end of this year
occur some characteristic comments on the true
sense of the word *Good* :—

. . . One of the noblest of the many noble words which
we owe to the grand old Anglo-Saxon. When the Anglo-
Saxon called God and Good by the same word (with a mere

difference of accent), he expressed two truths, which the
wisest of his successors have maintained with less brevity :
on the one hand, that the highest illustration of God
which the world has seen was, also, the highest illustration of human goodness, a Good Man, 'who went about
doing good ;' and, on the other hand, that when we so
assemble in our minds our highest ideas of *good* as to be
conscious of them without admixture, we have reached, so
far as we can reach in this body, to a contemplation of the
God 'whom no man hath seen neither can see.'

From these truths we may make two practical de-
ductions of high value at a time like this, when Papistry,
on the one side, and 'the flesh and the devil,' on the other,
are spoiling men's thoughts :—that nothing which is not
soundly and wholesomely manly can, for us here below, be
godliness ; and that nothing which is adverse to what we
know of the Divine can really deserve to be entitled
'manly.'

We may, perhaps, most fitly place here the
following reminiscences of Sydney Dobell, by one
whose brotherly love stood bravely and faithfully
by him to the end, doing all that the nature of
things permitted, to lighten and to soothe the
anxieties and the difficulties which beset his last
months, and hastened his death :—

May 18, 1878.

To record my own remembrance of Sydney Dobell is to review a lifetime, and to speak of a friendship in which there was never change, except that of deepening affection, for nearly fifty years. We were cousins, and I was married from his house and to his sister. I first remember him as a child not three years old, lying, wide-eyed, on the carpet, watching me, a boy of five, playing at the Transmigrations of Indur, in a drawing-room in a country town.

We lived in distant counties, and though always hearing of each other, my most distinct recollection of him is again at my own home, which was then a country house, with a garden. He was at that time a boy with a high forehead and healthy cheeks, and I recall his figure, standing among the evergreens and flowers, fresh and vigorous, with bright eyes and rounded limbs, in which there was no forecast of suffering and disease. His mind was already busy with thoughts that seldom trouble the heads of children; and the visit led to a correspondence on some points of religious difference, in which, though so much younger than myself, he was quite able to hold his own. Some time afterwards, at his own home in Cheltenham, I remember him deeply interested in some of the chemical experiments of boyhood, showing me with great glee, especially a piece of artillery made of a medicine phial with a lump of chalk in it, on which he poured some vinegar before putting in the cork. At that time he was an excellent walker, and was able to ramble over the Cotswold hills, and race across their breezy downs.

I am not sure whether we met again till after his marriage, and in the meantime that serious illness had occurred from which his health never recovered. It was my happy lot to be his travelling companion in three of the journeys which he took with his wife, who was with him always and everywhere. In the recollection of these journeys the wasting of his physical powers is painfully recorded, but to travel with him under any circumstances was too delightful for this to make itself prominent at the time.

The first journey was in 1850, among the mountains of North Wales. It was his first experience of mountain scenery. We drove through the pass of Llanberis, and he was able then to enjoy the ride up Snowdon. But, with characteristic instinct, he thought it always a higher pleasure to look upwards than to look downwards, and the grey precipices overhead in the craggy pass affected him more powerfully even than the wide view from the mountain-top. I have been with him on loftier summits and in wider chasms, and have always noticed this difference in his feelings. He looked at hills and valleys and golden plains below his feet with pure enjoyment and perfect admiration, but to the great heights above him with the reverence of a still higher mood.

Our second journey was in the following year, from London to Mont Blanc. We went by the Rhine and the Munster Thal, and through Geneva and Sallenches. He was, in fact, at that time already an invalid, but he scarcely recognised this, and his concern on grounds of health was chiefly for his wife, who of course was with us. He rode

up the rough ascent of La Flégère, and by the Tête Noire
to Martigny, when the roads were much steeper and
rougher than the French have made them in these later
years.

But it was in the Valley of Chamouni that he saw that
vision of the Alps which is reproduced in ' Balder.' I
remember well how glimpses of its nature revealed themselves from time to time, and how, standing in the star-
light and pointing to the spectral outline of the Glacier
des Bossons, he spoke there of the image immediately
suggested by it, the source of one of his finest metaphors.

No enjoyment could well be greater than that of being
with him on these two journeys. It was renewed every
morning, and prolonged through every day, by his good
humour, whatever happened, by the simplicity of all his
wants, by his power of enjoying everything, and by the
constant flow of his delightful conversation, which, even in
serious illness, very rarely failed.

My last journey with him was in 1866. I brought
him from Edinburgh to Clifton after a terrible attack,
from which, though he appeared to rally, there can have
been no true recovery. He was then so exhausted that we
had to divide the journey by sleeping at Carlisle, but
nothing ever seemed to affect the brightness of his spirit,
and he would have entertained us all the way in his usual
manner, if it could have been allowed.

This was characteristic of his whole life. I saw him in
his last years with increasing frequency, and through all
the stages of slow and fatal illness, but I never found him,
mentally, in any lower mood. He was always like one who

knew, indeed, what are the troubles of the world, and where
are its dark places, but who recognised about himself a
land of sunlight and beatitude, where Divine realities
were never absent, and where the joy of life and the
inward and outward beauty of all creation were perpetually
felt and seen.

But these fragments of memory, how little they
describe! In all his writings one of their highest charms
is the faultless perfection of their imagery. No likeness
is on the surface only, but the harmony between the
thought and its embodiment is always absolute and in the
essence of both. So in his own nature there was no outward seeming that was not the truest image of the real
life within, and to recollect his words and looks is to recall
his very self out of the grave. But to give the dear remembrance to others, in such short sentences as these, is
as impossible as to convey the full beauty of a completed
poem by quoting a few fragmentary lines.

ALBERT J. MOTT.

CHAPTER III.

1874.

THE winter of 1873–74, and the early spring of 1874, were quiet times, with even some promise of improvement: in several ways there was a little gain of strength and tone. He was himself thankfully conscious of this, and probably began to hope that recovery of working-power was at hand.

He is remembered to have said, more than once, that he had long thought of the year 1874 as destined to bring him some great good thing.

Twenty years before, he had written: 'How the Drama of Life with me has seemed cast into these ten-year acts!'[1]

Two letters, from which the following extracts are made, were addressed in January of this year to a young poet, the son-in-law of a valued friend, and the writer of a short poem, which appeared in.

[1] Vol. I., p. 369.

the 'Athenæum,' entitled 'Great Encounter,' with
the spiritual meaning of which he had been much
struck :—

That pen-and-ink hand-shake which I had the very
great pleasure of receiving from you the other day, was
not only so charming *in se*, but so suggestive, that, instead of attempting a representative grasp of thanks in
return, I am going to be so selfish as to try and persuade
you to bring your actual *coup-de-main* within reach of
my positive and grateful fist. . . .

. . . I am too anxious to win my cause to trust this
feeble and hasty pen with the picture of those defences by
which, up here at Barton End, we defy east and north
winds; but the fact that, at the height of five hundred
feet above valley-mists, we secure a climate more temperate than many a famous Italian sanatorium is a conclusion from which I will earnestly beg you, in more
senses than one, to arrive at the premises—viz., at Barton End House. Healthful to everyone, it should have a
special healing for you, since, as you'll easily perceive,
Barton is evidently either Bardon—the Bard's-hill, or
Baldon—the hill of Apollo (Bel, Baal, Belus). I incline
to the last derivation, because the Saxons have, in a kind
of territorial argumentation, named the opposite down
Horsley—the Leah of their god the Horse. . . .

Bard's down, or Apollo down, it should equally have
the spell of native land for the author of one of the few
poems, in our time, which may fairly claim to be (of its
sort and size) perfect. And far away in the Celtic ages

though it stands, it has the practical modern advantage, for anybody whose time is precious, that it is as easy of access from the world of to-day as anything in a fairy-tale.

To the Same.

Barton End House, near Nailsworth.

Duteous Nature, evidently aware of the present disappointment for me which your last letter unleashed—and slipped so gracefully, that even under the fangs I could not help cheering the noble and gallant manner of the huntsman—has provided so incessant a series of such days as shew our hills to least advantage (and at the same time usually prepare for an earlier date than ordinary the season to which you have pushed on the pleasure I hoped would have found us in a clear hard evergreen January), that, lying here, and looking through the incessant south-west drizzle, and past the waving green-darkness of a tall English fir—where, in the one dry hour, an over-early thrush was singing, and which inclemency is making a hive of smaller birds—to so much as I can see of Baal's hill, or Bard's down—as you please—I ———

Saturday.—I was interrupted yesterday in the foregoing unfinished sentence, which I am shocked to see had already 'stretched its slow length along' over the page. My invalidism is very much like that of a convict chained by the leg. *Valet* many things within the radius of his chain-measured circle, and *non-valet* anything beyond it . . . If my sofa is in a room liable to callers I am

valid to write, or pay compliments, or try philosophies,
or discuss the parish, or dogmatise on art, or sledge-
hammer politics, or descant on sweeter and more serious
things than these, to an extent which may be found by a
problem whereof the principal factors should be my in-
ability to change my place and my difficulty to do two
things at once.

Yesterday I was interrupted in a description of
'duteous Nature.' This morning the dawn-dusk shewed
a moony world which the rising light improved into the
first real snow-scene of this year—and the finest kind of
snow-scene, when frost and snow have worked together;
or, more truly, when Frost, the artist, has worked the
marvellous material which has such prevenient aptitude
to be the medium of his fancy.   If duteous Nature seemed
paying her homage by doing exactly the weather in which
I would not wish you to share the Baaldon, she has certainly taken a freak of asserting her freedom by juggling
in a single night the very thing you ought to see.   Could
anything be more essentially unlike London than what
has been silently added to everything since yesterday?
What can one call this immaculacy which, nevertheless,
is more positive than mere spotlessness?   Beside it, the
'white' snowdrop betrays the greenness of its blood, and
every other emblem of whiteness shows some differentiæ
that mark a separate category.   The last snow fell just
before dawn, and you might, therefore, have taken, when
the sun was illuminating every path, lawn, covert, shrub-
bery, and sacred grove on his own hill, one of the choicest

experiences of country winter—I mean you might have
read, utterly free from human workmanship, that involuntary record which the snow bears of the moving life that
goes on in such seclusions as these, before and soon after
sunrise. I may not see them with the bodily eye, but I
can see them as if I saw them . . . I was interrupted;
and, before I could resume, all chance of further pen and
ink was over.   Among other things, my nearest neighbour
—*i.e.* she lives about a mile off, across yonder glen—and
I had exchanged so much valuable information on the
famine in India and the *status quo* in Spain, that those
divine mediations by whom, while I am thus prisoner, my
objective life is ruled, decreed entire rest for so long a
time, that had I but a line to write, it could not have
been done before our early post.   I remember I was beginning to shew you in the spirit what I knew to be exist-
ing in matter (and only invisible to my eyes because of
an intervening wall of some hundred yards of distance),
to point out, on the snow-covered grass, the groove, with
small pricks and large pricks, where the stoat had chased
the mouse (for breakfast), and on the lawns, jungled with
laurels and other winter-fruit-bearers, the innumerable
tripods of those blackbirds and thrushes that (never shot
in this tree-full quarter of a mile) will repay their sanc-
tuary next month with three or four consentaneous generations of song; and, here and there, the larger prints of
scarcer birds—up to the long calmly-planted step of the
pheasant; or, in the copse the other side of the walk, the
tip-it, tip-it of the running, and the dip-and-blur, dip-

and-blur of the slowly moving hare—not to speak of the sidelong canter-marks of a fox, or—under the filbert-walk, near the highest ridge of Baaldon, the elfin-looking glove that the squirrel's long fingers have left. And, besides many more diagnostics than these, I know I was—for your hat's sake—going to warn you to keep clear of the rookery, since the black parliament were in full session—each member having brought in his own bill and vociferously supporting it—and the arrangements of the senate-house, like most Parliamentary provisions, being much to the convenience of the members, but entirely irrespective of ' the classes below.' I remember the debate was very loud that morning—the snowy invasion that had happened during the night being not quite understood, but evidently considered, from its exceeding whiteness, to be some device of the Opposition.

Tuesday.—While this letter has been lying in my blotting-book, ' duteous Nature,' I need not tell you, has swept out of sight her one-day's witchery and brought back as unlovely weather as she could suppose I desired. ' Duteous Nature!' how queer that must sound to the man of great capitals where ' the individuality of the individual,' as some one calls it, exists under such a weight of millions ! . . .

To a fair young niece, who had sent him a valentine, painted by herself, representing snow-drop, violet, primrose, and crocus, he scribbled these lines, in reply :—

> Tell me, Ethie dear,
> Hast thou given me, here,
> Such fair flow'rs of earliest spring
> As might make a blackbird sing?
> Or has Spring sent to me,
> These four miniatures of thee?
>
> Here, as where, all in white,
> Thou droopest prayer, morn and night;
> Here as, when the Muses meet,
> Thou sittest lowly at their feet,
> And, blue, indeed, but very sweet,
> What they say would'st fain repeat;
> Here as, morning's duty done,
> Thou art happy in the sun,
> And they who watch thy life disclose,
> See thee star, and name thee rose.
>
> Here, where made of line and line,
> That the graces might combine,
> By some skill to Graces known,
> Shown and hid, hid and shown,
> Thou art drest, Nature *in arte*,
> For a fairy's evening party :
> But (forgive a Tory fellow
> For the sigh), alas ! in yellow !

With the April of this year, and the death of
the man who had long managed his business affairs
—a man whom he had trusted and loved as a
brother—came a series of shocks he was ill-fitted
to bear, and of efforts which proved to be mortal.

Long letters had to be written, and written at
once ; long business discussions held, and complicated statements attended to.

The shocks were borne and the efforts were
made, in such a manner that even his almost daily
medical attendant was deceived into believing that
the necessity for exertion, and for attention to
external matters, had been a wholesome stimulus ;
as rousing the patient from constant indulgence
in abstruse and abstract lines of thought.

Members of his own family who visited him
were as much deceived ; taking away bright impressions of keen clearness of intellect and of fullness of vitality.

Only those who knew him to the core, and
knew him to be of the strain which will run till
it drops, apprehended the mischief that was being
done. His wife's repeated expression : ' These things
will kill him ! ' was considered to be passionate ex-
aggeration ; as was his mother's exclamation, ' Then
you have killed him ! ' when told of two or three

hours of close and uninterrupted business discussion, and of the mental vigour he had shown—only a month before the end.

By July, his physical weakness had so increased that even the effort of rising was almost too great an exhaustion; the change from bed to sofa was all he was equal to.

The distinctive mental features of his illness, as the end drew on, but while he still completely retained consciousness, were characteristic enough to demand an attempt at some slight indication. As life ebbed, it did not seem so much as if any definite disease were killing him, as that an intense over-susceptibility, a too acute accentuation of some of the highest qualities and finest functions of our nature, requiring an impossible perfection of conditions, made life, which for most of us is difficult, for him impossible. The mortal sheath was worn too thin and fine any longer to guard or to imprison the immortal spirit—the light in the lamp was so intense as to consume the frail medium.

It was no sick man occupied with his sickness with whom those close about him, while consciousness remained, had to do: intercourse with him was more what intercourse with one who had already put on immortality might be imagined to resemble.

Towards the end of July, the new and strange symptoms, which had followed on the long-protracted anxiety and exertion of this spring and early summer, began to increase in a marked manner.

Entirely himself and under his own control, he was subject to optical illusions; aware that they were illusions, and so describing them. People whom he knew not to be in the house would sometimes seem to him to cross the room; and objects, such as ships in full sail, would interpose between him and the furniture, as he lay on the sofa.

Neither to him, nor to those to whom he related these things, did they seem as remarkable as they otherwise would have done, because his eyes had always been of a peculiar sensitiveness. Looking at dusk or twilight from his window, for instance, he had often imagined and described a hunt with dogs and red-coated horsemen (even distinguishing the different colours of the horses), where no hunt was.

He had been always a wonderful dreamer of dreams—dreams so consecutive, so momentous, so vivid, that he often spoke of his first waking feeling as one of disappointment, and accompanied by a sense of the flat staleness and triviality of the ' real world,' compared with that glorious land of phantasy : at other times his dreams were so ghastly, so horrible, that it required the courage of a brave man to enter the realm of them.

Now they were visions rather than dreams that visited him. On two occasions the heavens had seemed to open, and he had felt himself drowned in an ineffable and indescribable effulgence.

The following fragments, found after his death, roughly scribbled on bits of paper, seem to be an attempt to reproduce some of the visions of his nights.

Armageddon was, probably, in his mind ; as, evidently, that passage in Joel which speaks of ' Multitudes, multitudes in the valley of decision : for the day of the Lord is near in the valley of decision,' is the sort of text of the attempt :—

A voice, a voice in the sky,
Like the voices of them that cry
In the market when a stranded fleet
Has buried the little street,
The little street by the sea,
In a tempest of wine and wheat ;

And they that there do dwell
Sit down to drink and eat
Of the years of wine, the harvests of wheat;
And the cry of them that sell
Brings no clatter of following feet,
Or clamour of voices that buy.

    .   .   .   .

Who are ye that cry
In the sky?
What is your cry, and why?
Is some Great Doom to be done?
Or do ye hold us mortals in derision?
Are these the cries that past
O'er Memphis, and o'er Babylon
And Nineveh,
Or but the words that pass
Thro' the black fight of greening (?) woods?

    .   .   .   .   .

Yea, all flesh is grass,
And there are multitudes, multitudes;
But where, oh, voice in the air,
Is the Valley of Decision?

    .   .   .   .   .

' We cry the cry
Of the sky;
Nor do we hold you mortals in derision.
And there are multitudes, multitudes, multitudes
In the Valley of Decision.'

    .   .   .   .   .

Ah! has it come at last?
Look up, look up on high,
To the very throne and crown of the domed sky!
And above the throne and crown,
What is this without colour and form?

This that shadows and broods,
 And looks down ?

 . . . . .

Make your white arms wings,
All ye soft-breasted things,
And flee, oh, doves, in flights,—
Like the flights and flights of the foam
Thro' wild nights of the monsterful main
Thundering nights of the monsterful main,
The mad white flights thro' the mad black nights
Before the hurricane ;
Every dove to her home,
The farm in the meadow, the house in the town,
To hut and castle, to cot and hall.

 . . . . .

By the hearth-stone,
By the bedside, by the graveside ;
By cross or shrine, by picture, or rag, or bone,
In lonely church or citied cathedral,
Wife and sister and mother,
  Pray, pray !

 . . . . .

Where'er, where'er
In all your lives you could ever discover
Anything whisper and hover,
Where'er, where'er
In all your lives you have known
Any hearer of prayer,
Any watcher and mover,
Any sprite, any saint, any ghost, any god, pray, pray !

 . . . . .

They are gone,
As if the fragments of a shattered moon,
Levelled to endless panic by the clash

And onset of some mad centrifugal star,
Snowed thro' the arrowy vast beyond the ring
Of systems, and were lost.

.   .   .   .   .

The earth is clear
For action ; under foot 'tis adamant,
And overhead
The blue is all too hot and proud
To stanch the parching wounded with a cloud,
Or shed above the slain
Some foolish ecstasy of rain
(Some passing folly of sweet rain).

.   .   .   .

I see the armèd earth career
As a great battle-ship
That some swift change of dynasty
Hath loosed from old allegiance due,
And none knows whether he or he
Should rule the shouting crew.
The flags are up, the decks are clear,
The splendid host divides,
And man to dauntless man they take their equal sides.

.   .   .   .   .   . Now War
Snatch from the arm of the archangel
The trumpet that shall raise the dead
And set it to thy lips,
And let the carnal difference of thy breath,
From world's end to world's end,
Raise up the innumerous lines of living men,
And blow them full of Death.

The later of the two visions—of the opening
heavens—occurred exactly four weeks before his

death. Writing of it to her friend, absent at the time for three days, his wife said: 'His symptoms seem to be undergoing a change—whether for good, or the contrary, is not yet given to us to know.'

That friend writes that, returning after three days' absence, she believed she saw a marked change for the worse, but had not the least apprehension of the end as near at hand, looking forward to years, rather than to days or weeks, during which he might linger with those who loved him. The change she saw was not only that of increased weakness. There was in his face a peculiar, inwardly-absorbed expression—as if the invisible world, more real and present to him than the visible, so occupied him, that it was only with effort he brought himself back from that far country to consciousness of what was passing around him.

She remembers on one of the last days of his being able to get down stairs, when reading to him —for, perhaps, the last time—his attention was attracted by a French epigram, of two lines, quoted in an article in the 'Athenæum.' He said it would be a useful thing to remember, and tried to fix it in his recollection. Failing to do so, and exhausted by the effort, he seemed for a few seconds to be plunged into profound melancholy : but only for a few seconds.

A perfect peacefulness and placidity was the general expression of his face at this time ; his eyes shone with a pure sweet light and a clear brightness ; seeing which, and feeling the strong warm grasp of his hand, those about him received an impression of insuperable vitality that would not allow apprehension of the great change. Possibly he himself realised its approach.

On one of the first days of August, from a sort of desperate sense in those about him that something must be done to revive him and give him strength, before colder weather should come and make all chance of open air impossible, he was persuaded, being too weak to walk, to lie out-doors a short time in his wife's invalid couch-carriage.

He lay there, on the sunny gravel sweep in front of the house, about a quarter of an hour, and seemed in a peculiar manner to delight in all that met his eyes. He was taking his last fully-conscious look at his beloved beech-woods, and the sloping terraced garden at the east end of the house, of which he had always been especially fond.

On going indoors, he fell into a profound sleep on the sofa. On his awaking, the evening was

passed as usual; but in the middle of that night
he woke in a strange trouble and confusion of
mind, from which his brain never wholly cleared.

Nearly a week passed, during which he did not
leave his room, but only rose from his bed to lie on
a couch near the window: sleeping a great deal,
and having when asleep a look of mortal illness;
talking little and with some slight difficulty—sometimes wandering for a moment, but the next, recalling and laughing at himself; and having one or
two fixed delusions.

No special alarm of danger close at hand was
felt, even then.   That he was temporarily affected
by a chill was the hypothesis.

But, after those still days, quite suddenly, on
the 8th of August, acute delirium set in.   From the
exhausting effect of this he never rallied.   It was
a glaring August day, and the keen light let into
the room by the raising of the dark green blinds
seemed at once to deprive him of sight and to
render him delirious.

He lay for two weeks, only partially and at
intervals conscious—consciousness always marked
by some gracious, pleasant, or tender saying or
recognition.   His incoherent talk was oftenest of
abstract philosophy — attempts to define such

abstract things as Faith—or expressions of love and anxiety and compassion for his wife. That he was never again sufficiently himself to take any conscious leave of her, was to her a source of great thankfulness, as sparing him an exquisite anguish.

'How beautiful!' was the comment of all who looked upon his face. At all calm times he looked so much less ill than those who had watched him in other illness had often seen him look, that hope would occasionally make itself felt, even now. But he never slept except under the influence of sedatives, and these so visibly lowered all powers of life, that to administer them was to hasten the end. Incessant restlessness wore him out.

On the evening of August 22—as his favourite rooks, winging home, were crossing the sky in front of his windows—his last breath was quietly drawn. Rest came to him.

The last sunshine of a gorgeous August evening lay rich and deep upon the scene he loved so dearly. The arms of his wife were round him, his hand was held by his mother.

Non può far morte il dolce viso amaro,
Ma 'l dolce viso dolce può far morte.

On the first day of September—his favourite month, the month of his wife's birthday, the month which in the old early days of happy courtship he passed at her home—his mortal remains were taken to the Painswick Cemetery, chosen for their resting-place as overlooking a district the ideal beauty of which was specially dear to him. The funeral service was read by Dr. Percival, who made a long journey from the place of his holiday sojourn to be present. His brothers and many old friends gathered round the coffin, which was lowered to its rest covered with fragrant white flowers.

On his coffin (by his own wish, expressed years before), the words, ' *Lord, remember me when Thou comest into thy Kingdom,*' were engraved.

At the head of the long green mound, in the midst of a little enclosed garden which love tries always to keep fair and sweet, has been erected by his wife a beautiful Runic cross of unpolished silver-grey granite.

SYDNEY DOBELL.

Fling lilies lightly on the laureate bier,
　　Where rests the garment of a soul as white,
　　Fled from the changing fields of bloom and blight.
Strew the late rose, and let the mourning year
Drop asters, fair as Hope outshining fear;
　　Plant the pure Cross that marks the finished fight—
　　The consummation of a Christian knight.
The world's regret, the heavens' recovered peer—
　　Let all things lovely where his relics lie
Hover around his sleep: may sweet birds sing,
　　And soft winds, gentle to the gentle, sigh,
Chanting his music, and from spring to spring
　　Castilian grace and English chivalry
Rise from his dust through ages blossoming.

J. N.

Painswick Cemetery: September 1, 1874.

In one of Sydney Dobell's note-books there is the following passage :—

Biographies, other than of the less by the greater, or of equals by equals, are really not biographies at all, and resemble those huts which the Achaian cottar builds with the broken pillars of a Grecian temple.

For the memorials contained in these volumes, therefore, no claim to the title of Biography is made. If against these records should be brought the charge that they afford no picture of the man, but merely catalogue his virtues, to such charge fit reply might be offered in words used, upwards of two centuries ago, by the writer of the Life of Colonel Hutchinson : 'To number his virtues is to give the epitome of his life, which was, nothing else but a progress from one degree of virtue to another, till, in a short time, he arrived to that height which many longer lives could never reach.'

A life lived, as it were, in the Divine Presence chamber, in unremitting endeavour to keep the Divine attributes constantly before the mental vision, and to bring its own being more and more into harmony with the glorified humanity of Christ, is not likely to hide ugly things in dark places; nor was Sydney Dobell's character, spite of his intellectual subtlety, difficult for any ordinarily intelligent love to read. The child's open heart was as signally his as the poet's open eye. He was most a hero for those most familiarly associating with him. His whole later life was heroic with that surely most difficult heroism—of submission.

No disappointment and no suffering ever soured or embittered one moment of his manhood; no murmur ever passed his lips. Yet his was never a stunned submission. The very breath of his life was sweet; his gracious pleasantness made all who served him, in things great or things small, find such service self-rewarding. His simplest words and deeds were dignified by the nobleness of his nature.

It has been objected by some of his friends that Sydney Dobell's life was, according to the cynical Italian proverb, 'so good as to be good for nothing' as regards any written history of it.

But, again quoting Colonel Hutchinson's biographer, we venture to say: 'Had I but the power of rightly disposing and relating his virtues, his single example would be more instructive than all the rules of the best moralists, for his practice was of a more Divine extraction, drawn from the Word of God, and wrought up by the assistance of His Spirit.' And to add, as she adds: 'I hope I shall be pardoned for drawing an imperfect image of him, especially when even the rudest draught that endeavours to counterfeit him will have much delightful loveliness in it.'

As some poor hound that through throng'd street and square,
Pursues his loved lost lord, and fond and fast
Seeks what he feels to be, but feels not where,
Tracks the dear feet to some closed door at last,
And lies him down and lornest looks doth cast—

So we, through all the long tumultuous days,
Tracing thy footstep on the human sands,
O'er the signed deserts and the vocal ways,
Pursue thee, faithful, through the echoing lands,
Bearing a wandering staff with trembling hands:

And now, one stride behind thee, and too late,
Yet true to all that reason cannot kill,
We stand before the inexorable gate,
And see thy latest footstep on the sill,
And know thou canst not come, but watch and wait thee still.

('*A Hero's Grave: England in Time of War.*')

THE END.

LONDON : PRINTED BY
SPOTTISWOODE AND CO., NEW-STREET SQUARE
AND PARLIAMENT STREET

www.ingramcontent.com/pod-product-compliance
Lightning Source LLC
Chambersburg PA
CBHW030948110726
47900CB00004B/1181